The Teleios Ring

The Teleios Ring

Adam Loxley

Matador
5 Weir Road
Kibworth Beauchamp
Leicester LE8 0LQ, UK
Tel: (+44) 116 279 2299
Fax: (+44) 116 279 2277
Email: books@troubador.co.uk
Web: www.troubador.co.uk/matador

ISBN 978 1848769 205

British Library Cataloguing in Publication Data.
A catalogue record for this book is available from the British Library.

Typeset in 11pt Bell MT by Troubador Publishing Ltd, Leicester, UK

Matador is an imprint of Troubador Publishing Ltd

Printed in Great Britain by the MPG Books Group, Bodmin and King's Lynn

To Elaine
For her unwavering belief

ONE

The *Grapevine Wine Bar* in Powder Lane, off Lombard Street was a typical City watering hole; a dark and gloomy old-fashioned wine cellar, full of suits and packed to the gills. Craven selected a bottle of Pinot Noir and two glasses, found himself a quiet table in the corner and then watched the boisterous crowd at the bar with some disdain. Essex boys made good. Thirty or forty alpha males; all spiky hair and loud pinstripes, pink shirts with double-cuffs, large footballer's ties, expensive loafers, signet rings, money clips and latest mobiles, all circling in macho groups and talking about deals and contracts and bigger bonuses.

Craven didn't understand much of the jargon – bankers or underwriters probably, but the estuary accents were unmistakeable. *Oscar Wilde was right,* he thought, *these days people know the price of everything and the value of nothing.* Thatcher's legacy. History would record her as the right-wing hardliner who broke the miners and stood for traditional conservative values but as far as he was concerned she would always be the great, unsung socialist; the conservative traitor. *Most of this lot would still be working in factories and living on council estates in Romford if it hadn't been for her enterprise culture, closing down the industrial heartland and worse of all, letting semi-illiterate yobs buy their own council houses and get on the property ladder. Still, if you're stupid enough to let a woman run the country what do you expect...*

Craven poured the wine into one of the glasses, checked his watch and took out a packet of cigarettes. He'd never had much time for the City but he had to admit that the wine was good, in fact it was very good, and it was one of the few remaining places where smoking wasn't regarded as a behavioural disorder. There was something very satisfying about unpeeling the cellophane wrapper off a brand new packet of cigarettes, pulling out the silver foil and looking at the rows of clean, pristine filters all neatly lined up, waiting to be selected one by one to share in that most personal and illicit pleasure. He checked his watch again. Five more minutes. Buchanan was never late. The suits had grown in number, a token female now the centre of attention, the language and laughter becoming more and more raucous. Craven lit a cigarette, inhaled deeply and returned to his newspaper, comfortable in the knowledge that whatever it was that Buchanan wanted, it wouldn't be long before he found out.

Charles Buchanan turned into Powder Lane more than satisfied with his choice of venue and with the anonymity that the City provided. He much preferred the clubs and wine bars of St. James's of course, but there were always too many familiar faces, too many drones straying over from Whitehall to make absolutely sure. The City was perfect. Far enough away from prying eyes, plus the place was always full of businessmen doing their squalid little deals over lunch. He descended the stairs into *The Grapevine*, pushed the door apologetically into the back of a young pinstripe and spotted Craven sitting in the corner with what looked like the foresight to have ordered a bottle of red wine and two glasses.

'Craven.' Even in a single word the cut-glass accent was unequivocally British.

'Charles.' Craven looked up and nodded as Buchanan pulled up a chair, inspected the label and then poured himself a decent measure of red wine into the vacant glass.

'This is rather agreeable.' said Buchanan approvingly, holding the wine glass up to the light and gently turning the contents to see the colour. 'Sorry about the venue. Serves it purpose though. The City boys look lively.' He nodded towards the suits, the jackets now off and the ties loosened, any semblance of refined behaviour now stripped bare by too much alcohol. 'So, how are you Craven? How's life in the real world?'

'Strange really, everything in the real world seems largely superficial.' Craven turned and nodded towards the crowd at the bar. 'Look at that lot, half of them look as though they've never read a book in their lives. Coloured a few in probably. How do people like that, barely educated, manage to earn all that money? What is it that they actually do?'

Buchanan smiled. 'They make money and they're probably very good at it. A poor education is probably an advantage. It makes them hungry.'

Craven pulled a face, unimpressed. 'Well, they don't look very hungry to me. They look under-worked and over-paid from where I'm sitting.'

Buchanan took another mouthful of wine and looked over at the suits again, another round of drinks being ordered and no indication of anyone getting back to work. 'You're probably right, but that's not what they get measured by. The only thing that matters is how much profit they make. Their behaviour isn't important. The City has a different value-set, totally different. The higher the buildings, the lower the morals.'

Craven grimaced. 'My point exactly. So much for the real world. I think I preferred your world Charles. It may be an artificially created nonsense full of people playing games all of the time, but at least you know the rules and feel that they make some sort of sense.'

'Well, it's an interesting perspective. I have to say the rules have never made any sense to me. You're not having any regrets are you?' Buchanan picked up the wine bottle, letting the question linger and settle into the silence as he refilled the glasses, pouring the last drop and the larger measure into his own.

Craven studied him carefully. Buchanan had spent the last twenty-five years navigating his way through the quagmire of politics and influences that contested back and forth across Parliament Square, observing the most brutal and retaliatory changes in organisation and governance with a detached relish. Normality was a constant maelstrom of shifting alliances, emerging powerbases and new paymasters – and Buchanan was the acknowledged expert at knowing how to leverage and manage them to his own advantage. *"All rising to great place is by a winding stair."* To witness Buchanan choreograph a meeting, outnumbered on either side by opposing parties was like watching a master-class in negotiation. Buchanan's way to high office was by a winding stair indeed, his ability to align conflicting viewpoints and agendas, or to drive them further apart in order to finesse his own third-way solution was breathtaking. And in Craven's experience, Buchanan had never acted spontaneously in his life. Every action, every sentence, every word was purposely selected for a reason. A meeting with Buchanan was like playing chess – in the dark.

'No Charles, no regrets. Do you fancy another bottle? I assume you're not driving.' Craven stood up, holding the bottle aloft as if the affirmative response was already assured.

'Excellent idea. I came by cab. Another bottle would be splendid.'

Craven nodded and threaded his way back through the crowd, indicating to a ring of six or seven suits that he wanted to get through to get some space at the bar. 'Excuse me.' he asked for the second time, leaning gently on the nearest pinstripe, trying to squeeze his way past.

'Why, what have you done?' A gelled-haired, pocked-faced Neanderthal stared blurry-eyed across the circle of pinstripes, his beer-fuelled colleagues sniggering obsequiously, waiting for the fun to start.

Craven smiled benignly. 'Nothing mate, just trying to get to the bar.'

'Yeah, well you want to watch out who you're pushing mate. Your clapped-out friend over there already shoved me in the back when he came in. If you want to start a fight why don't you just fucking well say so?'

The menace in the voice suddenly found its way across the bar, the silence descending in seconds. Heads turned. The room held its breath and darkened.

Craven paused. *Options. Always options.* Trying to argue with half a dozen drunken lunchtime bankers with a capital W was not going to be pretty. He held his hands up, palms facing outwards, the universal gesture of non-confrontation. 'Sorry mate, I'm just trying to get a drink. I'm not trying get in your way.' He turned and looked over at Buchanan, head buried in the paper, pretending to be oblivious but probably listening to every word.

The girl behind the bar had seen it all before and had the presence of mind to intervene smartly, sensing the opportunity to diffuse the moment. 'If you go and sit down Sir, I'll get you another bottle and bring it over to you.' She smiled at Craven, partly in sympathy, partly in gratitude.

'Yeah, "why don't you go and sit down sir", or better still why don't you just piss off before you get hurt?' The suits grinned. *Our turf, our watering hole.* The blonde bimbo gazed at the Neanderthal. *My brave soldier.*

Craven returned the smile to the girl behind the bar and headed back to join Buchanan. 'Sorry about that, I seem have upset the locals. Wine's on its way.'

'I noticed. Very restrained of you. I'm impressed.'

'Yeah, it's the new me. Anyway, how are things at *Vector?* I assume this isn't a social visit?'

'No, unfortunately not.' Buchanan paused as the barmaid arrived with a second bottle of wine and two clean glasses. Craven lit another cigarette and waited for Buchanan to continue. 'So, you were saying Charles – this isn't a social visit…'

'No – much as it's good to see you of course. Something's come up which I thought you might be able to help me with. A bit of a domestic issue that I can't really handle in-house.'

Craven relaxed back into the chair; reverse body-language ready for the negotiation that was about to begin. 'Domestic as in not foreign or domestic as in right in your own back yard?'

'Bit of both actually.'

Craven folded his arms, trying to read Buchanan across the table. 'And?'

Buchanan took a sip of wine, using the pause to full effect, choosing his words carefully. *Old habits.* 'Let's just say that the issue is a little sensitive and that your new freelance status would bring some advantages to the exercise.'

Craven raised his eyebrows. 'Everything you handle is sensitive Charles. Why can't you use your own people? They've all signed the Act. Everything they handle is classified to the hilt.'

'Well, that's the problem. This is more… unclassified.'

Craven concentrated on Buchanan's face, trying to work out the implication of what was being said. 'I assume by unclassified you mean it's totally off the radar screen and nobody else knows about it?'

'Something like that.' Buchanan reached into his inside jacket pocket and passed a folded sheet of paper across the table. Craven took it cautiously, well aware that once he unfolded and read its contents it would be difficult to turn down.

'It's not something I can let you keep unfortunately,' Buchanan added, nodding towards the document, 'protocols and all that – but the details are easy enough to remember.'

Craven unfolded the sheet and quickly scanned the document; a single side of typed A4, then re-read it slowly for a second and third time. He frowned, unimpressed. 'It's not exactly comprehensive is it. Who or what is Teleios?'

Buchanan shook his head. 'Not sure exactly. It's Greek – it means *completeness*, roughly translated.'

Craven shrugged, none the wiser. 'Okay, seems straightforward enough. I assume it's urgent?'

'Yesterday.'

'What about fees?'

'Let's say five hundred a day plus expenses.'

'Let's not.'

Buchanan smiled to himself and took another mouthful of wine. 'I wasn't aware that you were in a position to turn anything down.'

'It's one of the advantages of being freelance. It gives you the freedom to pick and choose. Besides, I'm very busy.'

'You don't look very busy.'

Craven nodded towards the suits still congregated at the bar. 'Neither do they, but they're very well paid. Like you say, it's results that count.'

Buchanan smiled to himself again, acknowledging the touché. 'What did you have in mind?'

'How about a thousand a day plus expenses?'

Buchanan winced and then shook his head. 'Eight hundred a day. That's as far as I can go.'

Craven stared at him across the table and said nothing for a moment, still circling his glass on the tabletop. 'It's not enough Charles. Make it nine hundred and you've got yourself a deal.'

Buchanan raised his eyebrows in surprise and took another sip of wine. 'Eight-fifty plus expenses. Final offer.'

'Sorry, it's nine hundred a day. Take it or leave it.'

Buchanan looked abstractedly towards the bar as if thinking about whether to push again for a lower price, maybe to split the difference. Eventually, he turned back towards Craven and gave him the slightest of nods. 'Okay, nine hundred plus expenses. Agreed.'

'Thank you. It'll be worth every penny Charles. How do I contact you?'

Buchanan reached inside his jacket again and slid a mobile across the table. 'Usual arrangement. The phone has only one number programmed into it. Don't use it for anything else.'

Craven nodded and pocketed the phone, passing the document back in return. 'Good. Just like old times. I'll give you a call in a couple of days and give you a progress report.'

Buchanan nodded in return, the agreement sealed. 'Thanks. I need to be getting back. I'll do the tab on the way out. Do you want to share a cab or are you going to finish off the bottle?'

Craven looked at the half-empty bottle of wine and thought better of it. 'No, I need to make a move as well, but I need to use the Gents first. You go ahead. I'll call you in a couple of days.'

He watched Buchanan pay the bill and leave and then wandered into the Gents, a narrow corridor of urinals, sinks and two cubicles all smartly finished in Italian tiles, white hardware and dark mahogany furniture. *Certainly no shortage of money in the City.* He used the urinal, washed his hands and started to use the hand-dryer fixed to the far wall, his back turned towards the exit, the noise of the dryer echoing around the tiled walls.

He was never really sure whether the small circular plate on the front of the hand-dryer was there to advertise the manufacturers name or was meant to act as a mirror, both probably but it was usually too small to effectively serve as the latter. On this occasion it was just big enough for him to make out the two pinstripes walking through the door making a direct line towards him – and just enough warning to give him two or three seconds to decide what to do next. *"The advantage of time and place in all practical actions is half a victory; which being lost is irrecoverable."*

Craven didn't flinch, but continued wringing his hands under the dryer, watching the advancing suits in the small mirrored plate, one immediately behind the other, the narrowness of the room not allowing them to walk side by side. *Foot soldier at the front, Neanderthal at the back.*

The hand-dryer was still pumping at full speed, the sound drowning out any other noise from the room. Craven stared intently at the mirror image and saw the first punch coming, the whole of the pinstripe's body unprotected as he raised his right fist high and backwards to launch the unannounced assault. In a split second Craven raised his right arm, twisted his hips sideways to get maximum torque and then turned and smashed his elbow backwards as hard as he could, using the mirror to aim perfectly into the side of the guy's head, straight into the softer space just between the temple and the cheekbone. *Just like reversing a car.* The elbow is one of the hardest bones in the body and Craven's delivery, aimed at the correct angle and with optimum force, was like a sledgehammer being driven into a watermelon. The suit hit the floor like a sack of potatoes and at the same moment the hand-dryer died, the sound of skull cracking on floor-tile reverberating round the room and bouncing off the walls like a ricochet.

Craven wheeled round and looked at the heap on the floor and then at the Neanderthal, a six-foot two, great lumbering unfit pen pusher, breathing heavily and still full of bravado but with not enough brain cells to weigh up the situation and get the hell out of there.

Too easy. Time to give him an opt-out. 'Why don't you dial 999 and get your mate an ambulance? Then you can turn round and walk out of here before it's too late.'

The suit narrowed his eyes and stepped forward menacingly. 'Oh, I'm going to walk out of here pal, which is more than you're going to do. You're full of shit.'

Craven saw the punch coming; a huge swinging right hook, but telegraphed and slowed by too much alcohol. He sidestepped and ducked beneath it easily, firing a single punch into the pinstripe, just at the point where the bottom of the ribcage joins at the front of the body. Craven knew all about pressure points, years of fieldwork had seen to that and this pressure point, if found correctly, hurt like hell from just the pressure of an index finger. Craven's punch, delivered with all his force and followed through with the momentum of his own body was perfectly placed and was like being hit by a train. The suit doubled up instantly, agonised in pain, his hands clasped to the centre of his body and his whole torso bent over, horizontal with the floor. In one swift movement Craven drove his knee up underneath the suit's chin and at the same time punched both fists down into the back of his neck. For the second time, a sickening crack reverberated around the room, bouncing off the walls.

Craven turned round and twisted the short metal tube on the front of the hand-dryer into the upwards position. He grabbed the Neanderthal's hair and then lifted his head, ramming it into the front of the machine, the rim of the steel tube slicing into his face near the top of his gum, just beneath his nose. Craven punched the dryer on, the blast pumping into the suit's mouth, the sound masking the terrified scream.

He stepped over the still unconscious foot soldier and walked towards the door, allowing himself one last glance back at the carnage behind him.

'Yeah, and you know what mate… you're full of hot air.'

TWO

Neil Ashton poured himself a large glass of red wine, took a backward glance at the room full of strangers and then stepped through the French windows into the garden of *Yew Tree Cottage*. The party was in full swing and he was relieved to be in the fresh and cooler air, away from the haze and chatter of guests behind him.

A summer get-together in rural Kent organised by his ageing aunt was not exactly the social highlight of the year for a twenty year-old undergraduate and besides, he felt sure that the only interesting person at the party, in fact the only interesting person he had seen all week had gone into the garden five minutes earlier and had not yet returned. Adjusting to the fading light he could just make out the far boundary where the gate had been cut into the beech hedge and to the left, beside the willow tree under which he had read earlier that day, a silhouette; small and slim and completely still, her neck craned upwards towards the sky as if waiting for some sign or confirmation from above.

Neil wandered into the garden, a familiar and comforting landscape which had shaped much of his early life. Years of boarding school meant that most of his summers had been spent in Appleden while his parents lived abroad, his father working in some of the most remote and inhospitable places in the world. *No place for a child*, he could remember him saying, *he'll be much better off at Hilary's,* impervious to the feelings that Neil felt as he watched the endless stream of parents arriving to collect the swarm of waiting boys at the end of each term. Standing on the steps at Collingfield he would wave despondently as car after car crunched slowly down the gravel drive, past Keeper's Lodge and then onwards, out of sight towards the main gate until there was just him and a handful of others, all feeling the same solitude at being left behind and all with the same yearning to one day have a normal home and a normal family to go home to.

Sometimes at Christmas and occasionally at Easter his parents would return on a flying visit and once, shortly after his 16th birthday, Neil made a trip to where his father's latest posting had taken him and where as always his mother had loyally followed. But for most of the time he whiled away his summer holidays in Appleden, a sleepy Kentish village of huddled cottages, a corner shop cum post office, a pub at either end of the village and a dark and musty antique shop that sold mostly junk to tourists travelling down from London on the way to Rye.

Dusk had brought an eerie stillness to a late May evening and with it a sense of change, the boughs and leaves of the much loved and tended garden still heavy from the earlier downpour that had washed across the Weald. Neil walked towards the herb garden, trailing his hand against the Wisteria and releasing its perfume into the damp evening air. Taking a mouthful of wine, he thought momentarily about the origin of the phrase "Dutch Courage" and wondered why it always seemed so difficult to initiate conversations with members of the opposite sex. Days of languid inactivity were now giving way to an unexpected distraction, but with it, a reticence which made him consider returning to the safety and comfort of the multitude indoors, the lighted windows and the muffled sounds of music and laughter becoming more attractive by the second.

A moment of indecision, not uncommon in Neil Ashton's life was followed by another large gulp of red wine (also not uncommon), some introductory words practiced under his breath and then finally a slow, meandering stroll across the still damp lawn, trying to look like a relaxed and nonchalant partygoer simply escaping the assembled throng and taking the evening air.

'Hello, I don't think we've met.' smiled Neil ambling up behind the girl and extending his hand. 'Neil Ashton – I'm Hilary Russell's nephew.'

'Hi, never mind all that now.' replied the girl abstractedly, maintaining her fixed stargazing position and not showing the slightest inclination to turn around and look at the source of the interruption. 'Here, hold this a minute will you…' a glass of white wine thrust unceremoniously towards Neil and eventually into his offered hand, '…second thoughts, put those down and just give me a leg up will you?'

'I don't want to sound like a killjoy,' said Neil, slightly taken aback by the girl's response, 'but I wouldn't climb up there if I were you, it's soaking wet, you'll get absolutely filthy.'

'Well, I'm going to have to, there's a cat up there, it's been up there for ages, I think it's stuck.'

Neil stood with a glass of wine in each hand and dutifully adopted the same craned neck position, although in the deepening twilight struggled to locate the offending animal, suspecting in any event that it was probably Tom and Doreen's ferocious beast from next door, which in his mind wasn't worth the effort or risk of rescuing at all.

'Gosh, this grass is wet. Come on then, are you going to put those glasses down and help me up?'

Neil turned away from trying to see anything in the tree and realised that the now barefoot, would-be rescuer was looking at him for the first time, hands on hips, eyebrows raised and wearing an earnest, impatient smile. She looked to him to be about eighteen or nineteen, dressed in a tiny grey sundress which barely covered her slender and suntanned body. The effect of her petite frame and her short, dark hair gave her an elfin like appearance, more so at this particular moment thought Neil as he stared at her shoeless feet, now wet and probably getting cold.

'Look, I really don't think this is a good idea,' he ventured, 'in fact it looks pretty dangerous to me. That tree is really wet, which means it's going to be absolutely filthy and more importantly it's going to be really slippery. I think we should leave it, it's bound to come down on its own eventually.'

'We can't just leave it,' the girl protested, 'besides, there's no way it's going to get down from there on its own, is there?'

Doing nothing and leaving the god forsaken cat to look after itself was exactly what Neil had in mind, but he sensed that this was not a good moment to appear indifferent.

'I don't think you need to worry too much. Cats are very resourceful. In my experience if a cat can climb up a tree it will always find a way down. Have you ever seen the skeleton of a cat in a tree? Besides, I can't even see the damn thing and I certainly can't hear any meowing or distressed animal noises. Are you sure it's still up there?'

'Look, it's up there, near one of the top right-hand branches, see?' the exasperation in her voice quickly transferring to her now pointed finger. 'Look, come here, put your face next to mine and follow the line of my finger,' and in that same moment she pulled Neil towards her, wrapping her arm around his waist and holding him so close that their faces touched and he could feel her hair and the warmth and smell of her skin and the thinness of her dress, and then suddenly someone let off a firework deep inside his body...

'You... didn't tell me your name,' he murmured, feeling the need to fill the silence, but not wanting to move and risk losing the proximity.

'Julia, everybody calls me Jules.'

'Julia, lovely name. Always reminds me of John Lennon.'

'The song or his mother?'

'Oh, the song... obviously.'

'I'm not sure that's what Mum and Dad had in mind, I think it's meant to remind you of Brideshead.'

'The house or the son?'

Julia turned her head and smiled. 'The book, silly. What did you say your name was again?'

'Neil – I'm staying here for a few weeks, well most of the summer probably. My parents work abroad so I tend to stay here quite a bit and… anyway, it's a long story, we ought to sort this cat out before it gets dark and to be honest, I think I ought to do it. I used to climb this tree every day as a child. I know every branch, even blindfolded.'

'Are you sure? – you'll get filthy.'

'Positive. Besides, I don't think I could handle standing here, looking up at you climbing the tree in that dress. The only thing is… I still can't see the cat.'

'What, you still can't see anything?'

Neil frowned in confusion and pointed aimlessly above his head, loosely in the direction where Julia had been staring. 'No… I think it's up there somewhere but to be honest I haven't seen it at all. I'm relying on you on this one.'

Julia dropped her head slightly and gave him a guilty smile. 'Sorry, I've a confession to make. There isn't any cat.'

'What do you mean, "there isn't any cat"?'

'No cat. Just me, standing out here in the dark for fifteen minutes wondering if you were ever going to come outside and then waiting another age while you wandered aimlessly around the garden. God, I thought you were never going to come over.'

Neil started to smile, the realisation slowly sinking in. 'Sorry, I didn't realise that I was late, I didn't know that I was expected.'

'Well, if we're going to go out with each other and you're only staying for the summer, we haven't got time to waste waiting to be formally introduced have we? Anyway, thanks for being so gallant and offering to climb up there, it was really sweet of you.' And then in one swift movement Jules stood on tiptoe, kissed him affectionately on the cheek and then ran off towards the house, barefoot across the wet lawn, laughing and shouting back, 'bring my shoes would you Neil? – I'll get us some more wine…'

*

Neil Ashton turned away from the window and refocused back on the harsh reality of the flashing curser on his screen and at Chris Fleming, colleague and friend, depositing a mug of something closely resembling coffee on his desk. 'There you go mate, two sugars, shaken not stirred. Are you okay?'

'Thanks Chris. Sorry, I was miles away.'

'Looked like it. Somewhere nice?'

'Yes, very – but a long time ago. Happier times...'

Chris looked at his colleague and gave him a knowing smile. 'Well, whoever she was, I hope she was nice.'

Neil grinned. In barely three years, Chris Fleming had become his closest friend and rather worryingly, had also developed an uncanny ability to read him like a book. 'Sorry, was it that obvious?'

'Yeah, you had that wistful, stupid grin on your face. The same one as when that little Italian girl from DiMarco's comes in with the sandwiches every day.'

'Mmm, no contest – this one was different. Very special.'

'They're all meant to be special Neil, at least while you're going out with them.'

'You being the experienced lothario and all that...'

Chris smiled and eased himself into the chair next to Neil's desk, waiting for a pause in the banter to allow him to change the subject. Neil Ashton had joined *The Chronicle* towards the end of a long, hot summer three years earlier, two months before his twenty-eighth birthday and six years after leaving Cambridge with a first class degree in English and a desire to become a successful and renowned front-line journalist. His father's career in Petrochemicals had posted him across five continents and because of his background in exploration, invariably to extreme climates and often into the middle of unstable and dangerous regimes. Two months after graduation, Neil's parents found themselves in the wrong place at the wrong time, caught up in a cocktail of politics, foreign policy and religious fanaticism. The telephone call that he took at 2.30 am on Sunday 8 September changed Neil Ashton's life forever. A promising career in journalism was suddenly put on hold for a six month period of doing his duty, of making arrangements, of learning how to deal with the endless bureaucracy that threatens to depersonalise the grief and ultimately, to close the final chapter on his parents' life.

And then somehow, inexplicably, a six-month delay drifted into years. Months of waiting for the right opportunity led to nothing, followed by a succession of temporary jobs and failed applications and in the end none of it materialising to anything of any substance. Eventually, impatient for something more than a life of telesales and rented bedsits, he embarked on a period of travelling; an un-timetabled, round-the-world trip funded initially by his parents inheritance and then by whatever casual work he could turn his hand to. What was meant to be a 12 month belated gap year turned into several years of "seeing the world" until in the end his original plans had become a memory and the prospect of ever becoming a serious journalist seemed to have finally disappeared, lost somewhere between the death of his parents and his sense of responsibility towards a family he hardly ever knew.

For no particular reason, when he finally returned to the UK he gravitated back to Cambridge and, with a renewed commitment, started his job search all over again. Miraculously, after nearly six years from when he first began, somebody at *The Chronicle* noticed his potential and decided to give him a chance. At the end of a long, hot August, dressed in a brand new suit and possibly the proudest employee they had ever seen, Neil Ashton walked through the front doors to join the local paper as a trainee journalist – and from that moment had struck up a brilliant working relationship with Chris Fleming.

Chris studied his colleague with concern and then chose his moment. 'Reception said that they put a phone call through to you from the police – is everything okay?'

'No, not really. Kent CID. Apparently my aunt died over the weekend.'

'Oh Neil, I'm sorry. Were you close?'

'Not so much lately. I haven't seen her for a few years, but at one point, yes, very close. Feeling a bit guilty about that actually. I'm going to have to go down there for a few days and sort things out. I'll need to ask for some time off – that'll go down well.'

'Hey, they can hardly say no. Anyway, I can cover for you. 'When do you need to go?'

Neil swivelled his chair back towards the window and gazed out at the greyness of the Cambridge Technology Park and then turned back and looked at the office, full of computers and telephones and piles of paper and all of it a million miles away from the memories of Appleden – and suddenly none of it important anymore. 'Straightaway. I have to go tomorrow. There isn't anybody else.'

Instinctively he started to tidy his desk, the decision in his own mind having been taken and the process of leaving having already begun. Chris watched him momentarily, recognising all the signs of someone about to pack a bag and walk out on the first and only stable arrangement in their life. 'Hey Neil, how about going for a beer after work, or maybe coming over to get something to eat tonight before you leave?'

'No it's okay, there are things I need to do tonight. Anyway, I've got some food in.'

'What, like beans on toast?'

'Beans on toast are good for you.'

'Yeah, but not five times a week. No wonder you can't get a girl under the duvet.'

Neil laughed. Chris Fleming had a wonderful knack of diffusing even the most serious of situations. Whatever the problem, however tense things became, he always seemed to say or do something inappropriate to make sure that Neil never took himself, or life in general, too seriously. 'Chris, you know, if someone ever accuses you of not being sympathetic and supportive when they've lost a close relative, be sure to refer them to me, I'll be happy to provide a reference for you. Anyway, thanks for the offer but like I said, I'll be fine. I've got things to do tonight before I leave.'

Chris shrugged and sauntered back to his desk, leaving Neil to spend the rest of the afternoon clearing emails and getting through as much outstanding work in his in-tray as possible. At 5.30 on Monday 25 September 2006 he finished tidying his desk, collected up the few personal effects that he wanted to take with him and at 5.45 turned off his desk lamp and switched off his computer for what he knew would be the last time.

Shortly after 6.30 he was turning the key and opening the door to number 12a, Grenville Road, a small but neat and tidy two bedroom flat on the western edge of Cambridge, which had been his home since joining *The Chronicle* three years earlier. *Not much to show for a thirty year-old Cambridge graduate* he thought for the umpteenth time, dropping his brief case on the carpet and looking around the sparsely decorated living room. *No wife, no girlfriend, no property, no prospects. Still, no reason to stay around,* he thought as he filled the kettle and went off to rummage on top of the wardrobe in search of his holdall.

Grenville Road was a street of Victorian terraced houses, bay windowed with short front gardens and red-tiled porches, the low front walls and metal gates now replaced by tarmac drives and too many cars, parked mostly askew with front wheels jutting onto the pavement. The multiple door buzzers gave confirmation to the amount of property conversion that had taken place in recent years. What was once a quiet, tree-lined road of smart private houses was now a depressing run-down assortment of separate flats or poorly maintained properties, overcrowded with students who didn't bother and owned by landlords who didn't care.

When he first arrived, buoyed by the enthusiasm of his first proper job, he'd initially had grand designs about updating and redecorating the flat, enjoying the prospect of imposing his own taste and personality into the property. But without much money and with increasingly little enthusiasm for the task, the fading 1970s décor had prevailed and number 12a remained a clean but spartan bachelor pad, a space used mostly for sleeping and storage, but not somewhere that he had ever considered calling "home". In truth, the lack of money had always been an excuse. Other than Appleden, he had never felt at home. Cambridge and *The Chronicle* had been an opportunity, but ultimately, an interruption – and Grenville Road had never felt anything other than a small and temporary footprint in his life.

Neil found the holdall and wandered back into the kitchen, thinking about what he needed to do before he left. *Fifteen minutes to pack, half an hour to have something to eat and then maybe a couple of pints down the Red Lion later on. Get up early, train to Liverpool Street, walk down to London Bridge and then get the train to Headcorn and call Detective Constable Whatshername.* Neil took the piece of paper out of his back pocket and looked at the name and contact number that he had noted down earlier – DC Page, Kent CID. The kettle clicked off just as the telephone rang.

'Hi Neil, it's Carol. Chris told me your news – are you okay?'

'Carol, I'm fine, stop worrying.'

'My useless excuse for a husband also tells me that he invited you over for dinner tonight and let you get away with turning us down – suddenly my cooking isn't good enough for you anymore?'

'Thanks Carol but I've got stuff to do tonight.'

'What stuff?'

'Well, like packing for a start.'

'Well that'll take ten minutes – what else?'

'I just won't be very good company tonight Carol. It's kind of you to ask but I'm better left on my own, honestly.'

'Don't be silly Neil, this is what friends are for, besides we've opened some wine especially. Stop mucking about and get yourself round here pronto…'

'Honestly Carol, it's nice of you and Chris to think of me, but I really do have things to do.'

'… and I made a rhubarb crumble.'

'What, with custard?'

'Of course with custard. How can you have rhubarb crumble without custard?'

'I'll be half an hour…'

Neil spent his last evening in Cambridge in exactly the same way that he had spent the evening after his first day of work – enjoying the company and hospitality of Chris and Carol Fleming, not to mention the delights of Carol's cooking. Neil had been paired up with Chris on his first morning and by the end of the day had been invited back to meet Carol, stayed for dinner and from that moment had come to regard them both as his closest friends. Chris came from a very different background, having been educated at the local comprehensive and joining the paper straight from school with few qualifications – but what he lacked in formal education he made up for in natural ability. By his own admission he would never write with the style and literacy of Neil Ashton but he had a streetwise antenna for sniffing out a story unlike any other journalist in the office. As a pair they were formidable and more importantly, they shared the same ideals and ambitions about the job and about journalism in general.

Neil made himself comfortable in the armchair, familiarising himself with the living room and started to exchange a shouted conversation with Carol, who was preparing dinner in the kitchen. 'Something smells good Carol, I hope you're not going to too much trouble!'

'No trouble at all Neil. Anyway, we grow all our own stuff in the back garden now so, it's just a case of getting out there after work and digging a few things up.'

'Really?'

Carol's head appeared around the kitchen door, grinning wickedly. 'Well it's either that Neil or I popped into *Marks & Spencer* on the way home tonight – what do you think?'

'Ignore her.' mumbled Chris, wandering into the living room and collapsing into the chair opposite Neil. 'See what I have to put up with? So, what did they say about giving you some time off?"

'Oh, they were okay about it, but they wouldn't give me more than a few days. They want me back at work next Monday, which to be honest won't be enough but I couldn't be bothered to argue with them. I'll get down to Appleden tomorrow lunchtime and if I need more time, I'll just have to ring and say I'm not coming back. It's probably time to move on anyway.'

Chris frowned, the thought of just giving up a steady job a complete anathema to him. 'You want to think carefully Neil, you don't want to do anything too hasty.'

'I'm not being hasty Chris. When I decided I wanted to become a journalist it was because I had ideals and ambition and I wanted to make a difference. I wanted to be a famous investigative reporter. I wanted to write leaders for *The Times*. I thought you and I could become the Bernstein and Woodward of Cambridge. I waited a long time to get the job at *The Chronicle* and it was all I ever wanted to do, but when it comes down to it, after three years where has it actually got me? I'm still reporting on broken street lights and lost dogs for a provincial newspaper. It's not exactly Fleet Street is it?'

Chris frowned in obvious disagreement. 'Come on Neil, everybody has to start somewhere. You're a fantastic journalist, nobody writes better copy than you. The paper's been great experience for you. I know you're upset about what's happened today but it's not worth giving up your career for.'

'But that's the whole point Chris, it's not a career, is it? It's just a job and it's not a very rewarding one at that – not at any level. I'm hardly being paid a fortune and like I say, it's not exactly Fleet Street, is it?'

'Listen mate, if I want to listen to some miserable bloke moaning about life and repeating the same old phrases over and over again I'll go and put a Morrissey record on. I can't believe that you heard that your aunt died earlier today and you're sitting there moaning about your lack of career prospects!'

Neil smiled and held his hands up in defeat. 'Sorry Chris. You're right, as usual. Anyway, I didn't mean to moan, I was just trying to convey how certain I was about it being time to move on. I'll shut up now.'

'Good. Now then, do you fancy some wine – red or white?'

'Red please.'

'Beaujolais or Beaujolais?'

'I'll have the Beaujolais then…'

*

The following morning, under a clear blue September sky, Neil Ashton caught the 11.07 from London Bridge to Headcorn and settled himself into a window seat for the hour or so journey to Appleden, uncertain about where his future lay, but for some reason confident that he was in some way drawing a line under his past and starting a new beginning. As with most late morning trains the carriages were only half full, an odd mixture of suited business people and families laden down with children and pushchairs and shopping. Neil gazed out at the passing landscape as it quickly changed from grey London sprawl to green Kentish fields, oblivious to the noise and conversations of his fellow passengers. *The trains might have changed* he thought *but the journey still looks the same.*

After about half an hour he spotted a number of oast houses clustered together at the edge of a Kentish farm, the memory of travelling this same route suddenly flooding back to him; visiting Appleden as a child with all the anticipation of a long vacation and a warm, endless summer stretching ahead. He thought of *Yew Tree Cottage* and of him as a small child, playing in the sunshine and in the puddles that used to collect between the back door and the shed, whilst Aunt Hilary would hang out the washing again and stare up at the fast moving clouds, waiting for the next passing shower. A fond memory now tinged with sadness but despite it all he felt happy and he felt contented. Today, finally, he was going home.

THREE

John Garrick ducked under the blue and white police tape and walked up the garden path to *Yew Tree Cottage*, reassured by the patrol car parked outside that there would be someone in. The front garden was deceptively wide and well maintained; a central path, now cracked and uneven with age, bordered on either side by lawns and cottage plants. An old weathered bench sat at an angle to the house and underneath it, a small black and white cat was curled dozing in the late September sun. Garrick gazed up at the house and then at the adjoining cottage next door, the house and garden of *Briar Cottage* seeming the mirror image of its next-door neighbour. What struck him most was how quiet and peaceful it all seemed. A few late wasps droned lazily here and there but otherwise everything was still and tranquil.

The two cottages sat on Parsonage Lane, just off a path which led from the church to a gate into the open fields which circled the village, dipping into the woods beyond and then sweeping across the Weald as far as the eye could see. It felt as though nothing could disturb the calm of the village, the only noise a distant sound of Bach floating across the churchyard; eternal music cascading gently into silence. A round, ceramic plaque on the wall by the front door spelt out *Yew Tree Cottage*, the words surrounded by a circle of blue and yellow flowers, the colours now faded and worn by years of sunlight and, next to it, a front door made of heavy, faded oak which he noticed was slightly ajar. Garrick pushed it gently and stepped inside.

The hall was cool and dark and he waited a second for his eyes to adjust, spotting the burly, dependable figure of PC Hughes resting on a stool in the kitchen at the end of the hall. He paused, uncertain as to whether his entrance had been noticed, but nothing stirred, the PC's back turned towards him, his face buried deep in the daily newspaper and oblivious to Garrick's arrival. The hall was old-fashioned but spotless. Polished oak floorboards, stairs on the right, two doors on the left, kitchen straight ahead and all of it exactly as he imagined it would be. Traditional, un-modernised, lovingly preserved. A vase of flowers stood on a small telephone table at the bottom of the stairs and above it, a matching wall mirror, and to its side, an umbrella stand placed just inside the front door. Garrick pushed the door hard behind him, making sure it slammed with impact, Bob Hughes looking up alarmed and then twisting off his stool in an instant.

'Sorry Sir, I didn't see you.' The top button and tie were being frantically re-arranged.

'No, that's because you had your head stuck in a paper, Bob. What are you doing here anyway?'

'Waiting for the chippy.' Bob nodded towards the bits of splintered doorframe lying by the back door in the kitchen. 'I thought you were still on holiday, Sir?'

'I was, came back early. Cornwall. Rain. Forensics been?'

'And gone, Sir.'

'Good. We got any water, electricity?' asked Garrick wandering into the kitchen and looking around at the mess.

'Don't know, Sir, haven't tried.'

'Well, now's your chance to find out, preferably with a cup of tea as a real live test. White, no sugar. I'm just going to have a look round.'

'Yes Sir.' Bob Hughes grunted and busied himself trying to find cups and tea bags, feeling unhappy about being caught off-guard and uneasy about opening cupboards and poking around in someone else's house, especially someone who had just died. Garrick wandered into what appeared to be the dining room; dark heavy furniture, dining table and four chairs, sideboard, bureau, the contents of the last two strewn across the carpet.

On top of the bureau were a couple of photographs, which he picked up and studied carefully. An old sepia photo of a couple, a husband and wife presumably, with two small daughters, hard to date and a colour photo of a middle aged woman and a young boy aged about ten or eleven standing in a park or a large garden somewhere. Garrick studied the faces, putting the photos carefully back in the same position as he had found them.

He moved onto the front room, similarly furnished in a traditional, old-fashioned style. In the corner facing the door was a high backed, wooden framed armchair, the cushion still crumpled as though someone had stood up and left it only moments earlier. A sofa in the same design stood under the window, less worn and therefore less used and in the corner, a small, very outdated television set. Garrick smiled. *I'm sure we had a telly just like that when we were kids.* Again, the same mess strewn over the floor. Books, magazines and the contents of a small chest of drawers which was now lying on its side, presumably tipped over to empty the contents as quickly as possible.

He wandered back into the kitchen to find Bob who was in the process of pouring boiling water into two delicate cups and saucers. 'No mugs Sir, all I could find were these. Best china by the looks of it.'

'Mmm. Looking at the house I suspect that's all she ever used Bob. Probably never drank out of anything else. Anyway, why don't you get me up to speed. What do we know so far?'

Bob passed the cup and saucer over to Garrick and started stirring milk into his own. 'Looks like the old girl interrupted a burglary sometime over the weekend, Saturday night or Sunday morning most probably. House is owned by a Miss Hilary Russell, about seventy-two, seventy-three years of age, retired, spinster, living on her own, obviously…'

'Obviously…' Garrick cupped the tea and blew gently across the surface.

Bob continued, unperturbed. '…Neighbours, a Mr and Mrs Webster, discovered the break-in yesterday morning. They'd been away for the weekend visiting friends and got back late on Sunday evening. On Monday morning Mrs Webster noticed something was wrong, came round and found the back door forced open and Miss Russell lying on the floor over there.' Bob nodded down the hall, indicating towards the bottom of the stairs.

Garrick raised his eyebrows in surprise. 'And what does the pathologist say?'

Bob snorted. 'Wouldn't commit himself – never do, do they? Said there were no signs of injury or any obvious signs of a struggle but that he should be able to give us a report tomorrow or Thursday morning, latest.'

'Well, that's something I suppose.' Garrick looked down the hall and frowned. Something didn't quite add up, but he couldn't put his finger on it.

'What about the burglary, Bob, do we know what was stolen?'

'Hard to say. Neighbours don't seem too sure and obviously she lived here on her own.'

'So basically we've got a burglary but we don't know exactly when it took place, we've no idea what's been taken and not much chance of finding out, and we've got a dead body but we don't know when she died or the cause of death.'

'That's about it Sir.'

Garrick sighed. *Wonderful. First day back and this.* In his experience there were three basic approaches to investigating a burglary. Forensics, witnesses and stolen property. *Yew Tree Cottage* had all the hallmarks of a case that was going to end up with lots of paperwork and precious little leads. He didn't know whether the forensics boys would come up with anything of course, but a house like this was normally full of prints and evidence of lots of other people having been there, especially in a kitchen. Good witnesses were always best, a door to door would have to be organised in due course, but this wasn't a housing estate with hundreds of neighbours and lots of potential for somebody to have seen something. It was a quiet, rural hamlet and the nearest neighbours had been away. So the default approach would be to get an itinerary of the stolen goods and trace the burglary back from there, checking out the markets, local pubs and newspaper ads, leaning on the usual suspects, but that wasn't going to be possible either, not unless somebody could come up with a list of what had been taken. Suddenly a rainy beach in Cornwall looked attractive by comparison.

'What about next of kin, Bob?'

'Just a nephew. Lives in Cambridge. Someone from the station rang him yesterday. Apparently he's on his way down today. Should be here sometime later this afternoon.'

Garrick finished his tea and passed the cup and saucer back to Bob. 'Okay, you'd better wash these up. I'm just going to have a look upstairs.'

The cottage upstairs was of a similar layout, a bathroom at the top of the stairs immediately over the kitchen and two bedrooms on the left, the main bedroom at the front and a smaller second bedroom at the back. The bathroom was surprisingly large and modern, having obviously been updated in recent years. Everything looked undisturbed and Garrick quickly moved into the back bedroom, a dark, old-fashioned room with fading wallpaper and large heavy furniture, much in keeping with the rest of the house. He could tell immediately that the room wasn't used for anything other than storage. The single bed looked as though it hadn't been slept in for years.

He opened the large mahogany wardrobe, the musty smell of wood and old clothes reminding him of his parents' bedroom and of him as a small child, secretly hunting for Christmas presents which were always wrapped and hidden from early December. At the bottom were some shoeboxes full of documents, birth certificates, old National Insurance cards, an assortment of letters and postcards and a number of loose photographs, mostly black and white, presumably pictures of friends and relatives from years ago. In the back corner was an old metal cash box, black with a red stripe around the side and a metal handle in the centre. Garrick tried to open it, but found it locked, the contents rattling inside as he turned it over. Again, nothing seemed to have been disturbed. He looked round at the rest of the room, a chest of drawers, a small bedside cabinet, a couple of photos in frames and over in the corner beside the window, a collection of bits of pieces; nothing of any value, but obviously personal possessions from a bygone age too precious to throw away.

Garrick wandered over and looked at the items, more out of interest than in relation to the enquiry. An old cricket bat stood propped up in the corner, the handle heavily taped and the yellowing wood dimpled and marked from innings played on village greens in summers long past. He picked it up, rubbing his hand over the batting surface to get the feel of the grain, wondering who it had belonged to and how many runs it had scored. A wooden tennis racket lay by its side, the strings now mostly broken and loose, but all carefully secured in a wooden frame, a butterfly screw in each corner. He knelt down and rummaged in one of the boxes, fascinated by the history and stories that must have belonged to each piece, but which now could never be told. A silver cigarette case, initialled with the letters *JWR*, a small, tortoiseshell penknife, a pair of men's hair brushes kept tightly inside a worn leather case, a pair of gold cuff-links, some playing cards with an old wooden cribbage board and four ivory pegs, a silver pocket watch, a pair of metal, elasticated armbands, an old Minox camera and finally two small, leather bound books; *Curious Anecdotes, Bon Mots and Characteristic Traits* by someone called the Rev. J. Adams, dated 1792 and a collection of poems by Wilfred Owen. Garrick looked around the room again. Whoever had broken in had not bothered to come in here, everything looked untouched and in its original place. Or maybe they didn't have the time, maybe they'd been disturbed before getting this far.

He poked his head around the door of the main bedroom, but quickly decided that he'd seen enough. The bed was unmade and the curtains were still drawn, testimony to the events that had taken place two nights before, but as far as he could tell, everything else looked normal and as it should be. A large, round alarm clock with luminous hands was ticking loudly on the bedside cabinet, a macabre rhythm, slow and purposeful and at odds with the stillness in the rest of the house.

Bob Hughes was still waiting in the kitchen when Garrick came back downstairs, leaning against the worktop and conscious to be seen doing anything rather than reading the paper.

'Find anything upstairs Sir?'

Garrick shook his head. 'No, not much. Some interesting junk in the back bedroom but nothing else. No evidence of anybody having been upstairs at all. My guess is that she was woken up by the intrusion and came downstairs. Beyond that we'll have to wait for the pathologist.'

He took another look around the kitchen, hoping for inspiration and then wandered over to the back door, inspecting the bits of broken doorframe that were still lying on the floor. 'They made a right mess of this Bob. What do you reckon?'

Bob nodded in agreement. 'Amateurs. Kids probably. Professionals would have been in and out much cleaner than that. Probably wouldn't have woken her up either.'

Garrick pursed his lips, deep in thought. 'You know, Bob, I think you might have something there. Do you know who was first on the scene yesterday?'

'DC Page Sir. I think it was her that phoned the nephew. She's probably seeing him this afternoon.'

Garrick nodded and smiled. *Well that's something at least. Nothing like being first on the scene to get a feel for what happened.* Steph Page would have been one of his first choices to spot anything that didn't add up. 'Look, I'm not sure there's much more that I can do here, I'm going to shoot off now. I'll catch up with DC Page when I get back and try and chase up Forensics. I'll see you later on.'

He left Bob to wait for the carpenter and walked back down the garden path, turning round to close the gate behind him and looking up again at the cottage as he left. The peace and stillness of the village was overwhelming. It felt quintessentially English, almost as though he had travelled back in time to a more innocent age, a paradox really, given what had happened. He paused by the car, still bothered by the nagging feeling in the back of his mind that he had missed something, all his experience and intuition telling him that something here didn't make sense. But worse of all was the frustration of not being able to identify what it was and knowing that as much as he wanted to work it out, for now it would have to wait.

Later that evening, Neil stood at the bar in *The Chequers* at Appleden with Tom Webster, bemused at how little it had changed and trying to recall the last time he had been in there. He could remember plenty of times with Jules of course, they had never really used *The Black Horse* at the other end of the village but the last time he'd been in *The Chequers* must have been seven years ago, a weekend visit to see Aunt Hilary just before he'd left the UK.

To his regret, he'd only been to see her once after that, which was three years ago, shortly before he started at *The Chronicle*. They'd driven out to Sissinghurst Castle that day and had stopped for lunch at *The Three Chimneys*, an old public house with flagstone floors and real ale still served from barrels racked up behind the bar. She had been so pleased to see him, wanting to know all about his travels and so excited and proud of him landing the job at Cambridge. He could remember promising to keep in touch and to keep her updated with his progress, but inevitably the distractions of a new job and a new circle of friends meant that it was a promise he hadn't kept. Over the last three years, contact had reduced to an occasional telephone call and the perfunctory birthday and Christmas cards, normally bought at the last minute and always posted with the faint but optimistic hope that they would arrive on time.

The Chequers hadn't changed at all, the same old tables and chairs, most of them empty were still scattered around the room, the locals much preferring to stand at the bar. The landlord would stretch to making a sandwich or two but this wasn't an updated, modernised pub for families and children with comfortable seating and an extensive lunch menu, it was a local pub where locals met and drank and enjoyed a gossip and banter with friends and neighbours at the end of the day. Most of them greeted Tom, who was clearly a regular, and a couple of them nodded at Neil, perhaps recognising him from years ago, or maybe they were simply acknowledging him out of respect. No doubt all of them had heard about Hilary Russell. It was a small village and reports about the burglary had been all over the local news.

'Now lad, what are you having?' asked Tom, squeezing his way to the front of the crowd.

Neil noticed that there were a few new beer pumps on top of the bar, mostly foreign sounding lagers with brightly coloured signs, *brewed in Northampton probably*, but everybody seemed to be drinking beer. 'Don't know Tom, what do you recommend?'

'Oh, the Harvey's or the King & Barnes, they're both good. Keeps a good drop of beer does Frank. I'm having a pint of King & Barnes.'

'Okay, I'll have the same then please.'

'Good. You go and grab a seat and I'll get them in.'

Neil wandered over to a table near the fireplace and waited for Tom to get served at the bar. The large inglenook was empty, although the logs were piled up either side, ready and waiting for the darker evenings which were just around the corner. He stared at the fireplace, remembering that he had sat at this table with Jules several years earlier, a colder September then, the smell of wood smoke forever reminding him of the end of summer and the last few days before they parted. He shivered, forcing himself out of the train of thought. *Too long ago.*

'There you are lad, one pint of King & Barnes – just what the Doctor ordered.' Tom put the pint carefully on a beer mat, taking care not to spill it and then sat down in the chair opposite.

'Thanks Tom, cheers.' Neil held up his glass and clinked it against Tom's. 'Thanks for calling round as well, I was starting to feel a bit lost in the cottage tonight – not sure where to start really.'

'That's all right lad, it's nice to see you again. I'm just sorry it's under such circumstances. If there's anything we can do…'

Neil smiled in acknowledgement, not knowing exactly what to say. Tom took out an old tobacco tin and started to roll up a cigarette, expertly licking the gummed paper between two fingers. 'Your Aunt Hilary was a lovely lady. She was also a good friend and a good neighbour. Both are hard to find these days. We'll miss her very much.'

'Thanks Tom. So will I. I wish I'd seen more of her in the last few years.' Neil stared into the distance, the feelings of guilt beginning to overwhelm him.

'She would have liked that lad, she thought the world of you.' Tom caught Neil's mood and quickly changed the subject. 'Anyway, Doreen says you must come round and have dinner with us tomorrow. She would have asked you round this evening but she's still a bit shook up from yesterday – I don't think she really felt up to it.'

Neil took a slurp of beer and gave Tom an appreciative look. 'Thanks, Tom, that's really kind of you. I won't deny, it'll be nice to have the company at the moment.' How is Doreen then? Must have been a real shock for her.'

'Aye, it was lad – but she'll be fine. The police are coming round to see us tomorrow to take a statement, which she isn't looking forward to. I think she'll be better once that's over.'

Neil gave an understanding nod. 'Yeah, I saw them this afternoon. They told me about the burglary, which was a bit of a surprise – they didn't mention anything about that on the phone yesterday. But beyond that they don't seem to know what happened yet. Waiting for forensic reports and the pathologist apparently. I get the impression that they think she was woken up and had some sort of stroke or heart attack, possibly from the shock of it all.'

Tom looked at him quizzically. 'Well, that'd be a first lad. Your Auntie slept like a log, always did. Slept through the great storm of '87 as I recall.'

'Really?'

'Absolutely. The whole village was up and out on the main street with torches. Never forget it. We didn't have any warning of it you see – totally unexpected. They keep showing that late-night weather forecast of Michael Fish on the BBC, but I don't know anybody who was up and saw that. We all went to bed as normal and then at three o'clock in the morning everybody was suddenly awake wondering what the hell was going on.'

Neil smiled, enjoying Tom's company and listening to him recounting stories from the past. 'And she slept right through it did she?'

Tom laughed. 'Like a baby. I've never known a storm like it. People were looking out of their windows thinking it was the end of the world. Pitch black it was, no lights as far as you could see. And the wind, well ...the houses shook – literally shook with the force of it. I thought all the windows were going to come in and all you could hear were trees falling, tiles coming off roofs, dustbins blowing up the street. The ice-cream sign outside the post office nearly decapitated old Mrs Brooker. There she was, outside her front gate in her dressing gown and slippers calling for her precious moggy and this sign comes whizzing up the street like some sort of demented frisbee. If she hadn't had ducked, it would have taken her head clean off. People reckoned it was only living with old Jim, who was a bit handy with his fists after a couple of pints, that gave her such good reflexes. Old bugger probably saved her life!'

Neil burst out laughing. Tom was clearly warming to his theme now.

'Anyway, a lot of people went over to the church – really frightened they were. You couldn't find out what was going on. No television, no radio. Just a pitch-black night and a storm blowing so hard that it was pulling down 500 year-old trees. Never seen anything like it. Me and Doreen were up and I thought I'd better go and check next door and make sure that Hilary was alright ...' Tom paused, taking a large slurp of beer. 'Well, I banged on the front door and then on the back door for what must have been about ten minutes. Couldn't wake her at all. Doreen was all for calling the ambulance but I said, "She'll be sound asleep, nothing wakes up Hilary once she's in bed," and true enough, next morning she appears on the doorstep asking all innocently, "I think our fence has blown over Tom, was there a bit of a storm last night?" Unbelievable. I'll tell you lad, if it was burglars that woke up your Auntie then they've got to be the loudest burglars you'll ever meet.'

Neil looked at Tom, a thought running through his mind. 'Well, something certainly woke her up Tom. If it wasn't burglars it must have been something else.'

'Well, I suppose so. But I'll tell you something else that doesn't add up...' Tom starting patting his pockets looking for his lighter, his roll-up still sitting on the tobacco tin waiting to be smoked. 'Hang on a minute lad I need to get a light, must have left mine indoors.' He leant over to ask for a light from a fellow smoker who was enjoying a quiet early evening pint at the next table. 'Excuse me, could I borrow a light please?'

'Sure.' The man smiled as he passed over some matches.

'Thanks.' Tom took the matches and lit his cigarette, inhaling the smoke with obvious pleasure and then spitting out the bits of loose tobacco. 'Where was I?'

'You said there was something else that didn't add up?'

Tom took another long drag, flicking the ash into the empty fireplace. 'Well it doesn't make any sense does it? No offence lad, but why would someone want to burgle your Auntie's house. I mean, me and Doreen aren't exactly at the cutting-edge of technology but we've got a fairly new television in the front room and a decent portable in the kitchen. We've got a DVD recorder, we've both got mobile phones and whilst I might look like an old fuddy duddy, the hi-fi in the back room is absolutely top of the range. That's the sort of stuff that burglars are interested in isn't it? Why on earth would someone want to break into Hilary's? There wasn't anything worth taking, not unless you're interested in old furniture. She didn't even have a CD player.'

Neil studied Tom, trying to work out the implications of what he was saying. 'Maybe she had something valuable in there, old jewellery or something.'

Tom pulled a face, unimpressed. 'Well maybe lad, but how would anybody know that? And another thing – me and Doreen were away all weekend. I bet if you're a burglar it isn't too hard to work out that one cottage is empty and full of modern stuff worth pinching, whilst the other one is occupied by an old lady surrounded by antique furniture. You tell me lad, which one would you break into?'

Tom's description of Aunt Hilary as "an old lady" made Neil smile. He wasn't sure exactly how old Tom and Doreen were, but there wasn't much to choose between them and Aunt Hilary. At best they were only a couple of years younger. He leant forward and dropped his voice. 'So what are you saying Tom, that you don't think it was a normal burglary?'

'Don't know lad, can't work it out. All I know is that it doesn't add up, does it?'

Neil paused for a moment, thinking about what Tom had said. 'No, you're right Tom, it doesn't. It doesn't make any sense at all. The only logical explanation is that they were looking for something specific, something that they already knew would be in there.'

Tom nodded. 'That's what I thought. Maybe you ought to try and find out what's been taken.'

Neil sighed. 'That's easier said than done. I haven't a clue what was in there in the first place. Maybe the police will come up with something.'

Tom snorted, obviously unimpressed. 'I wouldn't bank on it lad, they all look about fourteen these days. Who did you see at the station today?'

'A woman from CID, she must have been about thirty I suppose.' Neil smiled to himself. 'Quite attractive actually.'

Tom chuckled. 'Ah well lad, every cloud… do you want another pint?' Tom held up his own glass, clearly indicating that he was going to have another one whether Neil said yes or no.

Neil stood up, quickly getting his wallet out of his back pocket. 'My shout Tom. What do you want, same again or are you going to try the Harvey's?'

'No, I'll have the same again.' Tom grinned mischievously. 'Anyway, we can always try the Harvey's tomorrow before dinner.'

Neil grinned back and wandered up to the bar. He'd known Tom and Doreen for as long as he could remember and they were good people. They must have lived in *Briar Cottage* for most of their lives and like Tom had said, had been good friends and neighbours to Aunt Hilary for nigh on thirty years. *Most people don't stay in properties that long these days,* thought Neil, *everybody seems to be constantly aspiring to move and get something bigger or more expensive. Upwardly mobile. Trying to prove how successful or happy they are by how much they own. Consumerism gone mad. People buying things they don't need and which they can't afford with money they haven't even earned yet.* It struck him how happy and contented Tom seemed, living in his small world and not wanting much other than his good health, the security of his home, Doreen of course and the company of his friends and neighbours in the village pub.

Neil bought the beer and sat back down. 'You still working then Tom or have you retired now?'

Tom took a long pull of his pint and settled it down in the middle of the beer mat with a satisfied sigh. 'No lad, sort of in-between really. Semi-retired they call it. I've got a couple of part-time gardening jobs just to keep me busy and supplement the pension. Doreen also does a couple of mornings a week, so between us we manage quite well.'

'Well, that's good. Actually Tom, I was thinking about your old cat the other day, you know that big ferocious ginger thing you had, can't remember its name.'

Tom smiled. 'Ah, *Morse,* he was a real scrapper he was. "King of the Alley" we used to call him. Take your eyes out he would. Died about two years ago. I buried him under the damson tree in the back garden. He always liked the shade there in the summer. Got another one now. Small black and white thing. Pretty, but not the same as old *Morse.*'

Neil smiled, allowing himself a fleeting thought of the summer evening when he had first met Jules. 'I don't think I ever asked you Tom, why did you call him *Morse*?'

'He had these funny markings on his nose, three dots and then a dash, like a hyphen. I can remember Doreen saying "It looks like Morse Code," so I said, "Right, we'll call him *Morse* then," and that was that.'

'So, what's the new one called?' asked Neil.

Tom grinned. 'Well, *Lewis*, obviously.'

FOUR

Craven checked into *The Moon & Falcon*, dumped his bag onto the double bed and then went straight back downstairs again to the bar. He ordered a large glass of red wine, origin unknown, found a comfortable seat out of the way at the end of the lounge and then relaxed back into the armchair to enjoy his nightcap.

It had been a long day and he was tired. Yesterday's meeting with Buchanan had been eventful and under normal circumstances he would have taken a few days off before starting the job – but he knew that time was of the essence. The journey from London had also taken longer than he'd planned. He didn't know Kent very well and although he'd driven down to the Channel Tunnel a couple of times, that had been on the motorway of course. Tonight he'd got lost around the country lanes and it had taken him a while to eventually find the hotel; a small country residence noted for its restaurant and with only a handful of rooms. Nice and quiet and far away from the madding crowd.

He took a large gulp of wine and closed his eyes, thinking about his plan of action for the following day. Buchanan's briefing had been sparse, leaving out more details than it contained. Deliberate probably, but it was clear what he needed to do and obvious that he needed to move as quickly as possible. Every day was likely to make a difference. Still, much to his surprise it seemed a straightforward assignment. The phone call from Buchanan had been unexpected and he had turned up willing to listen and ready to negotiate – but also prepared to say "no", assuming it would be something slow and routine that they couldn't be bothered to handle or something toxic that they didn't want to dirty their hands on. But this didn't appear to be either. Uncomplicated, clean and as far as he could tell, no repercussions.

Still, he'd worked for Buchanan before and knew from bitter experience never to assume anything, other than that there would always be something undisclosed, some other undercurrent or separate agenda which wouldn't surface until events took their course, or until Buchanan decided it was unavoidable. Nevertheless, he trusted Buchanan. In fact he trusted him implicitly, more than anyone else he knew. He'd worked for him for too many years and on too many occasions to think anything else, but intuitively he also knew that the briefing yesterday had barely covered the basic facts. The only issue was whether he was going to find out what was really going on and why everything seemed to be so unofficial and off the record. Still, given his new independence, maybe it was better not to know.

The girl who had checked him in at the reception walked past carrying a tray of drinks, taking them through to the restaurant or maybe upstairs to someone who had ordered room service. 'Everything all right with your room Sir?' she asked, recognising him from only five minutes earlier and giving him a friendly smile.

Craven smiled back. 'Absolutely fine. It'll be perfect, thank you.'

'Well, if there's anything you need tonight Sir, don't hesitate to ask. I'll be on the reception until midnight.'

'Thanks.' Craven nodded and smiled again, wondering if the innuendo was intentional or just the product of his own imagination. 'Actually, I don't suppose there's any chance of getting anything to eat is there? I seem to have missed both lunch and dinner today.'

'Chef's gone home Sir but I'll see if I can rustle up something in the kitchen for you. I'll just take these through to the restaurant and then see what I can do.'

Craven gave her an appreciative nod. 'Thanks, that's really kind of you.'

The receptionist disappeared with the tray of drinks and Craven went back up to the bar to get another glass of wine. It was gone 11.00 and there were only two other people in the lounge, a local who was draining the last dregs out of a pint of beer and about to make his way home and a young businessman reading what looked like papers for some meeting or another that he was probably attending the following day. After the buzz of the City the place seemed dead and devoid of any atmosphere. Much too provincial for Craven's liking, but he guessed that was the norm for this part of the world. *"Early to bed, early to rise..."*

The barman seemed to be cashing-up, but happily poured Craven his glass of wine and then carried on counting the money in the till, not showing any interest in making conversation. Craven sat on a bar stool and watched him working for a while and then wandered out into the reception area and looked at the collection of tourist information leaflets which were stuffed in a wooden rack next to the front door. He flicked through a few; historic houses, country gardens, steam trains, butterfly farms, but none of them of any use. What he needed was a map, but none of these were detailed enough. *First thing tomorrow, find a local post office and get a decent map of the area.*

He smiled as he saw the receptionist coming back carrying the empty tray and heading off towards to the kitchen in search of some supper for him. She looked about nineteen or twenty he guessed and was wearing a charcoal suit and crisp white blouse, which despite its formality and uniform style seemed to somehow show off her figure. The buttons on the blouse were certainly straining under the promise of something less stuffy and formal. Either that or it was the high heels and the blonde hair which had attracted his attention. She caught him looking at her as she turned into the corridor and stopped and gave him another smile, pushing a strand of blonde hair behind her ear.

'You checking out the local attractions Sir?' she asked, nodding towards the leaflets but still with enough innuendo to leave him wondering.

Craven raised an eyebrow and held her gaze, unable to decide whether it was just an innocent, friendly remark or whether it was deliberate and something more flirtatious. It was a thin line as far he was concerned and one he couldn't read. Still, he'd never been able to read women very well. He opted for friendly innocence.

'No, not really. I was just looking for a map. Can't seem to find one though.'

She thought for a second and then put the empty tray on a side table. 'I'm sure we've got one behind the reception somewhere. Hang on a minute, I'll just go and have a look.'

Craven leant on the reception counter and gazed down at her whilst she squatted down and rummaged through one of the bottom drawers. 'There you are,' she said, suddenly standing up and looking pleased with herself at having found it. 'I knew we had had one in there somewhere. We'll need to have it back, but you can borrow it until the morning if you like.'

Craven took the map gratefully. 'Thanks, I'll pop it back to you before breakfast.'

'So, are you here on business or pleasure Sir?' she asked, an innocent question, but delivered with the same inflection that Craven still couldn't read.

'Oh business I'm afraid. I don't think I'm going to have much time for pleasure unfortunately.'

'Oh, that's a shame.' She gave him a disappointed smile, her head tilted slightly at an angle. 'Well, maybe you'll come another time.' Again the innuendo. Again the strand of hair pushed coquettishly behind the ear.

Craven watched her walk down the corridor towards the kitchen, immediately thinking that he'd chosen the wrong response. *Still, you never know, maybe there will be some spare time to check out the local attractions and have some fun. Uncomplicated, clean and no repercussions.*

It had gone midnight by the time he finished eating and had returned to his room. He moved his bag onto the floor and then opened the map and spread it out over the bed. It looked as though it was probably a couple of years old but that didn't matter – not where he was going.

The map went as far as Faversham to the north and down to Hastings in the south. Craven traced his hand along the villages that ran across the Weald; Goudhurst, Cranbrook, Sissinghurst, Biddenden, Appleden, trying to get his bearings and working out his route for the following morning. If he made an early start he could cover most of the ground in one day and with a bit of luck he could get everything done by the end of the week and get back to London and to some civilisation.

He looked around the room at the dark oak beams and heavy red and gold curtains and then looked back again at the map and smiled ruefully to himself. It wasn't long ago that he was working for Buchanan and staring at maps of Helsinki or Vienna or Prague, staying in grey, anonymous hotels and having to blend into the background, despite all the difficulties of language and culture. That was what he was trained for. If this was what the future of being freelance was going to be like he might have to think again. What on earth was he doing in this place, chasing around the countryside and sweeping up some domestic loose ends just to keep Buchanan's world clean and tidy? It was the sort of job that he'd have given to a trainee six months ago, some fresh faced, keen and eager Cambridge graduate whose bollocks hadn't dropped yet and who didn't know one end of a Glock 23 from the other.

Craven unzipped the pocket inside the bag and took out the pistol, turning it over in his hand to feel the balance. It was slightly lighter than the full size 22 but as far as he was concerned easier to use – and easier to conceal. He snapped open the magazine and checked the thirteen rounds of .40 calibre bullets, the smell of oil and gunmetal reminding him of another time and another place. He was starting to get angry and he knew it. Normally he'd sleep with it under his pillow or stuffed down the side of the bed, but there was no need to do that here – not in Sleepy Hollow.

He put the Glock back into the bag, made a mental note of the locations on the map and then folded it up and put it on top of the chest of drawers in the corner of the room. He took a final look out of the window before going to bed, but couldn't see a thing. The night was pitch-black and there wasn't a street light to be seen. It was also deathly quiet. He decided there and then that he hated the country. The place was full of apple pickers and dogs and 4x4 trucks, with not a wine bar or art gallery in sight. Craven preferred cities – he always had done. He'd lay in bed late at night and listen to the sounds of the city, the sound of traffic on the high road, the ceiling shadows moving across the room, the late night sirens fading into the distance, couples walking home, car doors banging, milk bottles clinking.

Comforting, familiar, alive. Real life. This place was dead. And tomorrow, someone else was going to be.

FIVE

Wednesday morning was clear and bright, but colder. Garrick stood by the window of the CID room drinking a cup of coffee and looking down at the people hurrying to work, most of them now wrapped up in coats and scarves against the autumnal weather, hands deep in pockets and battling against the northerly wind that had arrived overnight and without warning. The Indian summer had suddenly gone. The leaves in the park were starting to turn and soon the clocks would be going back. Then it would be that period of grey, misty afternoons, dark November evenings, cold white frosts and then onto Christmas. Another season, another year.

The only other person in the office that morning was Matt Isaacs, a thirty year old Detective Constable, two years in CID and making a name for himself for quietly getting on with the job and for his uncomplaining, professional attitude. Garrick had a lot of time for him. Unlike some of the others, Matt didn't seem to have a natural instinct for CID work – maybe it was just lack of experience, but what he did have was a systematic, logical, almost clinical approach to investigation; one which had predictably earned him the nickname of Sherlock, and one which because of his religious background had quickly changed to Shylock. Matt didn't mind. Being on the receiving end of a nickname meant that he'd been accepted by his colleagues. It was all part of the banter of being one of the team.

Garrick gazed over at the park opposite and at the small cafeteria that sold mostly ice creams and cold drinks in the summer and teas and coffee in the winter. The owner was opening up the shutters on the front of the building and putting out the metal chairs and tables for the day, busily getting ready for the early morning customers, although there would be fewer of them now that autumn was approaching. Garrick wondered whether he would ever know how much his daily routine was watched by the CID team, the window position in the CID room having established itself over time as the place to stand and think, the space to reflect and work things out without interruption from the noise and distractions of the desks and phones and paperwork.

Matt finished reading the file on *Yew Tree Cottage* and closed it quietly, waiting for Garrick to finish his coffee. House rules dictated that you didn't interrupt the DCI when he was thinking and Matt knew better than to get on the wrong side of him first thing in the morning. Eventually, Garrick sensed that Matt was ready, took one last look at a lone dog walker crossing the far side of the park and then turned away from the window. 'So, what do you think Matt?'

Matt paused, indicating that what he was about to say wasn't based on very much substance. 'It's difficult to say without actually seeing the scene of crime but I think I agree with Bob Hughes Sir. It has all the hallmarks of amateurs – kids probably.'

'Because of the mess at the backdoor?' Garrick was now leaning with his backside against the windowsill, arms crossed and staring keenly at his DC, hoping for a different insight but also ready to challenge.

Matt nodded. 'Partly. But also because of the style of the burglary. It looks very different to what you'd expect.'

Garrick finished the last dregs of his coffee and threw the paper cup expertly into the bin next to Matt's desk. 'Go on.'

'There were a few burglaries whilst you were away Sir. A couple of off-licences over at Ashford, which obviously don't compare, but also a couple of domestics which looked very professional and completely different to this one. Have you heard of Stuart Richmond?'

Garrick nodded. 'The fashion designer? The guy that owns all the retail shops. Always on the television.'

'That's the one. He lives over at Boughton Monchelsea. Huge house – iron gates, gravel drive, swimming pool, tons of bedrooms. Must have cost him a fortune. Anyway, he came back from a night out in London with his wife last week to find his house turned over. Steph and I covered it whilst you were away.'

Matt passed the file on Stuart Richmond across to Garrick who flicked through it, scanning the papers rather than reading them in any detail. 'So, how was it different Matt?'

'It just looked totally professional. Entry was via an upstairs window. It looked like they climbed onto a flat roof and then forced the lock – no mess, no damage and then went through the house from top to bottom. The first thing they did was strip the duvet covers off two of the beds and then used those to stash and carry everything away. The place was completely turned upside down. I reckon they started in the bedrooms and then worked systematically from room to room. Nothing was left untouched, but you could sense the speed at which they must have gone through the house. They exited by the front door with a couple of duvets full of stuff, but I bet it didn't take them more than ten minutes from start to finish. Professional job.'

Garrick thought for a moment, trying to visualise the scene that Matt had described. 'Well, I agree it's very different Matt, but it doesn't mean that our burglary is necessarily kids. Perhaps the backdoor was the easiest way in.'

'Doesn't really make sense though, does it Sir – on two counts. One; Richmond's place was full of expensive property and two; there was no one at home. My conclusion from that is that the burglary must have been planned. It must have been staked out and they waited for the right moment to strike...'

Garrick nodded. He couldn't argue with the logic. What Matt was describing wasn't an opportunistic burglary.

'...whilst the burglary at *Yew Tree Cottage* was exactly the opposite. One; the house doesn't look as though it contained anything of any great value and two; Miss Russell was at home, asleep upstairs – which is two reasons why it's unlikely to be a professional job. If you add that to the method of entry, which looks pretty amateurish, I'd say it's a fair bet that it was kids or someone who broke in on spec. Just someone trying their luck I would say.'

Garrick turned away and looked out of the window again, thinking through the implications of what Matt was saying. 'Well, it has a sort of logic to it Matt. But what about Miss Russell – what's your view on that?'

Matt picked up the file and started leafing through the papers. 'Again it's hard to say Sir. Obviously the pathologist will tell us one way or the other but if I had to take a guess, I'd say it looks like natural causes to me. Looking at the pictures that SOCO took at the scene, there don't seem to be any signs of a struggle.' Matt found what he was looking for and passed over a couple of photographs to Garrick. 'Look at the vase of flowers on the hall table.'

Garrick studied the photos carefully and smiled to himself. He knew when he'd been at the cottage yesterday that something didn't quite add up but he hadn't been able to put his finger on it. Matt was right. Hilary Russell's body was found in the hallway, just inside the front door. The vase of flowers was still on the hall table in exactly the same position as you'd expect to see it if someone had carefully placed it there. It would almost certainly have been knocked over if there had been any kind of a struggle. Even if someone had put it back on the table, there would have been remnants of flowers and water all over the floor.

Garrick passed the photos back to Matt as he wandered over to his desk. 'Thanks Matt, good analysis as always. We'll just have to wait for the pathologist and see whether you're right. What's the score on the Richmond burglary?'

Matt smiled. 'A lot easier. No forensics but we have got a detailed list of everything that was taken. We've also got some photos of some of the items. Seems like Mr. Richmond was very careful about cataloguing his possessions. Said his insurers insisted on it. We're chasing up all the stolen property at the moment. Some of it is bound to turn up before long.'

'Good. At least we've got one incident with a reasonable chance of clearing it up.' Garrick switched on his PC and groaned at the amount of spam that was waiting in his inbox. Technology had never been his forté. 'Do you know Matt, every morning I have to trawl through all this dross that gets delivered to my inbox every day. Where does it all come from? It's either the latest, hottest tips for stock investments in some company or other that I've never heard of, or it's some dodgy pharmaceutical company trying to sell me stuff that promises to give me a bigger penis. Is it just me?'

Matt laughed. 'No Sir, it's not just you. We all get it. Even Steph gets it.'

'And I'll tell you something else,' continued Garrick, banging his mouse on the desktop and starting to get visibly irritated. ' I notice that in both cases, whether it's for investments or pharmaceuticals, they don't seem to give you the obligatory warning that your assets could go down as well as up…'

*

Doreen Webster bustled about tidying up the sitting room whilst Tom sat in the armchair next to the fireplace, reading his newspaper and occasionally looking at her over the top of his glasses as she attacked the sofa with a dustpan and brush. Doreen ignored his silent look which she could read only too well, and continued plumping up the cushions and picking up the old papers and magazines that had collected over the past couple of weeks.

'It's no use you looking at me like that Tom Webster, she'll be here in a minute and I don't care what you think, I'm not having visitors thinking we live in a pigsty.'

Tom grunted and went back to his newspaper, studying the form guide for Kempton Park for the umpteenth time, trying to decide between two horses in the 3.40 race that afternoon. 'It's only a policewoman coming to take a statement Doreen, not the Queen of England coming to tea. She'll have to take us as she finds us.'

'Well, she'll find us living in a clean and tidy house. Now, make yourself useful and go and empty those ashtrays and go and get me some mint from the garden. I want to do some potatoes for lunch. '

Tom sighed and put his newspaper down, realising that he wasn't going to get any peace until Doreen was satisfied that the place was as clean as a new pin. It was probably better to get out of her way until she had finished – and the garden shed was always favourite for a bit of peace and quiet. He picked up the ashtrays and took them out into the kitchen and then wandered into the back garden, checking the vegetables as he walked down the path towards the shed.

Doreen busied herself dusting and tidying up and was just thinking about whether to get the hoover out, when she spotted the car pull up outside. She took one quick glance around the room to check that everything looked respectable and then went and called Tom back in from the garden. 'Tom, she's here. You go and get the front door and I'll put the kettle on.'

Tom muttered something unintelligible under his breath and came back indoors, just in time to answer the front door before Steph Page rang the bell for a second time.

She greeted him with a friendly smile, her warrant card already open and a black leather document holder under her arm. 'Mr. Webster? DC Page. I've come to take a statement from you and your wife – hopefully you're expecting me?'

Tom smiled. 'Come in luv. Oh, we're expecting you alright. Doreen's been getting ready for you all morning. I'm glad you've turned up, I don't think I could stand being hoovered and polished much more.'

Steph laughed. 'Sorry if this is putting you out Mr. Webster – it shouldn't take very long.'

Tom winked at her as he led her through to the sitting room. 'I wouldn't bank on it luv. This is going to be the social highlight of Doreen's year. She'll be talking to the neighbours about this for weeks. She's probably bought some new biscuits especially. 'Doreen – DC Page is here!'

Doreen came through from the kitchen, drying her hands on her apron and looking slightly harassed, as though she'd been busy cooking and had been unexpectedly interrupted. 'Oh, hello again dear, you're the one that came out on Monday morning aren't you? I thought I recognised you. Would you like a cup of tea before we start?'

Steph smiled. 'Yes please Mrs. Webster, that would be lovely. Milk, no sugar. Thank you.'

'Right, I'll just go and make the tea. Tom, you look after DC Page while I'll try and see if we've got any biscuits anywhere.'

Tom winked at Steph again and then pointed towards the sofa, indicating to her to take a seat. She looked about thirty and was dressed in a black trouser suit with a pale blue blouse and one of those posh silk scarves that Tom had noticed younger women wore these days. Her hair was obviously quite long but was tied up above her head, held in place by a large tortoiseshell butterfly grip. What struck him most were her eyes. They were a bright cornflower blue, which with her dark, almost black hair was very striking, as indeed was her overall appearance. *I don't remember policewomen looking like this in my day,* thought Tom, *most of them were old battleaxes.*

'So, you must be the one who saw Neil Ashton yesterday at the station?' said Tom, remembering Neil's comment in the pub.

Steph frowned quizzically, not sure as to why Tom was asking the question or how he knew that it was her who had seen Neil the day before. 'Yes, it was me actually. Why do you ask?'

Tom grinned mischievously. 'Oh, it was just something he said. I sort of guessed it must have been you. You don't mind if I smoke do you?' he asked, reaching for his tobacco tin and starting to roll up a cigarette.

Steph raised her hand in silent approval and passed the clean ashtray and matches over to Tom, which Doreen had put on the side table beside the sofa. 'You've been up to London recently then Mr. Webster,' she said, more as a statement than a question.

Tom pulled a face, confused by the thought of anybody thinking that he would want to go to London. He hadn't been for years and had no inclination to go either. He couldn't stand the place – full of crowds and traffic and litter. He couldn't think of anywhere that he wanted to go to less. 'Not me luv. Haven't been to London for years. What made you say that?'

Doreen suddenly arrived with a tray of teacups and a plate full of biscuits, giving Tom a disapproving frown as he proceeded to light his roll-up. 'There you are dear,' she said, offering the tray towards Steph and nodding towards the cup nearest to her. 'That's yours there, milk no sugar. What's all this about London?'

Steph took the tea and helped herself to a couple of biscuits, more out of politeness than hunger. 'I was just asking your husband whether he'd been to London recently, but he says he hasn't.'

'Not unless he's got another woman up there,' laughed Doreen. 'Can't see Tom wanting to go to London. He doesn't even like going out of Appleden, do you Tom?'

Tom shook his head, a mouthful of biscuit stopping him from replying.

'It's just the matches you've got there Mr. Webster.' explained Steph. 'It says *The Grapevine Wine Bar,* on the front. I assumed you'd been up to London recently.'

Tom finished his biscuit and picked up the book of matches and looked at the front cover, noticing the writing for the first time, *The Grapevine Wine Bar, Powder Lane, London. EC3* and then suddenly remembered. 'No, I borrowed these off a bloke in the pub last night. You wouldn't catch me going up to London in a month of Sundays.'

'Oh well, that's one mystery solved then.' joked Steph, putting her cup of tea on the side table and opening the document folder. 'Now, are you happy for me to start taking the witness statements?'

*

Neil decided to spend the day tidying up the cottage and then working through the papers in the bureau. Until the pathologist had finished the post mortem and released the body there wasn't anything he could do about getting a death certificate or arranging the funeral, so he thought he might as well get a head start on getting all the papers and documents in order. Fortunately, Aunt Hilary had never been a hoarder and years of working as a secretary meant that she had always had a very tidy, organised approach to paperwork and filing. It didn't take him too long to find a copy of the will, several insurance policies plus all the bank account details and by lunchtime he had more or less sorted everything that he needed to and had also filled one black bin liner full of letters and papers to be thrown away.

In one of the drawers of the bureau he had found a brown leather address book which seemed to be up-to-date; certainly his own address in Grenville Road was correct, so he reckoned it was no more than two or three years old at the most. At about one o'clock he decided to stop and have something to eat and then afterwards thought he should phone some of the names in the address book to let them know the news about Aunt Hilary. He didn't recognise any of the names of course, which would make the telephone conversations a bit awkward but he felt that it was his duty to try and let people know what had happened and to make a list of those who might want to attend the funeral.

Actually, making the telephone calls was the easy bit. Cooking lunch was the real challenge. Neil had always been hopeless at cooking. In fact he was hopeless at anything to do with the kitchen, a bit of a paradox really given the amount of time that he had spent on his own. He stared ruefully at the larder full of packets and tins, wondering where to start and grateful for the fact that Tom and Doreen had invited him round to dinner that evening. He was looking forward to that. A couple of pints in *The Chequers* with Tom and then some good, old-fashioned, home cooked food next door.

Eventually, he decided that he had stared at the larder long enough and that he could just about manage to cook himself some scrambled eggs on toast. He'd seen Carol do that a few times and it couldn't be that difficult. It was just a case of whisking up a few eggs and making some toast as far as he could remember. He found a couple of eggs in the fridge and some bread that was still fresh in the breadbin – at least it looked fresh and didn't have any of those green mouldy bits on it, which was the only thing he knew about bread that had gone off. He put the bread in the toaster and lit the gas under the saucepan full of eggs. After a couple of minutes, just as he was thinking about serving up, the front doorbell rang. *Damn – trust someone to come round just when I'm at the difficult bit.*

Neil left the scrambled eggs to look after themselves and went to open the door, showing his surprise at seeing DC Page again, having been with her only the day before.

'Hello, Mr. Ashton, DC Page. I'm sorry to call unannounced. I wonder, could you spare me a few minutes? Just a formality I need to go through.'

Neil smiled, the initial annoyance at being interrupted quickly replaced by the fact that it was her and by the fact that she looked even more attractive than he'd remembered her at the Police Station. 'Of course, come in. I'd offer you a drink or something but I'm just in the middle of doing some lunch and I'm not that good at multi-tasking in the kitchen.'

'Thanks.' Steph brushed passed him as he opened the door fully and directed her towards the kitchen at the end of the hall. 'Actually, I'm full up with tea thanks, I've just come round from Mr. and Mrs. Webster's next door.'

Neil grinned. 'Oh, I know what you mean; Doreen's famous hospitality. I'm hoping to get some of that myself later on.'

Steph walked towards the kitchen, reached the doorway and then suddenly stopped and looked back at Neil, who was a couple of paces behind her. 'What are you actually cooking Mr. Ashton? Lunch or some sort of pagan, sacrificial offering?'

Neil frowned, uncertain as to what she meant. 'It's only scrambled eggs on toast – or meant to be anyway. Why, what's the problem?'

As he poked his head around the door, looking over her shoulder, Steph pointed towards the saucepan on the gas stove, the flames at full speed, a flume of blue-black smoke billowing out across the kitchen.

Neil darted across the kitchen, whipped the saucepan off the oven and poured a jet of cold water into what was going to be his lunch as he deposited the pan into the sink. 'Bloody hell! Why is everything so bloody complicated!' As he turned round he was aware of Steph, leaning against the doorframe, her hand over her mouth, trying not to laugh.

'You left the gas on full then?' she said, trying her hardest to put on a sympathetic and consoling expression.

'Well, only because I had to answer the front door.' protested Neil, inspecting his fingers and realising the handle of the saucepan must have been hotter than he thought.

'Did you put some milk in it?'

'Milk?' Neil looked at Steph in bewilderment, as though she had just asked him a complicated question about quantum physics or the periodic table.

'Yeah, you know, milk? White stuff? – it comes from cows.'

'I know what milk is,' replied Neil indignantly, 'I'm not completely stupid.'

Steph burst out laughing. 'Scrambled eggs. Whisk the eggs, pour some milk in, heat on a low flame, continue to stir. Obviously that wasn't the recipe you were working to?'

Neil leant on the sink worktop and shook his head in mock despair. 'I didn't know there was a recipe. It was more like, whisk the eggs, turn the gas full on and leave to burn.'

Steph walked over to him standing at the sink and looked at the burnt remains which were now stuck firmly to the bottom and sides of the pan. 'You did use a non-stick saucepan didn't you?' she asked, instinctively knowing that he hadn't and that washing up was going to be the next delight in store for him.

Neil groaned. 'Probably not, knowing my luck. I don't suppose you're any good at cooking are you DC Page?'

Steph smiled, as much out of sympathy as in amusement. 'Stephanie. Steph for short. I'm not sure scrambled eggs qualifies as cooking but looking at your lunch, I think you need the services of the Fire Brigade, not the Police Force.'

Neil wasn't very good with women, in fact he had hardly chatted up anybody in his life before. For some reason he'd never needed to, it always seemed to happen the other way round. But there was something about Steph that gave him the confidence to ask, almost as though it was just an innocent invitation between friends. Stupid really, he didn't know her at all, in fact he'd only known her first name seconds ago – but all his instincts told him that this was the moment, that life changing events sometimes distilled down to a single opportunity and often to a single decision, to turn left instead of right, or in this case to stay silent and let the moment pass or to say what he had in his mind.

'Tell you what,' he said, with as much nonchalance as he could muster, 'how about you cook lunch and to repay the favour I take you out to dinner later in the week?'

Steph raised her eyebrows in genuine surprise. 'Gosh, you're very forward Mr. Ashton.'

'Neil, Neil for short.' *She's smiling. She's going to say yes.* 'Not very forward, just very hungry.'

Steph feigned her disappointment to perfection. 'Oh, so it's only my culinary skills you're interested in then?'

'Absolutely – the only thing on my mind is food.' replied Neil, pretending to be offended at the suggestion that there could be any other motive.

'Mmm – well, I'll say one thing for you Mr. Ashton, you're not backwards in coming forwards. For all you know I could be married or living with someone.'

'Hey, I don't even know if you can cook. I'm the one taking all the risks here!'

Steph laughed and held Neil's gaze for several seconds, trying to work out his intentions. This wasn't really in the rule book but she liked him. He was a nice guy. 'Okay, what food have you got in the cupboard then Neil?'

'Brilliant. I knew you'd say yes,' exclaimed Neil, skipping over to the larder and opening the door for Steph to inspect the options. 'Tons of stuff but all a complete mystery to me I'm afraid.'

Steph poked her head into the larder and started inspecting the various tins and packets for something quick and easy to cook. 'But I'll have to get back to you on the dinner invitation.'

For the first time Neil looked genuinely disappointed. 'Oh, that's a shame. Married? Partner?'

Steph shook her head. 'No, single. But it's not really allowed while the enquiry is in progress. Plus, I'd need to organise a babysitter. I have a daughter, Chloe, she's five.'

'Gosh, being a single parent must be difficult doing the job that you do.' said Neil, wondering what circumstances had led to Steph ending up with a daughter but no husband.

'Oh, we manage,' said Steph resolutely. 'My mum lives just round the corner and helps out a lot. In fact I don't know how I would have managed without her. Anyway, how do you fancy some pasta with mushrooms and sun-dried tomatoes? It'll take about ten minutes.'

'That sounds absolutely spot on.' replied Neil appreciatively. 'Thank you.'

Steph nodded and set about making lunch. It was a long time since she'd cooked a meal for a man, even if it was only a quick bit of pasta. Neil had disappeared into the dining room to lay the table. A thought suddenly struck her as she brought the water to the boil and added a dash of olive oil. 'Neil…' she shouted, not wanting to leave the stove.

Neil's head appeared in the doorway, cutlery in hand. 'What?'

'Steph smiled at him. 'As I'm here now…you may as well lay the table for two.'

*

It was mid afternoon by the time Steph got back to the station. Lunch with Neil had only taken an extra 30 minutes or so but the door-to-door enquiries had been slow and fruitless. Nobody had seen or heard anything, but it was a small village and everybody wanted to stand on the doorstep and gossip about the burglary or invite her in for a cup of tea and a natter. Steph felt as though she'd drunk enough tea today to last a lifetime.

When she got back to the CID room she expected the place to be full and buzzing but in fact it was empty, everybody seemed to be out except for Matt who as usual was at his desk, head down and working hard.

'Hey, Shylock, where is everybody?'

Matt looked up and blinked several times, the effect of staring at his computer screen for several hours clearly taking a toll on his eyes. 'Garrick's upstairs with Anderson. Everybody else is setting up the incident room. Briefing in ten minutes. You missed all the excitement.'

Steph sat on the edge of Matt's desk and pinched one of the mint humbugs which were always kept loose in his top left hand drawer. 'Why what's happened? Why is Garrick upstairs with the brass?'

Matt also took a sweet and then passed her the manila file which he'd been reading earlier in the day. 'The pathologist came through. The burglary at *Yew Tree Cottage* – it's just become a murder enquiry.'

SIX

The incident room was in truth, no more than a couple of meeting rooms with a dividing wall which had been commandeered for the purpose of focusing on the investigation. By the time Garrick turned up, the white board at the end of the room had been cleaned, the tables had been pushed to the sides and a number of extra chairs had been brought in to accommodate as many people as possible. Someone had put the SOCO photographs taken at the scene onto the white board, the remaining magnetic discs, red, blue, yellow and green clustered in the four corners, waiting for the additional information that would surely emerge over the coming days and weeks.

About fifteen officers were seated, waiting for Garrick to start and explain how the enquiry was going to be handled. This wasn't the Met or West Yorkshire. Murders in this part of the world were a rarity and as selfish and heartless as it seemed, everybody wanted to be involved in the case. Providing it went okay this was going to be good for the CV and besides, a murder enquiry was lot more interesting to work on than shop-lifting or car theft. It was cases like this that made you want to join CID.

Armed robberies – now they were ten a penny. Half the villains in South London seemed to have 'retired' down to Kent and the increasing number of Bank or Building Society jobs was no coincidence, which meant they weren't really a challenge. You could spot the primary suspects a mile off. They'd all bought smallholdings within a couple of acres in a triangle around West Malling, which was close to all the motorway links and meant that they could get around the county or back up to London in no time at all. And they all drove top of the range Mercs or Range Rovers and all drank together in the same pubs. Birds of a feather. Identifying the culprits was easy – it was nailing the evidence that took the time.

The Appleden case was different. Everybody sensed that this wasn't a straightforward murder and word had got around that there was precious little evidence to go on. Something complicated that was going to take weeks to unravel was something to get your teeth into, an opportunity for everyone to work together on a large-scale enquiry and a chance for the team to prove itself.

Garrick waited for the noise to quieten down and then stood up at the front of the room.

'Okay. Thanks for coming everybody. As you all know, we find ourselves with a murder enquiry, the first one I think for almost four years. Some of you worked on that investigation so should pretty much know what to expect. For the rest of you, it won't take long for you to get into the routine but I just want to say three things. One; this investigation takes priority over any other case that you've got on at the moment, but that doesn't mean that you stop working on everything else, so be prepared to put in some extra hours. Two; all leave is cancelled unless it has been specifically re-approved by me. See me afterwards if you've got something booked that can't be re-arranged. Three; nobody talks to the media without my express permission – in fact, refer all media enquiries to me or in my absence to Chief Superintendent Anderson. Everybody clear?'

A low murmur went round the room, people nodding in agreement.

'Do the media know yet Sir?'

Garrick looked at DS Cooper, a twenty-five year career veteran who'd seen it all before and knew the right questions to ask. 'Good question Andy. No they don't. We're briefing them at 4.30, straight after this, so expect some press activity this evening. They'll probably be on the phones to you as soon as we finish. Any other questions before we begin?'

Steph put her hand up. She wasn't sure why, it wasn't really necessary but it felt like the best way to get Garrick's attention. 'What about the nephew Sir? Has someone told him? I assume we don't want him to find out by hearing it on the local news?'

Garrick shook his head. 'No we haven't told him yet Steph but you're right, we ought to let him know. Perhaps you could do that once we've finished – while I'm briefing the press.'

Steph nodded, pleased that she'd made the point and feeling strangely responsible for the way in which they were dealing with Neil.

'He might already know of course Sir,' volunteered one of the newer DCs. 'I assume until we eliminate him, he's a prime suspect?'

Garrick nodded. 'Absolutely. We all know the statistics about murders being committed in the family, so we'll need to take a statement from him and check out his movements and any alibis over the weekend. Steph, you saw him again today, what's he's like?'

Steph could feel herself blushing slightly and could only hope that nobody else noticed. 'He just seems like a normal guy Sir. Very genuine I would say. I'm happy to follow up with getting the statement, but if we're looking at Neil Ashton as being a prime suspect then I think we're looking in the wrong direction. I'd bet the house on it.'

'Okay, thanks Steph. Still, it might be worth checking out the will. He's probably the sole beneficiary and we don't have a clear motive at the moment, let alone any leads, so we'll need to eliminate all possibilities.'

'I thought the motive was burglary Sir?' asked Steph, slightly confused by Garrick's reply.

'Well, it still is probably – but the information from Alan Wyatt, the pathologist, puts a new light on everything. I've asked Dr. Wyatt to explain the details to you personally. It's much better for you to hear it direct from him rather than from me trying to translate, plus you'll also get the opportunity to ask him any questions. Matt, would you mind going to get him – he's in interview room three at the moment catching up on some notes.'

Matt disappeared and returned with Alan Wyatt in tow. Some of the CID team recognised him from previous enquiries, others had spoken to him on the phone. He was about fifty-five, average height, quite wiry in build and had short greying hair and a close-cut beard of the same colour. Steph reckoned that there must be an unspoken dress code or uniform for pathologists; they all looked the same to her. Wyatt was wearing a tweed jacket with faded, leather patches on the elbows, a checked shirt with a mustard coloured tie, brown trousers and light tan shoes. His small, rimless glasses added to his overall appearance, as did the two pens sticking out the top of his jacket pocket. As far as Steph was concerned he looked like the archetypal chemistry or physics teacher from when she'd been at school.

Garrick introduced Wyatt to the assembled audience, offered him a glass of water and then sat to the side of the room, indicating to Wyatt that the floor was his. Wyatt nodded at Garrick, taking his cue, and then spoke very slowly and deliberately. In his experience, police officers were not the brightest bunch of people he'd ever met.

'Good afternoon. Let's start with the facts before we get into questions and any discussion. Hilary Russell was found dead in the hallway of her home at approximately 10.30 am on Monday morning and as you know I was the pathologist who attended the scene. As I indicated to DC Page on Monday morning and subsequently to DCI Garrick yesterday, there were no signs of external injury to the deceased and no obvious signs of a struggle. My initial diagnosis following a brief examination on site was that she had died either from respiratory failure or possibly from a cardiac arrest or a cerebral hemorrhage or infarction. At that stage it was not possible to ascertain whether death was as a result of foul play or by natural causes. Neither could be ruled out and consequently a post mortem and further tests were required.'

Wyatt paused, using the silence to full effect, making sure that he had everybody's full and undivided attention before delivering the news that they were waiting for.

'The post mortem carried out yesterday confirms my initial diagnosis that Hilary Russell did indeed die from respiratory failure, and from body temperature readings I estimate that time of death was somewhere between 3.00 and 4.00 am on Sunday morning. Unfortunately it's difficult to be more precise than that. However, there was no evidence of any cardiac symptoms to suggest any contributory cause and the deceased had no medical history to support the probability that death occurred by natural causes. Critically, there were one or two physical conditions, most notably facial colouring and pupil contraction which caused me sufficient concern to request some additional toxicology tests, which were carried out last night. The results of those tests arrived earlier today and confirm unequivocally that Hilary Russell died as a result of a lethal injection of *Fentanyl.* In layman's terms she stopped breathing as a result of being poisoned.'

A low murmur went round the incident room as Wyatt walked over to the white board and spelt out the word FENTANYL in large letters with one of the red markers.

'Re-examination of the body this afternoon finally located the point of injection, which was on the sole of the left foot. Almost impossible to detect. Any questions so far?'

Wyatt waited for a few seconds but predictably, no-one responded. They all had lots of questions but knew from experience that it was better to wait until he had finished speaking. Wyatt paused to make sure that no-one wanted to ask anything and then continued.

'Okay, now for the technical bit. *Fentanyl* is an opioid analgesic first synthesized in the late 1950s and developed specifically to treat chronic pain. It's in a class of drugs called "narcotic analgesics" and is a member of the same group of drugs to which opium and morphine belong. It works by acting on the central nervous system and most significantly has an analgesic potency of about 80 to 100 times that of morphine. In other words it's one of the most powerful pain killers known to man.'

Again, a low murmur and a few whistled exclamations went round the room. Wyatt ignored, or didn't notice the reaction and continued with his very deadpan, matter-of-fact delivery.

'*Fentanyl* was introduced into medical practice in the 1960s as an intravenous anesthetic and for those of you are interested in the technical details, opiate drugs work by binding to different types of opiate receptors throughout the nervous system. Different types of opiates tend to bind to different types of receptors, thus creating differences in effect between the different opiates. The "mu" receptor is responsible for the narcotic effects of euphoria, addiction and respiratory depression. There are also 'kappa' and 'sigma' receptors responsible for other effects. *Fentanyl* binds only to the 'mu' receptor and as I said, at levels approximately 80 to 100 times stronger than morphine.'

Wyatt paused again, sensing that some of the audience needed a moment to take in all of the information.

'Since its introduction in the early 60s, the pharmaceutical industry has developed numerous analogues or derivatives of *Fentanyl* over the years. These include a more potent analgesic, about 5 to 10 times more powerful than the original called *Sufentanil*, which is used in open heart surgery and also *Carfentanil*, which has an analgesic potency 10,000 times that of morphine and which is used in veterinary practice to immobilize large animals. Basically it's strong enough to knock over an elephant.'

A few of the CID officers laughed politely, realising that this was as about as light-hearted a comment as they were going to get from the taciturn Dr. Wyatt.

'In its traditional form *Fentanyl* is administered either intrathecally as part of spinal anesthesia or epidurally for epidural anesthesia and analgesia. More recent developments have seen *Fentanyl* manufactured as a transdermal patch. The patches work on the same principle as nicotine patches, i.e. by releasing the drug into subcutaneous fats, which then slowly release the drug into the blood stream over 72 hours, in this case providing long lasting relief from chronic pain. They have also developed a solid formulation of *Fentanyl* citrate on a stick, which is made in the form of a berry-flavored lollipop that dissolves slowly in the mouth for transmucosal absorption. The unit is swabbed on the mucosal surfaces inside the mouth to release the drug quickly into the system, again intended for opioid-tolerant individuals as an effective breakthrough treatment for cancer pain.'

Wyatt sensed that most of the officers were now in information overload so stopped and paused again for several seconds.

'Okay, I think that's probably enough of the science lecture for one day. The purpose of giving you all that background is to emphasise the fact that although you've probably never heard of *Fentanyl*, it has been around for over 50 years, it's manufactured in a variety of different formulations and it has been used before in cases of murder, albeit infrequently. Beyond that I just want to say two things. One; death from poisoning is extremely rare and is usually as a result of an accident or ignorance rather than murder, so this is a very unusual case indeed. And two; I don't know much about other types of crimes but intuitively I assume that armed robbery is more likely to be carried out by men rather than by women…'

Again, a few of the detectives laughed, the thought of female bank robbers somehow painting an unlikely picture.

'…and incidents of poisoning, whether fatal or not, are equally gender specific, except that in this case it's the other way round. Statistically, poisoners are much more likely to be female. I'll leave you with that thought. Now, any questions?'

Several arms went up in unison. Garrick decided he ought to manage the Q&As and pointed towards DS Cooper. 'Andy?'

Andy Cooper hadn't had any difficulty in keeping up with Dr. Wyatt and was already trying to translate this new information into possible lines of enquiry. 'You mentioned a lot about the medicinal and therefore legal use of *Fentanyl*. Has it transferred into the illegal drug market?'

Wyatt nodded. 'Absolutely. Illicit use of *Fentanyl* first appeared in the mid 1970s and, as is so often the case, initially in the medical community – and it continues today. The biological effects of *Fentanyl* are similar to those of heroin with the exception that there is less of a euphoric "high" associated with the drug and a stronger analgesic effect. It also has a shorter half-life than that of heroin. It's most commonly used orally, but like heroin can also be smoked, snorted or injected. Some heroin dealers mix *Fentanyl* powder with larger amounts of heroin in order to increase the potency or to compensate for low-quality heroin and therefore to increase the volume of their product. The mixture of *Fentanyl* and heroin is known as *"magic"*, amongst other names, on the street. Earlier this year, a mix of *Fentanyl* and either cocaine or heroin caused an outbreak in overdose deaths in the United States, heavily concentrated in the area around Detroit. There is also a clandestinely produced alpha-methyl strain called *"china white"* which is reported to be twice the strength of regular *Fentan*yl. The main advantage of the alpha-methyl formulation is that it provides a site of resistance to metabolic degradation, resulting in a drug with an increased duration.'

Again, Wyatt noticed that some of the officers were struggling to keep up and moved back into layman's speak.

'That said, the use of *Fentanyl* is extremely rare in the UK. Whilst you might be able to buy it on the streets of New York or Los Angeles, you'd be hard pushed to buy it on the streets of London or Manchester. To find *Fentanyl* in a small village in the Weald of Kent is frankly mind-boggling. I understand from DCI Garrick that there are very few leads in this case and of course, these are matters for you as detectives rather than me as a pathologist – but I would suggest that this very unusual choice of poison may be a useful place to start the enquiry and may help you target your investigation.'

Garrick waited a second to make sure that Wyatt had finished and then pointed to DS Taylor, another officer with over twenty years' experience. Paul?'

'Your last comment implies that the choice of *Fentanyl* over other possible poisons is significant? Why would someone want to use *Fentanyl* rather than something more easily available?'

Wyatt nodded. 'Good question, thank you. Firstly, the statement that other poisons would be more easily available to the murderer than *Fentanyl* is an assumption. Again, these are matters for you as detectives rather than me as a pathologist, but if the person that you're looking for works in the pharmaceutical industry or in medicine, perhaps as a doctor, or a paramedic or even a chemist, then it's likely that *Fentanyl* will be as readily available to them as most other poisons – indeed more so in some cases. Certainly access to the drug would be a sensible line of enquiry. However, in this case I don't think that access is the deciding factor. I'm fairly confident that the choice of *Fentanyl* would be dictated by two key facts. One; the speed at which the poison renders the patient unconscious and two; the difficulty it presents pathologists like me in diagnosis.'

Wyatt stopped and took a drink of water, the effects of talking at length starting to impact on his voice. Garrick got up and re-filled his glass as he continued.

'Let me cover the second point first. As police officers you will be aware of the case of Harold Shipman, even if you are not acquainted with the actual details. Shipman was a General Practitioner who it is now suspected may have killed as many as 137 patients during his time as a young trainee hospital doctor in Yorkshire between 1970 and 1974, in addition to the 215 murders that have already been attributed to him...'

The figures were clearly a surprise to most of the officers. Again, a number of comments and whistles went round the room.

'Unfortunately, Shipman hanged himself in his prison cell in January 2004, so we will never know the full extent of his crimes. The reason that Shipman's actions went undetected for so long is because he murdered most, if not all of his victims with a lethal overdose of morphine, or diamorphine to be more precise. Most of his victims were elderly and the advantage of using morphine is that there are very few symptoms for pathologists to look for and indeed, in hundreds of cases it was assumed that his patients had died from natural causes. Inevitably, most of his victims were cremated, but Shipman was finally caught following the exhumation of the body of one such patient, whose late changes to her will raised the suspicions of her daughter, who promptly went to the police. The exhumed body revealed lethal traces of diamorphine in her liver and thigh muscles.'

Wyatt paused for a moment again, deliberately giving some of the slower officers in the audience time to catch up.

'To answer your question, *Fentanyl* works in much the same way as morphine and for that reason, is an excellent choice of poison. Additionally, because *Fentanyl* is much more powerful than morphine, the effect of the overdose works that much quicker. The toxicology tests found 83 nanograms of *Fentanyl* in Hilary Russell's tissue, which is several times the amount required to kill her. If there is any consolation in this case I would estimate that it would have taken no more than five seconds following injection before Miss Russell went into coma – and if as I surmise she was injected whilst asleep in bed, then she would have hardly woken up.'

Garrick looked at his watch; conscious that time was moving on and that there was still a difficult press briefing to prepare for. 'Steph?'

'You said that time of death was somewhere between 3.00 and 4.00 am. Do you know what time the poison was injected?'

Wyatt nodded. 'Thank you DC Page. An obvious omission, I should have mentioned it. As I said, the dosage of *Fentanyl* given to Miss Russell would have put her into a coma almost instantly. I would estimate that it would have taken approximately fifteen minutes before she finally succumbed to the effects and stopped breathing, therefore I would estimate that the injection was administered somewhere around 3.00 am.'

'Burglar's hour.' one of the officers murmured under his breath. Garrick checked his watch again. 'Okay, five more minutes. Two more questions and then we'll have to wrap this up and let Dr. Wyatt get back to his day job. Andy?'

'I was just thinking about the choice of poison, which seems to be significant and wondered what are the other poisons that could have been used? Perhaps there's something significant about them which could help us – like maybe the murderer didn't have access to them.'

Wyatt paused for a moment, taking another drink from the glass of water and thinking about his response. 'Well, it's an interesting question. It's certainly looking at the problem from a different perspective which might be worthwhile, although I have to say that with one possible exception your suspect has chosen what is almost the perfect poison. Whilst you may regard him or her as something of an amateur with regard to the burglary, in terms of the choice of poison, they knew exactly what they were doing. However, with regard to alternatives, the short answer to your question is probably either morphine, the properties of which I've already covered, or nicotine…'

Wyatt sensed the surprise and slight amusement that this last comment produced, but carried on with his answer.

'There are other more popular or perhaps I should say, more well known poisons of course, such as arsenic or strychnine but neither of these would produce the same effects. Arsenic has probably claimed more victims than any other poison in history but crucially it needs to be administered in small doses over a long period of time, so that the cumulative effect of the poison, especially in the kidneys and liver, eventually kills the victim – normally with symptoms consistent with food poisoning. Strychnine is highly poisonous; one and a half grains or 100 milligrams will result in certain death but when dissolved, it produces a colourless solution with a strong bitter taste that still remains detected in dilutions as high as one part in 600,000 so is easily detected by post mortem. The effects of strychnine poisoning are also instantly recognisable to any pathologist. I don't think we've got time to go into the details now, fascinating as they are, but suffice to say, death by strychnine is truly one of the most horrific ways to die, the effects of which are written all over the face and body of the victim.'

A few disappointed comments went around the room, some of the officers clearly fascinated by the subject and by Wyatt's expertise. Wyatt smiled, pleased to have such an appreciative audience but nevertheless carried on, conscious that time was of the essence.

'Cyanide is a possible option perhaps. Cyanide is a synthetic organic is fatal in small doses and kills extremely quickly. It's found naturally in the stones of cherries, plums and peaches, the cores of apples and in the leaves of the laurel plant. Ingestion of moderate amounts of these natural substances causes headaches accompanied by mild heart palpitations. If a large dose is taken at one go, the heart will immediately be affected, causing a sudden collapse. The brain may also be affected, causing a seizure or a coma. Reaction to cyanide is rapid and deadly; as little as 50 milligrams causes death by anoxia within five minutes. It's often used in suicides of course, Hitler and Goering being two of the more famous examples. There is also some speculation that Steve McQueen may have died from cyanide poisoning caused by peach stone enemas given to him by a clinic in Mexico to treat his lung cancer. Finally, there are poisons such as ricin and thallium which are more well known these days because of the activities of diplomatic and terrorist organisations, which seem to favour their use. However, whilst both are deadly, they both take too long to take effect, the victim normally suffering for several days or possibly weeks before the poison eventually kills them. Ricin incidentally is obtained from the waste mash left over from the production of castor oil by the simple process of chromatography, hence its popularity. It's easy and cheap to make, is highly stable; and is affected little by extreme conditions. One gram is sufficient to kill about 30,000 people, so if you're feeling slightly out of your depth at the prospect of conducting an investigation that involves *Fentanyl*, you can imagine how your colleagues in the Anti-Terrorist Branch are feeling.'

Some of the officers looked stunned by the magnitude of the statistics.

'Because of its availability and sheer lethality, ricin has been linked with terrorist activity amongst anti-government militia in the US as well as Al Qaeda, and some of you may also remember the case of Georgi Markov, the Bulgarian dissident who was murdered in London in the 1970s, supposedly by the KGB, with a ricin poisoned dart fired in the so called "Umbrella Assassination". Let us just hope that the unthinkable never happens.'

Wyatt paused, indicating that the summary was over and looked over at Garrick who like his fellow officers had suddenly gone quiet, reflecting on the enormity of the terrorist threat and the consequences of a major incident involving ricin. Eventually, one of the longer serving DCs broke the ice.

'I was just thinking about going for a cigarette after this but I think I might change my mind now!'

Everybody laughed, including Wyatt, the comment bringing him back on track to Andy's original question.

'Yes, thank you for reminding me. Nicotine. Probably the most viable but least well-known alternative. Nicotine belongs to the same group of poisons as opium, morphine and cocaine. Nicotine is liquid at room temperature and is a highly effective poison, in large doses producing nausea and cardiac irregularity and then paralysing the respiratory system. The lethal dose for an adult is somewhere between 40 and 60 milligrams, which is the quantity contained in just two cigarettes. One cigar contains enough nicotine to kill two adults if it were administered by injection and death would take only a few minutes. An average human adult would probably die from eating two to three whole cigarettes because the amount of nicotine in an unsmoked cigarette is about 300 times as much as you get from smoking it. Of course, when tobacco is smoked most of the nicotine is burned off, the downside being that a number of carcinogens are produced instead. Crucially, nicotine inhalers and nasal sprays are readily available from Chemists and are essentially 100 milligram vials of 33% pure liquid nicotine with nothing more than a piece of plastic spray apparatus to stop you accessing the whole product. In summary, if you want to kill someone very quickly with a substance that is readily available, you could do a lot worse than buy a 100 milligram bottle of liquid nicotine, put the contents in a syringe and simply inject it into the victim. It would be fatal in seconds. Additionally, nicotine isn't found in serum toxicology screens and results from urine toxicology screens are rarely conclusive, mainly because any smoker or person who spends time around smokers is likely to have trace quantities of nicotine in their urine. In short, it's virtually impossible for the pathologist to produce a definitive conclusion.'

Wyatt looked over and smiled at the officer who had cracked the comment about going for a cigarette. 'But if you still want to go ahead and have your cigarette break, don't let me stop you.'

Again, everybody laughed, although a bit nervously this time. Quite a few of the CID team were smokers and the implication of Wyatt's information was definitely sinking in.

Garrick checked his watch again. 'Okay, one last question and then we really must finish. Anybody?'

Everybody seemed to have asked everything that was on their mind, or were still thinking through all the information that had been presented. Eventually Matt put his hand up. Matt wasn't a smoker and to be honest, he wasn't convinced about the relevance of Andy's question. Wyatt's information on poisons had been interesting but he wasn't sure how pertinent it was to the enquiry. Matt was still thinking about Wyatt's answer to the question before.

'Earlier, you said that you assumed that Miss Russell was murdered in her sleep, in bed, yet she was found dead in the hallway at the bottom of the stairs, which doesn't seem to make sense. Why do you think she was murdered in bed rather than where she was found?'

Wyatt nodded, as though he understood why someone should question his hypothesis. 'That, I have to say is the most interesting question of all. Thank you. I think the poison was administered while Miss Russell was asleep because I find it inconceivable that an injection could be forcibly given to the sole of the foot to someone awake and upright, without there being some sort of struggle, however brief. There were no signs of a struggle whatsoever, no bruising, no foreign material under the fingernails – nothing. It is as though she died peacefully in her sleep and was then carried downstairs, the reasons for which I can't explain. In moving the body, someone took a risk, whether they knew it or not. What I don't understand is, why?'

The room fell into silence again, everyone thinking through the implications of what Dr. Wyatt had just said. If the murderer deliberately wanted to give the impression that Hilary Russell had died from natural causes, why move the body? Why not simply leave her in bed? Elderly people died in their sleep all the time didn't they?

Garrick nodded at Wyatt, indicating that they needed to finish and then shook hands and thanked him for his time as he walked him to the door and then watched him wander off down the corridor. The CID team were busy conducting their own post mortem on Wyatt's performance. The general consensus was that it had been fascinating. Garrick quickly got their attention back before closing the meeting.

'Okay, I know this seems like a daunting enquiry but to put it into perspective, yesterday we had practically no information whatsoever and thanks to Dr. Wyatt and his team, today we know the exact location where the murder took place, the approximate time of death and the cause of death, which is considerable progress in just 24 hours. All we need to do now is work out why Hilary Russell was murdered and by whom.'

A few of the officers laughed at Garrick's over-simplification of the task ahead.

Garrick smiled, sharing the joke at his own expense. 'Right, I need to shoot off in a minute and do this press briefing, which will take about 30 minutes hopefully. Whilst I'm away what would be really helpful is if those of you who are working this evening could...'

Garrick stopped, conscious that Desk Sergeant Phil Edwards was standing at the door, looking out of breath from having walked upstairs and also visibly annoyed at having had to make the journey. Edwards was in his late fifties and over-weight and was not known for leaving his desk unless he really had to.

'Sorry to interrupt you John, I tried ringing the CID room but nobody's answering the phones up here.'

Edwards was one of the old guard and as in most stations, there was a healthy rivalry between uniform and CID. Garrick could sense his annoyance immediately and knew this would be the talk of the canteen tomorrow – CID swanning about in the incident room and not bothering to pick up calls. He apologised immediately. 'Sorry Phil, my fault. We were all in here. We're just finishing up. What's the problem?'

Edwards took a deep breath as though he was still recovering from having run upstairs too quickly. 'I thought you'd want to know. We've just been passed a 999 call from a Mrs. Sarah Richmond out at Boughton Monchelsea. She's the wife of Stuart Richmond, their house was burgled last week...'

Garrick nodded impatiently. He knew who Stuart Richmond was.

'...I've directed the nearest patrol car to attend. She says her husband's just been murdered.'

SEVEN

The Heath Road which ran from Boughton Monchelsea to Linton was long and flat, a single carriageway but very straight and very fast. Craven should have turned off into the safety of the back lanes and cut through to one of the local villages but he needed a cigarette and he needed it now. He didn't normally approve of taking risks but today he was going to make an exception. He drove the car as fast as he could towards the crossroads and as soon as he saw the lay-by, pulled over, unwound the window and lit up, needing a few minutes to collect his thoughts and decide what to do next.

It had been a close call. He'd only been in the house about fifteen minutes when he'd heard the car coming up the drive and then the key turning in the front door. He could argue that it was just bad luck, but he knew better than that. He didn't know how long Richmond's wife had been out or when she was coming back – but that was his own fault. Sloppy. He should have done some reconnaissance, staked the place out, watched some movements, established some patterns. Stupid. Going in on impulse and expecting to have enough time was crazy and against everything he'd been taught and trained to do. He took another drag on the cigarette and switched off the engine. Typical. The jobs that looked complicated were always the ones that went smoothly and the ones that looked simple and straightforward ended up being a pain in the arse.

He looked at the mobile phone which was lying on the front passenger seat and thought about phoning Buchanan but just as quickly changed his mind. There was no point in ringing him with a problem – much better to call him later with a solution. He just needed to wait until he'd decided his next move. *"The sufferings that fate inflicts on us should be borne with patience; what enemies inflict with manly courage."*

Craven could see the crossroads half a mile ahead and heard the sirens before he could see the flashing blue lights. The police car was travelling at full speed, heading towards him and obviously on its way to *Chart Place*. He quickly pulled out a map from the side pocket of the driver's door, unfolded it on the passenger seat and then held it up, shifting sideways so that his face was turned away from the road. The patrol car sped past and as far as he could tell, without taking any notice of him – just a motorist pulled over, looking at a map and checking his directions. Still, there was no point in taking unnecessary risks. He needed to get out of there as soon as possible.

He checked the rear-view mirror to make sure that the car was out of sight, put the map back into the driver's door pocket and finished the cigarette. There was only one thing for it. If he couldn't complete the assignment with Richmond's co-operation then he'd have to find another way. Start from the other end of the problem. He flicked the cigarette butt out of the window and heard the second siren approaching from the same direction. He could see from the height of the blue lights that it was an ambulance, also travelling at full speed, a line of cars pulling over to let it overtake. *Bit late for that*, he thought, *should have ordered him a hearse.*

Craven waited for the ambulance to pass and then started the car and drove off towards the crossroads. Plan B. Time to move quickly, not least because he needed to keep ahead of the local police. They hadn't a clue what they were dealing with, but it wouldn't stay that way forever. He was starting to lose his advantage. It wouldn't be long before they began to work out what was going on – either that or the inquisitive nephew and his nosey neighbour would start poking into things and he needed to get there first. Otherwise, things were going to get very messy indeed.

*

Neil put the phone down and sat down on the kitchen stool, partly in shock and partly because he just didn't know what to do next. He looked at the words that he'd written down on the pad that Aunt Hilary had left by the phone. *Fentanyl, morphine, pain killer* and *Sunday at 3.00 am* and stared at them for several minutes, trying to work out what it all meant. Suddenly his visit to Appleden was turning sour. First of all there was the burglary and now this. Tom was right. Something was going on here that didn't make sense. Who on earth would want to kill his aunt and why?

He got off the stool and went into the dining room where he'd remembered seeing some bottles of wine. Neil enjoyed a glass of wine now and again but seldom drank on his own and never at 4.30 in the afternoon – but he suddenly felt an overwhelming need to have a drink and it wasn't a cup of tea that he wanted. He took the bottle back into kitchen, found a corkscrew and opened the wine, pouring himself a large glass and staring back at the words on the pad. *Fentanyl* didn't mean anything to him. He needed to do something about this. Perhaps Tom was right – maybe the police were useless. Steph was friendly and very attractive but at the end of the day they didn't seem to have a clue. No suspects, no witnesses, no forensics and no leads. In short, no idea.

He took another large gulp of wine and could feel the effects kicking in. *Idiot. There you were thinking that she'd rung up to follow up on the dinner invitation and she's ringing to tell you about the case. She's not interested in going out for dinner – she's just doing her job.*

He poured himself another glass of wine and thought for a moment. What he really needed was a laptop and an internet connection, but even Tom and Doreen didn't have a computer. There was probably an internet café in Ashford or Maidstone but there was no way he was going to be able to get on the internet whilst he was stuck in Appleden – and he didn't even have a car. Instinctively he picked up the phone and called the office. The telephone rang only a couple of times before it was picked up.

'News Desk – Chris Fleming speaking.'

'Hi Chris, it's Neil.'

Neil could sense the surprise in Chris's voice. 'Hey Neil. How are you? Is everything okay?'

'I'm fine Chris but I need your help with something. Are you busy at the moment?'

Chris laughed. 'No, you were right mate. Lost dogs and broken streetlights. Actually, I'm meant to be covering the Modern Arts Festival this week but someone's just come back with some shots and I can't work out whether they're photos of the exhibits or a load of plastic bags full of rubbish waiting for the council to collect. Anyway, you shouldn't be worrying about work – what's the favour?'

It took Neil a couple of minutes to bring Chris up to speed with everything. He could sense that Chris was struggling to balance being sympathetic and concerned about what had happened, against his natural instincts as a journalist for a possible story. He was obviously worried about his friend but at the same time intrigued and excited by the prospect of investigating a real life murder enquiry.

'Leave it with me, Neil, I'll do some research and get back to you. If you get any more info give me a call or send me a text.'

'Okay Chris, thanks very much – and give my regards to Carol.'

'Will do. Hey actually, I've just had a thought. Carol's going to her Mum and Dad's this weekend, I'm meant to going with her...'

Neil smiled. He knew what was coming next. Good old Chris.

'...don't get me wrong, they're really nice people but it's not the most exciting way to spend the weekend. We were going by train – it's less hassle.

How about I try and get out of it and come and spend the weekend with you down in Kent? I could bring the car.'

'Chris, that would be brilliant. Wouldn't Carol mind?'

Chris laughed. 'You must be joking. She'll have a much better time without me. She spends most of the weekend worrying about me surviving the in-laws if I go with her. She'll be absolutely fine.'

'Well, if you're sure Chris, I'd really appreciate it. It'd be nice to have some company to be honest.'

'Good. Consider it sorted. I'll do as much digging around as I can and I'll update you at the weekend. I'll come down straight after work on Friday. Maybe we'll get the chance to do the old Bernstein and Woodward routine after all. Anyway, if not, we'll just have a good weekend. You can introduce me to some of that famous Kentish beer!'

Neil put the phone down and suddenly felt much better. He looked at the glass of wine that was still on the worktop and promptly threw it down the sink. That wasn't going to solve anything. Besides, he was going down the pub later with Tom and he didn't want to turn up at Doreen's having had too much to drink. For the first time in several days he felt that he was taking control of the situation instead of just waiting for events to unfold. He knew it wasn't strictly true of course but at least he felt as though he was doing something. It was about time that he tried to sort things out and there was nobody better to help him with that than Chris. *Still, wait until I tell Tom*, he thought, *he'll also have something to say about this. Maybe the three of us, if we put our heads together, will finally work out what's going on.*

*

By the time Garrick and Matt turned up at *Chart Place*, the ambulance had arrived and been sent away again and Alan Wyatt had more or less concluded his on-site examination. It had taken Garrick twenty minutes or so to persuade Chief Superintendent Anderson to cover the press conference, a decision that neither of them were particularly enamoured with. Anderson had spent the last five years sitting behind a desk and whilst he had enough political nouse to handle the boys from the local press without any difficulty, he wasn't that familiar with the details of the case. Going through the drafted statement would be straightforward, but answering questions on his feet was another thing altogether.

Garrick wasn't that pleased either. Running a press conference wasn't something that he could delegate downwards, but keeping everybody "on message" in a case like this was key, particularly in the early stages of an enquiry. Which meant there were only two options; either let Anderson do it, or do it himself and send a couple of the others out to *Chart Place*. That wasn't an option he wanted to consider. Being first on the scene was absolutely critical and not something he was prepared to miss.

Garrick gazed out of the car window as Matt drove up towards the house and pulled into the large turning circle which swept up to and across the main entrance. *Chart Place* was an imposing and substantial property, a fifteen bedroom Queen Anne residence with later Edwardian additions, sympathetically restored, immaculately furnished and set in ten or so acres of landscaped grounds. Garrick let out a low whistle as the first sight of the house came into view. 'Wow, look at the size of this place Matt – the guy must be worth a fortune.'

'Not much good to him now though, is it Sir?' said Matt, as he turned off the ignition and got out of the car, surveying the expanse of manicured lawns and low box hedging which dominated the front of the property. The patrol car and Wyatt's Volvo were already parked outside and the SOCO team had also arrived, their van parked at an angle to the house with the back doors still open.

Garrick got out of the car and walked briskly towards Alan Wyatt who was standing on the front steps, looking as though he was waiting for their arrival, although in truth he had simply stepped outside to get some fresh air after examining the body.

Garrick nodded as he walked up the steps towards the house. 'Alan – twice in one day. People will start to talk…'

Wyatt pulled a grim face. 'Mmm. I think twice in one week is probably the more pertinent statistic. And before you ask – no, it isn't another poisoning, although I have to say, in thirty years I've never seen anything like this before. You'd better come in and have a look.' Garrick and Matt exchanged a puzzled look as Wyatt turned and went back into the house, indicating to them to follow him inside.

The hall was large and wide with a long, open staircase which ran up the left-hand side and then swept majestically across the width of the room at the back. The décor had been updated in recent years and was finished in soft pinks and pastel blues in keeping with the period and lavishly furnished with occasional tables, original paintings and other period pieces. A large grandfather clock in a mahogany case stood to attention at the far end of the room.

Wyatt pointed towards the doorway ahead of him, in the top left-hand corner of the hall. 'The body's in the study, over there. The SOCO boys are still working at the moment so you can go as far as the door and look in, unless you want to get suited up.'

Garrick shook his head, knowing that he and Matt would only be in the way until the SOCO team had finished.

The study was a medium sized, square-ish room with two large, sash windows taking up most of the right-hand wall and overlooking a terrace and croquet lawn which led towards a small fountain and then out towards the rear garden. The wall opposite the door was dedicated to a bookcase which ran the length of the wall and which was filled from floor to ceiling with books of all conceivable shapes and sizes, both old and modern, including what looked like a number of sets of leather bound volumes, probably antique.

Because of the angle of the door which was hinged on the left, Garrick couldn't see much of the left hand wall, but through the crack in the door he could make out a substantial desk and chair, which was where Richmond presumably worked when he was at home. The two SOCO officers were busy brushing and dusting various parts of the room and there was a lot of mess and disturbance around them, but it was the body and the amount of money strewn across the floor which immediately caught Garrick's and Matt's attention.

'Like I said, in thirty years I've never seen anything like it.' Wyatt was leaning over Garrick's shoulder, also looking at Richmond's body, which was lying face up on the floor, about halfway between the door and the far wall. His eyes were open and bulging slightly but it was his mouth, wide open and stuffed full of crumpled £20 notes that Wyatt was referring to. 'I'll need to do a PM of course to confirm everything,' he continued, 'but I think it's fairly safe to say that he died of asphyxiation as a result of having his mouth crammed full of paper. Basically, somebody suffocated him by ramming a load of money down his throat...'

Garrick looked around the room and at the volume of banknotes scattered all over the furniture. Chairs, window seats, lamp tables, carpet – almost every spare inch of space was covered in money, some of it in £50 notes and a couple of bundles still wrapped in cellophane packets as though it had come straight from the bank, but most of it in loose £20 notes and scattered around the room like confetti.

'Phew, any idea how much there is in total?' asked Matt, equally taken aback by the sheer volume of cash in front of them.

Wyatt shook his head. 'No idea. A lot. Tens of thousands, certainly. A £100,000 perhaps? Anyway, the SOCO boys will want to check it all so you're in luck, somebody else it going to count it for you.'

Garrick looked round the room, trying to get a feel for what had happened and looking for anything else that might be significant. 'Do you know how long he's been dead?' he asked, still staring at Richmond's body and trying to take it all in.

Wyatt hesitated, indicating that what he was about to say was only an estimate. 'A couple of hours at the most – probably less. I'll be able to give you a more exact time once I've had a proper look at him. If it helps, his wife said that she went out at lunchtime and came back at about four o'clock, so at least you've got a definite window to work with.'

Garrick nodded, deep in thought. 'I'd better go and have a quick word with her. Do you know where she is Alan?'

'In the kitchen I think,' replied Wyatt, 'with one of your PCs. Not in very good shape I'm afraid.'

'No, suppose not. Is there anything else I should know?'

Wyatt nodded. 'There are a number of small burn marks to the body, consistent with the use of a stun gun. I've found three symmetrical pairs so far but there may be more. I would guess that the notes were pushed in his mouth while he was knocked out – but it's possible that he was awake and fully conscious by the time he finally stopped breathing.'

Garrick frowned, not really wanting to contemplate the implications of slowly suffocating on a mouth full of money, rammed so far down your throat that it's impossible to get out or cough up, desperately trying to catch you breath, lungs burning for air but nothing getting through. Choking and suffocating at the same time. He shuddered. Not a nice way to die. 'Anything else, Alan?'

'Just one. Does the word "Teleios" mean anything to you?'

Garrick and Matt looked blankly at each other and shook their heads. 'Never heard of it,' said Garrick, 'why?'

Wyatt indicated towards the part of the room behind the door. 'You can't see it from here but somebody's sprayed the words "Teleios" in red paint on the wall behind the door. I assume it was Richmond's visitor.'

Garrick tried to look through the gap again but couldn't see the wall that was immediately behind the door. He and Matt exchanged another look – part intrigue, part acknowledgement that they hadn't a clue what was going on. 'Matt, I'd better go and see Mrs. Richmond. Go and get suited up and get in there and have a look at it. And see if you can borrow SOCO's camera and get some pictures as well. I'll be back in ten minutes.'

Garrick left Wyatt and Matt talking to the SOCO officers and wandered down the hall to where he assumed the kitchen was. He could see a young PC standing in a doorway at the end of the corridor and stopped for a brief word before going in. 'Anything I should know constable?'

'Wife doesn't seem to know anything Sir,' replied the PC, instantly going ramrod straight, 'says she left here at about 12.30 to go and do some shopping and came back about an hour ago. She's very distressed. I don't think you'll get much out of her today Sir. WPC Evans is with her at the moment. We're waiting for a sister to arrive from Chislehurst. She'll probably be another hour.'

Garrick nodded. 'Okay, anything else?'

'Couldn't find any sign of forced entry Sir. That's it I think.'

'Okay, thanks.' Garrick walked into the room and saw Sarah Richmond and the WPC sitting at the kitchen table, both cupping a mug of something hot, tea probably, and neither of them talking. Sarah Richmond was starring into space, looking at nothing in particular and didn't even notice Garrick enter the room. The WPC was looking at the calendar on the kitchen wall, trying to keep herself occupied and not look too bored – but knowing that there wasn't anything that she could say or do that was going to make things any better. Sometimes being in the police force was one of the worst jobs in the world.

Garrick walked up to the table and sat down opposite Sarah Richmond, waiting for her to notice his arrival rather than announce it himself. Eventually, she turned her head very slowly towards him as if coming out of a trance and smiled, although only with her mouth; her eyes too red and swollen from crying to do anything else.

'Mrs. Richmond, can I just say how sorry I am…' Garrick's words faded into nothing. There wasn't much he could say that really meant anything. He didn't know her. He'd never met her husband. She didn't need his platitudes.

'Mrs. Richmond, I know this isn't the time and I really don't want to upset you any more than you are already…'

Her face changed in an instant – defiance, indignation, anger, the response hissed through clenched teeth. 'You couldn't upset me any more than I am already Chief Inspector, I've just lost my husband.'

Garrick held his hands up, desperately trying to defuse the situation and find the right words. 'I'm sorry, I just need to ask you a couple of questions Mrs. Richmond. I wish it could wait but it really is very urgent.'

She took a deep breath and nodded, indicating her consent for him to continue.

'Do you know of anybody, anyone at all who might want to do this to your husband? Somebody that he's fallen out with or had an argument with perhaps…?'

Sarah Richmond was already shaking her head. 'Not to my knowledge. He ran a large, successful business and knew a lot of people, but I'm not aware of anything. Sorry.'

Garrick held a hand up again, as if to indicate that there was nothing to apologise for and moved onto to the next question, conscious that they both wanted to get through this as quickly as possible. 'I assume that the money in the study belonged to your husband? Did he normally have that much cash in the house?'

Again she shook her head. 'Never. We pay everything by plastic – always have done. I doubt that we normally have more than £100 in cash between us…' Her eyes suddenly welled up, the realisation that her whole vocabulary was going to have to change. No more *we*, no more *us*.

Garrick smiled at her as a sort of encouragement. *You're doing fine. Two more questions.* 'Does the name Teleios mean anything to you Mrs. Richmond?'

For the third time she shook her head. 'No, other than it's written all over the wall of our study… my study. I've never heard it before,' she added, finding some composure, 'it could be the name of a label or a fashion designer for all I know, but I've not heard it before and I don't remember my husband ever using it.'

'No matter. One last question. Does anyone have a spare set of keys to the house?'

Sarah Richmond took a drink of tea and nodded towards a row of key hooks hanging up next to the back door. 'We have a spare set of everything, which we keep on the hook over there. Our neighbours next door have a spare key for the front door but we've known them for years. I expect whoever it was simply rang the bell and my husband answered it.'

Garrick nodded, recognising that this was the most likely explanation. 'Okay, Mrs. Richmond. We'll need to talk again, but for the time being, thanks for your help. Sorry about the poor choice of words.'

She smiled back, partly in apology. 'That's okay Chief Inspector, my fault. Oh, about the keys – we also have a cleaner who comes in a couple of mornings a week. She has a front door key as well – but we've also known her for years. I've got a phone number for her somewhere. Doreen Webster, she lives over at Appleden.'

Garrick forced a smile, trying his hardest not to give anything away. 'That's all right Mrs. Richmond. Don't worry about the number – I'm sure we'll be able to find her.'

EIGHT

It took Garrick and Matt about thirty minutes to drive back to the station, a journey which Garrick knew was precious time to process everything that they had seen and heard – and to try and work out what it all meant. The station was going to be in chaos when they got back and everybody would be looking to him to provide some direction. Problem was, he hadn't a clue what was going on. He needed time to think and he needed Matt to just drive and not talk.

That wasn't going to be a problem. Matt knew the road like the back of his hand and drove on autopilot, also needing time to think. He guessed this was likely to be the only period of peace and quiet that they were going to get and sensed that Garrick was not in the mood for bouncing ideas around. Time for some quiet reflection.

Matt pulled the car out onto the main road and headed back towards Sutton Valence, an old Kentish village perched on top of a steep hill, famous for not very much other than a rather ordinary public school. Or was it a private school? He never really knew the difference. Either way, it was nothing to do with education. It was all about nepotism and maintaining the English class system. Posh kids with rich parents trying to buy their children a head start in life. Iniquitous, privileged, medieval.

Matt let his mind wander for several minutes, unable to stop the images of boarding schools and playing fields from occupying his thoughts. Cold, decaying buildings, evening prep, dining halls, quads, *"non scholae sed vitae discimus."* He shook his head in disbelief and brought his mind back to concentrate on *Chart Place*. There had to be a connection between the burglary and Richmond's murder. The two incidents had to be connected and he wanted to try and work out why; develop some logical conclusions, some possibilities to explain the two events. What he hadn't expected was a connection between Richmond and the murder at *Yew Tree Cottage*.

Garrick was going through the same process but reaching different conclusions. He didn't believe in coincidences. There hadn't been a murder in this part of Kent for over four years and suddenly there were two in four days. There had to be a connection between the events in Appleden and at Boughton Monchelsea – he just didn't expect it to be Doreen Webster and he couldn't for the life of him work out how or why it was her.

Matt got to Sutton Valence, navigated the hill on the far side of the village and then drove out towards Headcorn, lost in his own thoughts and trying his hardest to find a rational explanation for the events at *Chart Place*. After a few minutes Garrick looked across at him and broke the silence. 'So, what do you think Matt? Any flashes of inspiration for me?'

Matt shook his head. 'I'm just trying to work through possible connections between the burglary and Richmond's murder. The obvious conclusion is that whoever committed the burglary came back and killed him – but for the moment I can't work out why. The answer has to be in the money and in the word "Teleios", whatever that means. What about you Sir?'

Garrick stared out of the side window. It was going dark and it was starting to rain. 'Actually, I was thinking about a possible connection between Hilary Russell and Stuart Richmond and trying to figure out how Doreen Webster fits into all this – but likewise, not getting very far.'

Matt raised his eyebrows, looking slightly surprised at Garrick's response. 'Oh, I assumed we'd interview her and hopefully she'd tell us – or am I just being naïve?'

Garrick smiled to himself. 'No, it's not naïve at all Matt. It's exactly the logical thing to assume and obviously what we're going to do. I probably could have spent the last ten minutes concentrating on something more useful.'

Matt was just turning into Headcorn and conscious that they weren't far away from Appleden. 'Do you want to go and see her now Sir?'

Garrick looked at his watch. It was nearly half past six. 'No, it can wait Matt. Anyway, we'd better get her into the station tomorrow and get it on tape. Best to have Steph there as well. We'll need a female officer with us and Steph's met her before. Besides, I expect Anderson's waiting for me to get back and give him an update. I think I'm going to spend a lot of time managing upwards on this one.'

They both went quiet for another minute or so, thinking about the ramifications of Richmond's murder. An anonymous old lady attacked during the course of a burglary was one thing. The murder of a high profile celebrity was completely different. The press were going to have a field day and everybody from Anderson downwards was going to be under enormous pressure.

'Do you think the two murders were carried out by the same person?' asked Matt eventually, concentrating on a particularly vicious bend and hoping that the question wasn't too stupid.

Garrick shook his head. 'I wouldn't have thought so. They look completely different to me.'

Matt threw him a look, indicating that he wasn't sure what Garrick meant and wanted him to explain further.

'Well, I'm no psychologist Matt but it strikes me that poisoning is a particularly cold and calculated way of killing somebody. It's very pre-meditated. It's also an act committed by stealth – in this case silently and in the dead of night. Strangely, it's also not particularly violent. In many cases the murderer isn't actually there when the victim dies. Think about it Matt, it's a crime committed by someone who is very controlled and very precise in everything they do. Look at the planning and preparation needed to make it happen and the lengths that someone went to, to try and disguise the evidence – the injection in the foot, moving the body. And it's a crime carried out without any confrontation. Someone very secretive who had to take a great deal of care to select the right poison, to administer exactly the right dose, to minimise all the risks – but who didn't need to be there to see the result of all of that coming together.'

Matt nodded. Garrick's hypothesis made a lot of sense.

'Whereas Richmond's murder looked exactly the opposite. Violent, confrontational, dramatic. It looked like retribution, a punishment even; someone wanting to tell the whole world why it happened. For god's sake, he even left us a message sprayed in twelve-inch letters all over the wall. Remember all the mess in that room and the banknotes spread all over the floor. There was nothing careful about it Matt and it certainly wasn't committed by stealth. Mrs. Richmond could be right. Maybe the murderer simply walked up to the front door and rang the bell. I don't know whether it was pre-meditated or not but I'd say it was a murder committed by someone who when they get angry can't help showing it, or doesn't even want to hide it. I'd bet any money that they were carried out by two different people.'

Matt gave Garrick an appreciative nod, clearly impressed with the analysis. 'Well, it makes a lot of sense to me Sir. Very logical.'

Garrick smiled. 'Yeah I know Matt. Worrying isn't it? I think I must have been working with you for too long.'

Matt laughed as he pulled into one of the parking bays at the rear of the station and switched off the engine. Despite the pressure, Garrick usually kept his sense of humour. 'So what's the plan of action then Sir?'

'Well, Steph and I can talk to Mrs. Webster tomorrow morning. What we need really quickly is a full profile and recent history on Richmond. I want to know his every movement, hour by hour since the night of the burglary. Where he's been, who he's met, who he's spoken to, bank records, credit card bills, telephone calls, everything. In particular we need to find out why he had £100,000 in cash at home. I want a dossier on him so detailed that it feels as though I've been by his side for the past two weeks.

'I can get started on that now Sir,' volunteered Matt.

'Good, thanks Matt. We also need to chase up the stolen property from Richmond's place. If we can trace anything back to the burglary then we've got a fighting chance of making some progress on the case. We also need to talk to the nephew again and see if he's managed to work out what's been taken from *Yew Tree Cottage*. Whoever broke in was obviously looking for something in particular and until we know what it is, we're working in the dark.'

'Anything else?' asked Matt, getting out of the car.

'We'd better get someone to do so some research on Teleios and *Fentanyl*. Find out what the hell Teleios means and see if we can identify every practice in say a twenty-mile radius that stocks *Fentanyl*. Other than that, it's probably just a question of keeping the press off our backs for 48 hours and being given the space to get on and do the job.'

Matt nodded in acknowledgement as they walked up to the rear door of the station. 'It's going to be a lot of work Sir but the whole team will pull together and do whatever it takes. I'm sure we'll get a result – and get one quickly.'

Garrick pulled a grim face. What Matt didn't realise was how little time they really had. 'Amen to that. So do I Matt. So do I.'

*

'I couldn't manage another mouthful Doreen, honestly,' said Neil, pushing his plate forward and leaning back into the chair to indicate that he was full up.

'Nonsense, you've hardly eaten anything. A growing lad like you needs to keep his strength up. There's plenty more left.'

'Doreen, I've had two whole platefuls, I couldn't eat another thing,' protested Neil, his eyes wide open at the suggestion that he hadn't eaten very much and that at thirty years of age he was still a growing lad.

Tom grinned at him from the opposite side of the table. Doreen always did have a different idea about of the size of portions.

'Well if you're sure. There wasn't anything wrong with it was there?' she added, frowning and suddenly worrying that her plain, home-cooked food wasn't cosmopolitan enough for someone as well travelled as Neil. 'I expect you're used to all sorts of fancy cooking these days.'

'Doreen, it was fabulous. Absolutely wonderful. I haven't had rabbit stew in years. It's the best meal I've had since I've been back in England. You should open a restaurant – you'd make a fortune. It's much better than any meal I've had out in Cambridge. Honestly, it was wonderful.'

'Oh, don't be so silly,' said Doreen, pretending to be modest but at the same time beaming at Neil's comments and at having such an appreciative guest to dinner. 'It was only a bit of rabbit with some vegetables and a few lentils. 'Now then, you two go and sit down while I wash up and then I'll make us all a cup of tea.'

'Do you want a hand with the washing up Doreen?' asked Neil, remembering his manners.

Tom threw him a withering look. There was clearly a very old-fashioned division of labour in the Webster household – most of it in Tom's favour and he didn't want anybody upsetting the applecart. Doreen had already gone back into the kitchen and either hadn't heard Neil or was pretending not to, so he joined Tom in one of the armchairs in front of the fire. Tom tossed another log onto the fire which spat and crackled under the flame. It was the first one that he'd lit since the weather had turned and in truth, it wasn't really cold enough for a real fire, but he knew it made the place feel warm and homely and thought that Neil would appreciate it.

'So, where do you do your gardening jobs then Tom?' asked Neil, sinking into the armchair and watching the flames take hold of the wood.

'I do the vicarage on Mondays,' replied Tom, reaching for his lighter and tobacco tin, 'and one of the big houses at the end of the village, Greenways, on Thursdays.'

'Oh, Doctor Keating's old place,' said Neil, still staring at the fire.

Tom finished rolling up his cigarette and gave him a knowing look. 'Of course, you went out with his daughter for a while didn't you. I'd forgotten about that. What was her name?'

'Julia,' replied Neil rather wistfully. 'It was just for one summer – years ago,' he added with as much understatement as he could manage. 'I don't suppose you know what happened to the Keatings after they moved away?' he asked, trying to make it sound as though it was just idle curiosity.

Tom shook his head. 'Haven't heard of them for years. Both the children went to university I think but the family moved before they'd finished. Haven't seen them since. The place is owned by a lawyer now. He works in London somewhere. Gets up at 5.30 and gets home at eight o'clock in the evening. Must be mad. Doreen might know where they are now.'

Tom was just about to call out to Doreen in the kitchen when they both heard the telephone ring and Doreen pick it up. Tom lit his cigarette and picked up the paper and Neil gazed at the fire, thinking about a summer ten years ago and the happiest period in his life.

After about five minutes Doreen came through into the dining room and sat back down at the table.

'You alright luv?' asked Tom, putting down the paper and noticing that she wasn't looking herself.

'Just had a strange phone call Tom. It was that nice policewoman who came round this morning. Apparently they want to interview me again. I've got to be at the station tomorrow at nine-thirty.'

'But we only gave them a statement this morning.' protested Tom. 'Why do they want to see you again?'

'I don't know, she wouldn't say,' replied Doreen, still looking as though the phone call had upset her. 'I did ask if they wanted to see you as well but she said they just wanted to see me.'

Tom and Neil exchanged a puzzled look. 'Well how are you going to get there?' asked Tom, suddenly thinking about the practicalities of Doreen not being able to drive. 'I've got to be up at Greenways tomorrow, I can't really take the morning off.'

'Oh, I'll be alright,' said Doreen, 'I'll get the bus. She did offer to come and collect me but I'm not having a police car turning up at the front door and taking me away. Whatever would the neighbours think?'

Neil smiled and Tom shook his head in despair. Only Doreen would put up with the inconvenience of traipsing all that way and back on the bus just to avoid giving the neighbours something to talk about. 'I suppose I could see if I can swap tomorrow to Friday,' suggested Tom, actually more worried about Doreen having to go on her own rather than the fact that she was going on public transport.

'Oh, stop worrying Tom, I'll be fine. Anyway, I can always get some shopping while I'm there and bring it back on the bus.'

Tom let out a begrudging grunt, clearly not impressed with the proposed arrangements. 'I don't suppose you're doing anything tomorrow are you lad?' he asked, suddenly looking at Neil.

'No, nothing Tom. I'd gladly take Doreen over, but I haven't got a car.'

Tom brightened up instantly. 'That's all right, you can borrow mine. It's only an old Escort but you'll be okay driving that won't you?'

'I suppose so Tom. Am I insured to drive it?'

Tom grinned. 'Oh, I wouldn't worry about that lad, it's not even taxed.'

Neil laughed. Tom really did live in another world. 'Of course I'll come with you Doreen. Anyway, it might be a good idea to have someone with you. Give you some moral support.'

'That's settled then,' said Tom, pleased that the practical arrangements had been sorted out and completely forgetting to worry about why they wanted to see Doreen again. 'Now then lad, can you remember how to play cribbage? How about 10p a point?'

Neil smiled. He did remember how to play cribbage but he had a feeling that an evening playing cards with Tom was about to cost him a lot of money.

*

It had gone nine o'clock by the time Matt decided that he'd had enough and that he ought to go home and get some sleep. Some of the others had gone to the pub to get something to eat and were coming back later but Matt had worked right through and needed to call it a day. He was tired and he was hungry and in the last hour he'd also developed a headache. Too many hours working on the PC and too much information buzzing around his head. He switched off the computer and looked at the list of items from Richmond's burglary for one last time, trying to find some inspiration and some sort of connection between the burglary and the murder. He didn't believe in coincidences any more than Garrick did and he felt certain that the answer had to be somewhere in the list of stolen property.

It was the same list that Craven had taken from Richmond's study and which he was also reading, laying on his bed in *The Moon and Falcon* whilst slowly working his way through a bottle of wine. As it happened, both Matt and Craven reached the same conclusion at exactly the same time. They'd both been at *Chart Place* no more than an hour apart and had both seen the original watercolours, the casement clocks, the Georgian silverware, the antique books. As Matt scanned down the list again he suddenly realised that he would have to tell Garrick that his original analysis had been wrong. Whoever had broken into *Chart Place* may have been streetwise enough to know how to commit a burglary without getting caught – but the list of items told a different story. These weren't professional burglars, they must have been kids looking to make a quick profit.

Craven filled his glass with more wine and also went through the list again. There was no doubt about it. The list was full of cheap, commoditised crap. Digital cameras, CD players, DVD recorders, camcorders, mobile phones, CDs, DVDs... All the really valuable stuff at *Chart Place* had been left untouched. Selling an original watercolour was a specialist business and not a quick process. You needed connections and you needed to be patient before you saw any profit. Weeks or months probably. Whoever had turned over Richmond's place was looking to get rid of everything and convert it all into cash as quickly as possible – probably within 24 hours. Kids. It had to be kids.

He scanned through the list several more times. All he needed to do was find one item, something unique and easily traceable and the job was more or less sorted. There was still a chance that he could recover the position without having to ring Buchanan. Five pages of closely typed A4 containing over 250 items looked promising at first but most of it turned out to be of no help. One digital camera or one DVD recorder looked much the same as another to Craven and the chance of finding one that belonged to Richmond was nigh on impossible. He wouldn't know where to start. There was some jewellery of course, which was probably quite expensive, but it was all too small and too difficult to identify – plus there were too many places that it could be sold on to. This part of the world was full of antique and second-hand junk shops.

Craven went through the list methodically and within half an hour had excluded more or less everything, other than the list of 200 or so CDs. He wasn't an expert on popular music, too many years working abroad had put paid to that – but he knew enough to recognise that Richmond's collection was a little bit out of the ordinary. Everybody had eclectic tastes these days; everything from ABBA to ZZ Top – but Richmond's musical taste looked a little more unusual. *The guy was a fashion designer for god's sake – he must have moved in fairly unconventional circles. He's bound to have a couple of rare CDs in his collection.*

It took him about five minutes to set up the laptop and get connected onto the internet. It was simply a question of putting the cable into the telephone socket by the bedside cabinet and then changing the dial properties to make sure that the modem dialled a 9 for an outside line. Within an hour he'd typed all the CD titles that he didn't recognise into *ebay* and had a list of half a dozen which looked pretty rare and a couple that he couldn't find at all. All he had to do now was get out there tomorrow and hope that his instincts were right.

Second-hand CDs were worth next to nothing. Whoever had broken into *Chart Place* wanted to trade everything into cash as soon as possible, so there wasn't any sense in trying to sell them one at a time. The obvious way would be to sell the whole lot together, which meant that they had to turn up on a market stall somewhere or in a second-hand record shop. Craven was banking on the latter. It was only two weeks since the burglary and by his reckoning they were still out there somewhere and probably not too far away.

Craven lit a cigarette and poured the last drop of wine into his glass. He thought about ringing the reception and asking if he could borrow some Yellow Pages – get a head start on tomorrow, but in the end decided against it. The friendly receptionist was on duty again and if anything, seemed even friendlier than the day before. The last thing he needed was a late night and not enough sleep. Plenty of time for that when the job was over.

Tomorrow he was going to get an early start, find the poor bastard who had burgled Richmond and then shut him up for good and put the job back on track.

NINE

Neil's morning wasn't going very well. He'd gone to bed the night before, also with the best intentions of making an early start and getting a few things done before driving Doreen to the station, but a couple of pints down *The Chequers* with Tom followed by a couple of nightcaps after dinner meant that he'd overslept. To be honest, it was the best night's sleep that he'd had in ages, but he needed to call round for Doreen and leave by nine o'clock at the latest and at 8.45 he was still sitting on the stool in the kitchen, hurriedly bolting down some breakfast and still wondering about the merits of parking a clapped-out old Escort on the forecourt of the local Police Station with no tax and no insurance.

He quickly finished his breakfast and dropped everything into the sink, deciding that he could wash up later when he got back. The last thing he needed was anything else to hold him up, but just as he was getting his jacket and was about to leave, the telephone rang.

Neil stood in the hallway, looking at the phone in the kitchen and for a moment thought about not answering it. He let it ring a couple more times but then changed his mind. Ever since taking the call about his parents nine years ago, he'd never been any good at ignoring the telephone. He darted across the kitchen and snatched up the receiver, unable to stop the irritation of being late translating into the brusqueness of his voice. 'Yes, hello?'

'Oh, hi Neil, it's Steph. Are you alright?'

Neil wasn't expecting it to be her and could have kicked himself for sounding so curt. 'Oh, hello Steph. Sorry, I'm in a bit of a hurry, running a bit late.'

'You sound out of breath.'

He could sense her smiling at the other end of the phone. 'Yeah, out of condition probably. Too many pints with Tom next door. Actually I'm coming in to see you in a minute.'

The surprise and interest in her voice were unmistakable. 'Really, what for?'

Neil grinned. There was definitely a natural chemistry with Steph that he hadn't felt for years. 'It's okay – I'm just driving Doreen over to the station. Apparently you want to see her again?'

'Oh, okay – for a moment I thought you meant…' Steph's words tailed off, hesitant, embarrassed.

He let the moment pass. Maybe teasing was a little out of order given everything that was going on. 'Anyway, why did you call? Has something happened?'

Again he could sense the hesitancy in her voice. Uncertain, cautious, unconfident. Not the same person that he was laughing and joking with in the kitchen yesterday lunchtime.

'No, nothing's happened. I was just wondering… well… when you said the other day about going out to dinner… whether you were serious… and well… whether you still wanted to?'

Neil's morning suddenly went from not very good to absolutely bloody brilliant. Luckily, Steph couldn't see him punching the air with delight like some sort of euphoric sportsman having just hit a winning shot. 'Absolutely, of course I meant it,' he said reassuringly, 'I'd love to go out to dinner. You know me, anything to avoid cooking.'

Steph laughed, albeit still nervously. 'It's just, things are very difficult at work at the moment, we're all working lots of overtime and it's difficult to know what time we're going to finish…'

'Go on…' Neil wasn't sure where this was heading.

'and like I said, it's not really allowed, well, it's not allowed at all to be honest while the enquiry is still in progress – it wouldn't be very good for me if we were seen sitting in a restaurant together…'

'Go on…' *This sounds more like a turn down than an acceptance.*

'But they know I can't work late unless I've got someone to look after Chloe and as it happens I can't get anybody to baby-sit tonight so…'

'Steph…'

'What?'

'If you're trying to invite me round to dinner at your house this evening, then I'd love to accept.'

Neil could hear the relief in her voice. 'Really – you don't mind?'

'Of course I don't mind. I'd love to come. Why did you think I would mind?'

'I thought you might think it was a bit underhand or a bit… I don't know… forward.'

Neil smiled. Steph really was very special. She was clearly taking a risk in agreeing to see him and inviting him to her own home conveyed a level of trust which made him feel very special. 'Steph, I don't think it's either of those things and if it helps, as far as I'm concerned it's just an innocent invitation to dinner from a friend. Nothing else. And no reason for anyone else to know about it.'

'Thanks Neil. That does help – a lot. I don't think I'm very good at this. Out of practice.'

'Well let's just hope your cooking is still up to scratch – I set very high standards you know!'

Steph laughed again. He was a nice guy. Easy to talk to. 'There's just one more thing Neil…'

'Go on…'

'I don't have strange men coming round for dinner very often, well…not at all actually, so you'll probably have to put up with a very inquisitive five year-old for a while, at least until she goes to bed.'

'No problem, some of my best friends behave like children. I can communicate at any level!'

Steph smiled. 'Okay, how about sevenish?'

Perfect, thought Neil. 'Sevenish will be fine,' he said, 'what's the address?'

Steph gave him the address and phone number, which Neil wrote down on the pad which was next to the phone. He didn't know Cranbrook very well but there was bound to be a local map in the house somewhere and anyway, he'd probably get a taxi there and back.

'Okay, I might bump into you later, but if not, I'll see you this evening – and thanks for ringing. I really appreciate it.' Neil put the phone down and looked at his watch. Nine o'clock. He was late. Doreen would be wondering what was happening. What he really wanted to do was rush upstairs and check what clean clothes he had left, he might even have to go out and buy something new but it would all have to wait for now. He needed to leave and needed to leave immediately.

He quickly tore off the top sheet from the pad on which he'd written the details about *Fentanyl* and the time of the burglary and then tore off the next sheet on which he'd written Steph's address and put it in his pocket. He guessed that he would have some time to kill waiting for Doreen at the police station and they probably had lots of local maps there. He could look up and see exactly where Steph lived. Maybe Tom would let him borrow the car.

Something made Neil glance back at the pad on the kitchen worktop. The sheet underneath the one that he'd just torn off had been written on and it was in Aunt Hilary's handwriting. There was no mistaking it. He'd received too many letters and Christmas and birthday cards over the years not to recognise her distinctive swirls and backward sloping style. *That's odd. Why write something on the pad but not write on the top sheet?*

He really needed to make a move, Doreen would be starting to get worried by now and it probably wouldn't look good for her to turn up late. But something in the back of his mind, some unexplained intuition made him think that this could be important and that he ought to look more closely at what she had written. It was a list of three telephone numbers, one with a 01242 number which he didn't recognise and the other two both 0207 London numbers and then a couple of words which he struggled to read. One of them looked like Carlisle. The other one looked like Rawlings or Rowlands. There were also a couple of dates, 1997 and 2003, plus a load of numbers, seemingly scribbled at random around the edge of the pad, as if Aunt Hilary had been doodling whilst talking to somebody on the phone.

Instinctively, Neil picked up the telephone and dialled the 01242 number, not sure what he was going to do next but happy to busk it and rely on his journalistic instincts. The call was answered almost before the first ring had stopped.

'Daniels.' The guy sounded busy, professional. It was clearly a business number rather than a personal phone.

'Oh, I'm sorry, I must have the wrong extension, could you put me back to the main switchboard please.'

'Who are you after?'

'Steve Walker in IT. Network Support.' It was a gamble but an old journalist's ploy. Most modern businesses had an IT department these days and were normally staffed by techies who most of the company never saw and didn't know. These were the guys who came in every day, worked anonymously in the backroom of the organisation, occasionally came out to fix things but nobody ever got to know their names. Half of them were usually contractors and in any case, turnover of IT staff was always high – the names and faces were always changing.

Neil and a few colleagues had once found themselves stuck in the bar of *The Great Western Hotel* in Cambridge just before Christmas and a few of the lads, buoyed by too many pints of Guinness decided to gatecrash an office Christmas party which was taking place in one of the large conference areas at the back of the hotel. They simply walked into the room, sat down at a table and when questioned about which part of the company they worked for, said they were in Network Support. No-one batted an eyelid. By all accounts they had a free bar, a full Christmas dinner with all the trimmings and spent the rest of the evening chatting up the girls on the dance floor. It had become something of a legend at *The Chronicle* and Neil still smiled at the audacity of it all.

'Sorry, never heard of him,' replied the guy on the other end of the phone. 'Do you mind redialling, I risk cutting you off if I try and transfer you. You need a degree in electronics to manage these phones.'

'No problem, we must have the same sort of phones this end,' laughed Neil, trying to keep the thing light-hearted. 'All I had was this direct line though, which is obviously wrong. Can you give me the switchboard number?'

'Same number but with 100 as the last three digits.'

'Thanks.' Neil put the phone down just as the front doorbell rang. It had to be Doreen, probably thinking that he'd forgotten or was still in bed. He picked the phone up again and quickly dialled the switchboard number. Again, it was answered almost instantly.

'GCHQ.'

Neil nearly dropped the phone. 'I'm sorry? What number have I got?'

'GCHQ. What extension do you want?'

He hadn't misheard her. An efficient female telephonist but with a local Cheltenham accent.

'Sorry, I must have the wrong number.' Neil put the phone down and stared into space for several seconds, not sure what to think. The doorbell rang again – three times in quick succession. It's amazing the amount of intonation that can be conveyed from just ringing a simple doorbell but in different ways. Cheerful, friendly (ding-dong), serious or foreboding (slow, with a long pause in between) and impatient or panic (fast, with no pause). Doreen's was definitely panic.

*

The Trading Post in Tenterden High Street was a small, independent record shop which sold second-hand CDs and which for over seven years had been more of a passion than a commercially viable business for its keen and dedicated owner. There were a few loyal customers who came in on a regular basis and the odd passing tourist who would wander in and browse through the thousands of CDs, lovingly kept in alphabetical order – but for most of the time the place was empty, waiting for the late afternoon rush of teenage school kids who would flood the shop with a cacophony of noise and enthusiasm, searching for the latest back catalogue that was back in fashion or for some long-forgotten masterpiece waiting to be re-discovered.

The shop was small and rather dingy, the rows of wooden CD racks banked up against every available wall space making it feel darker and more cluttered than it actually was. Thursday mornings were always quiet. A couple of customers, let alone a sale by lunchtime were a rarity. It was a good time for checking stock, getting up-to-date with the paperwork and generally tidying the place up. It was with some surprise therefore that the owner looked up from the other side of the counter as Craven walked through the door, a couple of minutes after nine o'clock and only several moments after the shop had opened.

Craven didn't think this was likely to be the place to find what he was looking for, it looked too legitimate and well-established to deal in stolen property, but having checked the phone book it was the nearest on his list and by his reckoning, just as good a place to start and test his theory. He had a preconception that these sorts of shops were all run by ageing hippies or scruffy twenty-something blokes wearing black T-shirts and listening to heavy rock music, but surprisingly, the guy behind the counter was smartly dressed in a conventional sort of way and looked to be in his early fifties. The music he was playing also sounded pretty good and he looked as though he was going to be friendly and helpful.

'Morning. I think you must win the prize for being the earliest customer I've had in here this week – all year probably!'

Craven closed the door behind him and returned the smile. 'I'm on a bit of a mission actually,' he said, walking up to the counter, 'I'm looking for something specific and thought I'd better make an early start. I wonder if you could help me?'

'Sure, no problem. What are you after?' asked the guy, standing up straight and pushing his paperwork to one side.

'I'm trying to buy a present for my nephew's birthday – he's a bit of a music buff and I've got a list of a few CDs that he wants. Just wondered if you've got in any of them in stock.' Craven took out the list that he'd made the night before and passed it over to the guy who scanned it quickly and raised his eyebrows in appreciation.

'Wow. How old is your nephew, if you don't mind me asking?' enquired the guy, still looking at the list.

'Seventeen,' replied Craven without hesitation. 'Why?'

'It's just unusual to see a youngster with such good taste in music. He must be a real enthusiast.'

'You can say that again – he's a bit of a collector actually.'

'I can see that. This one for example,' indicated the guy, pointing to the title at the top of the list. *Manfred Mann Chapter Three, Volume One.* I haven't seen anybody looking for that for years.'

'Never heard of it I'm afraid,' said Craven, being able to drop the pretence and tell the truth.

'Not many people have. Wonderful album. Released in 1969, one of the finest years of all time for British music.'

'Really?' said Craven, feigning interest but wanting to keep the guy talking and get as much information as possible.

'Absolutely. *Abbey Road, Let it Bleed, Liege and Lief, Tommy, Led Zeppelin I.* It was a fabulous year for music. But for those of us that were there, the crowning glory, the real undiscovered gem was *Manfred Mann Chapter Three.* One of the finest jazz-rock albums ever made. Really evocative of its time.'

'Well, I've heard of *Abbey Road*,' smiled Craven, again not having to lie.

The guy laughed. 'Music not your subject then?'

'No, not really. Don't suppose you've got a copy have you?'

The guy shook his head. 'Not a chance. Can't remember the last time I saw one. The internet is your best bet. It's still in production I think – you should be able to get hold of it easily enough.'

Craven pulled a face. 'No good I'm afraid. His birthday's tomorrow. I really need to try and get him something today. What about the others?'

The guy shook his head again. 'Sorry, unfortunately your nephew's set you a bit of a challenge. Most of these are pretty rare. In fact, a couple of them are like gold dust. I'm afraid I haven't got any of them – and two or three of them never likely to either.'

'Oh well, never mind,' said Craven, looking disappointed. 'Are they that rare then?'

The guy nodded emphatically. 'Absolutely. This one for example,' he continued, pointing halfway down the list. 'David Devant & His Spirit Wife – *Work, Lovelife, Miscellaneous.* Again. you should be able to get it on the internet easily enough but I don't think you'd ever find it on the high street. Wonderful album though. Very eccentric and very, very clever.'

Craven smiled. The guy was obviously passionate about his music and was clearly impressed by the musical taste of the imaginary nephew and also excited at seeing a list of so many rare CDs all on the same page. *Must have made his day.* 'What about this one?' he asked, pointing to one of the CDs that he recognised that he hadn't been able to find on the internet the night before.

'Same story I'm afraid. The Pineapple Thief – *Little Man*. Very sought after and very rare.'

'I wasn't sure which one was the title and which one was the name of the artist.'

'No reason why you should I suppose. The Pineapple Thief is the name of the band. Some people prefer their earlier work but trust me, this is the one to get. Absolutely gorgeous song-writing and their finest album by a mile. People have been known to pay up to £100 for it.'

'Wow!' Craven shook his head in disbelief. He couldn't imagine what sort of music could create such a demand and at such an inflated price. 'Oh well, thanks for the information. I guess I'll just have to keep looking. Are there any other independent record shops in the area?'

'Well, I think you're wasting your time trying to find anything on that list around here but for what it's worth, there are definitely a couple of shops in Tunbridge Wells and there must be at least one in both Ashford and Maidstone, but I think that's probably it. The internet is killing the second-hand market I'm afraid.'

Craven pulled a sympathetic face. 'That's a real shame. Actually, that sounds really good,' he added, nodding towards the noise coming out of one of the speakers. 'Who's that?'

The guy nodded in agreement. 'Yeah, nice isn't it? Gene – *Drawn to the Deep End*. A tenner to you.'

'Done, I'll take a copy – thanks.'

Craven got a ten-pound note out of his wallet while the guy took the CD out of the Hi-Fi, found the case and then put it into a small green plastic bag. He genuinely liked the sound and anyway, ten pounds was a small price to pay for the information and to get his theory tested.

Things were looking up. Half a dozen CDs which were about as rare as you can get and only three or four shops in the whole area to check out. With a bit of luck, there was a real prospect of tracking down Richmond's burglar before the day was out. He lit a cigarette as he left the shop and walked optimistically back to the car. Craven wasn't normally an optimist but that was the whole point. *"The nice part about being a pessimist is that you are constantly either being proved right or pleasantly surprised."*

TEN

Garrick stood with his back to the CID room and gazed out of the window at the park across the road, deep in thought. Matt had updated him on his latest theory about the burglary at *Chart Place* and he was trying to make sense of what it all meant – and he was worried. The whole case was turning out to be exactly the opposite of what they thought they were dealing with and every assumption that they had made so far was turning out to be wrong. Less than twenty-four hours ago he was certain that Richmond's burglary had been carried out by professionals and that *Yew Tree Cottage* had been broken into by kids. Now it appeared to be the other way round. Nothing was as it seemed and in the space of two days they'd moved from having no information and no leads at all, to more information than they could sensibly manage.

The CID room behind him was in chaos. Everybody was in and the place was crowded with too many people and too much activity and noise. It was starting to feel disorganised. Garrick knew that he had to get a grip on the enquiry and get some discipline into the team. Some of them were experienced but a lot of them were newly promoted and this was the biggest and most complex case that they had ever worked on. Enthusiasm and hard work were all well and good but disciplined, methodical detective work was another thing altogether. Hopefully Doreen Webster would give them a few answers and give the enquiry the breakthrough that it desperately needed.

And another thing was bothering him. He couldn't work out what was the matter with some of them this morning. Steph, in particular, had arrived at work looking nervous and edgy and had hardly spoken a word to anybody and then suddenly she'd disappeared for ten minutes and had come back all happy and smiling and talking to everyone as though she'd just won the lottery. Women…

Garrick checked his watch. 9.20. Just enough time to ring forensics before Doreen Webster arrived. He wandered back to his office and made the call. Ian Dawson wasn't his favourite person in the world, but for the moment he needed him onside so resolved to draw a line under past disagreements and to be on his best behaviour.

'Hi, Ian, it's John Garrick, returning your call. You rang earlier.'

'John, thanks for getting back to me. *Yew Tree Cottage*. Sorry for the delay, we're drowning a bit over here.'

Garrick looked out of the glazed partition of his office at the flurry of activity that was going on in the CID room. *You want to see drowning mate you should come over here*. He took a deep breath. 'No problem Ian, what have you got for me?'

'Something and nothing really. Not a lot of evidence I'm afraid but a couple of things which might be useful.'

'Go on ...'

'Well the bad news is your intruder wore gloves. No prints and interestingly, no trace of DNA.'

Garrick had expected as much. Nothing like forensics to state the bleeding obvious. He checked his watch again. He needed to speed this up a bit. Either that or keep Mrs. Webster waiting. 'Why do you say "interesting" Ian? Were you expecting DNA?'

'Well probably, yes. Even my boys suited up find it hard not to leave traces now and again. All you need is a loose eyelash or the minutest piece of skin flaking off and you've got a 24-carat, gold-plated DNA sample. Scratch your eye or the end of your nose whilst leaning over a body and it's almost impossible to avoid. Either your suspect was wearing a diver's suit or he was very careful indeed. More careful than most people we come across.'

'This guy really knew what he was doing didn't he?'

'I would say so – except that he made a mistake in the choice of gloves. He was wearing the latex variety, you know the sort that medics and dentists wear.'

'Really?' Garrick suddenly perked up.

'I know what you're thinking John, don't get excited. I've spoken to Alan Wyatt and I know all about the *Fentanyl* in this case. Twenty years ago, even ten perhaps, the use of latex gloves might have been significant but not these days. People use them for all sorts of things, DIY, car maintenance, gardening – you can buy them at just about every ironmongers or DIY store in the country.'

'Yeah, I know, I've got some myself at home in the garage,' said Garrick, somewhat deflated. 'So what was the mistake?'

'Well, I don't know whether you've noticed but they come in two varieties, powdered and unpowdered. Your man used the powdered variety and the thing about those is that they leave small traces of white powder wherever they touch, so we can see exactly where your suspect has been in the house.'

'Ah, now that could be interesting,' replied Garrick, starting to perk up again.

'Well it's actually better than that,' continued Dawson, sounding a bit too smug for Garrick's liking. 'The powder wears off after a while so the stronger traces will tend to indicate where he went first. That's why it's taken us so long to get back to you. It's not just a question of analysing the evidence; what we've done is measure the density of every residue sample that he left behind, which enables us to track his exact movements. In other words, in what order he went through the house.'

Garrick had to admit it – this was impressive. 'That sounds promising Ian. So what does it tell us?'

'Well, plenty of samples around the back door, confirming the point of entry.'

'Okay...'

'And then the strongest traces are on the inside handles of three windows upstairs; one in the bathroom, one in the back bedroom and one in the front bedroom. The windows were all shut when we got there so my guess is that he broke in through the back door and then went straight upstairs and closed the three windows, probably in the same order that I've just gone through. Bathroom at the top of the stairs, then the back bedroom and then the front bedroom where the victim was sleeping.'

Garrick was trying to process the information as fast as he was receiving it. 'Why would he do that?'

Dawson smiled at the other end of the phone. 'Well, you're the detective John but if you ask me I think it would have been to cut out the risk of any noise. Nobody takes any notice of a bit of noise on the middle of a housing estate but this was a small village and it was three o'clock in the morning. Even the slightest sound might get someone's attention and there's more sense of community in a small village – neighbours would be less likely to ignore it.'

Garrick rolled his eyeballs towards the top of his head. 'You're in the wrong job Ian, you should have been a detective.'

Dawson smiled again. 'You must be joking. All that paperwork and going round in circles. No thanks. The real work in solving crimes takes place over here.'

Garrick forced a laugh. It was common knowledge that the staff in forensics and pathology held the view that CID officers spent most of their time wading around in statements and red tape while the real detective work was being done in the labs. Maybe it was true. Advances in science and technology had certainly overtaken the methods that Garrick's team were using. Even the profilers and the criminal psychologists had a healthy disregard for old-fashioned police work. Still, it cut both ways. Most of the CID team didn't have a lot of time for their hurdy-gurdy methods either.

'Okay, so where next after the windows?' asked Garrick, conscious that time was moving on and that he had an interview to conduct.

'Reasonable traces on the bedclothes and then lighter traces in the front room downstairs and then in the dining room. Nothing in the back bedroom, bathroom or in the kitchen.'

Garrick thought for a moment, trying to visualise the intruder's movements through the house. 'So basically, he came in through the back door, went straight upstairs, closed three windows, murdered the victim, came downstairs, searched the two living rooms and then left.'

'That's about it.' Dawson paused, not offering any more information. Garrick could tell that there was something else but that Dawson was going to make him ask.

'So what's your conclusion from all that then, Ian?' asked Garrick in a rather laboured, "Do we have to play these sort of games," type of voice. *If he says, "Well, you're the detective John," I'm going to drive round there and shove a test tube right up his arse.*

Dawson seemed to be getting the message and backed off the one-upmanship for a moment. 'I'd say it tells us two things. One; your intruder didn't bother to search some of the rooms, which indicates that he knew where to look for whatever it was that he was after, which means that two; he went in there to get something specific. It could also mean that he's been there before of course – how else would he know where to look? But either way I think it means that you need to find out what's been taken. It might help you focus the enquiry. I hear you've been struggling on that front.'

Dawson was crossing a line now and Garrick was in danger of losing it with him on the phone. It was as much as he could do to contain his temper. 'Thanks Ian, that's really useful – even if it is a bit late. Anything else? You said that there were a couple of things.'

'Yes, we found traces of Poly-vinyl-chloride-acetate on the surface of the catch on the back door lock.'

'Polly what?'

'Poly-vinyl-chloride-acetate. PVCA. It's the plastic they use to manufacture credit cards. It looks like your man tried to break in by tripping the lock on the back door, but obviously without success, so he busted his way through the door frame instead. That's about it I think.'

'Okay, thanks Ian. When can I get the written report?' *Apply some pressure. Everybody else is working overtime.*

Dawson smiled. 'Well it's up to you really. I can either get on with writing up the report or get started on analysing the stuff that we took from *Chart Place* yesterday. Which one do you want first?'

'You'd better get started on *Chart Place,*' replied Garrick begrudgingly, recognising when he was onto a loser, 'particularly if it's going to take as long as it took you on this one. Is there much of it?'

'Tons of it. We've got more forensic evidence than you can shake a stick at. No blood but it looks as though we've got some saliva so we ought to get a decent DNA sample.'

'Not the same person then?' Garrick regretted the question almost as soon as he'd asked it.

'Don't know John, you're meant to be the detective. I just provide the evidence.'

There was a silence as both of them paused, recognising that the sparring had probably gone far enough. Dawson's tone suddenly softened. 'No, I wouldn't have thought so John. I reckon you're looking for two different people. One very careful. One very careless.'

Garrick softened his tone deliberately as well. 'Okay Ian. Give me a call when you've got something. And by the way – thanks, the stuff on *Yew Tree Cottage* is really helpful.'

'Okay, will do. By the way, we've counted the money. We had to, to get it indexed and logged. It's £99,460 exactly. Alan Wyatt must have a talent for counting bank notes from a distance.'

Garrick frowned at the other end of the telephone. 'That's an odd amount – are you sure you haven't missed some of it?'

Dawson resisted the temptation to score another point. 'Its £540 short of £100,000 John, which is probably twenty-seven £20.00 notes. Obviously we didn't have access to the notes that were stuffed down the deceased's throat. I think you'll find Alan will recover them when he does the PM.'

Garrick rolled his eyeballs up to the top of his head again. 'Thanks Ian. Like you say, it's obvious really once you've had time to think it through. I'll talk to you later.'

He put the phone down and checked the time again. Five past ten. The forensic information was impressive and potentially significant, but for now he'd had enough of Ian Dawson and his new-fangled technology and scientific jargon. Doreen Webster should be sitting in the waiting room, probably getting nervous and worrying about the interrogation that was about to begin. It was time to try out some good old-fashioned police-work and find out the connection between Stuart Richmond and Hilary Russell.

*

Neil sat in the waiting room and looked at his watch again, wondering how much longer Doreen was going to be. It was eleven o'clock and he had finished reading the newspaper that he'd brought in from home, as well as all the information leaflets and the crime prevention posters on the wall and he was starting to get bored and impatient. He was also beginning to worry whether Doreen was okay. She'd been in there nearly an hour and he wasn't sure how well she would cope with the ordeal of being formally interviewed inside a police station.

He also wanted to get back and check that he had something decent to wear for dinner with Steph tonight – plus he desperately wanted to go home and ring the two other telephone numbers that were written on the pad. He hadn't had time before he left and he was dying to find out who was going to be on the other end of the phone. He couldn't understand why on earth Aunt Hilary would ring anybody at GCHQ, but he felt sure that ringing the two London numbers would provide some answers. But whilst he was stuck in the waiting room of the police station, he couldn't get on with anything.

A succession of police officers trooped in and out of the double swing doors which led from the front desk into a corridor and then towards the interview rooms and the rest of the station. Neil watched the endless stream of uniforms going backwards and forwards, always with the same banter and humorous comments, invariably aimed at the desk sergeant, a greying "seen it all before" veteran who was leaning on the counter and dealing with the occasional customer who wandered in off the street. Neil half expected to see some excitement, some half-crazed madman bursting through the front doors, covered in blood screaming, "I've just killed my wife," but it was all slow and ordinary; a teenager coming in to show his driving licence and insurance documents, a women reporting a stolen handbag, a guy handing in a set of keys that he'd found. It was all very dull and all very boring.

Doreen couldn't remember the last time that she'd been in a police station but whenever it was, she knew that she'd never been beyond the front desk and she'd certainly never been in an interview room before. She wasn't impressed. Four cold, blank walls which badly needed a lick of paint, no windows, a metal table and four chairs plus some sort of machine on a side table to record the interview. Even the cup of tea that they'd given her had come out of a machine.

Garrick pushed his chair back, took a deep breath and looked up at the ceiling. They were going round in circles. He'd pinned all his hopes on Doreen shedding some light on things but they were getting nowhere. Like Neil, he'd also been worried that she might be overawed by the experience of being interviewed or perhaps too upset by the news about Richmond's death but he couldn't have been more wrong. Tom could have told him that. She might just be a local housewife living a parochial, humdrum life in a small and sleepy village but she was no fool. Push Doreen around and she pushed back.

Garrick looked at the clock again which was hanging on the back wall and thought about taking a break. 'Would you like another cup of tea Mrs. Webster?'

'Doreen, I told you before, my name's Doreen. The only person I knew who answered to the name of Mrs. Webster was Tom's mother and she's been dead twenty years. And no, I don't want another cup of tea thank you – I don't know how you can drink the stuff…'

Garrick and Steph exchanged a frustrated look. *Where do we go from here?*

'…besides, I haven't got all day to be sitting here. I need to get round Tesco's before I go home and I want to be back indoors before my husband comes home from work – he doesn't like it if I'm not there when he gets in.'

Garrick looked at Steph again, not sure whether they might as well call it a day or try just one last time. He opted for the latter. There had to be something.

'Okay, well we'd better keep going then. Are you absolutely positive that Miss Russell and Mr. Richmond didn't know each other?'

Doreen looked exasperated. 'Of course I'm positive. You've already asked me that twice and I've already told you – they didn't know each other. Why on earth would someone like Mr. Richmond know Hilary?'

'I don't know Doreen,' replied Garrick, using her name on purpose and trying his best to take the heat out of the situation, 'but you have to see it from our point of view. We've got two burglaries and two murders in the space of two weeks and the only thing that connects the two of them is you. You worked for one of them and lived next door to the other.

'I'm not a connection,' protested Doreen. You make it sound as though I've got something to do with it. It must just be a coincidence.'

'I don't believe in coincidences,' replied Garrick, leaning forward and starting to get irritated, 'which is why I am surprised that you didn't mention it when you gave the statement to DC Page. It must have seemed odd to you that you knew two separate people who'd been burgled in such a short space of time?'

Doreen frowned, looking affronted at the implication. 'It didn't seem odd to me at all Chief Inspector because I didn't make any connection between them. Finding out that there's been a burglary next door to you whilst you've been away is unsettling enough, but losing a good friend and neighbour so suddenly and under those circumstances was a real shock. I wasn't even thinking about the Richmonds. Anyway, why should I have to mention it to you? You already knew about the burglary at *Chart Place.*'

Garrick put his head in his hands. He couldn't work out whether Doreen was being deliberately obtuse or whether she genuinely couldn't see the significance of her own position in all of this. 'Doreen, there has to be something that connects Mr. Richmond to your neighbour and at the moment, the only thing we've got is you.'

Doreen stared across at Garrick, trying her hardest to think of anything that might help but as hard as she tried, she couldn't. Not a thing. 'Like I said, I work for Mr. and Mrs. Richmond two days a week from 9.00 until 1.00 and that's it. Mr. Richmond and Hilary didn't know each other, they never met each other, they never spoke to each other. I don't know what else I can say.'

There was another pause. Garrick was on the point of deciding that enough was enough. Like Doreen, he had better things to do.

Steph smiled at Doreen and decided to ask something neutral – maybe taking the pressure out of the interview would help.

'You said that you work on Tuesdays and Fridays Doreen, why do you work on those particular days?'

Doreen smiled at her, obviously more comfortable with Steph asking the questions than Garrick. 'Well, it suits both of us to be honest dear. Mrs. Richmond wanted me to work on Friday mornings because she likes to have the house clean and tidy for the weekend and I work Tuesdays because it's sort of halfway in-between. It also means that my husband can give me a lift. He works on Mondays and Thursdays.'

'So what happens if your husband can't take you,' asked Garrick, 'did Hilary ever give you a lift up there?'

Doreen pulled a face, clearly indicating that they were just asking the same question but from a different perspective. 'No, never. If Tom can't drive me up there for any reason then I get the bus, but it's only happened a couple of times. I know what you're thinking Chief Inspector, but I'm absolutely certain, Hilary never went to *Chart Place.'*

Garrick tried again – same question but the other way round. They really were going round in circles. 'Have Mr. or Mrs. Richmond ever been to visit you in Appleden?'

Doreen almost laughed at the absurdity of it. 'Good gracious me, of course not. Why would they want to come and visit me in Appleden? I'm their cleaner. I'm not a family friend!'

Garrick could see her point and decided that he'd had enough. He looked over at the clock again and then nodded at Steph, indicating that he was ready to finish. Steph held her hand up, suggesting that she wanted one last try.

'If you don't mind me saying so Doreen,' she asked, trying a different tack, 'you don't seem very upset or affected by the news about Mr. Richmond. Didn't you like him very much?'

For the first time, Doreen looked slightly taken aback and embarrassed by the question. It didn't do to speak ill of the dead. She shifted slightly in her chair and thought about her response, picking her words carefully. 'I do feel very sorry for poor Mrs. Richmond of course, she's a lovely lady, but like I said, I didn't know Mr. Richmond as well – he wasn't there most of the time when I was cleaning, he was usually at work.'

Garrick sensed a chink of light but knew well enough to stay quiet. Doreen was looking uncomfortable and Steph could sense it as well.

'But it does sound as though you didn't like him very much,' Steph repeated. 'Is that true?'

Again, Doreen looked unsettled and was picking her words very slowly and with care. 'It wasn't that I didn't like him, it was just that he wasn't an easy man to get on with. He was a bit moody and wasn't always very friendly. And if he was working at home he didn't like to be disturbed, which meant that I couldn't get in and clean the study, so I had to sort of work round him, which was a bit difficult sometimes. To be honest I used to keep out of his way if I could, so I didn't speak to him that much.'

'You must have preferred it when he wasn't there then,' said Steph, trying to move the conversation forward.

Doreen nodded. 'I did. Me and Mrs. Richmond would sometimes have a cup of coffee and a natter in the kitchen, but we didn't do it when Mr. Richmond was there. He didn't approve. Got quite cross about it once. Said I was paid to clean, not to sit around drinking tea all day.'

Steph gave her a sympathetic smile. Doreen was painting not a very nice picture of the late Mr. Richmond. 'Did you ever talk to Mrs. Richmond about Hilary?' asked Steph, steering the question as gently as she could back to the subject in hand.

Doreen shook her head. 'No. I used to talk about me and Tom sometimes but I'm sure I never mentioned Hilary. No reason to.'

'Did you ever mention Mr. and Mrs. Richmond to Hilary? I expect you had a coffee and a chat with Hilary sometimes, didn't you? It must have been difficult not to mention him if you'd had a bad day at work.'

Doreen smiled. She had happy memories of sitting down at Hilary's kitchen table, gossiping about village life and putting the world to rights while Tom was at work. 'Oh, I probably moaned about him a couple of times – you know what it's like.'

Steph looked at Garrick, not sure whether this was leading anywhere or not. 'Can you remember the last time that was, Doreen and what you said?'

Doreen thought for a moment, trying to make sure that what she was about to say was accurate. 'It was about a week ago, so it must have been on the Thursday, about a week after the burglary. Tom had gone to work at Greenways and me and Hilary used to have a coffee once a week, normally round at her house.'

'Can you remember what you talked about?' asked Garrick, not being able to resist butting in and moving the thing forward.

Doreen frowned at him as though it had now become a private conversation between her and Steph and that he was interrupting. She deliberately ignored him and looked back at Steph. 'Well, Mr. Richmond had been working at home on the Tuesday and as usual he was in the study. I knew to keep out of his way. He wasn't in the best of moods most of the time and he certainly wasn't very happy after the burglary.'

'So Hilary knew about the burglary then?' said Steph softly, trying her best not to upset Doreen's train of thought.

'Well, I might have mentioned it,' said Doreen, feeling slightly guilty about discussing the private lives of her employers with her neighbour, 'but she didn't seem very interested. She certainly wasn't surprised. I'd described the house to her before and she said that a large house like that, full of expensive things was bound to get burgled at some stage.'

'Was there anything else Doreen?' asked Steph, 'anything else you can remember talking about that might be significant?'

Doreen thought for another moment and then nodded. 'The only other thing that I mentioned was about one of the phone calls for Mr. Richmond. If Mrs. Richmond wasn't there, I had to write down the messages and leave them on the hall table because he didn't like being disturbed, not even by the phone.

On the Tuesday I took a call for him in the morning and the man was insistent that he spoke to Mr. Richmond and asked me to interrupt him. I told him that it was more than my job was worth but he wouldn't take "no" for an answer and said that it was very urgent – and that if I passed on a message, Mr. Richmond would want to speak to him. I can't tell you how nervous I was knocking on the door of his study.

Steph and Garrick exchanged another look. 'So, did he take the call Doreen?' asked Steph.

Doreen nodded. 'Yes he did. Surprised me, I can tell you. I expected to get thrown out of his study with a flea in my ear, but I gave him the message and he just smiled at me and said thank you. That's why I was telling Hilary over coffee. It was so out of character.'

'Doreen,' said Garrick, not able to keep quiet any longer. 'Can you remember what the message was?'

Doreen shook her head. 'No, I couldn't remember it because I didn't understand it. That's why I wrote it down. It's still in my handbag I think.'

Garrick and Steph leant patiently across the table as Doreen fumbled around in her handbag, searching for the scrap of paper. An assortment of keys and tissues and coins were deposited on the table, but after what seemed like an eternity she eventually looked up and gave them a half-smile and an apologetic shrug. 'Sorry, I think I must have thrown it away. Didn't see the need to keep it.'

Garrick was about to explode but Steph knew exactly how to deal with the situation. She took hold of Doreen's hand and gently squeezed it. 'Never mind Doreen, it doesn't matter. I expect you read it a few times. What do you think it said?'

Doreen thought hard, as though trying to remember the exact words. 'Well, I can't be certain and, like I said, it didn't make a lot of sense to me but I think it said, "I need to speak to you about Teleios." Something like that.'

Steph tried hard not to look at Garrick and give anything away. She was all for ending the interview there and then but Garrick couldn't take the chance. He needed to make sure.

'Doreen, this is really important, are you absolutely sure that what he said was Teleios?'

Doreen gave him a very strange, quizzical look as though he'd just said something, almost word for word that she'd heard before – which he had. 'That's funny,' she said, looking Garrick straight in the eye, 'that's exactly what Hilary said.'

ELEVEN

It was early afternoon by the time Craven got to *Seedy CDs*, an aptly named second-hand store located on the poorer side of Ashford town centre. Much to his annoyance, the visit to Tunbridge Wells had been a complete waste of time. *Discovery*, a loud and modern outlet at the upper end of the high street had turned out to be a shop specialising in vinyl and in particular in dance and drum 'n' bass music, a term that Craven hadn't heard of before and frankly one that he wasn't bothered if he never heard of again. He'd only stayed a couple of minutes, the sound blasting out of the speakers was enough to put anybody off and it was clear that the place didn't deal in CDs or the sort of music that he was looking for. It was also full of kids wearing expensive urban gear, talking about mixes and decks and conversing in a whole street language that he didn't understand at all. How anybody could listen to the stuff that they were playing was beyond him. As far as he was concerned it didn't even meet the definition of what music was meant to sound like. He remembered smiling to himself as he walked out of the shop. He was starting to sound like his father.

Rik's Records, situated amongst the smarter wine bars and antiques shops at the other end of town also turned out to be a wasted visit, the shop being much like *The Trading Post* in Tenterden, a more traditional and upmarket enterprise and one which Craven knew immediately was far too legitimate to deal in stolen property. The guy behind the counter had been helpful, confirming everything that Craven already knew about the rarity of his shopping list, but at the same time beginning to make him doubt his strategy. Maybe it was wishful thinking to expect to find one or two CDs that were stolen a couple a weeks ago in just three or four shops dotted around the county.

Still, this looks more promising, he thought as he peered through the window of *Seedy CDs*, looking at the tatty and run-down interior and at the handful of customers who were browsing inside. The kid behind the counter also met his expectations, an archetypal heavy metal fan, about twenty-one or twenty-two dressed in blue jeans, black T-shirt and the obligatory long hair and assortment of wristbands and silver jewellery. The words *Mummy's Boy* written in large yellow letters across the front of his T-shirt did nothing to fill Craven with any confidence. Other than the packet of Marlboro Lights and a Zippo lighter, they weren't going to have a lot in common.

Craven went into the shop and wandered over to the CD racks which ran along the left-hand side of the wall and started to casually browse through the cases, not looking for anything in particular but wanting to check out the prices and see what sort of help he was likely to get. The three other customers, a couple of teenagers and a guy in his early thirties were working their way through the racks on the opposite side of the room, methodically searching through them as if looking for something specific, but the kid wasn't taking any notice of anybody, his head bent over a guitar magazine which was obviously more interesting and holding all his attention. Clearly, there wasn't a strong customer service philosophy in this establishment and Craven sensed that the naïve uncle routine wasn't going to work here. He'd have to find a different approach.

Most of the CDs were the same price. There were a few cheaper and a few more expensive ones but as he flicked through the titles alphabetically the going rate seemed to be about ten pounds. Same as everywhere else. He recognised some of the artists, ABBA, The Beatles, Cream, but when he got to the 'D' section he immediately recognised something else and something altogether more interesting. *Work, Lovelife, Miscellaneous* by David Devant & His Spirit Wife. *Bingo.* He picked up the case, double-checked to make sure that it was the right one and then nonchalantly put it back in the rack. Within a couple of minutes he'd also found *Little Man* by The Pineapple Thief and another rarity that had been on the list, *Posthumous Silence* by Sylvan. All three were priced at thirty pounds.

Craven looked around the shop and at the other customers who were still browsing through the stock. They didn't look as though they'd found what they were looking for and didn't seem to be in any hurry – which was going to be a problem. He wanted to have a nice friendly chat with the kid but he needed to do it when no-one else was around. Impatient to get things moving he picked up the Sylvan CD and walked up to the counter. Mummy's Boy was still hunched over his magazine, drooling over a 1959 Gibson Les Paul with twin DiMarzio pickups and sunburst finish.

'Hi, I wonder if you can help me?' said Craven, deciding to start with an open, friendly approach.

The kid looked up slowly, seemingly annoyed at being interrupted. 'Yeah, what?'

'I was just looking at this CD and wondered why it's more expensive than everything else in here. Are you sure you've got the right price on it?'

The kid took the CD, glanced at it and then handed it back to Craven. 'Yeah, thirty pounds. Take it or leave it. It'll be gone by the weekend.' His head went straight back into the magazine. Conversation over.

Asshole. 'So why is it so pricey then?' asked Craven, for no particular reason other than he could see that the kid didn't like being interrupted and that asking him a stupid question was going to annoy him even more.

Again, the slow movement of the head upwards, dragging himself away from the more interesting read in front of him. 'It's German. The prices reflect how hard they are to get hold of.' He sneered at Craven as though he was an idiot. 'Anything else?'

Craven backed off. 'No, I'll think about it. Thanks.' As he walked the CD back to the rack he heard the kid mutter "Wanker" under his breath. Not a good move. He looked back at him as he reached the door and smiled. 'Thanks for your help. I might pop back later.'

Craven went outside, lit a cigarette and wandered up the street, idly looking in the shop windows while he considered his next move. The street was a mishmash of small, terraced properties, all of them privately owned businesses, the majority with just a single door and one flat or bay-fronted window. He stopped outside an electrical shop and looked at the array of kettles and smoke alarms and cheap digital clocks, wondering how on earth these sorts of places managed to compete with the large DIY stores out of town – but mostly thinking about what he was going to do next.

He needed to get the kid to talk. That wouldn't be a problem of course, five minutes would be more than enough time, but he had to wait until the place was empty – and as obnoxious as he was, the last thing he needed was Mummy's Boy kicking and screaming all the way to the police. For the moment they had no idea what they were dealing with and that's the way he wanted to keep it. Finding the CDs meant that he could put some clear blue water between himself and that useless detective and it was an advantage that he didn't want to throw away.

He could shut the kid up for good of course but a third dead body in the space of a week would trigger a media frenzy which would be uncontrollable. Buchanan would go apoplectic. No, what he needed to do to was make sure that he got the information he wanted but frighten the kid so much that he didn't talk – at least for a couple of days. All he needed was 48, possibly 72 hours.

Craven walked slowly up the length of the street, working out his options and then crossed over and came back down the other side. After about ten minutes he was back at *Seedy CDs*, peering through the window again to see if the other customers had left. The two teenagers had gone but the older guy was still there, standing at the counter and looking as though he was buying something and about to leave. Craven decided to be patient and lit another cigarette. Before he had finished it the guy had come out and the place was empty.

As he closed the door behind him, Craven quietly slipped the catch on the door lock and turned the sign on the door from *Open* to *Closed*. Again, the kid didn't bother to look up. There were a couple of bolts, one each at the top and bottom of the door but they looked as though they were going to be noisy so he decided to leave them for the moment. He walked over to the racks and picked up the three CDs that he'd found earlier, just in case the police did turn up. *No point in leaving good clues around*. As he approached the counter, the kid finally lifted his head out of the magazine, conscious that someone was making a multiple purchase.

Craven put the cases on the counter and looked him in the eye. 'So, where were we?'

The kid frowned at him, obviously confused by Craven's remark and then looked down at the CDs, recognising the titles and more importantly, recognising their origin. Craven had to hand it to him. He wasn't giving anything away. He must have done this a few times before.

'That'll be £90.00 then. Do you want a bag?'

Craven ignored the question and gave him a cold smile. 'So, you got a name, Mummy's Boy?'

'Yes thanks. How about you?'

Smart-arse. 'Sorry, I didn't introduce myself properly did I? DS Turner. Ashford CID.'

The kid looked him up and down, obviously unimpressed and gave him the same sneer as before. 'We don't give discounts.' The head dropped back into the magazine.

Craven looked down at the top of his head and for a moment thought about dragging him over the counter and beating the shit out him there and then. He stared at him for a couple of seconds, restraining himself from changing his plan and just teaching the kid a lesson. 'I'm not looking for a discount. What I want is some information.'

Again the long, slow raise of the head, dragged upwards from the counter. 'Sorry, we don't do information. The library's on the other side of town.' Sarcastic, indolent, disrespectful.

Craven looked at him and held his gaze. Mummy's Boy was starting to irritate him big time. 'We can always do this down at the station if you prefer.'

The kid looked him up and down again, not sure whether to believe he was a policeman or not. He didn't look like a copper and he certainly didn't sound like one. Too polite and definitely not aggressive enough. Most of those bastards over at Ashford would have had him pinned up against the wall by now. 'You got any ID?'

'Sure.' Craven put his right hand inside the left hand pocket of his jacket as if to get out his warrant card, split his index and middle finger into a V and as he pulled his hand out of his jacket, stabbed the two fingers as fast and hard as he could into the kid's eyeballs. Sudden, violent, effective.

The kid didn't see it coming, a portent really given that he wasn't going to see anything coming for the next couple of days. He hardly had time to scream before Craven smacked him hard a couple of times, once on the mouth and once on the side of the head. The kid's lip split like an over-ripe tomato and as he yelped and stumbled against the back wall, Craven swung a huge, conversion-kicking boot into his testicles and then smashed the back of his fist square into the front of his face. The force from the last punch clattered his head against the wall, the impact of which seemed to knock him senseless as he slid to the floor and lay motionless in a crumpled, groaning heap.

In the space of a few seconds his day had exploded into a dark and terrifying nightmare. Craven knew as soon as he hit him that the lip and several teeth had given way and that the cartilage in his nose had also collapsed on impact. The kid was having trouble breathing, the blood and mucous coming out of his nose and mouth starting to congeal and bubble and block his airways. His eyes were already closing; a sudden, enveloping darkness of constant, stabbing pain – but it was the effect of the kick that had made him throw up. Craven had never really played rugby, too busy smoking cigarettes behind the pavilion, but he'd watched enough matches on television to know that a decent kick needed a decent follow through. The dull, gnawing ache started in the kid's bollocks, went through his stomach, up through the spine and stopped in the bottom of his throat. Craven kicked him again hard, just to make sure. *"They'll be dancing in the streets of Pontypridd tonight."*

Craven walked over to the door and shot the two bolts across, just to make sure that no-one could get in. What he needed to do now was get him to talk, not beat him unconscious but he also needed to frighten him to the point that he would keep his mouth shut afterwards. Tricky combination. At the back of the room was a door, leading to an office or maybe a storeroom. He poked his head round and saw it was a small kitchen; sink, draining board, kettle, fridge, plus one old and very dilapidated armchair. This was obviously where the kid ate his lunch or made a cup of coffee. The place was a tip, full of cardboard boxes, magazines, old newspapers, unopened post and stank of food and stale tobacco.

The kid was still lying on the floor so Craven dragged him into the room and put him into a slumped position in the chair, out of sight from the front of the shop. Out of sight in every sense. His eyes were now swollen and fully closed and his whole world had suddenly become a dark and sinister place. Craven looked at him for several seconds and could see that he was petrified. He was in a bad way and he was crying.

'So, you got a name?'

No answer. The kid wasn't listening, too busy whimpering and trying to block out the pain. He just wanted to curl up in the chair and wait for everything to go away. Most of all he just wanted his mum to put her arms around him and tell him that everything was going to be all right. Mummy's Boy by name...

Craven slapped him hard across the face to make him pay attention, which instantly had the desired effect. The slap had come out of nowhere and it was the shock more than the stinging pain that brought him round. Everything was pitch-black and he was at Craven's mercy. Hearing was about the only sense he had left that was working properly and he was suddenly listening better than he'd ever listened in his life. It was the only way he could tell what was going to happen next.

'I said, have you got a name?' Cold, dispassionate, ruthless.

The kid whimpered again. 'Ray.' A large glob of blood and mucous fell out of his mouth and down the front of his T-shirt as he tried to speak, the split lip and loose teeth giving him difficulty in getting the words out.

Craven looked at him with disgust. 'Okay Ray, this is how it's going to work. I'm going to ask you a few questions and then you're going to answer them – in which case I'll be out of here in five minutes. Nod if you understand...'

Ray nodded. Ray was going to answer any questions that anybody asked him.

'...but just to be absolutely clear. If you start pissing me about, we'll be stuck in here together for a couple of hours – and then I'm going to rip your fucking throat out before I leave. Understood?'

Ray nodded again. There was a lot of whimpering and groaning but most of all there was nodding. Ray understood exactly how things were going to work.

'Good. Okay – question one. Who's your favourite guitarist?'

Despite all the pain, the closed eyes, the broken nose, the split lip, Ray still managed to pull a confused and contorted expression. 'I don't understand, what do you mean?'

Craven slapped him again, this time harder. Almost a punch. 'Don't piss me about Ray. Just answer the question. Who's your favourite guitarist?'

Ray was holding his head back, breathing through his mouth and trying to stop the blood from running down his nose. He didn't understand. He didn't understand anything at all. He wanted to tell Craven about the CDs. Surely that was what this was all about. He mumbled an answer – incoherent, unintelligible.

Craven looked at him without an ounce of sympathy, the voice still cold and ruthless. 'I can't hear you Ray. Last chance, I'm not going to ask you again.'

The kid knew he meant it. Finally, he mumbled an answer. 'Joe Satriani.'

Craven softened his tone deliberately and gently took hold of Ray's left hand. 'There, that wasn't so difficult was it?'

Ray shook his head in the darkness, terrified but hopeful.

Still the calm, reassuring voice. 'The good news Ray is that you're telling me the truth which means that we're going to get along fine. The bad news is – you're never going to play the guitar as well as Joe Satriani.' As he finished speaking, Craven took hold of the kid's middle finger and bent it back sharply, leaning all his weight on it until it snapped clean into two pieces.

Ray screamed, a terrified, high-pitched, glass-shattering wail. Excruciating pain, absolute terror. Luckily he couldn't see the finger, broken and dangling at a right angle across his knuckles. 'Please, I haven't done anything, please…' The pleading tailed off into blackness and into gentle sobbing.

Craven waited a couple of minutes until the kid had stopped. *Time to turn the screw.* He took hold of his hand again and gave him the same calm, reassuring voice. 'Okay Ray, question two. Who's your second favourite guitarist?'

Ray tried to scream again, his whole body tensing, waiting for the shock and the next jolt of pain. He started to hyperventilate, too terrified to do anything except wait for the impact. A rabbit caught in the headlights – except that he couldn't see any headlights. He couldn't see anything at all. Eventually the answer – desperate, trembling, petrified. 'Roy Buchanan.'

Ray arched his body, stiffened in readiness for the pain that didn't come.

Craven was still holding his hand, still talking in the same quiet, soothing voice. 'The good news Ray is that if you tell me the truth, I'm not going to break any more of your fingers and you'll never have to see me again. Do you understand?'

Ray nodded. Ray nodded vigorously. He just wanted this to be over.

'But the bad news is, if you tell anybody about me and what's happened here, I'm going to come back and pay you another visit – and when I'm finished, you won't even be able to hold your penis, let alone a guitar chord. Understood?'

Ray nodded again. He hadn't been able to see anything of Craven's face for the last five minutes but there was one thing that he was absolutely sure of. He never wanted to see him again.

Craven smiled. The kid was going to tell him everything he wanted to know and more importantly, once he'd gone, he was going to keep his mouth shut. He wasn't going to say a word to anybody. Mission accomplished. 'So... where did you get the CDs from?'

TWELVE

Garrick sat in the chair opposite Anderson's desk and looked at his watch for the third or fourth time. *Where the hell was he?* It had been nearly a quarter of an hour since Cheryl had telephoned and having dropped everything and come up immediately, he'd spent the last ten minutes kicking his heels waiting for him to arrive. Patience had never been one of Garrick's strong points, particularly when he had better things to do – like trying to solve a couple of murders.

He stood up and paced around the office a few times, looking out of the window at the view of the town centre and then browsing at the books and the photographs of Anderson and a variety of colleagues which were proudly displayed on the cabinet behind the desk. Most of the photos were taken years ago, the young, uniformed officers all looking happy and full of life, long before the years of suffocating red tape, political correctness and a soft and failing judicial system had worn them down, turning them into the hardened, cynical policemen that they had inevitably become. Garrick pulled a grim face as he stared at the young, smiling officers looking out at him from the photo frames. Thirty years ago. What happened to all that pride, all that ambition, all that hope and optimism for the future? Where did it all get lost? A collection of sad, defeated men with over-luncheoned waistlines, resigned to their future and acquiescing to the bureaucrats as they slid uncomplainingly towards retirement and to their over-protected pensions.

He took a deep breath and shook himself back into the present. This was pointless. There were more important things that he needed to be getting on with. He was just on the point of going back downstairs when he heard Anderson coming through the outer office, talking to his PA and then finally walking in behind him, carrying a large pile of papers which he deposited neatly on the desk.

'John, sorry to keep you waiting. Got held up at the Finance Committee. Has anyone offered you a coffee or something?'

'Yes thank you Sir, Cheryl's just getting me some.' Garrick watched as Anderson sat in the chair and took out a bunch of keys to unlock the drawers on the right-hand side of the desk. He was a neat and tidy man, a softly spoken Scot from somewhere in the Borders, an experienced officer from a quiet, rural background who learned his policing on the tough, uncompromising streets of Glasgow and who now, in his mid fifties had turned to a quieter, rural posting – albeit at the other end of the country.

'Good. Anyway, how are things?' Anderson unlocked the desk and started to search through the top right hand drawer, not bothering to look at Garrick as he continued to search for something that he had obviously mislaid.

Garrick shrugged, not sure what sort of conversation they were having. Polite, introductory small-talk or meaningful, detailed discussion. He opted for the former. 'Not bad – busy obviously.'

Suddenly the document searching had stopped. Anderson was leaning back in his chair, arms folded and staring at Garrick with undivided attention. He nodded but said nothing, as if taking it all in and thinking about his next question. Silence. The negotiator's ploy. They stared at each other for several seconds, a stalemate waiting to break.

'So, specifically John, what sort of progress are you making on the two murder enquiries?'

Garrick forced a thin smile. *And so it begins.* He'd been expecting the pressure from above with the same certainty that he expected the sun to rise tomorrow morning – but what he hadn't bargained for was for it to happen so quickly. Richmond's body had only been found yesterday afternoon and Hilary Russell's two days before that. The enquiry was only four days old and already they were preparing the altar. Politicians more concerned with saving face than solving crimes. It made him despair. He summoned up as much enthusiasm as he could manage. 'Actually, we're making good progress. We've identified a possible link between the two murders today which we're investigating further and we're also following up enquiries on the type of poison used in the Appleden case and on the message left at the scene of crime at Richmond's place. The whole team are working hard to move the enquiry forward and to solve both cases as soon as possible...'

Anderson held his hand up, indicating to Garrick to stop. 'Spare me the party political broadcast John, I assume everybody's working hard. What I'm interested in, is what actual progress are we making?'

Garrick looked taken aback. He'd always had a good relationship with Anderson but he'd never seen him like this before. Unsupportive, sarcastic, accusing. 'Like I said, we're making good progress...'

Anderson held his hand up again, impatient to cut straight to the key issue. 'Any suspects yet?'

Garrick flinched, part surprise, part indignation. 'No Sir. Richmond hasn't even been dead 24 hours. A suspect at this stage would be something of a record, don't you think?'

Anderson stared at him across the desk, arms still folded – unimpressed. 'Hilary Russell's been dead since Sunday morning John. Today's Thursday. Any suspects in that case?'

Garrick stood his ground. Being bullied by the Chief Superintendent was not something that he'd experienced before, but he was damned if he was going to be pushed around by someone who sat behind a desk for a living. 'No Sir. The body wasn't discovered until Monday morning and I didn't actually get back from holiday until Tuesday, which is two days ago. Like I said, given the timescale, any suspects at this stage would be unrealistic.'

Anderson said nothing and started rifling through the papers again, obviously still looking for something important and pertinent to the discussion. Eventually he looked up and gave Garrick a cold smile. 'What about motives? Have you got any ideas about why either of them were killed?'

The balance was shifting. Suddenly Garrick had an uncomfortable realisation that the screw was being turned and that the answers he was giving weren't good enough. He squirmed awkwardly in the chair. 'No Sir, nothing certain on motives as yet.'

'I didn't ask for anything certain John, I asked you whether you had any ideas.'

Garrick's head dropped slightly towards the floor. 'No, nothing as yet. We thought burglary in the case of Hilary Russell, but now I'm not so sure. For Richmond it's too early to say.'

Anderson drilled home the advantage. 'So, let me just get this right John; when you say that you're making good progress it doesn't actually mean that you've got any idea as to why either of these people have been murdered or indeed who might have done it. Is that a reasonable summary?'

Garrick nodded. It wasn't the time to argue. 'Yes Sir, very reasonable.'

Anderson looked at him with disdain and went back to searching through one of the piles of papers which were now on his desk. At that moment, Cheryl came in with a tray and two cups of coffee which she quietly put in front of the two officers, seemingly aware that there was some tension in the room. Garrick smiled up at her, appreciative of the interruption and the opportunity to say and do something other than talk about his lack of progress. 'Thanks Cheryl. How are you?'

She smiled back, not bothering to hide the unspoken chemistry which had always been there between herself and Garrick. 'Fine thanks John. Busy as ever.'

Garrick turned and watched her walk back to the outer office, closing the door behind her, a hint of perfume lingering in the air. It was no secret that they both liked each other, the whole station either knew or had speculated about it for years but it was also common knowledge that it was an attraction that neither of them had ever declared or done anything about.

Garrick had always been a confirmed bachelor. Committing to a career in the police force with all the sacrifices that that entailed meant that he'd never found the time to meet someone and settle down. Besides, he'd seen too many marriages and relationships destroyed by the dedication and commitment that was needed to do the job. Not to mention the hours. For some officers the police force gave them a sense of belonging and the work took one hundred percent of their focus, sometimes for weeks or possibly months on end. Immersing yourself in an enquiry like the Appleden case was bound to have a detrimental effect on your home life and in the end the wives or girlfriends always got fed up with waiting or being ignored, or worse of all, having to put up with being second best. Ultimately, the ultimatums were inevitable.

Still, there was something very attractive, almost seductive about Cheryl which he couldn't explain. He only had to be in the same room with her, or even on the telephone and there was an instant electricity, an unexplained frisson which sparked on both sides. One day he was going to have to pluck up the courage and ask her out, otherwise he was going to end up like John Betjeman, wistfully reflecting on a life that might have been.

Garrick picked up the cup of coffee and watched Anderson opposite him, still searching through the papers that were now stacked up in numerous piles on top of the desk. After a couple of minutes the elusive document was eventually found and passed across, this time with a smile and a warmer tone of voice.

'It's the press release and statement on Stuart Richmond. We managed to keep it out of the lunchtime bulletins, but it'll be released in time for the six o'clock news this evening – which means it'll be all over the front pages tomorrow morning. My money's on "Fashion Victim" being one of the less imaginative headlines. I cut you as much slack as I could John but by tomorrow lunchtime half the county is going to be swarming with journalists from every major newspaper, and by the evening the hyenas from the redtops will be crawling through everybody's dustbins and skeleton cupboards, including yours and mine. If you think the last five minutes with me have been difficult you haven't seen anything yet – and by the way, you'd better prepare some better answers than you just gave me. They'd tear you to pieces on that performance…'

'Yes Sir.' Garrick was reading the press release and looking contrite. Anderson had made his point and made it well.

'…now quit the crap and tell me how the enquiry's going.'

Garrick took a deep breath, preparing himself for the response. 'Well, the Appleden case is full of contradictions. It has all the hallmarks of a carefully planned, almost professional murder committed by what looks like a fairly amateurish burglar, which doesn't make a lot of sense. On the other hand, the Richmond case appears to be exactly the opposite – a spontaneous murder committed about ten days after a fairly professional burglary.'

Anderson raised his eyebrows, indicating that he agreed with Garrick's comments that it didn't add up.

'It's true, we don't have any suspects as yet but I'm fairly confident that we're looking for two separate people. The murders are just too different to be carried out by the same person. And whilst we don't have a clear motive for either killing, there is a possibility that the two events are in some way connected, which was the information that emerged this morning and which we need to follow up.'

Anderson nodded, still silent and still taking it in all in.

'We're also waiting for the pathologist's report on Richmond and for the forensics report from *Chart Place*. Until we've got those it's difficult to make any definitive conclusions.'

Anderson frowned, Garrick was straying into defensive territory again. 'Okay, well let's get a second press statement prepared on that basis ready for the calls that will be coming in this evening. "Actively pursuing several lines of enquiry but still waiting for the analysis of key forensic evidence taken from the scene of the crime," – something along those lines…'

Garrick nodded as he scribbled down the words.

'…and you'd better get everything cleared with somebody in Communications – I know you think that they're all a waste of space but believe me, it's at times like this that the PR boys really earn their money.'

'Yes Sir.'

'Anyway, so what's the connection?'

'Sorry?'

'The connection between the two murders. You said some information emerged this morning which you were following up.'

Garrick nodded again, suddenly realising what Anderson was talking about. 'Richmond received a telephone call last week from someone wanting to speak to him about something called Teleios. We don't know what Teleios means at the moment but we do know that it's significant. The murderer at *Chart Place* sprayed the word across the wall of the crime scene, so we're assuming that the caller and the murderer are one and the same person. It also appears that Hilary Russell was made aware of the phone call a couple of days before she died and it seems that Teleios meant something to her as well. It was certainly something that she recognised.'

Anderson wrote down the word Teleios on his pad, checking the correct spelling with Garrick as he did so. 'So I assume you're throwing everything at trying to find out what this Teleios means?'

Garrick nodded. 'Yes, we are – but since interviewing Mrs. Webster this morning the other priority is to try and trace the caller who rang Richmond last Tuesday. If we can identify who made that phone call it would be a real breakthrough. We're also investigating Richmond's movements over the last couple of weeks and researching possible sources of *Fentanyl*, the poison used at Appleden. To be honest we're spread pretty thin at the moment. We've got too many lines of enquiry running at the same time – but finding out who or what Teleios is and identifying the caller who telephoned Richmond are the two main priorities.'

Anderson stared at him for a couple of seconds, as if trying to decide whether to tell him something or not. He'd worked with Garrick long enough to know that what he was about to say was going to provoke a reaction. *Light the blue touch paper and retire immediately.*

'Well, as you mentioned being stretched a bit thin John, perhaps it's only fair to tell you that the Chief Constable rang me at lunchtime. He wanted to know how the enquiry was going.'

Garrick could immediately feel his hackles rising, unable to stop the irritation and sarcasm spilling out in his response. 'Well, it's good to know he's interested in what's going on at the coal face I suppose.'

Anderson gave him a disappointed look. 'He simply wanted to know how things were going John and the point is, there wasn't much I could tell him, was there? I think we'd better put something in the diary at the end of each day so that we can have a regular update.'

Garrick nodded. 'Okay, I'll talk to Cheryl. So what did you tell him?'

'I gave him the same bullshit that you were giving me earlier – which I have to say he didn't swallow for one minute.'

Garrick smiled, acknowledging the difficult situation that Anderson was in. 'Sorry. I'll leave the spin to PR from now on.'

'Good.' Anderson took a deep breath and hesitated, struggling to find the right words. 'But as it happens he also asked me whether we had enough resources and whether...'

'Whether what?' Garrick crossed his arms. He guessed what was coming next.

'...whether you and the team were up to the job.'

'Jesus Christ!' Garrick exploded out of the chair and stormed over to the window, too furious to look Anderson straight in the eye. 'What the hell does he know about managing a murder enquiry, he wouldn't recognise a murder suspect if it was shoved under his nose holding a smoking gun. We've only been on the case a couple of days and already he's watching his own back. Well if that's how things are going to be maybe you should get somebody else – frankly I've got better things to do than waste my time managing the press and a load of politics just to keep the Chief Constable happy. I'd rather concentrate on doing some real police work...'

Anderson had swivelled round in his chair to look at Garrick, who was still staring out of the window and shaking with anger. 'Don't be so bloody high and mighty John. Of course he doesn't know how to solve a murder enquiry, he hasn't been a front-line police officer for years. It's not his job to know. He's the Chief Constable for god's sake. He's managing an organisation of over 5,000 staff and a budget of over £250 million a year – and whether you like it or not he's doing his job and he's doing it properly.'

Garrick turned away from the window and strode back towards the desk, surprised that Anderson was pushing back but just as ready for an argument. 'Well if he's doing his job properly why doesn't he give us the space to get on and do ours?'

Anderson shook his head in despair and slammed the cup of coffee he was holding back onto the tray. 'You might like to think that policing starts and ends with catching criminals John but it doesn't. Grow up. This is the 21st century. It's also about making sure that the public have the trust and confidence in our ability to protect them and to do our job properly. Modern policing is as much about managing PR and communications as it is about solving crimes. To be honest he probably doesn't give a toss about any one particular case. That's our job. His primary concern is about the reputation and integrity of this force and making sure that we don't do anything to put that at risk. You know what happened at Soham. All he's doing is thinking ahead, knowing the amount of publicity that this case is going to attract. He's simply doing his job by checking that we've got enough resources and capability to do ours.

'So what did you tell him?' asked Garrick, starting to feel as though he was on the back foot.

'What do you think I told him? I told him that of course you and the team were up to it and that you had my one hundred percent confidence and support. What do you expect me to say?'

Garrick was now looking humble and slightly embarrassed. 'Thank you Sir, we won't let you down.'

'You'd better not John. And if you do think you need more resources or the help of someone more senior you'd better say so now. Don't tell me when it's too late.'

'Jump before I'm pushed you mean?' replied Garrick sullenly.

It was Anderson's turn to lose his temper, leaning across the desk on both knuckles and starting to shake with anger. 'No, I don't mean fucking jump before you're pushed. I mean we have a duty to the public to make sure that we're organised to solve these murders as quickly as possible and that it's better for us to take that decision and to control what happens, rather than let someone else reach that conclusion in a couple of weeks time and have something imposed on us. This isn't about you John, it's about the force doing the job properly and not setting ourselves up as targets for the tabloids or the politicians. Stop being so bloody precious about everything!'

Garrick held his hands up in defeat, recognising this was a moral argument that he wasn't going to win.

Anderson sank back in his chair and took some deep breaths. His face had gone bright red and there were beads of sweat glistening on his forehead and beginning to run down the side of his neck. He poured himself a glass of water, which he drank hurriedly and after a few moments started to calm down, his breathing beginning to subside and return to a more relaxed pattern. 'Anyway, what sort of hours are you working at the moment John?'

I'm getting in about sevenish and I normally make sure I don't work any later than ten.'

Anderson raised his eyebrows. 'That's a fifteen hour day. Don't forget to sharpen the saw.'

'Sharpen the saw?' Garrick frowned, clearly not understanding the last remark.

'It's management theory. Look it up. On second thoughts, don't. It'll only put you in a bad mood. You're a good officer John but you're a prickly bugger sometimes.'

Garrick smiled. 'Sorry Sir, it's probably being principled that makes me such a good copper.'

Anderson grunted and gave him a rueful smile. 'I don't know about your principles John but I do know what would do you a bit of good,' nodding towards the door of the outer office where Cheryl was working. 'You ought to make time for yourself. A bit of indulgence never hurt anybody. *"All work and no play..."* Might help stop you getting so bloody stroppy.'

Garrick gave him an old-fashioned look as he stood up and made his exit, realising that there wasn't any point in pretending that he didn't understand. 'Well, you learn something new every day Sir. I've never heard it called sharpening the saw before...'

By the time he got back to CID some of the team had moved into the incident room and were trying to integrate the information obtained from Doreen's interview into the enquiry. The whiteboard, which only a couple of days ago had consisted of no more than a few SOCO photographs was now overflowing with information and possible connections. Andy had written the time-line across the centre of the board and Paul had clustered the various leads and pieces of information around each date, connecting each one with different coloured pens. It was starting to look busy.

Garrick stood in the doorway and watched them for a moment, noting the level of enthusiasm and commitment that they were all giving. Matt and Steph were hunched over one of the desks, carefully checking through one of the files. The last thing they needed was to be told that they weren't working hard enough or that they weren't up to the job. For the moment he was going to keep his conversation with Anderson to himself. Eventually he wandered in and took a seat at the back of the room, not wanting to interrupt Andy who was summarising the information that had just been put on the white board.

'So, the first incident was on Tuesday 12th September. *Chart Place* was burgled sometime during the evening before Richmond and his wife returned home from London at around midnight. Second, exactly one week later, Tuesday 19th September, Richmond received a telephone call at home from someone wanting to speak to him about Teleios. We know from the phone records that the call was made at 11.08 am. Two days after that, Thursday 21st September, Doreen Webster told her neighbour, Hilary Russell, about the phone call and about the Teleios message. Three days later, Sunday 24th September, *Yew Tree Cottage* was burgled and Hilary Russell was murdered.

Finally, three days after that, Wednesday 27th September, Stuart Richmond was murdered. That's the timeline.'

Inevitably, the whole room turned round to look at Garrick, wanting to bring him into the discussion and to get some further direction. He nodded at the white board, indicating his approval. 'That looks good – helpful summary. Let's have a quick update. What's the latest?'

'It's not particularly positive,' replied Andy, looking serious and slightly disheartened.

Garrick smiled, determined to try and keep the mood as optimistic as possible. 'Well, it can't be any worse than the last fifteen minutes with Anderson. Come on, we haven't got time for shrinking violets, somebody update me. Let's start with the good news.'

Andy turned towards Matt. 'Over to you Shylock, let's run through it again.'

Matt picked up the file that was lying on the chair next to him and opened it to make sure that he had all the details to hand. 'Well, the good news is that I've completed the research on Richmond and we've pretty much got an hour by hour detail of all of his movements, meetings and phone calls since Monday 11th September, the day before the burglary. One positive development is that we know that the £100,000 in cash was definitely his. He drew it out of his local branch at just after three o'clock on Monday 25th September, a couple of days after he took the phone call and two days before he was killed. The bank obviously has records but the local manager remembered it straight away because of the amount and the fact that Richmond wanted it in cash.'

'So what conclusions are we drawing from that?' asked Garrick, fairly certain in his own mind that he knew the answer but wanting to give the team the opportunity to develop their own thinking.

'Well, we know that Richmond didn't normally carry that amount of cash,' replied Andy, 'so it's too much of a coincidence not to be connected to either the burglary or the phone call. Our view is that he was either being blackmailed or he was trying to buy something back that had been stolen in the burglary – but that either way it's connected to the phone call and to this person or thing called Teleios.'

Garrick nodded in approval. 'I agree, exactly what I was thinking.'

'The only problem,' interrupted Matt, 'is that we know there was nothing of any real value stolen from *Chart Place* and even if he was being blackmailed or trying to buy something back, why didn't the murderer take the money after he had killed him? Why leave £100,000 in cash behind? Like everything else in this case, it doesn't make sense.'

Garrick paused, deep in thought, realising that what Matt was saying was true. 'Anything else?'

Nothing else on Richmond I'm afraid,' replied Matt, looking suddenly apprehensive. 'We've trawled through every meeting, every lunch appointment, every credit card transaction, every phone call. There doesn't seem to be anything of any significance. And more importantly, we can't trace the caller who rang Richmond on Tuesday morning.'

The room fell silent as everybody looked at Garrick, waiting for the reaction. He sat still for a moment, saying nothing and then wandered over to the window and stared out at the car park which was immediately below, processing the news and thinking about what he was going to do next. They were running out of time. 'Do we have a number?'

Matt nodded. 'Mobile. Sent from a "Pay As You Go" SIM card which was bought in Ashford town centre on Monday 18th September, the day before the phone call. No personal details given. No other calls made or received. One anonymous number. One phone call made.'

The room fell back into an uncomfortable silence. Everybody shared the disappointment but only Garrick really understood the potential impact of Matt's news. Still, there was no point in worrying the team. He needed them pumped up and absolutely switched on about the enquiry. He turned away from the window, putting on a deadpan voice and the straightest face that he could manage. 'Okay. So, what's the bad news then Matt?'

It took a second for the absurdity of Garrick's remark to cut through the silence before a couple of the team and then most of the others started to smile. Only Andy continued to look serious. 'Actually the bad news Sir is that we're drowning in too much work trying to identify possible sources of *Fentanyl*. And despite two of us wasting the whole day on so called research, we don't actually know any more about Teleios than you can find out by typing the word into *Google*. Without the lead on Richmond's caller, I'm not sure where the enquiry's going or how we're going to make any real progress.'

The bluntness of Andy's response took most of the team by surprise, almost as though it was challenging Garrick's authority. It was unintentional but they all stared at each other for a couple of seconds, not knowing what to say.

'Sorry Sir, that didn't come out as I meant it to. I didn't mean...'

Garrick held his hand up and waved Andy's apology away. Besides, he was right. The enquiry was going nowhere and worse than that, if it went on much longer there was a risk of him losing the confidence of his most experienced officers. Maybe Anderson was right. The case was too important to worry about pride or personal ambition. The most important thing was to make sure that the team had the best possible chance of success and if that meant bringing in someone else, so be it.

'There's a message on your desk to ring Dr. Wyatt,' offered Steph, trying to sound as positive and optimistic as possible. 'He rang just after you went upstairs. He says he's got the PM results on Richmond – maybe there will be some better news there.'

Garrick gave her a weak smile. He knew that it was probably too little, too late. What he needed to do was get back upstairs and see Anderson as soon as possible. He stood up and was just about to leave when the telephone in the far corner of the room rang. Someone from the front desk must have put the call through knowing that they were in the incident room. Steph picked it up and almost instantly offered the phone to Garrick. 'Its Bob Hughes Sir, says he wants to speak to you urgently.'

Garrick took the receiver without much enthusiasm. Bob Hughes wasn't the brightest officer the force had ever employed. He was probably still sitting in the kitchen of *Yew Tree Cottage*, waiting for a carpenter and after three days asking whether he could go home yet.

'Bob. What can I do for you?'

'Other way round Sir, it's what I can do for you.' Garrick could hear traffic and people in the background. Bob was obviously out and about.

'Make it snappy Bob, we're in the middle of something here. What's happening?'

'I'm standing outside a Jewellery shop in Canterbury Sir, one of the back streets. I was just looking in the window and right in the centre of their display are two of the items from *Chart Place*. Just wondered whether you wanted me to bring the owner in or whether you wanted to come out?'

Garrick looked at the rest of the team as he listened to Bob on the other end of the phone and couldn't help breaking into a broad grin. In the space of a few seconds he'd gone from the depths of despair to pure elation. It was moments like this, turning points in an investigation, that he always remembered and which despite all the low points, made it all worthwhile. 'Bob, are you absolutely sure it's two of Richmond's pieces?' The rest of the team were hanging on to every word, trying to interpret what was going on from one end of a telephone conversation.

'Absolutely Sir, they're items 38 and 61 if you've got the list in front of you. They've both got photographs. Sergeant Edwards made sure that we all had copies and I'm looking at mine now Sir. There's no mistaking it. A necklace with matching earrings and a bracelet. There could be others of course. I haven't gone inside. I thought it best to call you first. What do you want me to do Sir?'

Garrick clenched his fist and shook it firmly. 'Just stay there Bob and do nothing. We're on our way.'

THIRTEEN

It was three o'clock by the time Neil eventually got back to the cottage. The journey back from Ashford had been slow and frustrating, not helped by Doreen's insistence that they go round the local supermarket, and then taking ages, complaining repeatedly that it wasn't laid out like it used to be and that she couldn't find anything. Neil had tried to explain that supermarkets kept moving things around so that regular customers would have to wander up and down the aisles, enticing them to spend more by making more impulse purchases – but Doreen wasn't having any of it.

She'd said that it was a complete waste of time as most of the regular shoppers were women who knew exactly what they wanted and who weren't that gullible – and that if supermarkets really wanted to make bigger profits then all they had to do was encourage more men to go shopping. Apparently, taking Tom with her was guaranteed to add an extra five or ten pounds to her bill because he normally trailed behind her, usually bored and periodically lobbing things into the trolley, mostly luxury items like sweets and chocolate which were a complete waste of money.

Neil felt that this damning generalisation of the whole male race was a little unfair, a thought that had struck him particularly as he stood patiently at the checkouts, watching three separate women wait for their shopping to be scanned and packed and for the total bill to be run through the till before they even thought about rummaging through their bags to find their purses. And then all three of them started fumbling around for coins, trying to count out the exact amount in loose change. *Why can't they get their purses out ready before they start and then just hand over the nearest amount in whole notes?*

The drive back had also taken longer than expected, but at least it gave Doreen the chance to recount the details of her interview with Steph and Garrick, a story that Neil sat through for a second time when they got back home and she had to go through it all again for Tom. To her credit, she told it exactly the same the second time around and as far as he could tell, without any embellishment. Tom had never heard of the word Teleios and whilst Doreen busied herself making some lunch, he and Neil tried to look it up in an old

Chambers Dictionary – but inevitably without any success.

They spent half an hour or so after lunch, sitting in the armchairs in front of the fire, musing about the possible connection between Aunt Hilary and Stuart Richmond. Neither of them could think of a rational explanation and as their theories got more and more far-fetched they eventually gave up and moved onto more mundane matters, including the merits of Tom getting a new car. Apparently it was on its last legs and he had recently decided that it was time to treat himself to something a little more up-to-date and upmarket.

'What, like a Hillman Imp or a Morris Traveller?' teased Neil, 'Or maybe something with a bit of suspension and power steering?'

Tom smiled at him ruefully. 'You can laugh lad – but it's never let me down that old car. And I run it for next to nothing. You wait until you're a poor pensioner scrimping and saving on a fixed income. You won't want to be wasting your money on expensive cars then.'

Neil laughed. 'I don't waste any money on cars now Tom – never have. Anyway, I thought we were talking about you. Who's this poor pensioner scrimping and saving on a fixed income? I don't think I've met him yet!'

In the end, Neil decided not to ask if he could borrow the car that evening. He'd promised Steph that he wouldn't tell anybody about their meeting and although he trusted Tom implicitly, he didn't want to break the promise that he'd made. He also didn't want to get into the complication of borrowing the car but not being able to tell Tom what he wanted it for. Besides, it was probably better to get a taxi, which meant that he could have a glass wine or two without worrying about driving home. Driving an uninsured old banger with no road tax on top of several glasses of wine was probably not the best way to endear yourself to someone on your first date, particularly as she was a member of the local constabulary.

Eventually he thanked Doreen for the lunch and made his excuses and left. As soon as he got back to the cottage he headed straight for the kitchen, impatient to finish off the phone calls that he had started that morning and in particular, to find out who was going to be at the other end. He picked up the telephone and dialled the second of the London numbers. It was the last one on the list, so presumably the last one that Aunt Hilary had rung. Maybe that was significant. He sat on the kitchen stool, looking again at the piece of paper and the three telephone numbers and the two words written in Aunt Hilary's distinctive handwriting. He half hoped that one of the words might be Teleios but it was nothing like it. There was the Cheltenham number followed by two London numbers, the word "Carlisle" and then the final word, which looked like either "Rawlings" or "Rowlands." Either way, it wasn't Teleios. It wasn't even close.

'Jean Pettipher.'

Neil had the pen and paper ready and quickly scribbled down as many details as he could make out from the other end of the phone. Female, middle-aged, fifties probably. Educated, polite, articulate, definitely in control. So much information from just two words. There was no background noise, and from her response no way of telling whether it was a personal or business phone – but instinct told him that it was business. He tried the same approach as before. 'Oh, I'm sorry, I must have the wrong extension, could you put me back to the main switchboard please.'

'I'm sorry, you must have the wrong number. We don't have a switchboard here.' The voice purred. Smooth, confident, professional.

'Gosh, I don't know how that happened,' apologised Neil as quickly as he could, trying his best to keep the conversation going and prevent her from cutting him off. 'Can I just check what number I've got?'

'What number were you after?' The response was instant. Controlled, unflappable.

Neil repeated the number that he'd dialled. 'I was after Steve Walker in IT. Network Support.' Again, the same approach, but he already sensed that it was leading nowhere.

'I'm sorry, you really must have the wrong number. We don't have a Network Support department.'

'Okay, I'm sorry to have bothered you.' He was about to put the phone down and then suddenly it just blurted out. He didn't know why he said it. It was pure impulse. Maybe it was frustration or maybe he just wanted to try and provoke some sort of reaction from the calm and unflustered Ms. Pettipher, whoever she was. Either way, he knew it was his parting shot. His last attempt to try and find out who he was really speaking to and whether it had any relevance to Aunt Hilary's death. 'Oh, I don't suppose there's another Company in your building is there? The Company I'm after is called Teleios?'

'Teleios? How do you spell that?'

Neil sensed a millisecond pause and a slight change in tone. An almost imperceptible difference, no more than a one-degree shift in intonation – but a shift nevertheless. For some reason, he also felt that she wasn't writing the word down as he spelt it out to her over the telephone, as though she already knew it and was just playing for time. He knew it was irrational but that's how it felt.

'Just hold the line and I'll check for you.'

He sat patiently as the phone went dead and looked at everything that he'd written down on the pad. There was no background music on the phone, no *Fugue* by Bach or *Four Seasons* by Vivaldi, just a silent, dead line as though he'd been cut-off completely. He expected her to get back to him in a matter of seconds but it was almost a full minute before the line clicked back in and he heard the smooth, apologetic voice of Jean Pettipher again.

'I'm really sorry, there's no Company of that name here. All I can suggest is directory enquiries I'm afraid.'

Neil put the phone down and stared out of the kitchen window into the back garden. *Well that was a complete waste of time.* Suddenly, he also felt very reckless about having mentioned the word Teleios. The only thing he knew about it, other than it was probably Greek of course, was that Doreen had mentioned it to Aunt Hilary a couple of days before she died and that didn't bode well. And why on earth were the police so interested in it, particularly if the interview with Doreen was meant to be about the murder of Stuart Richmond a couple of days later? Did Teleios have something to do with that?

He turned away from the window and decided to try the other London number. It was the middle number that Aunt Hilary had rung and for some reason in Neil's mind, probably the least significant of the three, but he dialled it anyway and unlike the previous call, it was answered within seconds.

'Middle East Desk. Adam Saxby.' Neil felt the same jolt of surprise as when he'd rung GCHQ but managed to concentrate on capturing as much information as possible. Male, thirties, no discernable accent – and despite the speed at which the phone had been answered, a relaxed, almost lazy response. He could imagine the guy leaning back in his chair, top button and tie undone, slightly bored. Waiting for something to happen.

'Oh, I'm sorry, I must have the wrong extension, could you put me back to the main switchboard please.'

'I can transfer you from here if you want. Who are you after?' The guy sounded helpful and friendly.

'Steve Walker in IT. Network Support.'

'Not here I'm afraid, they're all centralised.'

Neil tried to keep the conversation going, thinking on his feet. 'Oh, sorry about that, I'm sure he said that he was working in your building today.'

'Well he might be but you'd have to get him on his mobile, he won't have an extension here at King Charles Street. Do you want me to put you back to the switchboard, they might have a mobile number for him?'

Neil grinned. 'No it's okay, I've got his mobile number somewhere. Thanks for your help.'

He put the phone down and blew a low whistle. His geography of central London wasn't that good but he remembered a school trip to the Houses of Parliament when he was about fifteen. A typical coach load of adolescent schoolboys, more interested in trying to slope off and have a quick fag or visit the seedier sights of Soho than wandering around the hallowed corridors of power. The trip had included a visit to Downing Street and a tour of the old war rooms, chaperoned by "Beaky" Middleton, the long suffering history master who all the boys ridiculed, but who in reality quietly commanded their respect, somehow producing outstanding exam results from his underachieving pupils year after year.

Neil could remember that they all had to make a map of the visit when they got back and he could still see his now – a carefully drawn plan of Westminster and Whitehall, painstakingly recreated on graph paper, including all the important roads and buildings. Parliament Square, Downing Street, Horse Guards Parade, The Cenotaph, Admiralty Arch and the least well known of them all; King Charles Street. It ran parallel to Downing Street with The Treasury on one side, opposite the Churchill Museum, and The Foreign & Commonwealth Office on the other. There was no doubt about it. Middle East Desk and King Charles Street meant only one thing. Aunt Hilary had telephoned the Foreign Office. The question was; when had she rung them and why?

Neil slid off the stool and went into the dining room to get the brown leather address book out of the bureau. It took him about ten minutes to page through all the entries, checking the names and the telephone numbers but there was nothing. Aunt Hilary had kept everything organised and up-to-date but there were no London numbers matching the ones that he'd just rung and no numbers at all in either Cheltenham or Carlisle. He checked the surnames for Daniels, Pettipher and Saxby but also drew a blank. Eventually he put the address book back in the bureau and wandered back into the kitchen. Just like yesterday, there was only one thing for it. He checked his watch and then picked up the phone and dialled Chris's number at *The Chronicle.*

'News Desk – Chris Fleming.'

'Hi Chris, it's Neil again. How are you doing?'

'Not bad mate, keeping busy. How are you?'

Neil could picture Chris swivelling round in his chair and putting his feet on the desk, like he always did when speaking to someone familiar. It used to drive his boss mad. 'Okay. Just ringing to see whether you had any joy with the *Fentanyl* research?'

'Yes and no really. Plenty of info but I don't know if it's of any use. I've printed most of it off so I'll bring it with me when I come down, but basically it's a painkiller – but very powerful. It's used in hospitals mostly as far as I can make out. Does that help or mean anything to you?'

Neil shook his head. 'Not sure what it means Chris, to be honest, but like you say, bring the stuff with you and we can go through it at the weekend. Thanks for checking it out anyway.'

'No problem. So, any progress your end?'

'Likewise, yes and no really.' Neil pulled a hesitant face before asking the follow-up. 'Actually I was ringing to ask another favour if that's okay?'

Chris smiled to himself. Typical Neil. He was a fabulous copywriter but he always hated doing the research. 'No problem, what is it?'

'I don't suppose you know anybody who can trace mainline telephone numbers and get hold of telephone records do you?'

'Wow, that sounds a bit serious. Isn't that illegal?'

'Yeah I know, that's why I thought of you.'

Chris laughed and then thought about the question for a couple of seconds, trying to remember whether he knew of anyone who could help. 'I might know someone Neil, but it depends which network you want checking out. Do you know which one it is?'

'Sorry, no idea. I've got three different numbers so they could be on three different networks for all I know. Actually, I think I've already identified two of the numbers and they're probably in the public domain – you might be able to confirm them just by doing an internet search.'

'Okay, well that shouldn't take long. So what about the third one?'

'No idea I'm afraid. It's a London number but beyond that I haven't got a clue. It was answered by someone called Jean Pettipher, but it sounds like a business line.'

Neil could hear Chris reaching for a pen and paper and then writing the name down. 'Okay, give me the numbers and I'll see what I can do.'

Neil read out the three numbers and also gave Chris the names of Daniels and Adam Saxby. 'Any information you can get on those two would also be really helpful…'

'Blimey Neil, you don't want much do you?'

'…and the final thing is, I think all three numbers were called by my Aunt from this phone, possibly just before she died. I really need to find out if the calls were made from here and if so, when.'

'Do you know which network you're on at the cottage?'

Again Neil shook his head. 'Sorry – I haven't found any old bills so again, no idea. Marconi probably, knowing this village.'

Chris laughed again. 'So what's going on then Neil? Sounds like there have been a few developments.'

Neil checked his watch. It was a long story which was going to take a while to explain. Personally, he had the time but he really wanted Chris to get on and start checking out the information as soon as possible. He needed to change the subject and knew exactly what sort of bait was going to work. 'Actually Chris, I'll tell you when I see you at the weekend. I'm going out to dinner tonight and I've got a few things I need to do before I leave.'

'Dinner? That sounds a bit posh for you mate. You mean pie and chips down the local pub?'

Neil pretended to be offended. 'No, I don't mean pie and chips down the local pub. I mean a proper dinner invitation with real food and fine wine and good company and intelligent conversation...'

'What, good company as in members of the opposite sex?'

Neil was grinning from ear to ear. The disbelief in Chris's voice was so predictable but at the same time, so enjoyable. 'Well, only one member of the opposite sex. It's a dinner date, not a party.'

'Dinner date? What do you mean it's a dinner date? You've only been there a couple of days. You don't do dinner dates. Who is she?'

Neil was still grinning. Oh, this was wonderful. Worth the price of the phone call alone. 'Chris, I'm really sorry, I really do have to go. I'll tell you all about it when I see you.'

'Neil, don't do this to me. I'll do the research this afternoon and ring you later this evening with an update. You can tell me all about it then.'

Neil started to laugh. 'Sorry Chris, I don't know what time I'll be back tonight, it'll probably be late. You'll be tucked up in bed fast asleep by the time I get in. I'll talk to you at the weekend.'

'Neil... Neil... don't do this to me... you know that you'll be running to me for advice in a couple of days... you'll be desperate to talk about it then... Neil... Neil?'

*

Craven eventually found *The Bricklayer's Arms,* an old, dilapidated pub on the corner of Marsham Street, wedged at the end of a residential road of small, terraced Victorian houses on the eastern outskirts of the town centre. He pulled the car up outside and stared at the fading brickwork and the run-down and grimy exterior, looking for signs of life. A wisp of smoke was curling out of one of the chimneys but the place was in darkness and he realised immediately that it was shut. Obviously all-day opening had not yet taken off in the poorer, working-class areas of Ashford.

He wound down the window and lit a cigarette, thinking about what he was going to do next. It was four o'clock, which meant that he had a couple of hours to kill before the towels came off and the doors were unlocked to welcome the early evening regulars. Reconnaissance followed by hours of waiting was familiar territory but he was starting to get impatient.

Richmond's death had added a complication which he could have done without and he knew that the police, incompetent as they were, would not be far behind. The nephew was also getting inquisitive. Craven didn't like journalists very much – he didn't trust them. He didn't really trust anyone to be honest, but journalists and politicians were the worst. He didn't trust them as far as he could throw them. He let his mind wander and thought about Dr. David Kelly, an honest, principled but ultimately naïve man who put his faith in the journalistic profession and in his government employers to protect his identity and to defend his reputation; but in the end they all betrayed him and then hung him out to dry. All for the sake of a good story and to preserve their own careers. They were as bad as each other.

And as always, it was passed to Buchanan to tidy things up. A situation far too critical and politically sensitive to trust to the drones over at Thames House. A brief, after-dinner conversation in a smoke-filled dining room, somewhere in between the pudding and a glass of Chateau Suau Sauternes, the arrangements discussed with an eloquence and a practiced finesse, almost as a sub-text to the finer points of the extensive wine list or the merits of the latest exhibition at The Royal Academy. Grace and favour, the tentacles of power curling their way to bind another promise, another debt, paid or re-called. It all amounted to the same. History would record a different story but the real unknown brokers, the mandarins and bureaucrats were always lurking in the shadows. Balancing the scales, moving the pawns, laying the grate.

Craven glanced up at the long-bladed knife which he kept discretely behind the driver's sun visor, remembering a summer's field in middle England, the sun burning on the back of his neck, the nodded "good afternoon" to the friendly, bearded walker who passed him by and then the screech of rooks, rising out of the trees and echoing into the silence that quickly followed. He looked into the driver's mirror and caught a glimpse of himself, barely recognising the fleeting moment of conscience written across his face. He frowned as it passed as quickly as it came. He was one of Buchanan's outriders and there was no room for doubt or self-reflection. A moment's hesitation and you were lost.

He flicked the cigarette butt out of the window and drove off towards the ring-road, looking for one of the bigger supermarkets, which were always located just off the main carriageway. What he needed was a petrol station and one that was really busy – where there were so many customers that nobody noticed or remembered anything, not even with the help of CCTV cameras. He found what he was looking for just off a large roundabout leading to the motorway on the southern edge of town. He pulled into the forecourt, topped up the car and then filled up the spare petrol-can that he kept in the boot. He went into the shop, bought a sandwich and a large bottle of water and then stood in the queue and waited patiently to pay for everything. Always in cash. No credit cards, no record of having been there.

When he got back to the car he drove into the large supermarket car park and found the quietest place to park, near a row of metal roller doors, presumably delivery bays located near the back of the store. These were the spaces that always filled up last and which at 4.30 in the afternoon were mostly empty. He switched off the engine, ate the sandwich and then smoked a cigarette and drank some of the water. When he'd finished he got out of the car, dumped the sandwich wrapper into the nearest bin and poured the rest of the water onto the ground. Then he went to the boot and took out the spare petrol-can, carefully filling the empty water bottle with petrol and replacing the screw-cap top, making sure that it was tight and that nothing could spill out. By ten to five he'd put both the petrol can and plastic bottle back in the boot and was ready to go.

The problem was, he had another hour to kill which was a real pain. He needed to find somewhere better to wait, a coffee shop perhaps or maybe a motorway service station. *Somewhere nice and crowded. The ideal place to go unnoticed.* He pulled the car onto the roundabout and took the second exit onto the motorway, heading towards Maidstone and the services at Leeds Castle. Within fifteen minutes he was sitting in the services coffee-shop, drinking a double expresso and thinking about what the next couple of hours were going to look like.

Not knowing where Jamie Collins lived was disappointing, but it was hardly a show-stopper. And he felt fairly certain that Ray hadn't been holding out on him – the kid had been too scared to risk not telling the truth. Besides, it all made sense. A guy who came in with a load of second-hand CDs and wanted to trade them for cash meant only one thing. He was hardly going to hand over his name and address. The kid had said that he'd been back a few times, normally three or four weeks apart and always with another consignment to offload. The stuff was obviously stolen, but nobody was going to ask any questions – it was better not to know anything. All Ray knew was that his name was Jamie Collins, that he lived on the Connaught Estate somewhere and that he drank in the *Bricklayer's Arms* on Marsham Street. Every night, regular as clockwork.

The guy was obviously a creature of habit. Probably liked his routines, regular schedules, familiarity. Probably didn't like his normal arrangements being upset. Didn't like surprises. Craven smiled to himself as he folded his arms and closed his eyes, sliding down the chair and hoping to get a quick cat-nap before the fun began. *"Attacking is the only secret. Dare and the world always yields; or if it beats you sometimes, dare it again and it will succumb."*

FOURTEEN

Howard Thorpe was a small, thin, humourless man, not known for his generous nature or for his sparkling personality and as he sat in interview room one, staring across the table at Garrick and Matt he was not a happy man.

Life had not been kind to Howard. Too many years struggling to manage a small, independent, family business had taken its toll and left him with a sour and bitter outlook on life. For thirty years he had owned and run *The Jewel Box*, a once thriving, successful enterprise located in the centre of Canterbury, nestled in one of the narrow back lanes and within sight and earshot of the historic Cathedral. In some ways, the shop had always been impractical; an old black and white Tudor building with ridiculously low beams and sloping floors, but it oozed a certain charm and originality, and over the years had managed to attract a loyal and regular customer base plus a multitude of inquisitive tourists through its 500 year-old door.

Once upon a time it was the perfect location – but not anymore. Times had changed. Being a private shopkeeper used to be a position that carried some respect in the local community. A local businessman, a member of the Chamber of Commerce, a Rotarian perhaps. It wasn't like that any longer. No-one had any respect these days, let alone manners and people weren't interested in old-fashioned customer service or proper jewellery. Nobody bought emeralds or rubies anymore, or real pearls or decent watches. Everything was either fake or it was cheap, mass-produced crap. It was all solitaires or white gold and platinum rings bought from bright, fashionable high-street chains, staffed by trendy young girls in stiletto heels with manicured nails and too much make-up. Or else it was large, ugly gyppo gold bought from cheap, tacky discount shops that were here today and gone tomorrow.

Going to the jewellers used to be a special occasion. Customers used to make appointments, particularly if they were buying something really special, like an engagement ring. The gentlemen would wear a collar and tie, or a suit perhaps and the ladies would dress up especially for the visit. It was nothing like that now. No-one had proper standards or common courtesy anymore. In they'd come, dressed in their tracksuits or pedal-pushers or whatever it was they wore these days. Coarse, vulgar women with their fat arses and cropped tops and butterfly tattoos; airplane blondes, chewing gum and hardly able to speak the Queen's English. Most of them couldn't even hold a pen properly, let alone write their own name.

Or else it was all flashy cabriolets, designer sunglasses, fashion labels and skinny lattés. Aspiring women with fake tans and too much money, most of it spent on fashion, none of it on style. It was like putting lipstick on a pig. Howard despised them. He despised them all. A semi-illiterate working-class, brought up on a diet of fast food, soap operas and reality TV and not an ounce of culture in any of them. The country was going to the dogs. The whole world had changed in the last thirty years and he saw the manifestation of it every day, walking through the front door of his shop. The slow, miserable decay of social values. It was soul destroying.

But despite it all, he had always maintained an honest business and in all that time he had never been in trouble with the police. Not once. And now here he was, six months from retirement, staring at the photographs of Richmond's jewellery laid out on the table in front of him, unmistakeably the items he had bought in good faith only two weeks before. Stolen property. A receiver of stolen goods. He stared across at Garrick and then put his head in his hands and sighed. What a bloody mess.

Garrick raised his eyebrows and exchanged a knowing glance with Matt. This wasn't going to take long.

Howard took his head out of his hands and held them open, palms facing upwards, trying to protest his innocence. 'I don't know what I can say. I bought them a couple of weeks ago. I had no idea they were stolen.'

Garrick shrugged, keen to apply as much pressure as quickly as possible. 'To be honest Mr. Thorpe, it doesn't much matter whether you knew they were stolen or not. Receiving stolen property is a criminal offence. It's our job to charge you. It will be up to the courts to decide whether you were complicit in the offence.'

Howard's head dropped into his hands again. His whole reputation, thirty years as an honest and respected trader was suddenly going down the drain. 'There must be something I can do?' he pleaded, looking alternately between Matt and Garrick, still not sure which one of them, if any, was going to give him the more sympathetic hearing.

'How much did you pay for them?' asked Garrick, remaining stony-faced.

'£300 in cash. Five pieces for £300.'

'And how much are they worth?'

Howard shrugged. 'Difficult to say. Seven hundred and fifty pounds, maybe a thousand if I sold them separately. It's not what they're worth that matters, it's whether I can sell them. No-one wants this sort of stuff anymore.'

Matt flicked through the list of stolen items from *Chart Place*, quickly totting up the values that Richmond had marked against the pieces. 'That's not what it says here Mr. Thorpe. According to the owner, or more importantly his insurers, they're valued collectively at somewhere between four and five thousand pounds.'

Garrick blew a low whistle, whilst Howard stared across the room, blinking several times and trying to think of a response. 'Well...there's a big difference between the second-hand value and the insurance cost of a new replacement. People aren't prepared to pay that sort of money for...'

Garrick held his hand up, indicating that he'd heard enough. 'I think you should stop wasting our time Mr. Thorpe. Paying £300 in cash for jewellery worth up to five thousand pounds is hardly going to convince a jury that you didn't know it was stolen...'

Howard opened his mouth as if to reply but nothing came out. He opened and closed it a couple of times, a goldfish drowning for air.

'...and if, as you say, you've been in the business for over thirty years, it wouldn't take a good barrister, in fact it wouldn't even take a half-decent barrister very long to prove that you must have known the real value of what you were buying. It doesn't look very good does it?'

There were several more seconds of silence as Howard stared across the room again, processing as fast as he could. 'I think I'd better have a solicitor with me.'

Garrick gave him a thin smile. 'Yes, I think you should. Have you got a lawyer Mr. Thorpe or would like me to arrange for the duty solicitor?'

'Um... well, I don't know. Only the solicitor that acted for me when we bought our last house. Would he be any good do you think?' Howard gave Garrick an embarrassed smile. He was out of his depth and he knew it.

For the first time Garrick looked back at him sympathetically and then paused, as if thinking through a proposal that had suddenly occurred to him. 'I'll tell you what Mr. Thorpe. I don't believe for one moment that you thought this jewellery was only worth £750 and I don't think any jury in the land would believe you either. However, I suppose it is possible – just possible that you didn't realise that it was stolen and that, let's say, you simply took advantage of a naïve customer who didn't realise the true value of what they were selling. Unethical but strictly speaking, not illegal.'

Howard started nodding enthusiastically. He'd been in business long enough to recognise a deal when it was being offered. He leant forward, indicating his support for the way the conversation was going. 'Absolutely, absolutely. That's exactly how it was.'

Garrick glanced at Matt again. This was pitiful. 'And to be honest with you Mr. Thorpe, I'm a busy man at the moment and the last thing I'm interested in is processing a load of paperwork simply because you've made an error of judgement...'

'A very uncharacteristic error of judgement,' interrupted Howard, trying to help Garrick with the explanation that was being built.

'Quite so. And of course what I'd rather spend my time doing is talking to the individual who sold you these items, who almost certainly acquired this jewellery by dishonest means.'

Howard nodded again, slower this time. The penny had dropped. Identify the seller and things might be easier. 'I'll give you whatever help I can Chief Inspector but I've never seen him before, he was just a lad.'

'What did he look like?' asked Matt, cutting to the chase. 'Can you give us a description?'

Howard thought for a moment, as if trying to picture the transaction that had taken place a couple of weeks earlier. 'Like I said, he was just a lad. White, early twenties, medium height, medium build, dark hair. He was very ordinary looking. There wasn't anything that was particularly noticeable about him.'

'Can you remember what he was wearing?' asked Garrick as Matt started to scribble down a few notes.

'Jeans, trainers, a leather jacket, brown I think, yes I'm sure it was brown, very faded. And he was wearing a football shirt, dark blue, shiny. It had some writing on the front.'

'Chelsea?' Matt had the pen poised, ready to confirm the football team in question.

Howard gave an apologetic shrug. 'Sorry, I'm not really into football but it was definitely blue. Blue with white lettering I think.'

Matt nodded and wrote down Chelsea followed by a question mark. 'Anything else?'

'Yes. He was wearing a Patek Philippe watch. It's the sort of thing I'd notice. It didn't really go with the rest of his appearance.'

'Patek Philippe?' Garrick's knowledge of watches was close to zero.

'It's a quality timepiece, hand made. Very expensive.'

'How expensive?'

'Ten, fifteen thousand pounds perhaps.'

Garrick spluttered in disbelief. 'Fifteen thousand pounds! Who the hell pays fifteen thousand pounds for a watch...?'

Matt smiled to himself. Garrick wasn't exactly the last of the big spenders.

'…and you're trying to tell me that some local oik came into your shop trying to flog second-hand jewellery wearing a fifteen thousand pound watch, and you didn't suspect anything?'

Howard didn't know what to say. He just stared back at Garrick and shrugged.

'Was it like one of these maybe?' Matt was flicking through the photographs from *Chart Place* and then picked out a couple which he laid out on the table.

Howard immediately pointed to the photo on the left. 'That's it. Definitely. A Patek Philippe Calatrava. You don't get to see many of those close up.'

Matt picked up the photos and put them back in the file. 'Must have kept it as a momento. Do you think you'd recognise him again Mr. Thorpe?'

Howard pulled a face, clearly not sure. 'I don't know to be honest. He was very ordinary looking. I'd probably recognise him if I saw him face to face but I'm not sure I'd recognise him from a photograph…'

Matt and Garrick exchanged a disappointed glance. *No point in going through the mugshots then.*

'…but I'd certainly recognise him if I heard him speak.'

Both Garrick and Matt suddenly sat up. 'Why, did he have an accent?' asked Garrick.

Howard shook his head. 'No – well only a local one. It was just…well I don't know whether he was nervous but I'm sure he had a stammer. Not a very pronounced one but just now and again, he seemed to have trouble with certain words. I'd definitely recognise him if I heard him speak.'

Matt and Garrick looked at each other again, both wanting to check that they were thinking the same thing. Garrick nodded his head towards the door, indicating to Matt to go and wait outside. Garrick watched him leave and then turned back towards Howard and smiled. 'Okay Mr. Thorpe, thank you. I'm just going to pop outside for a second and have a word with my colleague. I'll be back in a moment.'

Garrick closed the door behind him and looked enquiringly at Matt who was pacing impatiently up and down the corridor, like some sort of expectant father outside a maternity ward. 'You thinking what I'm thinking?'

'Jamie Collins?'

'Exactly, has to be. Have we got a mugshot on file?'

Matt nodded. 'I think so, do you want me to go and check?'

'No, somebody else can do that. You and I can go and pick him up. See if you can organise a car and I'll get someone to sort out Thorpe.'

Matt hurried off down the corridor and Garrick went back into the interview room. Howard had his head in his hands again, still unable to believe the mess that he had found himself in. He looked up anxiously as Garrick came through the door and then checked his watch. *Six o'clock.* 'Will I be able to go home soon Chief Inspector? My wife will be starting to worry.'

Garrick slid into one of the chairs opposite Howard and started to tidy up the photographs, which were still spread out across the table. 'Not much longer Mr. Thorpe. We need you to provide a statement before you go and I'm just arranging for another officer to come and take that now. After that, you can go.'

'And no charges?' asked Howard, hopefully.

'Possibly not. It looks as though we've identified a suspect from your description and providing you can give us a positive identification and are prepared to stand as a prosecution witness, then I don't think it will be in the public interest for us to pursue the matter.'

Howard let out a huge sigh of relief and relaxed back into the chair. He knew exactly what the score was. At that precise moment he would have identified the Prince of Wales if he thought it would have got him off the hook.

Within ten minutes, Matt and Garrick were speeding along the A20 towards the outskirts of Ashford and to the Connaught Estate. Matt, as usual, was driving and Garrick was speaking to Andy on the mobile, trying to get the exact address for Jamie Collins. 'I know it's on the Connaught somewhere Andy, we just didn't hang around to look it up before we left.'

It took Andy a couple of minutes to log-in to the system and get into Jamie Collins's details. Matt had already turned off the main road into the housing estate by the time Andy was back on the phone, relaying the information through to Garrick. 'It's 23 Dorset Rise, just off West Park Road.'

'Thanks Andy. Talk to you later.'

'Oh Sir, before you go…'

'Yes?'

'It's gone six. You know where to find him if he's not at home don't you?'

'No, go on.'

'*The Bricklayer's Arms* on Marsham Street. He's normally in there most evenings…'

'Okay thanks.'

'…but you might want to think about back-up. He drinks with Lee

Matthews.' Andy could hear the deafening silence at the other end of the phone.

'What, Lee Matthews as in "Pitbull"?'

'That's the one.'

There was another period of silence as the information was obviously being shared and digested in the car. Eventually Garrick came back on the phone. 'Well, let's just hope he's having a quiet night in. If not, we'll probably see you later.'

Andy put the phone down and smiled to himself. Either way, it was going to be an eventful evening.

FIFTEEN

Craven had been in some rough pubs in his time but it was a long while since he'd been in one as rough as *The Bricklayer's Arms.*

Even from the outside he could tell that it wasn't the sort of place that welcomed strangers or attracted passing trade. Virtually everybody who went in there was going to be a regular and by default, anybody who wasn't a local was going to be treated with suspicion. As soon as he pushed through the door he could feel the atmosphere, an ominous, hostile silence as the whole bar turned and stared at him, everyone wanting to check who was coming in. Everybody on guard. *Just like the Wild West. "I've come for my boy."*

Craven deliberately ignored the menacing looks and walked purposefully up to the bar, concentrating on the beer pumps and the small TV fixed at an angle high up in the left hand corner of the room. He lit a cigarette and perched on a bar stool, sensing within seconds that the mood was starting to shift, the regulars apparently satisfied that he was nothing to worry about and the conversation levels returning to normal. Blending in was always the secret. Camouflage wasn't about dressing up or being in disguise – it was about making yourself look like everybody else and making yourself anonymous.

He'd parked the car a couple of streets away and it had taken no more than a couple of minutes to put on an old jumper and a pair of workman's boots which he kept in the back of the vehicle. He used the jumper for gardening and sometimes working on the car and it was filthy; just the sort of thing you'd find a guy wearing on a building site in late September as the weather was turning colder. He also kept an old canvass tool bag in the boot which he slung over his shoulder. It made him look the part and besides, a hammer and few screwdrivers might come in handy later. After he locked the car he rubbed both his hands around the tread of the front tyre and then wiped them around his neck and across the top of his forehead before squatting down in front of the wing mirror to ruffle his hair into an untidy mess. Simple. In no time at all he'd transformed himself into just the sort of punter that would drink in *The Bricklayer's Arms;* someone getting a well-deserved couple of pints on their way home after a hard day at work.

Craven kept staring up at the TV as if he was distracted by the programme and then turned and looked at the landlord who was standing behind the beer pumps waiting to serve him. He was a heavy, middle-aged guy with a pockmarked face, greasy, swept back hair and a large beer-belly hanging over the top of his trousers. The guy looked as though he needed a good scrub; his hands and fingernails were dirty and the shirt was frayed and stained around the collar. There was also a button missing just above his waist, which meant that a bulge of stomach was poking out of his shirt, just above his belt. The place was a shit-hole and this guy wasn't doing anything to raise the standard.

'What can I get you?' asked the landlord, the question delivered with a tired indifference. He looked like a man who had given up on life. Craven wasn't surprised. Obviously there were a lot of worse jobs in the world but running an almost derelict pub for a bunch of local yobs wasn't exactly a great career choice. He checked the beer pumps and couldn't help noticing that the bar surface was also filthy. From a hygiene point of view he fancied something out of a bottle rather than from one of the pumps but this wasn't the sort of place to drink designer beer – and asking for a glass of red wine was an absolute non-starter. Besides, he needed a drink that was going to last as long as possible. No point in having too much alcohol.

'You got any Guinness?'

The landlord nodded. 'Pint?'

Craven nodded back and then twisted round on the stool, looking around the bar for the first time, while the landlord went off to pull the beer. *The Bricklayer's Arms* was a large Victorian building with high ceilings and large, ugly sash windows, similar to some of the pubs on the Old Kent Road that he remembered his Dad drinking in when he was a kid. The place didn't look as though it had been modernised at all and it certainly hadn't been decorated in years. The walls and ceilings must have been a different colour once upon a time but years of neglect had turned them into a grimy, tobacco-stained brown, not unlike the worn and faded lino on which he was now standing and which felt slightly sticky under foot. The bar, which occupied the middle of the room, was horseshoe shaped, facing the door and there was a collection of small, circular brown tables and thin, wooden chairs dotted in no particular order around the room. Every table had a round, glass ashtray and a couple of square, dog-eared beer-mats. Craven noticed what must have been original picture rails running the length of the walls and also what looked like an original black, iron fireplace located just inside the front door. Other than the TV, the only concession to modernity was a fruit machine, flashing silently in the far corner.

The pub was about half full, a predictable collection of tradesmen, factory workers and van drivers, all drinking beer and swapping stories about what sort of day they'd had. There was an old couple sitting motionless at one of the tables, staring into space and holding onto their half-empty glasses, an occasional sip of beer, but otherwise a contemporary, silent tableau. They looked poor and tired and defeated. A sad and poignant reflection of modern life. A few local lads were standing at one end of the bar, close to a door which presumably led to the toilets. Almost without exception, everyone was smoking. Craven wondered how on earth a place like this was going to enforce the smoking ban when it came in next year.

Suddenly the landlord was back, the Guinness half-poured and waiting to settle. 'Anything else?'

'No, that's it thanks.' Craven passed over a fiver and looked around the room again while he waited for his pint and his change. A couple of young lads were sitting at a table about half-way down the left-hand side of the bar. One of them had to be Jamie Collins. Ray had said that he was pretty ordinary looking but that he was a fanatical football supporter and usually wore his team's shirt. The lad in the jeans and the faded, brown leather jacket was wearing a blue Millwall shirt. It had to be him. The other kid looked to be about the same age and was similarly dressed in blue jeans and a brown jacket, although his was suede and he was wearing a white polo shirt. In truth, compared to most of the other customers Craven thought that they looked fairly normal and innocuous.

Eventually the landlord came back with the pint of Guinness, the beer spilling down the outside of the glass and onto the towel that was laid on top of the bar. Craven mopped up the beer with the edges of the towel and then picked up the glass and took a sip, pocketing the wet change with his left hand. 'Cheers.'

The landlord nodded in acknowledgement. 'Good health...but I wouldn't sit there if I were you. It's reserved.'

Craven looked down at the stool that he was sitting on and frowned. There were two other empty stools, one either side of him in the centre of the bar. 'Yeah, reserved for who?'

'Regulars. They're not in yet.'

'Well, if they're not here they won't mind me sitting here will they?'

The landlord shrugged. 'It's up to you mate.' *Don't say I didn't warn you.*

Craven shrugged back, as if to indicate he couldn't care less and then picked up the pint and wandered over to a table a couple down from Jamie Collins and his mate, close enough to hear what they were talking about but far enough away not to make it obvious. He dumped the bag of tools onto the floor next to him, pulled out *The Sun* that he'd bought twenty minutes earlier and settled down for what appeared to be a quiet, relaxing pint and a read of his newspaper. His plan was simple. Get a positive ID on Jamie Collins and then get out of there as soon as possible and wait for him outside. There was no point trying to tackle him in the pub. There were too many people about, too many regulars who might try and interfere and more importantly, too many witnesses who would remember his face. The future for Jamie Collins wasn't looking very bright and Craven knew from experience that his best chance of dealing with the situation was to see him on his own. *"Suddenly, massively, decisively."*

It didn't take him long to realise that his original opinion of Collins and his mate had been pretty accurate – they seemed just like a couple of ordinary lads. Craven kept his head buried in his paper, pretending to be engrossed in whatever he was reading but all the while listening to them talking about music and television and cinema and girls and football – in fact all the things that lads were talking about in thousands of pubs up and down the country. Collins mate appeared to be a Charlton supporter and there was a lot of banter and healthy rivalry going on, some of it very sharp and very funny, which made Craven smile to himself. The humour of football supporters had always appealed to him. He could always remember being in the crowd at White Hart Lane a few years ago when Tottenham Hotspur were playing an evening cup-tie against Cardiff City and the Tottenham fans, ever ready to bait the travelling Welsh supporters at the other end of the ground started singing, *"Does your shepherd know you're here?"* It still made him smile.

He was just starting to wonder whether he'd got the right kid when one of the locals standing at the end of the bar downed the last dregs of his pint and decided to make his way home, much to the derision and amusement of his drinking companions who were trying to persuade him to stay and have "one for the road". As the guy walked past Craven and headed towards the door he looked over at the two lads and waved his hand. 'See you later Jamie, see you Gary.'

That was all the confirmation Craven needed. It was time to drink up and make himself scarce. Part of him wanted to tackle Collins there and then but there was no point in being impatient. The kid might be planning to spend the whole evening in the pub, but it didn't matter, he would just have to wait for him – and waiting outside was a much better option than sitting in the bar, drinking alcohol. Apart from the first few seconds when he'd walked in, no-one had taken any notice of him and that was the way he wanted to keep it. Anyway, there was no rush. Finding the CDs had been a bit of a breakthrough and he reckoned he had at least a couple of days' head start on the local police. All he had to do now was wait for Collins to leave, follow him home and then as soon as the kid was on his own, make his move. Put some time and distance between him being seen in the pub and someone finding his body.

Craven drank the last of the Guinness and was about to get up and leave when the front door of the pub swung open and three more regulars came in, a loud and aggressive entrance as they banged through the door and then settled themselves noisily onto the three empty stools at the centre of the bar. The atmosphere inside the pub changed in an instant. Not the hostile, unwelcome silence that had greeted Craven's arrival but an uneasy, nervous mood as the locals dropped their voices and seemed to visibly shrink back into their seats. By any sort of standard most of the regulars were a pretty rough crowd but the three who had just walked in were a different proposition altogether.

Craven watched them with interest as they ordered three pints of lager and then walked over to the corner to play the fruit machine. He noticed that the beer was served without any money changing hands and wondered whether the landlord had lost control of the pub – the new arrivals were certainly acting as though they owned the place. They all looked to be in their late twenties, maybe early thirties and all three of them were smoking, all holding their cigarettes inwards between their thumb and middle finger – the same way that Craven used to when he was smoking furtively on the way home from school.

The tallest of the three was about six foot and well built, covered in tattoos and scruffily dressed in combat trousers and an old T-shirt. His hair was shaved in a type of skinhead cut and he looked as though he worked out in the gym regularly – either that or he had a job which kept him pretty fit. The second guy was about five foot ten, average build and dressed a lot smarter in jeans and a light-blue shirt with a button down collar. He seemed a lot calmer than the other two and maybe a bit brighter. But it was the third guy that really caught Craven's attention. He was the smallest of the three, about five foot six and slightly built in a kind of wiry, whippet sort of way but there was a menacing, intimidating feel about him which seemed to pervade the whole pub. Everyone could sense it. The guy was a bundle of nervous energy, constantly shifting from one foot to the other and continuously looking round to check what everybody else was doing. No-one was looking back. The guy looked like he was spoiling for a fight and nobody in this pub wanted to get involved. He obviously had a reputation and it didn't look good.

Craven decided that he'd seen enough. He'd drunk in enough bars to recognise when things were about to kick off and the last thing he needed was to get embroiled in some sort of punch up in a local pub. Anonymity was the primary objective and having got a positive ID on Jamie Collins he just needed to get out of there as quickly and as discreetly as possible. He left the paper folded on the table and bent down to pick up his bag of tools, just as the smaller guy walked over from the fruit machine to the table where Jamie Collins and his mate were sitting.

'Hello Jamie, I want a word with you.' The words were spat out. Malevolent, sinister, threatening.

Craven couldn't help looking across at the table as he sat up straight from picking up the tool bag. It was only for a second but as the guy noticed Craven's movement and turned round to look at him, their eyes locked; a cold, hard stare going in both directions. Craven looked away almost instantly. This was nothing to do with him and there was no way that he was getting involved. The guy continued staring at Craven for a couple of seconds, just to make sure that he'd backed down completely before turning his attention back to Collins.

'That digital camera you sold me the other week. It's doesn't work properly.'

Collins didn't seem to know what to say. The kid had pushed himself as far back into his chair as possible but there was no escaping. His mate started to shuffle his seat sideways to try and get out of the way and as he did so, gave Craven a quick, worried, sideways glance. Craven could see that he was scared. They both knew what was coming next.

'What do you mean it doesn't work properly?' asked Jamie timidly, unable to think of anything else to say.

By now the pub was virtually silent, the whole bar mesmerised by the act of violence that was about to explode. Everyone grateful that it was someone else and not them. Everybody ashamed but too frightened to help.

'What do you think I mean when I say it doesn't work properly? I mean it doesn't fucking work properly.' The silence in the room was unbearable. Everybody was listening, nobody was watching.

Jamie stared at him for a few seconds, trying to work out his options. None of them were good – and he knew it. 'I don't understand Pitbull, it was definitely working when I sold it to you. Honestly.'

Pitbull put his hands on the tabletop and leant across it slowly, pushing his face right into Jamie's so that they were literally nose-to-nose. He gave him a long, cold stare. 'So what are you saying Jamie? Are you calling me a fucking liar?' The kid looked as though he was going to wet himself.

Craven was still sitting at his table, his pint glass empty and the tool bag in his hand ready to go. He didn't feel any sympathy for Jamie Collins whatsoever and he was normally happy to let public disagreements run their course but there was something about the confrontation that made him feel uneasy and want to stick around for a moment. Besides, he needed Collins in one piece and able to talk, not unconscious and wired up to some machine in a hospital bed for a couple of days, or even worse, in police custody. The one thing that he was sure about was that the kid was about to get a good kicking but that he was Craven's only real prospect of being able to complete Buchanan's assignment, certainly within the next 24 hours. He needed him in one piece – at least until he'd finished with him himself.

Meanwhile, Jamie's stammer was back with a vengeance, much to the amusement of Pitbull and his two mates. The taller one with the skinhead haircut had wandered over to join in the baiting and apply a bit of extra pressure. Jamie was squirming in his chair, trying his hardest to talk himself out of trouble. Trying but failing. 'Do you want me to look at it for you and see if I can fix it?'

'No I don't want you to look at it for me. I want my fucking money back. And I want it now.' Pitball was starting to rock up and down in a sort of impatient, aggressive foreplay and the words were being spat out through clenched teeth. He could smell the kid's fear and it always goaded him on.

Jamie looked terrified and was starting to sweat. 'I haven't got that sort of money on me. You know I haven't.'

Pitbull sneered at him with disgust. 'Sure? Last chance Jamie. No-one takes the piss out of me.' The empty beer bottle in the middle of the table was already being picked up by the neck, ready to smash and jab. Craven had seen and heard enough. He suddenly pushed his chair away and stood up with his empty glass as if to get another drink, the noise and movement more than enough to distract what was going on at the next table, not to mention everybody else in the pub. As he stood up Pitbull turned round to look at him and again, their eyes locked in a cold, hard stare, both of them waiting for the other to look away. This time Craven didn't flinch He'd played this game too many times and with too many professionals. Bosnia, Johannesburg, Gaza. The other guy was always going to be the first to speak.

It took only a matter of seconds for Pitbull to get fed up with waiting. The words snarled across the bar. 'What the fuck at you looking at?'

Craven took his time, starting at the top of Pitbull's head and then looking him up and down really slowly. Head to toe and then back up again. 'Not a lot.' he sneered. Still the same cold, hard stare.

There was almost a gasp in the pub. Suddenly everybody was watching but nobody could believe what they were seeing. Jamie Collins didn't know what the hell was going on. He was just glad that someone other than him had suddenly become the centre of attention.

Craven turned away with disdain and walked slowly over to the bar, putting his empty glass on top of the counter and sitting down on the middle stool that he had sat on earlier. He looked up at the landlord and smiled. 'I'll have another pint of Guinness please. Same glass.' The landlord looked completely stunned but took the glass and walked over to the Guinness tap which was at the other end of the bar. He didn't understand what was going on either. Nobody had ever interfered in an argument with Lee Matthews before – at least, not survived to tell the tale.

Craven was now sitting with his back to the rest of the pub, indifferent to the stares that were coming across the room from Jamie's table. The middle guy who had been playing the fruit machine exchanged a confused and puzzled look with Pitbull, who shook his head and frowned back, equally baffled. He stared across the room at Craven, trying to work out whether he'd seen or met him before somewhere and then nodded to the skinhead, swiping his finger across his throat as an instruction to go and sort it out.

Craven could almost feel the floor moving as the footsteps lumbered up beside him. Six foot tall and built like a brick shit-house. The skinhead leant onto the bar and looked sideways at Craven, giving him a disbelieving, *you must be suicidal mate*, kind of look. He nodded down at the stool that Craven was sitting on. 'There's someone sitting there mate.'

Craven smiled back at him. 'Yeah, I know. I am.'

The skinhead shook his head and smiled to himself. *Okay pal, it's your funeral.* He stood up slowly and put both hands on the bar, arching his back and stretching his arms in preparation for the explosion that was about to come.

Craven was still sitting on the stool, looking up at him, knowing that the assault was going to happen in any second. The screwdriver that he had taken out of the tool bag and put in his back pocket was really old and had been filed and sharpened down to a razor point, almost like a gimlet or a bradawl used for making holes in wood or leather – except this was a full size screwdriver, the blade probably eight or nine inches long. The speed at which he pulled it out of his back pocket and rammed it into the skinhead's right hand took everybody by surprise, not least the landlord who darted backwards a couple of paces as the speed and movement made him jump.

The skinhead didn't have time to react. He was much too large and cumbersome for that. One second he was standing at the bar, about to unleash a haymaker into the smartarse troublemaker standing next to him and the next second he was staring down at his hand, palm faced downwards on the counter with a screwdriver driven all the way through it and into the wood underneath. It took a second for the visual recognition of what had happened to run up and down his spinal cord, before the searing pain hit his hand and took his breath away, just as the crimson pool started to flow out from under his palm and seep across the bar. He tugged at his hand a couple of times to pull it free but Craven had driven the screwdriver into the counter with all his force and it wouldn't move. The effect of tugging made the pain even worse and then suddenly there was a sort of rushing noise in his ears which he'd never experienced before and then his legs started to feel like jelly and everything started to go black.

Craven pushed one of the empty stools beneath him just before the guy fainted and collapsed forward onto the bar, his hand still firmly staked into the counter. As he wheeled round and picked up the other stool, feet facing outwards like some sort of lion-tamer, his abiding memory would always be the picture of Jamie and his mate, staring at him in complete disbelief, their mouths wide open in astonishment and then Pitbull, smashing the empty beer bottle on the edge of the table and advancing towards him.

The silence that only seconds before had been almost suffocating suddenly erupted into an explosion of crashing furniture and breaking glass. Craven noticed the other guy moving towards him from the fruit machine, shouting instructions at the other locals to get off their backsides and Pitbull, taking two strides forwards, the bottle raised high above his head, ready to strike as soon as he got close enough to attack. Seconds away. Craven stood his ground and waited. *Come on then. Let's get it over with.* It was at that moment that the front door pushed open and Pitbull stopped and turned and then everyone froze in an instant as Detective Chief Inspector John Garrick and Detective Constable Matt Isaacs walked silently through the doorway. A second later, Detective Sergeants Andy Cooper and Paul Taylor came through the rear door by the corner of the bar, just in time to block off Jamie Collins who was trying to make a discreet but hurried exit out the back.

It was like watching a film and suddenly hitting the pause button. Garrick looked at Pitball, breathing heavily, the adrenalin still pumping through his body and the broken bottle still primed for action in his clenched and shaking fist. Paul looked across the room at what appeared to be someone slumped across the bar with their hand skewered into the top of the counter and a pool of blood dripping slowly onto the floor. Matt looked at Jamie Collins who was being held by Andy by the scruff of the neck. A blue football shirt. *Millwall, not Chelsea. Bingo.* And Andy looked at Craven, a face he didn't recognise, sitting on a stool and casually lighting a cigarette and not showing the slightest interest in what was going on. Craven didn't look at anybody. He was too busy trying to keep his head down and work out how in God's name the police had managed to catch up with him that fast – not to mention what the hell was he going to do next.

It was at that moment, in those couple of seconds of frozen silence, with everybody staring at everybody else and everyone waiting for someone to make the first move, that the phone in Craven's pocket, Buchanan's phone, started to ring.

SIXTEEN

Neil stood with his head bent sideways, reading the book titles with interest as he thumbed his way slowly along the spines, taking care not to spill the glass of red wine which was balanced in his other hand. He'd always been fascinated by other people's books and had often said that you could tell a lot about someone from their choice of reading or from their taste in music or films. He smiled to himself as he realised that he and Steph must have a lot in common – quite a few of the books were identical to those he had bought over the years and which were still on his shelves back in Cambridge.

The collection was a mixture of classics, modern paperbacks, a couple of biographies and a fairly extensive collection of poetry. He picked up a volume at random; *Selected Poems* by Pablo Neruda and flicked through the pages, suddenly noticing a hand-written inscription inside the front cover which he realised too late that he probably shouldn't be reading. It made him feel that he was intruding on something that was personal and private. He put it back carefully into the space and moved onto a collection of DVDs that were stacked neatly at the end of the bookcase.

Steph's choice in films was unusual. There were a few black and white classics and a number of romantic comedies but her passion, surprisingly was World Cinema. There must have been thirty or forty subtitled films, some of them quite obscure and in a variety of foreign languages. Neil had a keen interest in cinema and recognised some of the more popular titles but even he hadn't seen or heard of most of the others. Again, he smiled to himself as he spotted a copy of *The Butterfly's Tongue,* a little known Spanish film, but one of his favourites. He'd seen it in London a couple of years earlier but hadn't met anyone else who had even heard of it, let alone had a copy of it on DVD.

He took a gulp of wine and looked around the living room again. The house was a compact, modern, terraced property built on a small and recent development on the outskirts of Cranbrook. He guessed that most of the houses must be owned either by young couples or single professionals – there wasn't enough living space for larger families and the plots were positively tiny. Steph certainly didn't have to spend her weekends trying to keep the garden under control. Inside, the décor and furniture was modern and fairly minimalist but the combination of books and pictures and subtle lighting succeeded in making everything feel warm and homely.

Dotted around the room were a few photos of a small, pretty girl, which was obviously Chloe. Neil looked at each of them in turn and then wandered over to the kitchen and stuck his head around the door to see how Steph was getting on. She had her back to him preparing some food and he gazed at her for a couple of moments. Secretly he couldn't wait to tell Chris all about this. 'Anything I can do to help?' he asked.

Steph turned round and smiled, visibly pleased at having someone to dinner and the chance to cook a proper meal for once. Dinner with Chloe was normally a rush and was always a battle. 'No, I'm fine. I'm just making a starter. You go and sit down and make yourself comfortable. It'll be about ten minutes.'

'Okay. As long as you're sure.' Neil went back into the living room and picked up another book and sat down on the sofa. After a minute or so he looked up, conscious that a small, inquisitive child was standing in the hall doorway, dressed in pink pyjamas and holding a very ragged, knitted rabbit whilst staring at him intently with the sort of unashamed curiosity that only small children can convey.

'Hello,' he said, in his friendliest voice. 'Are you Chloe?'

Chloe continued clutching the rabbit close to her chest and nodded her head very slowly and very seriously, still watching Neil intently with her large, round eyes.

'Shouldn't you be in bed Chloe?' asked Neil, unable to think of anything else to say. He wasn't very experienced at dealing with children, particularly ones who seemed to be so fascinated by him.

Again, Chloe cuddled the rabbit and nodded her head, still unable to take her eyes off Neil.

'I like your rabbit,' he said. 'What's his name?'

Chloe started to smile. 'Mr. Rumpus. Mummy bought him for me.'

Neil smiled back. 'He's nice, isn't he?'

Chloe nodded again and smiled even more. Mr. Rumpus was now being cuddled tighter than ever.

Suddenly Steph had emerged from the kitchen and was looking across at Chloe with hands on hips, trying her hardest not to smile, but maintain a stern, disapproving look. 'And what do you think you're doing out of bed young lady?'

Chloe put on her saddest, pouting face to show that she wasn't happy. 'I could hear you talking.'

Steph smiled. Certainly, Chloe wasn't used to hearing people talking once she had gone to bed, but Steph was fairly sure that it was something else that had made her come downstairs. 'Mmm. I think you just wanted to get up and say hello to Neil didn't you?'

Chloe began to look shy and embarrassed but in the end nodded her head. She was still staring at Neil intently, almost as though she'd never seen a man in her home before.

'Sorry Neil, I did warn you, she's just not used to us having visitors – are you poppet?'

Chloe shook her head and hugged Mr. Rumpus again.

'Well, you've said hello to Neil now, so now it's time to go back to bed. I'll come up and tuck you in properly in a minute.'

Chloe put on the sad, pouting expression again which was obviously well practiced. She hadn't come all this way downstairs just to be sent straight back up again. 'Can Neil read me a story?'

Steph burst out laughing. 'I don't think so darling, Neil's been very busy today and he's tired. You can have two stories tomorrow.'

'But I haven't had a story today.'

Steph looked at Neil and gave him an apologetic look. 'Sorry about this. Five years old and she's already twisting me round her little finger. I'll just go up with her and settle her down.'

Chloe still wasn't happy. The bottom lip got even lower and the sadder face got even sadder. 'But I wanted Neil to do it.'

Neil smiled at Steph and stood up, putting the book he was reading at the end of the sofa. 'I don't mind, honestly. I'm not sure I'll be very good at it but you finish getting the dinner ready and I'll read her a story.'

Chloe started clapping and jumping up and down excitedly. Steph gave him an appreciative look. 'Gosh, you are popular Neil. She doesn't normally take to visitors like this. Are you sure?'

Chloe was already out the door and on her way up to her bedroom. Steph followed her and called up from the bottom of the stairs in her firmest, most parental voice. 'One story young lady and no more. And no playing about.' She turned round to look at Neil, who had followed behind her and shook her head in exasperation. 'Thanks Neil, it's really kind of you. Now don't let her take advantage of you. She has one story and then it's lights out.'

Neil smiled and touched his forelock, pretending to salute his obedience to the very precise and explicit instructions. 'Yes M'Lady.'

Steph laughed and went back into the kitchen while Neil went upstairs and found Chloe's bedroom at the top of the landing, on the right-hand side. Chloe was already in bed with the covers tucked right up to her chin, still clutching Mr. Rumpus and waiting expectantly for her bedtime story. Her room was exactly how Neil imagined a little girl's bedroom should look; lots of pinks and yellows and pastel blues and lots of soft, cuddly toys placed strategically on the window sill and on various bits of furniture. At the end of the bed was a pine bookcase which was full of children's books, most of them fairly worn and well-read.

'So, what story would you like tonight Chloe?' he asked as he squatted down and looked at the different titles.

Chloe had propped herself up on her elbows and was looking down at him at the end of the bed. She didn't need any thinking time. She wanted her favourite. '*The Three Billy Goats Gruff*' please.'

It took Neil a moment or so to find the book and then he sat down on the bed and started to read, while Chloe snuggled down under the covers. "*Once upon a time there were three billy goats who were called Gruff. In the winter they lived in a barn in the valley. When spring came they longed to travel up to the mountains to eat the sweet, lush grass.*" Chloe started sucking her thumb and stared wide-eyed at Neil as he concentrated on reading the story. She knew the words off by heart.

Downstairs, Steph brought the bottle of wine into the living room and put it on the middle of the table. Then she lit the two small candles and straightened the place mats and the cutlery to make everything look perfect. Finally, she flicked through the CD collection and picked out something quiet and atmospheric. She put it on the CD player and pressed the play button, smiling to herself as she looked around the room, the soft music playing in the background, the smell of cooking coming from the kitchen and the sound of Neil's voice reading upstairs.

It took about ten minutes for Neil to finish the story. He put the book back into the bookcase and then walked over to the door, smiling at Chloe as he turned off the light. 'Goodnight then Chloe.'

Chloe stared back at him. 'You have to say goodnight properly, like Mummy does.'

Neil shook his head in mock exasperation. 'Go on then. How does Mummy say goodnight?'

'She kisses me on the forehead.'

Neil duly bent over the bed and kissed her on the forehead. 'Goodnight then Chloe.'

'No, you have to say, "Night night, mind the bed bugs don't bite." That's what mummy says.'

'Night, night, mind the bedbugs don't bite.'

Chloe finally seemed satisfied that all the proper customs and rituals associated with going to bed had been correctly observed and eventually cuddled Mr. Rumpus and snuggled down under the covers again. As Neil got the door she suddenly sat up and said. 'Neil, are you going to be mummy's boyfriend?'

Neil stopped, not sure what to say for a second. 'I don't think so Chloe. I'm just a friend of mummy's at the moment.'

Chloe looked at him, her eyes starting to look tired and heavy. She seemed to be thinking long and hard about what she was going to say. Eventually she laid back down and stared up at the ceiling. 'Well, I think you're mummy's boyfriend.' And as if to signal that was an end to the matter, she promptly turned over and went to sleep.

He closed the door gently behind him and went downstairs, just as Steph was putting the starters on the table. 'How did you get on?' she asked, indicating to him to sit down.

Neil sat in the chair opposite and spread the napkin on his lap. '*The Three Billy Goats Gruff.* I think I did okay.'

Steph smiled and picked up her glass of wine. 'Ah, I should have guessed. That's her favourite. She knows it backwards. So do I, come to think of it.'

Neil laughed. 'Yes, I guess you would. Well you'll be pleased to know that it's years since I've read it!'

Steph looked across the table and smiled at him again. 'I think she likes you.'

'Mmm. Beginner's luck probably. I'm sure it will soon wear off. Anyway, this looks good,' he added, looking at the starter that Steph had put on the table. 'You shouldn't have gone to all this trouble. I was meant to be buying you dinner, remember?'

'Oh it's nothing,' said Steph dismissively. 'Besides, I love cooking. I don't often get the chance to do it properly.' She picked up the bottle of wine and leant across to refill Neil's glass. 'Good idea about getting a taxi as well. It means you can have a glass of wine. I was given a bottle of this at Christmas and haven't had an occasion to open it yet.'

Neil picked up the glass and took a sip, nodding enthusiastically. 'Gosh, this is good, what is it?' He twisted the bottle and looked at the label, raising his eyebrows in appreciation at the Chateau and vintage. '*Lussac St. Emillion.*

It's really good. You're right, getting a taxi was definitely a good idea!'

'What time did you book one to go back?' asked Steph, also taking a sip.

'I haven't ordered one yet.' replied Neil, picking up his knife and fork, 'I wasn't sure what time to book it for, so thought I'd just ring up and get one later.'

Steph cupped her wine in both hands and gazed across the candlelight at Neil as he started to eat, watching him with the same, intense curiosity but knowing instinctively that he was oblivious to the thoughts that were going through her head. 'Oh well,' she said rather wistfully, 'I'm sure we'll sort something out.'

SEVENTEEN

Even as a child, Lee Matthews had never wet the bed. And in all the years that he'd staggered home from the pub having drunk countless pints of lager, invariably collapsing into his pit in a drunken stupor, he'd always woken up to go to the toilet and had always somehow managed to stumble around in the dark and find his way to the bathroom and back again without any trouble. Last night had been a heavy session but that was nothing unusual – that was situation normal four or five times a week. But as he suddenly woke up in the pitch black of his bedroom he knew immediately that something was wrong.

Despite the amount of alcohol that he'd drunk and the soundness of his sleep, something had disturbed him and the first thing he noticed was that the bed was soaking. He padded the sheets all around him and then felt the pillow. They were drenched. Even his body and his hair seemed to be wet. He sat up on one elbow and frantically felt the sheets again. He'd never known anything like it. They were absolutely sopping. He couldn't believe it. Surely, he couldn't have done. He twisted sideways and squinted at the clock on the beside cabinet, the green, digital display confirming that it was 03.08 am. It was a millisecond later that he smelt the overpowering smell of petrol and then a millisecond after that when he heard the unmistakeable sound of matches being rattled inside a matchbox. Someone was standing on the other side of the bed, invisible in the darkness but close enough to touch him. He wobbled on his elbow, trying to drag himself out of his drunken sleep and work out what the hell was going on.

Craven put a cigarette in his mouth and struck a match, the flare allowing Pitbull to see where he was standing and who he was. He lit the cigarette and blew the match out, the black and red embers glowing in the dark.

'Jesus, what the fuck ...' Pitbull was still leaning on one elbow, still trying to come to terms with everything. Too drunk and too dumbstruck to move.

Craven drew on the cigarette, the glow of burning tobacco lighting up his face in a sort of sinister, ghostly shadow. He flicked the ash from the end of the cigarette onto the bed. 'Shut up.'

'JESUS!'

Craven rattled the box of matches again. 'I said, shut up.' The instruction was absolute. Cold, ruthless, unequivocal.

Pitbull froze. His breathing was heavy and rapid and his elbow was starting to hurt but he didn't move an inch. He looked at Craven smoking the cigarette and then his brain suddenly kicked into gear, remembering the night before. The guy driving the screwdriver into the bar, picking up the stool and getting ready to fight, the long, hard stare across the room.

Craven took anther drag of the cigarette, his face lighting up again momentarily. 'Remember me?'

Pitbull nodded. Craven's face was one he was going to remember for as long as he lived. Problem was, he didn't know how long that was going to be.

Suddenly, something was tossed onto the bed. A small, white, shiny tablet. He felt it thud gently on the sheets. Then another one. And another one.

'Put them in the bed.' Again, the instruction was absolute.

Pitbull scrabbled around in the dark and found the tablets. They felt greasy and cold and he knew what they were as soon as he touched them. Paraffin blocks. Firelighters. He did as he was told and put them under the covers. He wasn't in a position to argue and besides, it gave him the chance to move off his elbow, which was starting to go numb. He lay on his back, his head twisted sideways on the pillow trying to see what Craven was doing. Prostrate and defenceless. A sacrifice waiting to happen.

'Don't move.' Craven leant forward and poured another third of the bottle over his face and over the pillow. Pitbull screwed his eyes shut as tight as possible, not daring to even move to wipe the petrol away from his lips as it started to run down his chin and then down the back of his neck. He started spitting to try and stop it going into his mouth.

Craven looked at him and said nothing for several seconds, letting the silence and the darkness apply its own pressure. The smell of petrol was overwhelming. He rattled the matches again, just to remind Pitbull who was in control. 'You got a receipt for that digital camera you bought?'

'No, of course I haven't.'

'You can't get your money back then, can you?'

Pitbull was still spitting out bits of petrol, still too scared to move and too confused to argue. He didn't understand what was going on but he had enough sense to know what to say – even if it wasn't true. 'I don't want my money back. I've written it off.'

Craven looked at him and took another drag on the cigarette. This time he flicked the ash on the carpet. 'Good. Where did Jamie get the camera from?'

Pitbull stared up at the ceiling. His neck was starting to ache from twisting round to look at Craven and he was trying to work out what this was all about.

He hadn't got a clue who Craven was or why he was so interested in a poxy digital camera – but he reckoned that if he gave him the information he wanted, then he was likely to go away. The guy was hardly going to torch the place if he got what he came for. *Live to fight another day.* Or so he thought.

The only problem was that there was an underlying principle that you never grassed up your mates. Not under any circumstances. Honour amongst thieves. Still, Jamie Collins was hardly a mate. He was just some toe-rag who drank in the same pub, trying to look big and knock about with the likes of Pitbull and some of the others. It was like a 'first-year' hanging around a load of sixth formers. Living off scraps. Not that Pitbull ever made it to the sixth form of course. He made sure he got out of that dump as soon as he could. No, it was an easy decision. It wasn't a decision at all really. He was covered in petrol and he'd seen enough of Craven the night before to know that the guy was capable of almost anything. Time to tell him whatever he wanted to know. He took a deep breath. 'He got it from his mate. Gary Parkes.'

Craven raised his eyebrows. 'The mate that was with him last night?'

Pitbull nodded. 'Yeah, the kid he was sitting next to in the pub.'

'And where did his mate get it from?'

'Where do you think? He nicked it.'

Craven smiled ruefully to himself. Typical. He'd been chasing the wrong kid and the one that he was really after had got away. Not only that, but unlike Jamie Collins, his mate wasn't even in police custody. 'So where does this Gary Parkes live?'

Pitbull shook his head. 'Don't know. On the Connaught somewhere.'

Craven shook the box of matches again. 'Wrong answer. "Don't know" isn't what I want to hear.'

Pitbull continued staring at the ceiling. 'I don't know where he lives. It's on the Connaught somewhere but I don't know the address.'

Craven thought for a moment. He hadn't detected any sense of friendship between Pitbull and the two lads in the pub, so maybe he was telling the truth. Given his current predicament, he couldn't think of any reason why he would try and protect anybody. Maybe he really didn't know where Gary Parkes lived. 'Okay. What did he do with everything else he nicked?'

'How should I know?'

Craven's punch came out of nowhere. A huge, slamming blow with the side of his fist, straight onto the bridge of Pitbull's nose. It broke instantly. One second he was lying on his back, just starting to feel that he had a measure of what was going on and the next moment it felt like he'd been hit by an express train in the dark. His head bounced up and down on the pillow before he could even shout, just as the second punch, delivered with the same side of the fist, smashed into the top of his mouth. At least three or four teeth cracked and moved under the impact. His head slumped to one side, trying to avoid the third punch that he felt sure was coming next.

Craven stood up straight and gave him a couple of seconds to recover. He couldn't tell whether Pitbull was terrified or angry. Both probably. He shook the matches again. 'Wrong answer. Try again. What did Gary Parkes do with all the stuff he nicked?'

Pitbull was lying on his side groaning, a searing pain throbbing in the centre of his face and the area around his neck now a sticky mixture of blood and petrol. Suddenly things weren't going the way he expected. If there was any doubt before, he now realised that the only way he was going to get out of this alive was to tell the guy everything he wanted to know. Just like Ray at *Seedy CDs*, the broken nose and teeth were giving him difficulty in talking. The words spluttered out, mumbled and barely coherent, his breathing now heavy and laboured. 'He sold a few things to the lads in the pub. A mobile phone, computer games, the digital camera – that sort of stuff.'

Craven took a final drag on the cigarette and flicked it across the other side of the room. 'And?'

'I don't really know. I'm only guessing but he probably unloaded some CDs and DVDs to Ray Holland.'

'At *Seedy CDs*?'

Pitbull twisted round and looked at Craven. 'Yeah. You know him then?'

Craven nodded back. 'I met him yesterday. He won't be buying stolen CDs again.'

Pitbull groaned and looked back up at the ceiling. He didn't know what Craven meant by that remark but he didn't really want to think about it. Craven was happy for the ambiguity to leave him wondering.

'What else?'

'He probably had some jewellery. There's always jewellery. There's half a dozen places he could get rid of that. It could be any of them.'

Craven let it pass. He wasn't interested in jewellery. 'Anything else?'

'Anything electrical, hardware, he would have sold onto Graham Colley. TVs, CD players, that sort of stuff.'

'Graham Colley?'

'He's got a shop in the town centre. *GC Electrics*.'

'Ashford?'

Pitbull nodded again. 'Same road as *Seedy CDs*.'

Craven shook his head in disbelief. It had to be the shop window that he was looking at yesterday afternoon when he was waiting for the CD shop to empty. Not only had he missed Gary Parkes but he'd actually walked past the place that he was ultimately looking for. He couldn't believe it. The job was turning into a nightmare. 'Anything else?'

Pitbull shook his head. 'No. Can't think of anything else.'

'Good.' Craven leant forward and poured the rest of the petrol over Pitbull's face and body, watching it run down either side of his nose and then under his ears and down the side of his neck. *Just like a baptism. A baptism of fire.* 'Tell me, are you a religious man?'

Pitbull snorted. Nothing could have been further from the truth. 'Not especially.'

'No-one you want to pray for then?'

'Only me.'

'Bit late for that.'

Pitbull kept staring up at the ceiling. 'You don't really want to set fire to anything. You know it and I know it.'

'Really? What makes you so sure?'

'You set fire to this bed and I run out the front door, screaming my head off. The place will be crawling with coppers within minutes. And it something happens to me, they'll remember you from last night.'

Craven looked at him. He was right. The last thing he needed was that useless detective on his tail again and a load of woodentops crawling over a pile of ashes looking for DNA. It was only because they were so intent on arresting Jamie Collins last night that everyone else in the pub got away without so much as a second look. It wouldn't stay like that for very long, particularly when they realised that they'd got the wrong kid. Problem was, he didn't know whether he could trust Pitbull to keep his mouth shut. He didn't look like the sort of bloke who would go running to the police, but then again, why take the risk?

Pitbull was still staring at the ceiling. He'd never been a religious man but at that moment he felt that he wanted to believe in God. The only problem was, he wasn't sure whether God still believed in him. He closed his eyes and started to pray. He didn't see Craven put his hand inside his jacket pocket and pull out the Glock. He didn't see him take out the silencer and screw it slowly into the end of the barrel. And he didn't hear him check the magazine and click it silently back into place.

'What do you do for a job?' Craven picked up the spare pillow that was lying next to Pitbull on the bed.

'I drive a skip lorry.'

'And what happens if you don't turn up for work tomorrow?'

Pitbull opened his eyes and swallowed hard. He sensed that Craven had made up his mind. 'I don't know. I don't suppose they'll be sending out a search party. Don't suppose anybody will really care.' He twisted round to look at Craven and saw the Glock pushed into the back of the pillow. And then for the first time in his life, he wet the bed.

Craven looked at him. It was the brutal honesty, the tragic admission of Pitbull's reply that struck him. Surely life couldn't get any more meaningless than that. *"Among the attributes of God, although they are all equal, mercy shines with even more brilliancy than justice."* He lent over the bed and put the pillow back in its place. 'Right answer. One word to anybody and I'll come back and see you again. Always in the middle in the night. You breathe one word of this to anybody and you'll never sleep properly again.'

Pitbull closed his eyes and started to cry. Maybe there was a God. It felt like a baptism.

The next time he opened them, Craven had gone.

EIGHTEEN

'So, are we ready to re-convene?' Garrick folded his arms and looked impatiently across the table at Jamie Collins and his lawyer, trying his best to convey that whether they wanted more time or not, he intended to move on. Having to wait all night before he could interview Collins had not put him in the best of moods and another fifteen-minute delay for an adjournment requested by Jamie's lawyer, the eponymous Nigel Bentley of Bentley, Simmons & Peacock was not helping matters one iota. Garrick checked his watch again, more to indicate his frustration than to check the time. He knew it was 9.45 and he still hadn't had any breakfast. He was tired and irritable and he was also hungry.

Bentley nodded at Garrick and Andy and then leant forward, clasping his hands together and adopting a serious and earnest pose. Garrick groaned and sunk back into his chair. He'd dealt with Bentley before and could tell that there was a speech coming. One of those rehearsed soliloquies that provincial solicitors seemed to favour so much. He also had a problem with men that wore bow ties. He understood and accepted the hygienic advantages for doctors of course but in all other circumstances he felt it was a rather bizarre and inappropriate choice of dress. As far as Garrick was concerned it either made the wearer look slightly comical or something of a dandy, and in Bentley's case it was definitely the latter. The overall effect of the tie, together with the pinstripe suit and the over elaborate handkerchief stuffed in the breast pocket was all too flamboyant for Garrick's liking.

'I've taken instructions from my client,' began Bentley somewhat pompously, 'who has asked me to assure you that he will of course co-operate fully with your enquiries...'

'I don't think your client has any choice on that particular point,' interrupted Garrick, looking at Jamie and giving him a particularly cynical look. To his credit, even Jamie Collins seemed slightly embarrassed at his solicitor's performance.

Bentley carried on regardless. '...but my client does wish to make it absolutely clear that he had no involvement in the burglary at *Chart Place* and furthermore, that he has never visited *Chart Place* or met Stuart Richmond at any time. Needless to say my client had no involvement in the murder of Mr.

Richmond and indeed was not aware of his death until you informed him of that fact yesterday evening. As you are aware, my client was in a public house in Ashford town centre when information regarding Mr. Richmond's murder was first released via the six o'clock news.'

Garrick spotted the opportunity to interrupt again as Bentley paused for breath. 'Is there any possibility that your client could speak for himself?'

Bentley smiled to himself as if Garrick had just asked a naïve or stupid question. 'This is a murder enquiry Chief Inspector. My client has certain rights and it is my duty to advise him of those rights and to make sure that he is properly represented.'

Andy ignored Bentley's response and looked straight at Jamie. 'We have a witness who has provided a statement and who is prepared to testify in court that you sold him five items of jewellery which were stolen from *Chart Place.*'

Jamie looked at his solicitor waiting for guidance as to whether he should answer or not. Bentley shook his head. In his experience these matters were always handled much better if the client remained silent. 'My client admits to selling the items of jewellery but does not admit to knowing that the items were stolen. And he is prepared to make a statement to that effect. As I said, my client is keen to cooperate fully with your enquiries.'

Garrick looked across the table, first at Jamie, then at Bentley. He'd had just about enough of this. It was turning into a circus and he was starting to lose his temper. 'As you say, Mr. Bentley, this is a murder enquiry. I have to advise you that we have information that absolutely connects the burglary at *Chart Place* to Stuart Richmond's subsequent death. We also have positive information which connects your client to that burglary. Unless your client starts to cooperate I shall assume that your client has something to hide and we will treat your client accordingly. Is that clear?'

'Is that a threat Chief Inspector?'

'Frankly you can interpret it any way you like, but until I am able to eliminate your client from this murder enquiry, he will be treated as a prime suspect.'

'And what exactly does that mean?' asked Bentley, starting to get irritated.

'It means that we will continue to keep your client in custody until he cooperates…'

Bentley snorted. He knew that Garrick wasn't allowed to keep Jamie in custody for more than 72 hours – not unless they were going to charge him.

'…and it also means that I can't promise that information relating to your client "helping us with our enquiries" doesn't leak to the twenty or so journalists who are camped outside the front of this police station – or that his name and photograph won't be all over the front pages of the national newspapers tomorrow morning.'

Bentley practically exploded. 'This is outrageous. If you have any evidence whatsoever that connects my client to Stuart Richmond's murder then I suggest you...'

'Of course I knew it was nicked!' Jamie's blurted admission, shouted at the top of his voice came out of nowhere and took Bentley, as much as any of them by surprise. They all stopped in mid-conversation and looked at him.

'What did you say?' asked Andy, wanting Jamie to repeat himself.

'Of course I knew the stuff was nicked. Obviously it was nicked.'

Bentley was starting to look flustered. 'You don't have to say anything. Unless they have any evidence they can't...'

'There's no point.' interrupted Jamie again, looking as though he was fed up with whole charade. 'I was only fencing a bit of stuff. It's hardly the crime of the century. I'm not going to have my name dragged into a murder enquiry.'

Garrick looked across the table at Bentley, unable to stop the smug satisfaction in his voice. 'It seems to me that your client has more sense than you give him credit for. Shall we get on with it?'

Bentley said nothing and just shrugged. 'Yeah, let's get it over with,' said Jamie, 'I want to get out of here.'

'Right. Where did you get the jewellery from?' asked Andy, getting straight to the point.

'I bought it in a pub.'

Andy leant back in the chair and stared up at the ceiling in exasperation. Garrick folded his arms again and sighed. 'Come on Jamie, do we look like complete idiots?'

Jamie's head dropped, looking down at the table, trying to hide a grin. Under other circumstances he would have given a smart-arse reply to that particular question. 'It's true, I bought them off a bloke in a pub.'

'Which bloke? Which pub?' asked Garrick, deciding to humour him for the moment.

'The bloke that was in the Bricklayer's Arms last night. Sitting on the stool.'

'What, the one that was about to have a punch up with Lee Matthews when we walked in?'

Jamie nodded. 'Yeah, that was him. He sold a load of stuff in the pub a couple of weeks ago.'

Garrick and Andy looked at each other, not sure whether to believe him or not.

'So who is he?' asked Andy. 'I assume this guy has got a name?'

Jamie shrugged. 'Dunno. Never seen him before.'

'What do you mean you've never seen him before? You just said you bought some jewellery off him a couple of weeks ago.'

'I meant I hadn't seen him before a couple of weeks ago. Either way, I don't know his name.'

Garrick and Andy exchanged another glance. Neither of them were convinced.

'So, what was the argument about?' asked Andy

Jamie shrugged again. 'Dunno. I think Pitball bought something off him and wasn't happy. I think he wanted his money back.'

'And then what happened?'

'What do you think? Pitbull doesn't need much of reason to get into a fight.'

Garrick smiled to himself. It was the first thing that Jamie Collins had said that had any ring of truth about it. The rest was jackanory. 'So what else did he sell?'

'What do you mean?'

'You just said he sold a load of stuff in the pub a couple of weeks ago – so what else did he sell?'

Jamie shrugged for the umpteenth time. 'Dunno. I only bought the jewellery. I just know he was selling other stuff.'

'So who else was buying?' asked Andy, also beginning to get tired of the whole charade. He didn't believe Jamie's version of events for one minute either.

'Dunno. I bought the jewellery, that's all I know.'

Garrick looked at his watch. It had gone ten o'clock. The canteen was now shut and he still hadn't had any breakfast. The day was going from bad to worse. He could tell that Jamie wasn't going to give up any information voluntarily. Time to put the kid under a bit of pressure. He closed the file of papers that was in front of him and pushed his chair back as if he were about to get up. 'Okay Jamie, thanks very much. You've been really helpful.'

Andy didn't have a clue what was going on but likewise, took his cue and picked up his file and stood up.

Jamie and Bentley exchanged a puzzled look, both of them still seated and both of them now looking up at Garrick and Andy who were standing side by side, waiting to leave.

'Is that it then?' asked Jamie, 'Can I go?'

Garrick nodded. 'Yes. Thanks for your help.'

'What, you're not charging me?'

Garrick waved his hand dismissively in the air. 'No, like you say, it's hardly the crime of the century. I've got a murder enquiry to investigate. More important things to do…'

Jamie started to smile and stood up. He couldn't believe his luck. Bentley remained seated. He'd had dealings with Garrick before and didn't believe what he was hearing. There had to be a punchline.

'…besides, I'm much more interested in taking someone like Lee Matthews off the streets than you. I'm more than happy to do a deal and not charge you in return for the information about him.'

The smile that had been on Jamie's face suddenly disappeared as he slowly sat back down in his chair. 'What deal? We haven't done any deal?'

Garrick kept a straight face. 'That's not the way he's going to see it I'm afraid. What's going to happen now is DS Cooper and I are going to get in a car and drive over to Lee Matthews' house and then we're going to kick his front door down and arrest him for buying stolen property. And on the drive back to the station we're going to make sure that he knows that it was you that grassed him up.'

'Yeah, right.' The sarcasm in Jamie's voice clearly indicated that he thought Garrick was bluffing.

Bentley, who hadn't said anything constructive since he arrived looked over the top of his glasses at Jamie and spoke for the first time in several minutes. 'I have to advise you that I've worked with Chief Inspector Garrick before and regretfully, from experience, I have to say that the course of action that he's just outlined is wholly consistent with his normal methods and *modus operandi*.'

'What does that mean?' asked Jamie, struggling to keep up with Bentley's turn of phrase.

'It means, he means what he says.'

'I haven't grassed anybody up!' shouted Jamie, starting to get agitated.

By now, Garrick was at the door and on the point of leaving. 'Anyway, we need to talk to Matthews. He might remember the name of this guy who sold him the stuff, even if you don't.'

Jamie's head dropped down, looking at the table. He knew when he was in a corner. There was a golden rule, an unwritten code that you didn't grass to the police, especially about your mates – but sticking to that code wasn't going to be worth anything if Pitbull thought that he'd done a deal with Garrick. His life wouldn't be worth living. Everybody in the pub knew that he'd been arrested and what's more, everybody in the pub knew that it was really him that had been selling the stolen gear. If the police let him go without so much as a warning he was in real trouble, particularly if they then started arresting some of the others for buying the stuff. Pitbull would go absolutely mental. He wouldn't think twice about telling Garrick who he really bought the camera from and then the situation would be even worse. He'd still be in the frame for fencing the gear but he'd have Pitbull and half the estate thinking he was a grass. He wouldn't be able to go out the front door. Jamie was processing as fast as he could but he knew he was out of options. Gary Parkes was his best mate but he didn't have any choice. Hopefully Gary would understand. He took a deep breath. 'There's no point talking to Pitbull.'

'Why's that then?' Garrick still had his hand on the door handle as if he was about to leave.

'Because it was me who was selling the stuff.'

Garrick and Andy looked across the room for a couple of seconds and said nothing, letting the impact of what Jamie had just said settle into the silence. Eventually, they walked back over to the table and sat down. 'Right,' said Garrick. 'Let's start again. Where did you get the jewellery from?'

Jamie's head dropped down, looking at the table again. This was going to be harder than he thought. 'It's hard for me to say. I'd be shopping a mate. I can tell you who I sold it to.'

Garrick shook his head. 'We know who you sold it to. We've already told you that. We need to know who carried out the burglary.'

'He couldn't have had anything to do with the murder.'

'How do you know that?' asked Andy.

'I just do. He just wouldn't have.'

Garrick looked at him. He could tell that Jamie meant it. He leant forward across the table, trying to encourage a response. 'Come on Jamie, we're running out of time. If whoever it was didn't have anything to do with the murder, then they haven't got anything to worry about. Just a domestic burglary. It's not what we're really interested in at the moment.'

Jamie knew that he was just delaying the inevitable. Finally he took another deep breath and, against all his instincts, against all of the feral code by which he lived, he delivered up his best friend, head on a platter. 'It was Gary Parkes. I got the stuff from Gary Parkes.'

'Just the jewellery?' Garrick was asking the questions, Andy was taking notes.

Jamie shook his head. 'No, everything. There was loads of stuff. He had a car full of it.'

'And it was Gary who carried out the burglary on *Chart Place*?'

Jamie nodded. 'Yeah. About three weeks ago.'

'And when did he give the stuff to you?' asked Garrick, trying to get a fix on the sequence of events.

'Next day. It was all in the boot of his car. Still in the duvet covers that he used to carry everything out of the house. I don't think he'd even looked at it. Gary wanted to get the stuff sold as soon as possible. He needed the money and anyway, there's no point in having a load of stolen property in the back of your car is there?'

Garrick smiled. 'No, I suppose not. So how much did you give him for it?'

Jamie shook his head again. 'Nothing. It didn't work like that. I haven't got that sort of cash. Gary turned the place over but he hasn't got a clue about how to get rid of anything. I sold it for him and then we split the money. Fifty, fifty.'

Garrick nodded, taking it all in while Andy continued scribbling. 'And how quickly did you get rid of the stuff?'

'Straight away. Next couple of days. It doesn't take long if you know where to go.'

'And has Gary mentioned *Chart Place* or Stuart Richmond since?'

Jamie shook his head again. 'No, not since I sold the stuff and we split the cash.'

'What about Appleden. Has he mentioned anything about Appleden at all.'

Jamie screwed his face up, clearly not understanding where the line of questioning was going. 'Appleden? No, he's never mentioned anything about Appleden. Why?'

Garrick waved away his question. 'It doesn't matter. Just a thought. So where did you sell the rest of the stuff?'

Jamie leant back in the chair and stared up at the ceiling. He felt like a Judas. Not only had he shopped his best friend but now he was going to have to shop everybody else as well. He took another deep breath. There was no turning back. 'I sold a few things to the lads in the pub…'

'*The Bricklayer's Arms*?'

Jamie nodded. 'Yeah. A couple of mobiles, some computer games, that sort of stuff.'

'What else?

'I unloaded some jewellery to a shop in Canterbury.'

'We know that. What else?' Garrick was getting impatient. In truth, he wasn't that interested in where Richmond's property ended up, but he knew that he had to go through the motions and get all the information. What he really wanted to do was get this over and done with as soon as possible and get out there and pick up Gary Parkes.

'There were a load of CDs and DVDs. I sold those onto a shop in Ashford.

'Which shop?'

'*Seedy CDs*, in the town centre.'

Garrick and Andy exchanged a glance. They'd heard of it but it wasn't really on their radar screen. 'Anything else?'

'Most of the other stuff, the hi-fi, a couple of TVs, a DVD recorder and the laptop I sold onto Graham Colley.'

This time Garrick nodded in recognition. Graham Colley was a name that had definitely come up before. 'Anything else?'

Jamie shook his head. 'No that was about it. There were a couple of watches. Me and Gary kept one each.' He smiled to himself at the absurdity of it all. 'Mine's in a plastic bag which I had to leave with your lot at the front desk when I came in.'

Garrick smiled back. The kid had delivered up his mate, which couldn't have been easy. 'Okay Jamie. Anything else we should know?'

Jamie thought for a moment but there wasn't anything else he could think of. He shook his head in silence. The last few minutes had been really difficult but in a way, the worse was still to come.

Garrick closed the file in front of him, this time for real and stood up. 'Okay Jamie. We need to go and pick up Gary and bring him in for questioning. If it helps, I'll try and make sure he understands that you didn't have any choice. Whilst we're doing that I'll arrange for another officer to come and take a statement from you. Do you want a cup of tea?'

Jamie nodded. He knew only too well what the process was from now on. Garrick looked down at Andy who appeared to be engrossed in paging through the list of stolen items from Richmond's burglary, which were in his file. Garrick was impatient to get going as soon as possible. 'Andy, are you ready?'

Andy held his hand up, indicating that he needed another moment or two. He flicked backwards and forwards through the list, scanning the items for the third or fourth time and then eventually looked up at Jamie. 'Tell me again, what items did you say that you sold onto Graham Colley?'

Jamie looked slightly surprised, obviously not sure why he was being asked the question for a second time. 'There was a hi-fi, one of those miniature things that plays CDs with a digital radio. There were a couple of small TVs, a portable CD player, a laptop, a DVD recorder...'

'You sure about the laptop?' interrupted Andy.

'Yeah, of course I'm sure. Why?'

Andy ignored the question and looked over at Garrick, nodding towards the door. 'Can I have a quick word Sir?'

Garrick nodded and the two of them left Jamie and the now redundant Bentley in the interview room and went out into the corridor, just as Garrick and Matt had done the day before.

'What's the problem?' asked Garrick, sensing that whatever was troubling Andy was potentially significant.

'There's no laptop on the list.'

'Are you sure?'

Andy nodded emphatically. 'I've double, triple checked it. Anyway, I knew before I looked. There was definitely no laptop on there.'

'Well, maybe Richmond forgot. It's a long list. He lost a lot of stuff.'

Andy gave Garrick a very old-fashioned, sideways look. Richmond's list was one of the most detailed and comprehensive itineraries that he had ever seen. There was no way that Richmond could have forgotten.

'Well maybe Gary Parkes got the laptop from somewhere else,' added Garrick, trying to think of a logical explanation.

'Maybe. It'll be easy enough to check. We can ask him when we get him back here for questioning. But all my instincts are telling me it was part of the same burglary.'

'So what are you thinking Andy?

'I don't know Sir. Still trying to work it out but at the moment it looks like Richmond got burgled and in the process lost a laptop which for some reason he didn't want us to know about.'

Garrick nodded slowly, taking it all in. If there was something significant about Richmond's laptop, it might be connected to why he received a mysterious phone call and why he drew out a hundred thousand pounds. It might even explain why he was murdered. 'Well spotted Andy. Let's get back in there, I just want to double-check something '

When they walked back into the room Jamie and Bentley were still sitting in silence, side by side at the interview table. As before, Garrick sat down opposite Bentley and Andy sat down opposite Jamie. Again, Garrick asked the questions, Andy took the notes.

'I know we've already asked you this Jamie but are you absolutely sure about this laptop?'

Jamie looked at him as if he was offended. He'd put his neck on the line to tell the truth and now they didn't believe him. 'Of course I'm sure. I'm not stupid. I know what I sold.'

'But are you sure it came from *Chart Place*, like the rest of the stuff?'

'Yeah, of course it did. It was at the bottom of one of the duvet covers. All the gear was together in the boot of his car. He wouldn't have got it from anywhere else.'

'Did you have a look at it?' asked Garrick.

Jamie shrugged in a sort of "yes and no" type of response. 'I lifted the lid up just to look at the keys to see what sort of condition it was in but I didn't try and switch it on. They all have passwords on them don't they?'

Garrick nodded. 'Yes, normally. Can you remember exactly when you sold it on to Graham Colley.'

Jamie thought for a moment. 'It must have been at the end of the same week that I got it off Gary. Probably the Friday?'

Garrick checked the calendar in his file. 'Friday 15th September? Two weeks ago?'

'Suppose so. Does it matter?'

Garrick looked at Andy. Oh it mattered all right. Two people were dead and Graham Colley was suddenly the prime suspect. He'd had the laptop several days before the phone call to Stuart Richmond and more importantly, before either Hilary Russell and Stuart Richmond had been murdered.

'Thanks for your help Jamie.' said Garrick standing up to leave. 'There'll be another officer down in a moment to take your statement. I'll organise that cup of tea.'

Jamie looked up at Garrick and Andy in some bewilderment. He didn't really understand what was going on anymore. 'Are you going to pick up Gary now?' he asked, still worried about what his best friend was going to think of him.

Andy looked at Garrick for unspoken confirmation and then back at Jamie. 'No. Change of plan, Jamie. Gary Parkes can wait. Right now, we're going to pick up Graham Colley.'

NINETEEN

The walk from Queen Anne's Gate to Carlton Gardens took no more than ten or fifteen minutes and was a route all too familiar to Charles Buchanan, a journey that he had made back and forth, rain or shine, almost twice a day for as many years as he could remember. Under other circumstances it would have been a pleasant morning to take a relaxed and leisurely stroll through St. James's Park, an opportunity to get some fresh air, to watch the seasons turn, to put the world back into perspective. The weather had changed again and the forecasters were promising a warm and settled weekend, but Buchanan's mind was on other matters. The weekend could wait. Nor was he in the mood for a leisurely stroll. Matters of State required attention and as usual, one couldn't rely on the politicians or the civil servants to handle things properly. Not that one would want to. Most of them couldn't run a bath, let alone a ministerial department.

It took him less than ten minutes to get back to the office, a purposeful stride through the park, not stopping as usual on top of the bridge across the lake to admire the view of Buckingham Palace, framed by trees and fountains to the west, or the Foreign and Commonwealth Office, similarly framed in the opposite direction. Buchanan loved all the Royal Parks, he was after all a historian by education and a monarchist at heart, but St. James's had always been his favourite. Bordered by The Mall to the north, Horse Guards Parade to the east and Birdcage Walk to the south, it was the oldest and in his view, the most beautiful and romantic of them all.

Many an evening he would take a slow, meandering walk through the criss-cross of lanes to the tube station on the other side, invisible amongst the crowds of tourists and hurried office-workers, often thinking about its heritage and its rich and colourful past. The deer park created by Henry VIII, the pageantry and pomp of the Elizabethan fetes, the flower gardens and exotic birds of James I, the games of *Pelle Melle* played on long-fenced courts and the infamous assignations of Charles II and Nell Gwyn. At one time it had become notorious as a meeting place for sexual degenerates, a fact vividly captured by John Wilmot, 2nd Earl of Rochester in his celebrated poem, *A Ramble in St James's*. Buchanan had a rare, priceless, second edition at home. In Hampshire of course – not in the flat in Pimlico.

It was nearly 10.30 by the time he got back to the office, a large, imposing building, unmarked and as anonymous as all the other large, anonymous buildings that made up the nameless maze that was Whitehall. As he walked through the lobby, he gave an authoritative nod to Jenkins, the desk security officer and then took the wide sweeping staircase up to the first floor, running his hand up the polished banister and looking down at the marbled floor below.

Number 1, Carlton Gardens was one of seven large houses situated in a cul-de-sac beside Carlton House Terrace, the street of two-terraces of white stucco-faced houses which sat majestically on the south side of Pall Mall, overlooking St. James's Park. Each terrace consisted of nine large houses, designed by John Nash and built around 1830, the east and west terraces divided by the Duke of York column and steps which led down from Waterloo Place and onto The Mall. The freehold was still owned by the Crown Estate and over the years, Carlton House Terrace had become one of the most fashionable addresses in London. Lord Palmerston had lived at Number 5, Earl Grey at Number 13 and William Gladstone at both Number 4 and Number 11.

Carlton Gardens was developed around the same time and, much to Buchanan's approval, was no less famous. Lord Kitchener had once lived at number 2, whilst number 4 had served as General Charles de Gaulle's headquarters during World War II. In architectural terms, the houses were perhaps less grand than their more imposing neighbours, but they were still late Georgian properties of huge, symmetrical proportions with large sash windows, high, decorative ceilings and room after room of glittering chandeliers. In all other respects, Buchanan's office looked like an expensive London residence and it was only the ubiquitous net curtains, ever ready to catch the splintering glass of the terrorist's bomb that gave confirmation to the fact that this was government property. It may have looked like a private home but Number 1 Carlton Gardens was unequivocally part of the establishment.

Buchanan walked into the outer office and hovered impatiently over the large mahogany desk which sat imposingly in the centre of the room, anxious to get back to his own office as soon as possible. 'Any messages?'

His PA looked up from her screen and gave him an efficient smile, picking up her notepad and then putting on her glasses which had been dangling around her neck on a gold chain. She flicked efficiently through several pages of notes. There had been a lot of messages, there always were but she sensed from Buchanan's tone that he was only interested in the really urgent ones. The others she could type up later. She looked up from the notepad to make sure that he was paying attention. 'The JIC meeting has been moved to four-thirty. Apparently the Chairman is stuck in Scotland.'

'Good. Gives me a spare couple of hours this afternoon. Anything else?'

'Sir Michael Hamilton returned your call. I said you'd ring him back.'

'Okay. Anything else.'

She flicked through the pad again and then shook her head. 'No, that's it. Oh, other than Robert Bellamy confirmed lunch. One o'clock at Boodles.'

Buchanan nodded. 'Thank you. Could you organise some coffee and take my calls for a while. There are a couple of things I need to get on with.'

Buchanan left her without waiting for a reply and closed the door behind him as he went into his office. He walked over to the desk and sat down in the leather upholstered chair, taking a bunch of keys out of his jacket pocket to unlock the drawers on either side. He opened the middle left hand draw and from a pile of documents pulled out a slim, manila file which he opened and put on the desk in front of him. From the inside pocket of his jacket he then took out a mobile phone and hit the green call button, swivelling round in his chair to look out of the window while he waited for the call to be answered. It rang no more than twice before Craven answered it. 'Hello?'

'It's me.'

'Obviously.' Craven smiled to himself. It was like going back in time. Same old routines. *"No names, no pack drill."*

'Sorry about earlier, I was just crossing the park when you rang.'

'That's okay. You back at *Vector* now?'

'Yes. What happened yesterday? I expected you to call back.'

'I was tied up. Local dispute. Then I needed to get something sorted before I rang you.'

'Everything okay?'

Craven looked across the room at Graham Colley, curled up, trembling and crying in the corner of the kitchen He smiled to himself again. 'It is now. I've located and secured the merchandise.'

Buchanan breathed a huge sigh of relief. Only he would ever know the true value of what Craven had just accomplished. 'Where did you find it?'

'Local. It's been through two or three pairs of hands. That's why I'm ringing. The most recent owner is with me now.' Craven looked across at Graham Colley again and then at the laptop which was sitting on Colley's kitchen table. 'He's neutral but I think …'

'You think he's opened it?' interrupted Buchanan, unable to stop the sense of urgency in his voice.

Craven turned away from Colley so that he couldn't hear the whispered reply.

'He says not…but it's hard to tell. He's has the ability.'

Buchanan swivelled back round so that he was facing the desk and quickly scanned through the papers in the file again. He wanted to ask Craven the guy's name but he knew he couldn't. Not on the mobile. 'What's your view?'

'Grey. Seventy-thirty black.'

Buchanan pursed his lips, thinking through the options. Grey meant that Craven wasn't certain. Seventy-thirty black meant that he thought it was more probable that they had a problem. Seventy-thirty white would have been the other way round. It was an easy decision. 'Then it's checkmate I think.'

Craven nodded. He wasn't surprised. 'Anything else?'

'What about the others? You said it's been through several pairs of hands.'

'Grey. Seventy-thirty white.'

'Are you sure?'

'Just kids. Don't think they had the ability. Or the time.'

Buchanan breathed another sigh of relief. 'Okay, one more thing.'

'Go on.' Craven looked round at Colley again, just to make sure that he wasn't thinking of trying anything funny.

'The nephew. Could you pay him a visit? He's starting to make a nuisance of himself. A friendly word should do it.'

'Okay, leave it with me. I'll be back sometime over the weekend.'

'Thanks.' Buchanan put the phone down and put the file back in the drawer. A great weight had been lifted off his mind. Suddenly, lunch with the Home Secretary was going to be a lot easier.

Craven switched off the phone and put it back in his pocket. Colley was still curled up in the corner, still trembling and still whimpering like a child. The pain was starting to throb but worse than that, he was worried about what Craven was going to do next.

Craven looked at him and for a moment thought about asking him what was on the laptop. He didn't mind Buchanan not telling him – not at first. But now that he had found it, surely it wouldn't make any difference? It was starting to annoy him that he didn't really know what this was all about. Then he let the moment go. Perhaps it was better not to know. He looked at Colley again, trying to decide what to do. A single bullet behind the ear, an *OBE* as the paramilitaries in Northern Ireland liked to call it, would have been the most clinical but it was going to be too messy. He needed to keep the local police off his trail, which meant that he needed to hide the body. Which meant no disturbance and no mess. He looked over at Colley again who was staring back at him, terrified but expectant. 'Okay, get up. We're leaving.'

'Where are we going?' asked Colley, struggling to his feet.

'A safe house. Put your hands behind your back, I need to put some plastic cuffs on you.'

Colley turned round and dutifully put his hands together behind his back. The previous thirty minutes with Craven had taught him not to question or try and resist what was happening. The outcome had been too painful.

Craven took out the plastic ties and tied one around each of Colley's wrists, tight enough to stop his hands getting through but loose enough to allow some movement. Then he threaded a third tie through both wrists and pulled them close together. Colley stood patiently waiting for Craven to finish, appreciative that the handcuffs had been put on without digging into his wrists.

Craven then took out a fourth tie and threaded the end through the clip to make a loop, just big enough to get over Colley's head. Colley still had his back towards him, unaware what was going to happen next, still waiting patiently with his hands clasped together behind his back. Craven slipped the plastic loop over his head and before Colley could react to what was happening, pulled the plastic strip as hard as he could around his neck. Within seconds he wished that he hadn't.

Colley reeled round in an instant and then stumbled against the kitchen worktops, his eyes bulging, gasping for air, the plastic tie digging into his neck. He tried to scream but Craven had pulled it so tight that the only sound coming out of his mouth was a rasping, choking, growl. His natural instinct was to put his hands up to his throat, to try and loosen the pressure around his neck but he couldn't – they were still tied behind his back. Not that it would have done him any good. The plastic clip only locked one way. Once it was on, it couldn't be loosened.

He started to panic, thrashings his arms and kicking and banging his body against the kitchen cupboards, anything to try and fight against the dying light but he knew it was useless. He was snared, like a wild animal in the woods. So all of a sudden he stopped. And then he just stood there, trying to catch his breath, unable to speak, unable to fight, unable to do anything except slowly wait, looking at Craven with all the pain and terror in his eyes. Choking to death. Craven wanted to look away but he knew he couldn't. It would have been weak. So he held his gaze and they stared at each other. Executioner and victim. A slow, painful exchange which both of them knew was going to last a couple of minutes.

Colley dropped to his knees, the struggle of trying to stand upright now too much for him. He looked up at Craven, his eyes pleading, silently begging for mercy, sweat running down his face. Desperately trying to breathe, desperately trying to swallow. Unbearable pressure in his head. The world starting to go black.

Craven couldn't stand it any longer. An OBE would have been better than this. A knife across the throat even. Anything but this. He'd killed a lot of people in his time and usually in cold blood, but this was awful. *"Is there a crime beneath the roof of heaven that stains the soul of man with more infernal hue than damned assassination?"* He put his hand in his pocket and walked behind Colley who was still kneeling on the floor, his head starting to drop and bend forwards. Colley caught Craven's movement and raised his head momentarily, a last, desperate plea for help, a final, flickering hope that Craven would take pity on him and cut him loose.

Craven pulled the garrotte out of his pocket and held the small wooden handles at either end of the rope in each hand. Then he put the rope over Colley's head and crossed his arms so that the rope tightened around his neck. Then he pushed his knee into the middle of his back and pulled as hard as he could. Colley's body started to twitch in a sort of involuntary movement and then, after what seemed like an eternity, it started to go limp. Craven knew from experience that you had to keep the pressure on for a good thirty seconds after the twitching had stopped. Eventually he let go. The garrotte was barbaric but it was efficient and clean – and most of all, you didn't have to stand in front of the victim and watch him die.

Colley's body was still bent over in the kneeling position, frozen in the exact same pose as when Craven had first put the rope around his neck. Craven nudged it gently with his foot and it slumped sideways onto the kitchen floor. Mission accomplished. He spent the next five minutes tidying up the house and then started looking for the car keys. Colley's car, a silver Mercedes was parked outside and the keys had to be somewhere. Craven needed to get rid of the body and hiding it in the boot of the car was going to be favourite.

He'd learnt a long time ago that disposing of a body was always the most difficult part of an operation. The actual killing was easy. Anybody could be taught to do that. Getting rid of a body, particularly getting rid of it permanently, was a real challenge. It required ingenuity and fortitude and perseverance. Everybody had heard the stories about people being buried under concrete pillars on the M1 or bodies being put through agricultural mincers and then fed to pigs. He didn't really know if any of those stories were true but what he did know was that if you wanted to hide a body for a few weeks, then the boot of a car parked in a long-term car park was almost perfect. The best place to hide was always in a crowd and the larger the car park, the longer it was likely to go undiscovered. Gatwick Airport would have been ideal but it was too far away. The drive there would have taken a couple of hours and then he'd have to get the Gatwick Express back into London Bridge and then a train back to Ashford. Too many people, which meant too many opportunities to get noticed. Not to mention all the cameras. The International Station at Ashford was his best bet. There were thousands of cars parked in the long-term car park, which meant one more would go unnoticed for days on end, possibly weeks. And he could be in and out of there and back in Ashford town centre in thirty minutes. Perfect.

It took him a couple of minutes to find the car keys, still in Colley's jacket pocket hanging over the back of a chair, where they had been since the night before. And once he'd found them he quickly managed to put the body in the boot, lock up the house and then turn the car out of the drive and into the lane that ran all the way down to the main road. The lane itself was narrow and on two occasions he had to pull over into the hedge to let through another car which was coming the other way.

Craven was concentrating on driving the Mercedes and thinking about the laptop which was lying safely beside him on the passenger seat. He was toying with the idea of getting back to the hotel room and then trying to switch it on. He didn't take any notice of the second car that he had to pull over for, a dark blue saloon being driven in a hurry and with two people in the front. And Garrick and Andy were too busy trying to get to Colley's house as soon as possible to take any notice of a silver Mercedes. They'd already wasted half an hour waiting outside his shop and were impatient to ask him a few questions. None of them knew how close they had been as they passed each other, no more than thirty seconds after Craven had left the house.

TWENTY

It didn't take them long to realise that there was no-one at home. Garrick pressed the doorbell a few times and then squatted down to peer through the letterbox, while Andy wandered off to investigate round the back of the house. It was obvious from just looking through the windows that the place was lived in; the rooms had that casual, untidy feel about them as though someone had just got up and left – but it was also clear that there was nobody in at the moment. Everything was still and quiet and the place was clearly deserted. Andy returned from the back garden within a couple of minutes, shaking his head to indicate that he hadn't found anything, other than a plastic slide and some children's toys on the back lawn. 'There must be a wife and kids. Maybe we ought to try and contact her.'

Garrick was still peering through the front window, shielding his eyes with his hand to try and stop the light bouncing off the glass. 'Probably. What do you reckon then? Do you think he's done a runner?'

Andy shrugged, not sure what to think. 'He could have done I suppose, particularly if he saw the news bulletin about Richmond last night. It seems odd that he's not at home and he's not at the shop.'

'I guess he could be out delivering,' replied Garrick, 'or fitting a washing machine or something.' He pressed the doorbell again, more out of frustration than with any expectation that it was going to be answered.

The two of them stood there in silence for a few moments, wondering what they should do next. Garrick leant back and looked up at the top of the house, as if he were a building inspector surveying the roof or the chimney. He wasn't sure why he was doing that, he wasn't looking at anything in particular – just killing time while he thought about what their next move was going to be. What he really wanted to do was force his way through the back door and have a good look around the house. Maybe the laptop was in there. That would be a result.

'We'd need a warrant Sir,' cautioned Andy, sensing that Garrick was getting impatient and on the point of taking matters into his own hands. 'Anyway, if he's done a runner, he's bound to have taken the laptop with him.'

Garrick pursed his lips, thinking through the implications of breaking into private property without a warrant. Anyway, Andy was right. The fastest way to find the laptop was to find Graham Colley, not to break into an empty house. 'Mind you, I suppose the mobile could be in there – the one that was used to call Stuart Richmond. We know it was bought in Ashford. If we could find that we could definitely link Colley to Richmond's murder.'

Andy smiled to himself. He could tell that Garrick was desperately trying to find a reason to break in and search the place. 'He didn't buy a mobile Sir, just a SIM card. He probably swapped it over with his usual card just to make the call. Trying to find a SIM card would be like trying to find a needle in a haystack.'

Garrick pulled a face, obviously not convinced. 'I'm not so sure Andy. Lots of people have spare handsets these days. Besides, the guy runs an electrical shop. Just the sort of person to have a spare mobile lying around.'

'It could be anywhere Sir,' persisted Andy, 'I think we should get back to the station and try and locate his wife. We could always drive past the shop again and see if he's turned up.'

Garrick nodded reluctantly. He knew that Andy was right.

'And I guess while we're out here,' added Andy, 'we could go and pick up Gary Parkes – take him back in with us?'

Garrick nodded again, although not with any enthusiasm. 'Make's sense. Although I have to say I'd rather concentrate on trying to find Graham Colley.'

Andy knew what he meant. Talking to Gary Parkes wasn't going to move the enquiry forward one iota. They already had all the information they needed about the burglary and already knew that Gary had passed the laptop onto Jamie Collins. They would just be going through the motions of interviewing him and getting a statement written up. None of that was urgent. What they really needed to do was find out what was on the laptop, which meant finding Graham Colley as soon as possible. 'I suppose we could have a quick word with him out here,' suggested Andy, 'and bring him back in for formal questioning later on?'

Garrick grinned. They were on the same wavelength. 'Exactly what I was thinking. Come on, let's drive back via the Connaught and see if he's there.'

It took them ten minutes or so to skirt round the Ashford ring-road and get to Gary Parkes's place, a grey, pebble-dashed council house on one of the rougher parts of the Connaught estate. On paper, number 36, Cambridge Close sounded like an upmarket, respectable address but in reality it was anything but. Garrick gazed at the rows of scruffy, neglected houses as he got out of the car. A few of the properties had been bought, the tell-tale signs of replacement windows and new doors or porches advertising the transfer to private ownership but the majority were still owned by the council and most of them were in a state of disrepair. Testimony to the fact that this was one of the poorest and most deprived areas of town.

The front garden to number 36 was rundown and overgrown and it was also full of junk. Someone looked as through they'd been repairing a car on the front lawn; there were tyre marks and oil patches in several places and there was also what appeared to be a discarded refrigerator rotting in the corner of one of the flower beds. It looked as though it had been there for some time. The edges and corners had gone rusty and a clump of weeds had started to overtake and cover the back of the machine. Garrick walked up the path and rang the doorbell. Andy waited by the gate, just in case he needed to nip round the side to stop anybody slipping out the back.

It took Garrick a couple of seconds to realise that the doorbell didn't work. He could hear voices inside but nothing was happening. Eventually he rapped the knocker attached to the letterbox three or four times and almost immediately the door was opened by a woman in her early forties wearing a pair of slippers, a tight blue skirt that was far too short and smoking a cigarette. Her hair, which was several shades of reddish-brown, was long and curly and tied up on top of her head in an untidy mess. The smell of fried food and stale tobacco hit him as soon as she opened the door.

'Mr. Garrick – as I live and breathe.' Stella Parkes looked him up and down as though he was a piece of dog shit underneath her shoe and then took a long, theatrical drag on her cigarette.

'Hello Stella. Can we come in?'

Stella titled her head back and blew the smoke up into the air. 'You got a warrant?'

Garrick shook his head. 'No. Why, do we need one?'

'Spose not.' She moved to one side to let Garrick through and waited for Andy to walk up the path and follow him into the house. 'Excuse the mess. If I'd known you were coming I would have put the red carpet out.'

'DS Cooper,' said Garrick, waving an introductory hand towards Andy's direction.

'Yeah I know. We've met.' Another long drag of the cigarette.

'Gary about?' asked Garrick, walking into the living room. Stella had been watching the television which was still on in the corner of the room. A girl in her late teens or early twenties was sitting on the sofa, legs crossed, filing her nails. 'Hello Becca. No work today then?'

The girl looked up from the sofa and gave him a sarcastic smile. 'Wall Street doesn't open for another couple of hours.'

Garrick gave her a sarcastic smile back. Becca Parkes worked on the checkouts at the local supermarket. Either she was skiving or she was on the late shift.

'So, is Gary about?' asked Garrick again as Andy and Stella followed him into the room.

Stella walked over to the television and switched the sound off, stubbing out her cigarette in a glass ashtray which was on the side. 'Yeah, he's upstairs. Why, what do you want him for?'

'Just a quick word,' replied Garrick, starting to think that maybe this wasn't such a good idea. Perhaps it would have been better to have seen him down at the station.

'A quick word about what?' replied Stella. 'He hasn't done anything.'

Garrick gave her a look which conveyed more than he could ever have said in words.

Stella muttered something under her breath and then went back out into the hall and called up the stairs. 'Gary! The police want a word with you! Chief Inspector Garrick. Are you coming down?'

Andy suddenly had this horrible feeling that he was going to see Gary Parkes dropping out of a bedroom window onto the back lawn and then legging it across the garden. He was just starting to think that maybe he should position himself by the back door when he heard footsteps coming down the stairs and then Gary walked into the living room, still wearing the blue jeans and white polo shirt from the night before. He nodded at Garrick and Andy as he walked over to the sofa and sat down next to his sister. 'I wondered when you lot would be turning up.'

'Expecting us were you?' asked Garrick, declining the invitation to take a seat. The place looked filthy.

'I saw it on the news when I got back from the pub. I wondered why you were mob handed last night. Didn't make sense for just a burglary. I suppose Jamie told you did he?'

Garrick nodded. 'It's a murder enquiry Gary. He didn't have any choice.'

Gary nodded back as if he understood and then leant forward as though he was about to get up off the sofa. 'We going down the station then?'

Garrick held his hand up, indicating to Gary to stay put. 'We can do that another day. We just wanted to hear your version of events first.'

'What do you want to know?'

'Just tell us what happened.'

'I didn't kill him if that's what you mean.'

Garrick smiled. 'We know that. Just tell us about the burglary.'

Stella stood up and went off to the kitchen. She couldn't stand listening to Gary confessing everything to the police. Becca stayed on the sofa, still filing her nails, seemingly oblivious to the conversation that was going on around her.

Gary shrugged. 'Not much to tell really. Richmond and his missus went out and I turned the place over after they left. I watched them leave. I knew they were going out for the evening cos she was all dolled up. It only took me about twenty minutes. Getting in the house was a piece of cake; they'd left a bedroom window unlocked on the first floor. All I had to do was climb onto a flat roof and push it open. Crazy really.'

'What did you do with all the stuff?' asked Andy, picking up and casually looking at a photo of Gary and Becca which was sitting on top of the television, an old faded picture of them taken when they were small.

'I just put it in the boot of the car and went home.'

'I meant after that.' said Andy, irritated by Gary's response. Surely it was obvious what he meant?

Gary started to look uncomfortable. Like Jamie, he wasn't happy about shopping his mate. 'What did Jamie say?'

'Never mind what Jamie said. Just tell us what happened.' Andy's tone was getting less patient and less sympathetic by the second. They didn't have time to play games.

Gary sensed the changing mood and took a deep breath. 'Okay. I saw Jamie in the pub the following night...'

'*The Bricklayer's Arms?*'

Gary nodded. 'I still had the gear in the boot of the car. We just transferred it from my car to his. That was it. I never saw the stuff again. Jamie unloaded it and we split everything down the middle.'

'Can you remember what was there?' asked Garrick, keen to move the line of questioning onto the matter in hand.

Gary shrugged. 'More or less. Why?'

'Do you remember a laptop?' asked Andy, getting straight to the point.

'Yeah. It was on his desk in the study.'

'Did you have a look at it?'

Gary shook his head. 'No, it was switched off and closed when I found it. I just put it in one of the duvet covers with everything else.'

'You didn't try and switch it on then?' asked Garrick.

'No, I wouldn't know how to.'

Garrick and Andy exchanged a quick glance. There was nothing for them here. Everything Gary had just said corroborated with what Jamie Collins had told them a couple of hours earlier. The explanations were identical and the pair of them certainly weren't clever enough to have agreed a set of rehearsed answers in advance. Garrick decided that he ought to try one last line of questioning. 'Have you been to *Chart Place* since?'

Gary shook his head again. 'No. No reason to.'

'And you didn't speak to Richmond after the burglary? You didn't telephone him about a week later?'

Gary almost laughed at the suggestion. 'Course not. I thought I'd got away with it. The last thing I'd do is ring him up.'

Garrick gave Andy a quick nod, indicating that it was time to go. He'd heard everything that he wanted to hear. This was getting them nowhere. 'Okay Gary, thanks for your help. We'll need a statement, but like I said, we'll do it another day.'

Gary shrugged again. 'Okay, suits me.' He stood up and waited for Andy to fold up his notebook and put it back in his pocket. 'I'll see you out.'

Garrick looked at him across the room. Despite everything else he was a polite kid. He might have been on the wrong side of the law but he wasn't like some of the pond-life that they had to deal with. At least he had some manners. Garrick called out goodbye to Stella who was still in the kitchen but didn't get a response. Becca predictably gave them a thin smile as they left.

'So, what do you think?' asked Garrick as he and Andy walked back to the car.

'I think we need to find that laptop as soon as possible, which means we need to find Graham Colley.'

Garrick turned the ignition key and started up the car. 'So do I Andy. And the sooner the better. Maybe we can get the details of his car and get uniform out there looking for him as well.'

'Good idea,' said Andy, pulling the seatbelt across his shoulder and locking it into place, 'if he's in the area and we've got the registration number, he can't be that difficult to find, can he?'

Garrick pulled the car out onto the road and said nothing. He didn't want to tempt fate and besides, they didn't even know if Colley was in the area or not. And even if he was, finding him might not be as easy as Andy reckoned. What was worrying him, was that without Colley and without the laptop the whole enquiry was stuck again. As usual, too much depended on one line of enquiry and on one vital piece of evidence.

He smiled to himself as he turned the car onto the main road. He suddenly realised that he'd forgotten to ask Gary Parkes to hand back the stolen watch; the Patek Philippe. The kid didn't look as though he knew where the price of the next meal was coming from and there he was, wearing a £15,000 designer wristwatch. He probably didn't even know what it was worth. Garrick thought about telling Andy but then decided to let it pass. Knowing Andy, he'd probably argue that they ought to go back and get it, which was the last thing that Garrick wanted to do.

Besides, it could wait. Gary Parkes wasn't going anywhere. They could afford to leave him where he was for a couple of days. He wasn't going to come to any harm. Gary Parkes was as safe as houses.

TWENTY-ONE

Craven got to the International Station at Ashford in no time at all and drove all the way up to the top of the car park and then back down to the ground floor again. Level five turned out to be the best place to park. It was on the same level as the walkway that went over to the main building, which meant that you didn't need to use the stairs or the lift to get to and from the terminal. Given that most people would be carrying luggage that was a real advantage. As a consequence, whilst some of the other floors were only half full, finding a parking space on level five was something of a challenge. Every time a space became vacant it was taken again within minutes. Craven however decided that being patient was going to be worth the wait. It virtually guaranteed that Colley's car would be surrounded by hundreds of others, which meant that it was going to be practically invisible. Just another silver, executive-saloon waiting for its owner to return back from an extended business trip in either Paris or Brussels. He drove round the floor several times and eventually managed to find a space near one of the fire escapes at the far end of the building. The Mercedes was a bigger car than he was used to but after a couple of attempts he managed to manoeuvre it neatly into the gap and then reversed it tight up against the wall. Even if someone wanted to break into the boot they wouldn't be able to without moving the car first. As he turned off the engine and was about to get out he deliberately put the CDs that he'd taken from *Seedy CDs* into the front glove compartment. Sooner or later the police were going to turn up and that should confuse them nicely. Craven's fifth rule of fieldwork. *If you're being followed, leave plenty of diversions.*

Finally, he picked up the laptop and then locked the door manually with the key, double-checking as he did so that the car alarm hadn't set. The last thing he wanted was to run the risk of it being triggered accidentally or by the battery running down. He wanted Colley's body to go undiscovered for as long as possible. He took the car park ticket with him and dropped it, together with the car keys, down a road drain just outside the stairwell on the way out. All he had to do now was walk the short distance along the dual carriageway into Ashford town centre and then get back to his own car, which he'd parked a couple of streets away from Colley's house. It wouldn't take him more than half an hour in total. Anyway, it was a nice morning. Some exercise and a bit of fresh air was just what he needed.

The walk back to Ashford gave him time to clear his head and think about what he was going to do next. Ideally he wanted to check out of the hotel and drive straight back to London there and then. He could be back home by the middle of the afternoon. As far as he was concerned the job had been completed and with the minimum of fuss. Buchanan's brief had been clear. Recover the laptop and deal with anybody who had accessed its contents – which was exactly what he had done. There were a couple of casualties along the way of course but they weren't really serious. Pitbull had been frightened more than anything else and even the kid in the record shop had only suffered a broken finger and a couple of black eyes. Still, neither of them were going to be running to the police, so there weren't any loose ends to be tidied up as far as he was concerned.

The two kids in the pub, Jamie Collins and Gary Parkes would probably remember his face and might be able to work out what had happened, especially once Colley's body was discovered, but it would all just be supposition. They didn't really know anything. No, now that the laptop had been found it was better to stop and let the dust settle. It was only Buchanan's request to sort out the inquisitive nephew that was preventing him from packing up and getting back to London as soon as possible. Pity. He could have made it back in time for a Friday night drink down at the Lamb & Flag on the Whitechapel Road. Still, Buchanan was paying his expenses and it wasn't going to take long. At most, it meant one more day and another night at the hotel.

Craven decided to drop the laptop off in his hotel room for safe keeping, so it was nearly half-past one by the time he eventually got to Appleden. As usual the village was quiet and he took care to park outside the antique shop and walk in the last few hundred yards. A strange car pulling up outside one of the cottages was bound to get noticed – particularly a cottage where there had been a burglary and a murder within the last few days.

He hadn't gone more than a few yards when he spotted the inquisitive nephew and his neighbour walking towards him, both of them obviously off to The Chequers for a lunchtime drink. Craven never ceased to be amazed by the speed and power of the human brain and particularly its ability to judge a combination of time and speed and distance. He could always remember standing on the corner of Leadenhall Street, watching the endless stream of Brokers crossing the main road to and from the Lloyd's building, normally weighed down with huge files of paper and always in a hurry to get to their next appointment. You could see them dashing up Lime Street, taking a quick glance right and left at the traffic moving in both directions and then computing in a millisecond the speed and trajectory which they needed to cross the main road without being hit. It was the same computation by which he realised that they were going to arrive at *The Chequers* at exactly the same time. The pub was roughly equidistant between them and they were both walking at about the same pace. He thought for a moment about slowing down or speeding up but it would have looked too obvious. He got to the front door of the pub a matter of seconds before Neil and Tom and held it open to let them go in first.

'After you gents, you look as though your need is greater than mine.'

Neil and Tom both grinned at the friendly stranger holding the door open. 'Thanks very much,' said Tom, wiping his feet on the doormat as he went in. 'That's very kind of you.'

The three of them trouped into the bar and as usual, most of the regulars said hello to Tom and a few of them nodded in acknowledgement to Neil. Nobody took any notice of Craven. Tom and Neil peeled off towards the end of the bar which was full of locals and Craven wandered up to the other end, which was quieter and less crowded.

'Right lad, what are you having?' asked Tom, putting his hand in his back pocket to get out his wallet.

Neil pulled a face, clearly undecided about what to have. 'Not sure Tom, I don't usually drink at lunchtime. What are you having?'

'A pint of Harveys, followed by another one straight away probably. Just what the doctor ordered after four hours in the back garden. It was quite hot out there today.' Tom lifted his cap and wiped the back of his hand across the top of his forehead. It was definitely warming up for the weekend.

'Okay. I'll have the same then,' relented Neil. 'Mind you, I'll have to see if I can get a sandwich or something, I haven't had anything to eat yet. I'll be falling asleep this afternoon if I try and keep up with you.'

They both stood at the bar for a while, chatting to the locals while they waited for their pints to be served and for the landlord to rustle up a cheese and tomato sandwich. Craven ordered a pint of Guinness and then sat down at a table in the centre of the bar, far enough from the crowd not to look suspicious but near enough to the inquisitive nephew and his next-door neighbour to hear most of what was being said.

In the event, the conversation was very ordinary and in truth, he wasn't that surprised. He wasn't really sure why Buchanan was so worried. The laptop had been recovered and as far as he was concerned, the nephew didn't even know it existed, let alone what was on it. Frankly, he seemed harmless compared to most of the other characters that Craven had met in the last 48 hours. Still, Buchanan was the paymaster, so it was simply a question of biding his time and then picking the right moment. The old boy from next door couldn't be with him all afternoon.

Craven drank his Guinness slowly whilst Tom tucked into several pints of Harveys and Neil struggled valiantly to keep up with him. The sandwich eventually arrived and they decided to leave the crowd at the bar and also find a table. There were plenty to choose from. Only the one occupied by Craven and one other was taken. By half-past two, Neil was downing the last dregs of his fourth pint whilst Tom stood beside him, patiently waiting with his own empty glass, ready to get another round in.

'Think this better be my last one Tom.' said Neil, trying to contain an involuntary belch and stop his words from slurring. 'I think five pints in a linchtime – lunchtime is about my limit.'

Tom grinned. 'Nonsense – big strapping lad like you. Besides, I should think you need a couple of drinks after being stuck indoors all morning.'

Neil nodded. He couldn't disagree with that. After all the distractions of the last few days he'd decided to knuckle down and try and finish sorting out Aunt Hilary's paperwork. He'd spent all morning sifting through the stuff in the bureau and by lunchtime was in need of a break and a chance to get out of the house. He was delighted when Tom had knocked on the door with the offer of a quick lunchtime beer. Neil smiled to himself. A quiet pint was more what he had in mind but he should have known better. He gazed across at Tom who was standing at the bar, getting into a lively conversation with some of the locals about the breathalyser and its impact on the country pub trade. There was lots of laughter and animated gestures and it looked as though Tom was settling himself in for an afternoon session.

'There was one thing I meant to ask you.' said Neil as Tom came back from the bar carrying two more pints of bitter. 'Do you ever remember Aunt Hilary mentioning somebody called Adam Saxby?'

Tom put the glasses on the table and sat back down in the chair, picking up his tobacco tin and lighter with an almost Pavlovian response. He shook his head as he pulled out a cigarette paper and started to fill it with tobacco. 'Adam Saxby? No, don't think so. Doreen's probably a better person to ask than me, but I don't remember her mentioning anybody of that name. Never heard of him I'm afraid.'

Craven was still listening attentively and made a mental note. The name didn't mean anything to him either but he could always check it out later.

'Or somebody called Daniels,' continued Neil, 'possibly from Cheltenham.'

'She used to watch Paul Daniels on the telly sometimes,' chuckled Tom, not taking the conversation at all seriously, 'but I'm not sure he came from Cheltenham.'

Neil grinned. Maybe the questions were a bit silly, but what did Tom expect after four pints of beer? 'Or Jean Pettipher,' he persisted, 'possibly from London?'

Tom lit his cigarette and then shook his head again, blowing a thin stream of smoke into the centre of the bar. 'Sorry lad. Never heard of any of them. Doreen might have done but not me.'

Craven drank the last of his Guinness and put the glass silently back on the table. No wonder Buchanan was worried. *Vector* had been established more than fifty years ago but most of the people in the Security Services barely knew it existed, let alone the names of anybody that worked there. Some of the field agents were so undercover that nobody knew their names. Nobody except Buchanan of course. And his PA, obviously. Jean Pettipher had worked for Buchanan for almost twenty years and with the exception of her boss, knew more about internal security than anybody else in the country. She saw the underbelly of the establishment on a daily basis and more importantly, she knew where the bodies were buried. What Craven couldn't work out was how the harmless nephew knew her name. And who the hell were Adam Saxby and Daniels? He hadn't heard of either of them but he knew there and then that they were names that he ought to check out.

Tom and Neil were by now halfway down their fifth pints and the combination of too much alcohol and not enough food was taking its effect on both of them. Neil was starting to feel decidedly light-headed and had started swaying slightly in his chair. Even Tom was beginning to feel the effects of too much sun and too many pints. 'Did she really watch Paul Daniels?' slurred Neil, frowning with a sort of earnest, confused expression.

Tom put on a funny, high-pitched voice. 'Not a lot,' he squeaked and then the pair of them collapsed into uncontrolled, childish giggling. It was the first time that Neil had laughed so much in ages.

Craven drank the last of his Guinness and put the glass silently back on the table. This was ridiculous. Even if he managed to get the nephew on his own for five minutes he was going to be too drunk to take any notice of anything. There was no point in hanging around this afternoon. He was going to have to come back and visit him later when he'd sobered up a bit.

'Anyway, talking of London...' said Tom, taking another large swig of beer.

'Were we?' interrupted Neil, still frowning and swaying in his chair. He started to giggle again.

Tom grinned at him. 'Yes, you asked me about somebody called June Pettipher. "Probably from London," you said.'

Neil tipped the glass to his mouth and drank the last of his pint, banging the glass on the table with a flourish and a bit more loudly than he intended. All of a sudden his actions seemed rather laboured and in slow motion. 'Jean Pettipher. *Jean*, not June.'

'Quite right,' replied Tom, not really listening and also finishing off his pint. 'Anyway, as I was saying, talking of London. Did you know that there's only one station on the London Underground that doesn't have any of the letters from the word *Mackerel* in it?'

Neil tried to stop himself from swaying for a moment and looked at Tom across the table, not sure whether to believe him or not.

'Are you sure? *Mackerel?*

'Absolutely. Every station on the London Underground has at least one letter from the word *Mackerel* in it – except one.'

'Really? How could anybody think up a question like that?' Neil started to run through some of the underground stations in his mind, *Charing Cross, Oxford Circus, Victoria, Tottenham Court Road* but they all had letters from the word mackerel in them and he'd drunk too much alcohol to give it any serious thought. 'What's the answer then?'

Tom tapped the side of his nose with his forefinger in a silent, knowing gesture. 'You'll have to work it out lad. Find yourself a map of the underground and work it out.'

'Well here's one for you then,' said Neil, suddenly remembering an obscure fact that he'd read somewhere. 'Did you know that there isn't one word in the English language that rhymes with the word *Orange?*'

Tom grinned. 'Oh, someone told me that years ago,' he said dismissively, 'but you must have heard that they've now worked out that it's not actually true. Didn't you know that if you say the word *Gullible* really slowly, it rhymes with the word O*range?*'

Neil looked at him, again not sure whether to believe him or not. 'Really? Are you sure?'

'Absolutely. Try it. Say it really slowly and you'll see.'

Tom looked across the table and grinned as Neil tried to pronounce the word *Gullible* several times, very slowly, syllable by syllable, whilst still swaying in his chair and with the same serious, confused expression on his face.

Even Craven had to laugh. The pair of them were just too comical for words.

TWENTY-TWO

'So, where are we John? Update me on what's been happening.' Anderson unlocked the bottom right-hand drawer of his desk and pulled out a half-bottle of scotch and two tumblers. There was no question of him asking Garrick whether he wanted a drink or not, or indeed of giving Garrick the option to refuse. It was the end of a long, hard week and sharing a glass of finest malt whisky with a senior colleague was an established ritual, not just under Anderson's command but in CID offices up and down the country. He unscrewed the cap and poured a large slug of scotch into both glasses, passing one over to Garrick who was sitting opposite him across the desk.

Garrick took the tumbler and then took a small sip, more out of politeness than with any real enthusiasm. He had never been a great fan of whisky – or of any other spirit for that matter. He much preferred a pint of beer or a glass a wine. Also, it was only half-past five in the afternoon, which was much too early for him to start drinking. He checked his watch as the thought went through his mind. Some of the team would be on their way out by now. Most of them were working either Saturday or Sunday and some of them, like Garrick, had volunteered to work both days. It had been a tough week but today had been particularly productive and Garrick was keen for the whole team to get away on time and enjoy a well deserved Friday evening. There weren't going to be too many opportunities for everyone to have a night off but he knew that it was important to let them recharge their batteries before the long haul ahead. Besides, "sharpen the saw" was what Anderson had said, so that was exactly what he was doing.

'Well, it's a been a long week Sir,' replied Garrick, putting the tumbler on the desk and resolving not to pick it up again, 'but I think we've made some positive progress – particularly today.'

'What's the latest on Colley?' asked Anderson, swirling the whisky in his glass and savouring the moment before he finally tasted it.

'Well, we managed to contact his wife fairly easily – she's a teaching assistant up at Danehill. As far as Mrs. Colley was concerned her husband was at home when she left after breakfast this morning and she assumed that he'd be at the shop all day today. To be honest she didn't seem unduly worried about

190

him until we told her that we'd run a GPS trace on his mobile phone, which indicated that it was still in the house. Apparently, the likelihood of him going out without his mobile is almost unthinkable. It was at that point that she came home and let us in to search the property.'

'Who went up there?' asked Anderson, keen to get a picture in his mind of everything that had been going on.

'Andy Cooper and Steph Page. Colley was nowhere to be found and his car was also missing. Needless to say, there was also no sign of the laptop. Steph found his mobile in a suit jacket, still hanging over the back of a chair from the night before – but more importantly she also found this.' Garrick suddenly produced a plastic evidence bag and put it on the desk, sliding it across towards Anderson. 'It was switched off and therefore not traceable under GPS but it has the same SIM card that was used to call Stuart Richmond.'

Anderson picked up the bag and turned it over a couple of times to look at the contents; a small, modern handset, probably with a camera and all the latest features.

'It means that not only have we identified Colley as the receiver of the stolen laptop but also as the caller who rang Richmond wanting to speak to him about Teleios. It links him unequivocally to the murder.'

Anderson gave Garrick an impressive nod. This certainly was progress. 'So where is he?' he asked, sliding the mobile back across the desk.

'We don't know at the moment. Our working hypothesis is that he's done a runner. Either that or someone else got to him before we did.'

'Why do you think someone else is looking for him?' Anderson's frown indicated that he was struggling to keep up with the line of thinking.

'Ray Holland.'

Anderson shook his head, still none the wiser.

'Ray Holland runs a second-hand record shop called *Seedy CDs* in the town centre. It's actually in the same road as Colley's electrical shop. Like Colley, Holland bought some of the stolen items from Richmond's burglary. We went out to pay him a visit this afternoon and like Colley's shop, *Seedy CDs* was closed.'

'That's a co-incidence isn't it?'

'Exactly. We eventually managed to track down the owner who then directed us towards Ray Holland, who is the young kid who basically runs the shop on his behalf.'

'So why was it closed?'

'The kid's off sick. It looks like someone's beaten him up and whoever it was has done a really professional job.'

Anderson pulled a face. 'Could be unrelated I suppose?'

Garrick shook his head. 'The kid's not talking. Says he had an accident on his bike. I'd say he's frightened to death. Besides, I don't believe in co-incidences. I think someone paid him a visit because they were looking for Colley.'

'So basically, we still need to find Colley and the laptop.'

'Absolutely. There's something on that laptop that Richmond didn't want us to know about and which he was prepared to pay a lot of money to get back – which means finding it is key.'

Anderson picked up his glass again and swirled the contents in a circular motion on the desk. 'Teleios presumably. Any progress on that?'

Garrick shook his head again. 'No, nothing I'm afraid. Not a thing.'

'What about Hilary Russell. Any progress there?'

Garrick took another sip of scotch. He suddenly felt the need for a bit of Dutch courage. He genuinely felt that they were making significant progress but every time he went through the details of it with Anderson, it always sounded less convincing. It was barely 24 hours since Bob Hughes had found the jewellery in Canterbury and in the space of a day they'd interviewed Howard Thorpe, arrested Jamie Collins, identified Graham Colley, talked to Gary Parkes, found Ray Holland and worked out all of the key information relating to the laptop. But as he was trying to explain it to Anderson, he knew it all sounded inconclusive.

'No real progress on Hilary Russell Sir,' he said almost apologetically, 'although interestingly, Alan Wyatt has done some further tests on the *Fentanyl* and has identified the type used in Appleden as being of a street variety, rather than a pure pharmaceutical version. Apparently the substance had traces of heroin and talcum powder in it.'

Anderson raised his eyebrows in obvious surprise. 'Really? Who on earth around here is going to have access to that sort of stuff?'

Garrick shrugged. 'London's only an hour away Sir. It's not that improbable really.'

Anderson shook his head in disbelief. He didn't know what the world was coming to. Hard drugs normally found on the streets of Detroit turning up in a Kentish village. It beggared belief. 'Anything else John?'

'Just one thing Sir. Alan Wyatt found nine pairs of stun-gun marks on Stuart Richmond's body. Excessive to say the least.'

'Excessive?'

Garrick nodded. 'A single blast from a stun-gun would have rendered Richmond useless for up to a minute at a time. Depending on the voltage it could have been longer. Some people are so disabled that they lose all control of their bodily functions. Whoever killed him wouldn't have needed to have used it more than a couple of times in order to push the money down his throat. In fact once might have been enough.'

'So why nine?'

'Good question. Whoever it was put him through a lot of pain before he died.'

'Colley presumably?'

'Exactly. We know that he telephoned Richmond about Teleios, so it's reasonable to assume that it was him that went to the house.'

Anderson finished his scotch and poured himself another small measure as the telephone on his desk started to ring. Cheryl had gone home for the day so he was having to answer his own calls.

'Anderson.'

Garrick put the glass back on the desk. He really didn't like the stuff. He looked across at his boss and for a moment thought about making an exit. They'd just about finished and if it was going to be a long call he might as well shoot off. Then he decided to wait. Anderson might not be happy about him disappearing and anyway, listening to one end of a telephone conversation was always intriguing.

'When was this?' Anderson suddenly leant forward and picked up a pen and started scribbling some notes on a pad in front of him. Garrick instantly picked up the sense of urgency but couldn't tell what was going on. It wasn't the Chief Constable – he knew that much. Anderson always sat upright and fiddled nervously with his tie when he was talking to him.

'So who was it?' There was another pause as information was being relayed down the phone and Anderson scribbled furiously. 'Have you told anybody else yet?' Garrick leant forward and twisted his neck, trying to read Anderson's notes upside down, but the handwriting was too untidy for him to make any sense of it.

'And you're sure it's Teleios?' He looked up and stared intently at Garrick across the desk. Garrick frowned back at him. *What's going on?*

'DCI Garrick. John Garrick. He's with me now.' Anderson stopped writing and relaxed back into his chair. Obviously the conversation was about to finish. 'Okay. I'll get him to call you back. Five minutes.'

Anderson put the phone down and gave Garrick a knowing look. 'You'd better get your team back in John. There's been another murder.'

*

Neil didn't know what time it was when he woke up but it had gone dark. It took him a couple of seconds to realise where he was and then suddenly it dawned on him. He was in the front room of the cottage. He must have fallen asleep when he'd got back from the pub. And then the next thing that struck him, almost in the same moment, was that he had a blinding hangover. His neck was aching and his arm was numb because of the awkward angle that he'd been sleeping in the chair. But his head was absolutely hammering. A real grade 'A' hangover. One of the worst he could remember. And his mouth tasted like the bottom of a birdcage – he was dying for a glass of water. That was the last time he was going to go out drinking at lunchtime with Tom Webster. He shook his head in disbelief. Fancy drinking five pints of beer on an empty stomach. Or was it six?

Neil groaned as he moved gingerly out of the chair and stood up, stretching out his arms to try and get his joints and muscles to work properly. Everything ached. Even his teeth hurt. That was it. From now on he was only going to drink at weekends. Tom Webster was leading him astray. He was just at the point of going into the kitchen to get something to drink when he heard a noise outside and realised that something must have woken him up.

For some reason, he felt instantly that the noise was furtive, unwelcome, sinister. As though someone was deliberately trying not to make a noise. A faint rustle on the ground, a footstep moving stealthily over a paving stone. And then having made the noise, suddenly stopping and making no noise at all. He froze where he was standing and listened as hard as he could, his heart pounding in his chest and his breathing getting faster and faster. Was the person outside doing exactly the same? Nothing. The village was as quiet as a grave. He stood there for several seconds, motionless and listening to silence. He started to breathe through his mouth, breathing though his nose was making too much noise. He was just starting to think that he had imagined it all when he jumped. He heard it again, someone walking quietly down the side of the house towards the back door.

Neil moved out of the front room and tiptoed slowly and silently down the hall and into the kitchen. He thought about putting the lights on to let whoever it was know that he was at home – but for some reason decided that wasn't a good idea. Besides, if he switched the lights on he wouldn't be able to see what was going on outside. At the moment, although it was dark he could still make out some shapes and movement. It was then that he saw the silhouette pass the kitchen window on its way towards the back door. His pulse was still racing and he was starting to sweat. Even from just a fleeting glimpse of a dark outline, Neil could tell that it wasn't anyone that he knew. Male, certainly but not anybody that he recognised.

He tiptoed over to the worktop behind the back door and waited, his heart beating even louder and faster than before. He could feel it pounding in his ears. Was someone trying to break in? Again, there were several seconds of silence as if the person outside was also frozen, listening and waiting. And then the handle on the kitchen door turned. Neil gasped under his breath.

He couldn't remember whether he'd locked the back door or not. He looked around him for something to pick up, something to protect himself. There were plenty of knives but he was scared of using those. He wanted something that he could swing. Something large and heavy. He picked up a frying pan. A huge, old cast-iron thing which Aunt Hilary must have had for donkey's years. It had a long wooden handle and was blackened with years of use. But it was also as heavy as hell. If anybody was coming through the door, this was what they were going to get.

The door handle twisted a couple of times but didn't open. The tension was unbearable. Neil thought that he was going to faint with the shock. And then he heard a scuffing noise, as if someone was playing around with the lock. Suddenly he saw the edge of a thin plastic card, like a credit card, poking through the gap between the lock and the door frame, and then a second later the door popped open. He started to hyperventilate and then the adrenalin began pumping through his body, primed to attack. He held the frying pan up behind him, ready to swing it as soon as anybody came through the door. The weight of it was making his arms ache.

He didn't have to wait long. A second after the door opened, a head and then the full body of the intruder came through the door. Neil unleashed the frying pan as if his life depended on it. He didn't know that he possessed so much strength. A vicious, wielding, hammer of a blow, driven with all his force and with as much follow through as he could manage. The power of the swing nearly took him off his feet and he let out a blood-curdling howl as the bottom of the frying pan smacked the guy firmly on the side of the head. *Take that you bastard!*

Matt heard the movement a millisecond before the frying pan hit him. It was like lying at the bottom of a lift shaft watching a ton of moving metal hurtling towards him. He looked at Neil for a second with a glazed, confused expression, *what did you want to go and do that for?* before he slumped into an unconscious heap onto the kitchen floor.

Neil dropped the frying pan with a clatter and then bent over, hands on knees, emotionally exhausted and totally out of breath, just as the second person walked through the back door and into the kitchen. Neil looked up at him and gasped in surprise – for the second time in as many minutes.

'Hello Neil,' said Chris, grinning wickedly, 'glad to see you've got everything under control.'

TWENTY-THREE

Neil and Chris propped Matt up against one of the kitchen units and then unloosened his tie to try and make him more comfortable. The pair of them managed to get him semi-upright, still sitting on the floor but with his back slumped up against the wall and his head resting to one side against one of the cupboards. Neil had been worried about moving him at all but Matt had starting groaning almost as soon as he'd hit the floor, so any loss of consciousness had only been for a few seconds.

'Do you think we ought to call an ambulance?' asked Neil, suddenly realising that neither he nor Chris knew anything about first-aid. Matt still had his eyes closed and seemed to be in a lot of pain.

'No, I think he's all right – I think he's coming round now. He's going to have a massive headache though.' Chris was looking down at the lump on the side of Matt's head which was getting larger by the second. Like something out of a *Tom & Jerry* cartoon.

'Good. Serves him right. We'd better call the police then.'

Chris stared at Neil in disbelief and then started to laugh. 'What do you mean? He is the police!'

Neil looked down at Matt and then at Chris again, the significance of what he had just done beginning to sink in. 'Oh God, I could have killed him!'

Chris was still grinning. 'Well I don't think you're out of the woods yet mate. I think assaulting a police officer is still a criminal offence. Custodial sentence probably.'

Neil ignored Chris's teasing and squatted down next to Matt to inspect the damage more closely. Surprisingly, there wasn't any blood, but the lump on the side of his head was still getting larger and looked really nasty. He didn't like the look of it at all. 'How do you know he's the police?' he asked, suddenly turning round and looking up at Chris.

'I met him on the front doorstep. I'd been ringing the bell for ages when he turned up. He said he'd come to see you to try something out. "Test out a theory," he said…'

Neil put his head in his hands and groaned.

'…anyway, you weren't answering the door and there were no lights on so we assumed you were out. I told him that I was visiting for the weekend and that I needed to get in. That's when he suggested going round the back to try the back door.'

Neil shook his head in disbelief. *Oh God, what have I done?*

'Anyway, why weren't you answering the door? And why were all the lights off?'

Neil stood up and started to look embarrassed. 'I fell asleep. I didn't hear anything.'

'You fell asleep? What, at seven o'clock in the evening? What's the matter, is all this fresh country air getting to you or something?'

Neil waved his hand away in a dismissive gesture. He really didn't want to talk about it. 'It's a long story – I'll tell you later.'

Chris studied him carefully. He always knew when Neil was trying to hide something but for the moment he let it pass. Matt was opening his eyes and was starting to come round. He looked up at Neil and Chris and then groaned, the realisation of what had happened suddenly kicking in. His vision was still blurred and his head hurt like hell.

'Do you want me to call you an ambulance?' asked Neil, squatting down next to Matt again. He was still concerned about the bang on the head and the fact that Matt had been knocked out, albeit for only a few seconds.

Matt shook his head, very slowly but very deliberately. The last thing he wanted to do was spend a Friday evening in casualty. He knew what that was going to be like. Waiting for hours on end, surrounded by drunks and yobs and then eventually being told to go home and take a couple of Paracetamol. He couldn't think of anything worse. He tried to pull himself up to demonstrate that he was alright but quickly slumped back down again when he started to feel dizzy. It eventually took Neil and Chris about five minutes to move him into the front room and get him settled into the armchair. Neil went off to make him a cup of tea while Chris sat with him to make sure that he was okay. Matt didn't say much at all. His head was thumping and his vision was still blurred, so he closed his eyes and sat still for a while and said nothing. Maybe just resting for ten minutes or so would help.

Neil returned with the tea and after about twenty minutes Matt started to look and feel a bit better. His head was still thumping, but at least he wasn't feeling so groggy.

'I'm really sorry,' apologised Neil for the umpteenth time, 'I thought you were the person who broke in on Sunday. I thought you'd come back for some reason.'

Matt forced a weak smile. 'Don't worry about it – it's my fault. Stupid of me.'

198

'What were you doing? Chris said that you were trying something out. Testing a theory?'

Matt nodded and then screwed up his face as the pain in his head started thumping even more. Neil recognised the symptoms only too well and disappeared into the kitchen, returning with a glass of water and some painkillers. 'So what was the theory?' he asked, handing over the water and tablets.

Matt swallowed a couple of painkillers and passed the glass back to Neil, nodding in thanks. 'I can't really say anything, I haven't even spoken to my boss about it yet.'

'I guess we could always ring him up and ask him.' said Chris, trying to apply some gentle pressure. 'I'm sure he'd be happy to explain why you were breaking into the cottage...'

Matt smiled ruefully to himself. The fact that he'd been attacked and injured was neither here nor there. Neil was simply protecting himself. Not unreasonable given that his Aunt had been murdered only a few days before. Explaining to Garrick why he had broken into private property was not going to be pretty. Definitely not a good career move. The last thing he needed was it being reported. Maybe he could persuade them not to say anything.

'...or I guess we could just hit him again with the frying pan,' said Chris, looking at Neil and giving him a wink. *Bernstein and Woodward.*

'I suppose if I tell you what I was doing,' volunteered Matt, 'then we won't need to report anything about this evening – either about me breaking in or about you assaulting a police officer.'

Neil and Chris exchanged a quick glance. That suited them fine. They hadn't lost anything and getting information about the police enquiry could only be to their advantage. 'I think that's a good idea,' said Chris, holding out his hand to properly introduce himself. 'I think we might be able to help each other. Chris Fleming.'

Matt shook his hand in return. 'Matt Isaacs. Detective Constable.'

Neil and Matt also exchanged a formal introduction. 'So what's the theory then Matt?' asked Chris, sitting down on the sofa underneath the window.

'Have you found out what was stolen yet?' asked Matt, looking at Neil.

Neil shook his head. 'No, no idea. Don't think I'll ever know. I don't know what was in here in the first place.'

'Neither do I,' replied Matt, 'but I think I know exactly what was stolen.'

'Really? What?'

'Nothing.'

'Nothing?' Both Neil and Chris spoke at the same time and then looked at each other. It wasn't the answer that either of them was expecting.

'Exactly. Nothing. And the reason nothing was taken, was because there was never a burglary in the first place.'

Neil was by now looking totally confused. 'You're going to have to explain that in words of one syllable. I don't understand. Of course there was a burglary.'

Matt shook his head. 'I don't think there was. And breaking in through your back door with my credit card has just proved it.'

'You'd better start from the beginning,' said Chris, also not following Matt's line of reasoning.

Matt picked up the glass of water again and took another sip. 'Last Sunday somebody broke into this cottage and murdered your Aunt. What they wanted us to believe was that she either died of natural causes or as a result of a burglary gone wrong. What they also wanted us to believe was that they broke into the cottage by busting their way in through the back door.'

'Well they did didn't they?' interrupted Neil. 'I saw all the mess. The carpenter had to put a new door frame in.'

Again, Matt shook his head. 'That's what they wanted you to believe. We know from forensic tests that the first thing that they did when they got inside was to close all of the upstairs windows. The only explanation for that, is that they were trying to keep everything as quiet as possible. That doesn't make any sense if they broke in through the back door. They would have already made too much noise getting in.'

Neil and Chris exchanged another glace. They were still struggling to keep up.

'Okay,' said Matt. 'I'll keep it simple and get straight to the point. Whoever murdered your Aunt the other night broke into the cottage by using a credit card to spring the lock on the back door. They broke in silently because they couldn't run the risk of waking her up, or of waking up the neighbours. They crept upstairs, closed all the windows, murdered your Aunt in bed and then carried her downstairs and lay her on the floor in the hall, just inside the front door.'

'But what about the burglary?' asked Neil. 'All the stuff overturned in here and in the dining room? They made a hell of a mess.'

Matt nodded. 'Yes they did – but they did it on purpose simply to make it look like a burglary. That's why they moved the body after they killed her. And that's why they busted the doorframe on the way out – not on the way in.'

'But why would someone want to make it look like a burglary?' asked Chris. 'I don't understand. Why would someone want to murder his Aunt if it wasn't a burglary?'

Matt pulled a face. 'To try and conceal the real reason why they killed her. I can't say more than that I'm afraid.'

There was a moment of silence and then Neil gave him a knowing look. 'It's Teleios isn't it?'

It was Matt's turn to look surprised. As far as he was concerned the details about Teleios had not been made public and he couldn't work out how Neil even knew the name, let alone that it was the probable reason for his Aunt's death. Neil could see the puzzlement in Matt's face. 'I drove Doreen Webster in to see your boss yesterday morning and she mentioned it on the way back. I put two and two together.'

Matt nodded slowly, trying to work out what else Neil already knew. 'Do you know what Teleios means?'

Neil shook his head. 'No, do you?'

Matt likewise shook his head. 'No, but I do know one thing. I spent a whole morning the other day trawling through all the movements and phone calls of Stuart Richmond when what we should have been doing was going through exactly the same process, but on your Aunt. If Doreen Webster had a conversation with her about Teleios on the Thursday, then she must have done something or spoken to somebody before she was murdered three days later on the Sunday. We've been concentrating on the wrong person.'

Neil and Chris exchanged another look. 'Actually,' said Chris, 'we know who she spoke to. Like I said, I think we might be able to help each other.'

Matt suddenly forgot all about his headache and leant forward, eager to hear what Chris had to say next. Everyone at the station had been concentrating on Richmond and on finding the laptop and they all seemed to have forgotten about Hilary Russell. To everybody else the case seemed straightforward but as far as Matt was concerned, some things still didn't make sense – and in his experience, if you applied enough logic you could normally work them out. Now it looked as if a couple of other people were on the same wavelength.

Chris smiled at him and then nodded towards Neil. 'I was following up on some research that Neil did yesterday. I've got the details in my bag, in the car. I'll go and get them.'

Chris left Neil to explain about the phone calls and went outside, hitting the remote control to unlock his car which was parked in front of the cottage. It didn't take him more than thirty seconds to unlock the boot, take out his bag and then re-lock the car again. He was thinking about the murder and a possible front-page story and then he smiled as he thought about Neil, attacking a CID officer with a cast-iron frying pan. You couldn't make it up. He didn't notice the saloon car parked thirty yards up the lane, or the man, smoking a cigarette and watching every movement at the cottage.

Craven tossed the cigarette butt out of the window and then fired up the ignition. This was a waste of time. At lunchtime the nephew had been with his next-door neighbour and now he had a visitor who was going to be there all weekend. There wasn't a hope in hell of being able to get near him. He waited for Chris to go back inside and then pulled the car out and drove off towards the hotel, resigned to the fact that he wouldn't be able to carry out Buchanan's last instruction. He would have to telephone him in the morning and let him know that the nephew was just too difficult to get close to. It wasn't critical. Craven knew that the most important thing was that the laptop had been recovered and that the only person who had accessed it had been dealt with. Mission accomplished. The rest he could leave.

By the time he got back to the hotel he was hungry and needed a drink. He hadn't eaten all day and other than a pint of Guinness at *The Chequers*, he hadn't drunk anything either. He thought about going straight into the restaurant and having an early dinner, but he was also impatient to get back to his room and see if he could get into Richmond's laptop. In the end he decided to order some room service. That way he could get on with things and eat at the same time. Besides, there was nothing worse than eating on your own in a restaurant. Drinking in a bar by yourself was okay but eating on your own was just awful.

He ordered steak and chips and a bottle of red wine and then started to set up the laptop. It took a couple of minutes for the operating system to go through its start-up sequence and then eventually the front page popped up, predictably with a password prompt. Craven looked at the screen for several seconds, cursing himself that he hadn't thought to ask Colley whether the laptop had been password protected. Colley would have told him anything he wanted to know, but it was a bit late now. Craven knew enough about technology to find his way around someone's files and directories, but he wasn't a computer expect by any means. Hacking into a laptop was another thing altogether. Unless he could guess the password he didn't have a hope of getting any further.

He tried typing in a few words but none of them worked. He didn't even know if the password was originally put on there by Richmond or whether it was a later one put on by Colley. Trying to guess what it might be was impossible and after a couple of minutes he gave up and closed everything down. Maybe Buchanan would tell him once the job was finished. Then again, perhaps it didn't really matter. In a few weeks time he'd be working on another job and Teleios would just be a distant memory. Maybe it was time to draw a line under everything and move on. He'd just finished putting the laptop into the bottom of his bag when there was a knock on the door. It looked like one of the benefits of ordering room service early was that you didn't have to wait too long for the food to arrive.

Craven opened the door and found himself staring at the friendly receptionist. She was carrying a tray with his order but that wasn't what immediately struck him. She was wearing the same crisp, white blouse as on the previous evening but on this occasion he could tell that she wasn't wearing anything underneath. The material was semi-transparent and he could see the outline of her breasts, firm and pert, pressed up against the fabric. The tight, black skirt was also incredibly short and her legs, accentuated by the high, stiletto heels seemed to go on forever. The overall effect, together with the long, blonde hair and the brilliant smile that she flashed him as he opened the door was of one very hot and expectant nineteen year old.

'Hi, you ordered room service. Where would you like it?' Her voice was breathless and Craven could tell that she was pumped up and excited. Her hands were trembling as she tottered passed him and bent over to put the tray down on the table in the middle of the room. 'Gosh, it's warm in here,' she said, nervously running her fingers through her hair and then fumbling to undo another button at the top of her blouse. Craven looked at her for a moment and couldn't work out what was going on. Was this some sort of schoolgirl bet? She looked as though she was working through the summer holidays – except of course the summer holidays had finished. He couldn't believe what he was seeing, but the signals were unmistakeable. If she was trying to get a reaction, it was working.

'Now, is there anything else I can get you?' Her breathing was becoming even more rapid and as if to convey the innuendo further, she circled her right hand lightly over the curve of her left breast. She murmured softly as the nipple stiffened instantly. Craven saw her pinch it gently between her thumb and middle finger and then close her eyes for just a second. A droplet of perspiration trickled slowly the down the nape of her neck.

'I see you brought two glasses,' said Craven, nodding towards the tray and then staring back at the girl.

'I didn't know whether you had anybody with you. I brought an extra one just in case.'

Craven shook his head. 'Just me I'm afraid. Seems a shame to waste it though.' He picked up the bottle and poured out two glasses of wine, passing one over to her. 'I don't even know your name.'

'Sophie.'

Craven picked up his glass and took a sip, watching her intently as she gulped hers down greedily, almost as though she was thirsty and drinking a glass of water. The wine disappeared in a couple of large mouthfuls and the effect of the alcohol on her already heightened state was almost instant – a heady mix of excitement and intoxication. He picked up the bottle and refilled her glass, conscious that they were standing about as close as you could get without actually touching. He could feel her breath as he poured the wine. There was almost a heat coming off her.

Sophie gulped down the second glass. Her world was becoming warm and blurred and fuzzy but at the same time her nerve endings were tingling, as though they were on the outside of her body. A shudder ran deliciously through her as she felt Craven trace his fingertips lightly across the contours of her body. She closed her eyes and let out a soft moan, gently biting her bottom lip. Again, she could feel her nipples stiffen, protruding hard up against the taut, white cotton of her blouse. She opened her eyes and stared at him as he slowly undid the buttons and stroked the back of his hand across her belly button and then down towards her abdomen, breathing in the scent of her body. She arched her hips towards him in an involuntary movement.

Craven glanced down at her empty glass, resting on the table. 'Would you like another drink?'

Sophie moved her hand and touched him between the legs, giving him a gentle squeeze. She smiled. 'No, I think I ought to eat something first.'

Craven closed his eyes and groaned as she dropped to her knees and started to undo his belt, her mouth only inches away from touching him. *Uncomplicated, clean and no repercussions.*

TWENTY-FOUR

'Bloody hell Shylock, what have you been up to?' The whole of the CID room looked up as Matt came through the door, curious to see what Andy was talking about.

Matt smiled grimly and gently touched the lump on the side of his head. Even he was surprised at how bad it looked when he'd got up this morning. The bruising had started to come out and there was no doubt about it – it looked as though he'd been in a serious punch-up. He hadn't slept that well either, mostly because of the pain, so all in all he was looking decidedly rough. All of which might not have been surprising had it been one of his colleagues walking through the door, some of whom always seemed to be getting into scrapes, but for Matt it was definitely unusual. He could tell that they were all dying to know what had happened. 'Oh, it's nothing,' he replied dismissively, walking across the office and secretly enjoying the prospect of acquiring a slightly tougher reputation, 'you should see the other bloke.'

Matt ignored the teasing and sat down at his desk, ready to start another long day on the case. He was looking forward to today. Everyone else was concentrating on Graham Colley and on Richmond's laptop but he had a different line of enquiry that he was impatient to get on with. Neil and Chris had updated him on the phone calls to Cheltenham and London and Neil had also given him the details of Hilary Russell's bank accounts and credit cards. Something to get his teeth into at last. 'Where's Garrick,' he asked to nobody in particular, switching on his computer and unlocking his desk.

'Stockbridge. He'll be back later.'

Matt looked up and then across at Andy, who had answered his question.

'Stockbridge? Where's that?'

'Hampshire. We tried to ring you last night but couldn't get hold of you. There's been another murder. Garrick and Steph went down there first thing this morning.'

'Stockbridge?' Matt was looking confused. He'd never heard of the place and didn't understand what was going on. Why would there be another murder? And why in Hampshire?

'Yeah, Stockbridge Matt, we've just told you that. What's the matter, has that bang on the head scrambled your brain or something?'

'Who's been murdered then?' he asked, not taking any notice of the banter.

'We don't know yet. We're waiting for them to get back. Anderson got a call last night apparently.'

Matt frowned and then wandered over to the large map which took up most of the far wall in the CID room. It showed the counties around Kent in some detail, as far as Suffolk to the north and Hampshire to the west. A pin had already been stuck in the town of Stockbridge, located to the west of Winchester and south of Andover. It meant nothing to him but it sounded like an important development. Still, there was no point in speculating. Like Andy had said, they would just have to wait for Garrick and Steph to get back. There was plenty to be getting on with in the meantime.

It took him about an hour to find what he was looking for. A few years ago, trying to check out bank or credit card transactions over a weekend would have been impossible but times had changed. Everything was 24/7 these days. Trawling through the bank accounts told him nothing, but it was the credit card history that came up trumps. He didn't have a statement of course so had to rely on the information being conveyed to him over the phone, but the guy on the other end was absolutely certain. On Friday 22 September there was a transaction for a rail ticket bought at Headcorn station. It was the day after Doreen Webster had told Hilary Russell about Teleios and two days before she had been murdered. Matt knew intuitively that it was going to be a return ticket to London, but he rang the station just in case. The amount matched exactly. The cost of a return ticket from Headcorn to London Charing Cross.

Matt updated the file and started to think through the sequence of events. He already knew from Chris's research that Hilary Russell had made the three phone calls on the afternoon of Thursday 21 September. She must have decided to ring them almost as soon as she'd had the conversation with Doreen Webster. Whatever Teleios meant to her, it was important enough for her to act immediately. And now he'd discovered that the following day she had travelled up to London. It must have been to meet one of the people that she'd telephoned the day before. It was the only logical conclusion. And whoever it was must have something to do with the fact that she was subsequently murdered. It felt like a real breakthrough.

Matt looked at the notes that he'd taken the night before and dialled the first of the London numbers. Chris had confirmed Neil's assumptions about GCHQ and the Foreign Office but he'd drawn a blank on the one answered by Jean Pettipher. It was ex-directory and despite his journalistic contacts, he hadn't made any progress in trying to trace it. Matt let it ring and ring for what seemed like ages and then eventually hung up. No answer and no answer phone. No matter. He'd been at Hendon with a guy who had joined the Anti-Terrorist Branch who could get access to just about anything. They'd kept in touch and he had always told Matt to give him a call if he ever needed a favour. Well now was the time. Matt picked up the phone and dialled his number. There was a natural pecking order in the police force and these days, Counter Terrorism Command, as it was now known, was absolutely top of the tree. You could forget about Special Branch or the Flying Squad or the Royal Protection Branch. Everyone else was subject to budget cuts and procurement controls and finance reviews but the guys in SO15 never had a problem with any of that. They always got exactly what they wanted.

Matt was going to find out who Jean Pettipher was, even if it was the last thing he did.

*

Garrick and Steph stood inside the sitting room in Winton Lodge and surveyed the scene of crime with interest. Garrick would have liked to have said that he'd never seen anything like it before, but unfortunately that wasn't true. The chaos and upheaval were all too reminiscent of Richmond's study and more importantly, the word *Teleios* had been sprayed in bright red letters, almost one foot high on the wall over the fireplace. Just standing in the room felt exactly the same as when he and Matt had been at *Chart Place* and he didn't need a forensics report to tell him that the two murders were committed by the same person.

'What time was the body found?' he asked, looking across the room at DS Hewett, a rather plodding, uninspiring detective from Hampshire CID.

'About 2.30 yesterday afternoon Sir. The pathologist thinks he'd been dead about twelve hours.'

Garrick raised his eyebrows and smiled to himself. A pathologist committing himself so early to the time of death was a rarity; he'd been trying to get Alan Wyatt to do that for years. It put the death somewhere between Thursday night and the early hours of Friday morning. 'And he's fairly certain about cause of death?'

'Absolutely. The housekeeper found him over there, hanging from the top of the banisters.' DS Hewett nodded through the doorway towards the stairs which ran up to the bedrooms on the first floor. The three of them wandered out into the hall and looked up towards the landing which ran across the top of the house. The body had been removed of course, but everything else was preserved and untouched, the rope still hanging, limp and still, in a silent, chilling image of what had taken place.

Steph walked over to the spot and looked up at the ceiling, trying to get a feel for what had happened. She pursed her lips, deep in thought and then looked back towards the sitting room again. 'If you didn't know any better, you'd think it was suicide.'

Garrick nodded. That was exactly what he was thinking. If it hadn't been for all the mess and the word Teleios, he would have jumped to the same conclusion. Was it possible that this was the murderer, spraying his own message on his own sitting room wall, before tying a rope around his neck and taking his own life? He dismissed the thought almost as soon as it occurred to him. It was absurd. Twenty years' experience and every bone in his body told him that this was a murder. You could almost smell it. Besides, High Court Judges weren't the type of people to commit suicide. Especially this one. He looked over to where Steph was standing and tried to visualise what Worsley's body would have looked like, twitching and swinging on the end of a rope. It wasn't a pretty sight.

'Do you want to see anywhere else?' asked Hewett, trying to encourage Garrick and Steph to move away from the stairs. He was nervous about them being near the actual murder scene and wanted to get them out of there as soon as possible. If anything got contaminated he knew that his life wasn't going to be worth living. He wasn't in charge of anything. Just the chaperone told to keep a close eye on the visitors from Kent. *"Don't let them touch anything."*

'Anything taken? Any sign of a burglary?' asked Garrick, still staring up at the rope and wondering what on earth could connect all of this with Stuart Richmond and Hilary Russell.

Hewett shook his head. 'Not as far as we know Sir. No sign of forced entry.'

The three of them stood in the hall and looked up at the wide, stone staircase that swept majestically up to the first floor. Winton Lodge was an old, imposing building, built in the late 1800s with large, baronial style rooms and a distinctly cold and draughty interior. Every room seemed to have a huge, stone fireplace but none of them looked as though they had been used for years. If the central heating worked, it certainly wasn't switched on. Garrick shivered. It was quite mild outside, but for some reason it felt several degrees colder indoors. He really didn't have the appetite for this. The house probably had five or six bedrooms and at least three or four reception rooms downstairs. He could see that every one was closed and shut off behind a heavy, oak panelled door, dressed in black, cast-iron hardware and styled into the shape of a Norman arch. It was going to take hours to do a thorough search.

'I don't need to go through the whole house,' he offered, 'but I do need to try and establish a connection between Worsley and Richmond. Did he have a study?'

'There's a sort of office down here Sir.' Hewett wandered down the hall and then opened one of the doors on the left. Garrick and Steph followed him and found themselves in a large square room, the window on the far wall overlooking the drive at the front of the house. Garrick shivered again. If anything, it was even colder. The office was frankly in such a mess that he couldn't work out whether it had been ransacked or whether this was just Worsley's normal state of untidiness. The room was packed full of filing cabinets, cardboard boxes and plastic crates and there were an array of files and books and old magazines and newspapers. At the centre of the far wall, underneath the window, was a large, old desk; a twin pedestal monster in dark mahogany with a worn and faded green, leather inlay. On top of the desk was a PC monitor, linked to a computer which was standing on the floor.

Garrick tried one of the drawers and found it open. The state of the drawers pretty much confirmed that Worsley was not the tidiest man in the world. 'Has anyone been through this yet?' asked Garrick, rummaging through the pile of papers that were stuffed in the top right hand drawer.

Hewett shrugged, obviously not sure. 'Don't know Sir. Sorry, I'll have to check.'

Garrick threw Steph an exasperated look and continued hunting through the drawers. What he was looking for was an address book, but he knew that they'd have to go through the desk with a fine toothcomb to do the job properly. Just one piece of paper might be enough to establish a link between Worsley and Richmond. There had to be a connection and Garrick needed to find it as soon as possible. He looked up at Hewett who was frowning down at him, obviously concerned that he was disturbing potentially vital evidence. 'I know you'll need to get this cleared,' said Garrick, 'but I'd like to send a team down here this afternoon to conduct a detailed search of the property – and particularly to go through the desk. I'd also like to take Worsley's computer away with me for analysis – we need to check his on-line address book and any email history.'

Hewett looked as though he was going to have a nervous breakdown there and then. Inter-force cooperation was all well and good in principle but in reality, cross-county rivalry was as healthy as it had ever been. And this was a murder committed in Hampshire, not in Kent. He knew instinctively what the answer was going to be.

Garrick and Steph wandered out into the hall, deliberately to give him some privacy to make a phone call. Conveying Garrick's request was not going to be easy. They both poked their heads around the sitting room doorway again to get another look at the mess and the message, sprayed above the fireplace. 'So what do you think?' asked Garrick.

Steph blew out her cheeks, indicating that what she was about to say was mostly guesswork. 'Well, I didn't actually see Richmond's study, but from the photographs and Matt's description, it looks almost identical. It looks like he was murdered by the same person, doesn't it?'

Garrick nodded. 'No doubt about it. The problem is we still don't know why. And what on earth could possibly connect a famous fashion designer with a Head of Division?'

Steph started to look slightly embarrassed. 'I'm afraid all that stuff about Heads of Division completely lost me. I've not heard of it before.'

Garrick gave her a sympathetic smile. 'Don't worry Steph, not many people have. The Judiciary have their own hierarchy, just like everybody else. District Judges, Circuit Judges, High Court Judges. The Heads of Division are simply the guys at the top.'

'How many of them are there?'

'Five. They effectively make up the Court of Appeal. The Lord Chief Justice is the most senior permanent judge in England and Wales, second only in rank to the Lord Chancellor. Then there are four others; The Master of the Rolls…'

'Oh I've heard of him,' interrupted Steph.

Garrick nodded. Everybody had. '…and then there's The President of the Queen's Bench, the President of the Family Division and the Chancellor of the High Court. They're all appointed by the Queen on the recommendation of the Prime Minister. To say that Worsley was a senior and influential member of the establishment would be something of an understatement. He was basically one of the most senior judges in the country.'

'How do you get to know all this stuff?' asked Steph, visibly impressed at Garrick's knowledge.

He grinned. 'I looked it up last night after Anderson told me who he was. I hadn't heard of him either.'

Steph smiled. That made her feel a lot better. Not half as stupid. 'It's odd isn't it,' she said, a thought suddenly occurring to her, 'that we've got a businessman who had a load of money stuffed down his throat and now we've got a judge who's been hanged. Unless of course that's just a coincidence.'

Garrick pulled a face. He didn't need to tell Steph what he thought about coincidences. The pair of them fell silent, partly thinking through what she had just said and also because Hewett had just come out of the office having finished his phone call.

'I've relayed your request to DCI Stenning Sir, he's coming straight over.'

'Thanks.' *That means it's a "no" then.*

'He'll be about five minutes.'

'Thanks.' Garrick and Steph exchanged a knowing look and wandered outside. There wasn't much point in hanging around indoors and Garrick wanted to call the station to get an update on how everything was going. The last thing he wanted was Hewett listening to every word. He walked over to the car and leant against the door as he made the call. 'Andy, what's happening?'

Steph wandered off down the drive, for no reason other than to get a breath of fresh air and to get some exercise. The journey from Kent had taken a couple of hours and she was starting to feel stiff and lethargic. She hadn't heard of Sir Julian Worsley before and didn't know anything about him, but as she walked further down the drive one thing was certain; he must have been a keen gardener. Either that or he spent a small fortune on employing some very professional staff. The grounds of Winton Lodge were absolutely stunning. It was a glorious, late September morning and the reds and copper-golds of the heavily laden branches were bathed in the amber glow of a pale, autumnal sun. It dropped in hazy, dreamlike shafts between the trees and sparkled on the dew soaked lawns.

Steph followed the drive which curved away from the house in a slow, long arc towards the front gate, her feet crunching over the private gravel. In a couple of weeks it would feel totally different; a deep, irresistible carpet of damp, rustling leaves. As she walked down towards the main entrance she could see a pair of tall monkey-puzzle trees, standing to attention as if guarding either side of the large, wooden gates. An odd, suburban concession in an otherwise natural and indigenous landscape.

Garrick heard the car coming up the drive, just as he finished the phone call. Moments later a dark grey saloon pulled up outside the house and a guy, probably in his early to mid forties got out. Garrick wasn't expecting Stenning to be either friendly or helpful and certainly wouldn't have blamed him for being cautious and overly protective about his own patch, but in the event he couldn't have been more wrong. As soon as he got out of the car it was obvious that the guy didn't have any time for politics. He smiled and held out his hand as he walked up to Garrick, who was standing just outside the front porch. 'John. Tony Stenning. Good to see you. Welcome to Hampshire.'

Garrick smiled back and the pair of them shook hands. 'Tony. Likewise, good to meet you. John Garrick.'

'So what do you think, John?' asked Stenning as they both turned towards the house and to the matter in hand, 'Do you think it's the same guy?'

'Absolutely. No doubt about it. The murder scene looks almost identical.'

The pair of them walked into the hall and immediately made their way over to the sitting room. Hewett was standing by the door and seemed to stiffen as he saw his DCI approaching. Garrick followed Stenning's lead and walked into the room, paying careful attention to where he walked and making sure that he didn't touch anything.

'So what about this then, John?' asked Stenning, arms folded across his chest and staring up at the letters sprayed in red paint on the wall above the mantelpiece. 'Have you lot got any idea what Teleios means yet?'

Garrick shook his head. 'No, unfortunately not. We think it's something to do with a laptop stolen from Stuart Richmond but beyond that we're not sure. But whoever murdered him on Wednesday left us exactly the same message, sprayed in exactly the same paint.'

'So who are we looking for?' asked Stenning, looking around the room at the chaos and mess that had been left behind.

'Graham Colley. He's a local retailer in Ashford. He's also a receiver of stolen property. We went to arrest him yesterday morning but he'd already disappeared. Now we know why.'

The pair of them fell silent as they stared at the wall again, concentrating on the letters and on the possible message that someone was trying to convey. Stenning eventually shook his head. He'd never seen anything like it. 'You'd better send me some details on Colley so that we can get our lads to start looking for him down here.'

Garrick nodded. 'I'll make a call in a minute and get them emailed over to you.'

'Thanks. Anyway, I understand that you want to send a team down to carry out a search?'

'If that's okay with you.' Garrick smiled but knew that he was pushing his luck.

'Well, it's pretty unorthodox but I'm happy to agree to it, if that's what you want to do. I think I ought to have my own people here supervising what's going on but otherwise, it's fine by me.'

Garrick raised his eyebrows. It wasn't the answer he was expecting.

Stenning caught the surprise in Garrick's expression and smiled. 'Look John, I think we both know that by Monday morning this is going to turn into a turf issue and that people more senior than you and me are going to be arguing about who should be in charge of what. I think the important thing is that you and I try and maintain communication between ourselves and not get involved in any of the politics.'

Garrick nodded emphatically. 'Thanks Tony. I couldn't agree more. Like you, I'm not interested in playing games. I just want to get the case solved.'

'Good, so do I. But I understand that you also want to take Worsley's computer away. That could be trickier to be honest.'

Garrick frowned, feigning disappointment. He wasn't really expecting Stenning to let him take anything away, but it was worth a try.

'I don't know a lot about computers,' Stenning continued, 'but intuitively I think it probably makes sense for us to do any diagnostics here on site rather than risk moving the PC. There doesn't seem to be any advantage in disturbing the evidence, which means we can probably organise everything much quicker from here. But again, I'm happy for your boys to be involved when we do it and for us to treat it as a joint operation.'

Garrick smiled. He couldn't argue with the logic. Besides, Stenning had agreed to more than he had hoped for. It was a result as far as he was concerned. 'Thanks Tony, that's really helpful. I appreciate it.'

'Good. Now then, has anyone offered you a coffee or a bite to eat or anything? You must have left Kent pretty early this morning.'

The pair of them walked back into the hall. The front door was still open and Garrick could see that Steph had walked back up the drive and was waiting patiently by the car. 'No, thanks for the offer Tony but I'd like to get back and see how the rest of the team are getting on. We'll get something on the road. I'll call you later and let you know when our people will be coming down. I'll try and organise something for this afternoon or tomorrow morning.'

Garrick shook hands again on the front step and then waved briefly to Stenning as they drove off, back towards Winchester and then on towards the M3. He checked his watch as they left. It was half past ten. With a bit of luck they should be back before one o'clock. The sooner the better. There was a lot to do and he sensed that they were running out of time. Stenning's response had been helpful but if anything, they were further away from solving Richmond's murder than before, let alone Hilary Russell's. Worsley's death had told them nothing and it just added another complication, not to mention a huge amount of work to try and establish another link between the three incidents. The team were already tired and overworked and this was simply going to stretch them even further. He wondered what progress the rest of them were making. Andy had mentioned that Matt was following up on some interesting developments and he started to think about what they might be. He couldn't remember exactly what Matt had been working on, but whatever it was, they needed a breakthrough and they needed it now.

Craven watched them leave as they turned out of the drive and onto the main road. So much for drawing a line under everything and getting back up to London. This was starting to become more than just a little irritating. He picked up the mobile and hit the send button. Buchanan wasn't going to like this. He wasn't going to like this at all.

TWENTY-FIVE

'Neil, this is ridiculous, you must know where she worked!'

Chris was standing in the dining room, hands on hips and shaking his head in despair as Neil continued to sift through the contents of the bureau which were spread out in an ever increasing pile across the table. The pair of them had spent most of the morning systematically going through all the paperwork and with Chris's help, Neil had finally finished writing to all the various banks and institutions to notify them about the death. Aunt Hilary had turned out to be something of an astute investor and because of the limit on saver's compensation had wisely spread her nest-egg across four separate bank accounts. There were also three different credit cards, two life-assurance policies, some premium bonds and national savings certificates, plus a small number of shares that she had bought some years ago in one of the utility companies. All in all, the process of informing everybody had turned out to be more involved than Neil had ever imagined, but it was the process of notifying her ex-employer about her pension that was really causing the difficulty.

'I keep telling you Chris, I haven't a clue where she worked. I can see the pension amount being paid into her bank account every month but I can't tell who it's being paid from and I can't find any paperwork at all relating to who she worked for.' Neil held up the bank statement as though it was primary evidence in some sort of courtroom drama and then went back to shuffling through the documents, more for effect than with any hope of actually finding anything. He'd been through it all three or four times now and he knew that there was nothing there.

'Well, don't you remember?' asked Chris, still in the same high-pitched, incredulous voice that was starting to get on Neil's nerves. 'She must have talked about who she worked for, surely?'

Neil stopped what he was doing and gave Chris a very tired and frustrated look across the table. 'Chris, she retired nearly twenty years ago. I must have been about eleven or twelve at the time. I was at boarding school. She was a secretary – that's all I know because that's all I remember. By the time I'd got to an age where I would have taken any notice, she'd already retired.'

Chris held his hands up, gesturing to Neil that he didn't want to get into an argument. 'Okay, okay. I believe you. It just seems strange to me, that's all. Anyway, it has to be the Civil Service. If she retired twenty years ago then she could only have been about fifty-five and as far as I know, the only people that can afford to retire that early are civil servants. If she'd worked for them all her life she probably retired on a full pension.'

Neil started to tidy up the papers on the table, obviously satisfied that there wasn't any point in trying to look through them any longer. 'Well, it's easy enough to find out – I can talk to the bank on Monday. Anyway, Tom and Doreen will know. We can ask them later.'

Chris nodded in agreement. 'Okay. Anyway, never mind the pension. The important thing is that it might explain the phone calls to Cheltenham and London. If your Aunt did work for the Civil Service, then maybe Adam Saxby and Jean Pettipher were people that she used to work with.'

'Not to mention Daniels,' replied Neil, 'whoever he is.' He started to pull a face, not sure whether to go along with the logic or not. It was hard enough trying to imagine Aunt Hilary knowing anyone from GCHQ or the Foreign Office, let alone her actually working with either of them. It didn't seem very likely as far as he was concerned. His memories of Aunt Hilary were always of a rather gentle, grey-haired old lady; as bright as a button certainly, but hardly someone who had worked in the corridors of power.

Chris helped Neil tidy up the paperwork and then the pair of them went into the kitchen to make a cup of coffee. It was actually lunchtime, but they had both got up and eaten breakfast so late that neither of them were really hungry. After the altercation with Matt, the three of them had stayed up talking into the early hours of the morning and it must have been almost two o'clock by the time Matt eventually left and they finally got to bed. For his part, Neil had also struggled to get to sleep – there were just too many things running through his mind and it had kept him awake for most of the night.

Neil put the kettle on whilst Chris sat at the kitchen table, leafing through the newspaper and thinking about the conversation the night before. Matt had shared a lot of information with them, in fact he had told them about as much about the case as he knew himself and Chris was now churning it all over in his mind, using all his journalistic instincts to try and work out what their next move should be.

'You know what I think?' he said, folding up the paper and tossing it onto the worktop with a theatrical flourish. 'What I reckon we should do is, get on the Internet and find out as much as we can about the Civil Service – see if we can find out how all the different departments and sections fit together.'

Neil grimaced as he carried the coffee cups over to the kitchen table, handing one of them over to Chris as he sat down. 'What's the point of that? We don't even know if she actually worked for the Civil Service.'

Chris took a sip of coffee and shook his head in despair. 'Come on Neil, she retired at fifty-five and she knows people who work at GCHQ and the Foreign Office. What other conclusion are you going to reach? She must have worked there somewhere. Besides, what else are we going to do? We haven't got any other leads and all that stuff on *Fentanyl* hasn't got us anywhere.'

Neil pulled another face, still not convinced. 'Okay, it's worth a try I suppose, but what exactly are we looking for? I'm not sure how trawling through the Civil Service organisation on the Internet is going to help us?'

Chris stood up, beginning to get exasperated at Neil's lack of enthusiasm. 'Neither am I Neil, but sometimes you just have to go on a fishing expedition and see what comes up. Sometimes you don't know what you're looking for until you find it. A bit like life really.' He shook his head to convey his frustration. 'I'll go and get the laptop.'

Chris went upstairs to get his bag and left Neil sitting at the kitchen table, mulling over Chris's remark. Maybe there was some truth in that. Only a week ago he thought that his life was pretty much on track but in truth it was all drifting along fairly aimlessly. Living and working in Cambridge was all well and good but he wasn't really achieving anything and he certainly wasn't pursuing any specific goals or ambitions. Looking back, there didn't seem to be any real purpose to anything. Just a combination of fairly uninspiring work and a very dull and boring social life. There had to be more to life than that. And now suddenly, he'd found himself in Appleden and everything seemed to have changed. Meeting Steph certainly had a lot to do with that. Perhaps Chris was right. Maybe they should just follow their instincts and see where it led them.

Chris returned with the laptop and started to set it up on the kitchen table. Within a couple of minutes he'd booted up the computer and had used the toll-free software to dial onto the Internet. 'Right, let's see what we can find out.'

The pair of them sat side by side, paging through the various sites and after half an hour had built up a comprehensive picture of the Civil Service and how all the various departments fitted together. They didn't have a printer of course so Neil was diligently taking notes. Neither of them had much experience of the Civil Service, but it was clear that there were two different types of government departments; ministerial departments such as The Home Office, led by a Government Minister, normally a Secretary of State, and non-ministerial departments such as The Crown Prosecution Service, for which direct political oversight was deemed unnecessary or inappropriate. These were headed up by a senior civil servant, usually a Permanent Secretary or a Second Permanent Secretary. The important distinction was that without exception, civil servants were all crown employees, whereas the politicians who they supported were responsible to the Sovereign and to Parliament. Whitehall, the main area in which most of the ministries were located, was still synonymous with the profession, much like the Quai d'Orsay in Paris or the Wilhelmstraße in Berlin.

There was a lot of information on the history of the Civil Service, going back to the 18th century and a lot of stuff about reforms and development, particularly since the Second World War. What was clear was that there had been a lot of change and consolidation in recent years. The Department of Employment had become the Department for Work and Pensions, the Ministry of Agriculture, Fisheries and Food had become the Department for Environment, Food and Rural Affairs and even the Inland Revenue had now merged with Customs and Excise to become something called HM Revenue and Customs. It seemed that even the mandarins at Whitehall were not immune to the world of corporate restructuring. There appeared to have been an almost constant process of review and reorganisation in the last twenty years.

'Let's have a look at The Foreign Office,' suggested Neil, beginning to get bored with reading the same, generalised descriptions. 'Maybe there's something more interesting there.'

Chris paged through two or three different sites, but the focus was very much on travel advice and consular services for British nationals abroad, rather than on current organisation or recent developments. Admittedly, it was important information to anybody who was travelling overseas, particularly if they were going to a political hotspot or to an area prone to tropical disease, but it wasn't exactly what Neil or Chris were looking for. There was also a whole section on Britain's position in the European Union with page after page of treaties, policies and bureaucratic publications which frankly would have taken them half a day to plough through, assuming of course that they didn't fall asleep halfway through. It was all very disappointing.

'I think you were right mate,' said Chris, slouching back in his chair and looking decidedly fed up with the whole thing. 'This looks like a complete waste of time.'

Neil nudged him out of the way and took over the keyboard, sensing that Chris was on the point of giving up. 'Come on, let's have a look at GCHQ, that ought to be a bit more exciting.' It took him only a matter of seconds to get into the site, which even on first appearance seemed to have a more modern and business-like feel about it.

'It says here,' said Neil, scanning through the narrative and trying to pick out the key facts, 'that GCHQ is the Government Communication Headquarters and is one of four principal intelligence organisations within the UK.'

'What are the other three then?' asked Chris, scribbling down some notes as Neil was reading out loud.

'The Security Service, more commonly known as MI5, which is at Thames House, Millbank, the Secret Intelligence Service, which is MI6, based at Vauxhall Cross and the Defence Intelligence Staff, which is at Feltham in Middlesex. It says that they all come under the guidance of the Joint Intelligence Committee.'

Chris raised his eyebrows in surprise. He'd never heard of The Defence Intelligence Staff. He also wasn't that sure of the difference between MI5 and MI6, but he let that pass for the moment.

Neil scanned through the pages, reading out anything that he thought looked interesting, even if it was just as useful background. There was a lot of information about signals intelligence and on something called *asymmetric key algorithm*, which was invented by a mathematics graduate and which apparently revolutionised the practice of cryptography in the 1970s. There was also a whole section on something called ECHELON which seemed to be some sort of super-duper monitoring system.

'ECHELON?' Chris looked over Neil's shoulder to check that he'd got the correct spelling. 'Must be some sort of codeword.'

'Like Teleios you mean?'

'Exactly.'

Neil smiled to himself and continued paging through the site. Chris was dying to turn this into some sort of conspiracy theory. 'The rest of it seems to be mostly about the history of the place. There's a lot of stuff about somebody called Geoffrey Prime, who was convicted for espionage in 1983. There's also a fairly large careers section. Looks like you can apply for vacancies on-line these days.'

Chris shook his head in disbelief. 'Blimey. I didn't know you could apply to be a spy via the Internet. I thought they did all their recruiting at your old college.'

Neil gave him a sarcastic smile. 'Very funny. Anyway, these guys aren't really spies, they're just technicians. The spies are the ones working at MI5 and MI6.'

'Let's have a look at them then – maybe we'll find something there.'

The two of them spent another half hour or so looking through various sites relating to MI5 and MI6, taking notes about locations and organisation but beyond that not getting very far. Again, most of the content seemed to be about the history of the departments, notable operations and details about some of the more high-profile leaders. It was all very interesting but it wasn't really what they were looking for. Even Neil was starting to get disheartened. According to Chris's logic, sooner or later they were going to experience some sort of eureka moment and stumble across a significant piece of information – but the longer they looked, the less likely it seemed that it was ever going to happen.

'Let's just have a look at the Joint Intelligence Committee,' said Chris, sensing that they were running out of steam and trying to delay the point at which they finally gave up. 'That seems to be the forum that governs everything from a security point of view. Let's see what it says about that.'

Neil leant forward again and typed in the website address, scrolling through the pages at speed, by now having become expert at quickly scanning information and picking out the key facts. Chris waited patiently, ready to capture anything that he read out, but after a minute or so it was clear that there was nothing of any real interest. The Joint Intelligence Committee was part of the Cabinet Office and was responsible for coordinating the activities of GCHQ, MI5 and MI6 but beyond that, there was very little information.

'It just says that it meets once a week,' said Neil, leaning back in his chair and looking thoroughly bored with the whole process, 'but there's nothing else really. Apparently it's chaired by the Permanent Secretary, Intelligence, Security and Resilience, whoever that is.'

'Well, look him up,' suggested Chris, trying to remain optimistic that they might still find something, 'he sounds as though he's the top dog as far as anything to do with security goes.' He looked over Neil's shoulder again as Neil typed in the enquiry and the page popped up on the screen.

'Actually, he's not the top dog,' said Neil, 'the JIC Chairman reports to the Cabinet Secretary.'

'So who does the Cabinet Secretary report to?'

'Nobody. The Cabinet Secretary is the Head of the Civil Service. You can't get any more senior than that. Everybody in the whole organisation reports to him. MI5, MI6, GCHQ, they all ultimately report to the Cabinet Secretary.'

'Okay, so who's the Cabinet Secretary?'

Neil typed in another enquiry and waited for the page to pop up, scanning through it as he tried to find the name. 'It's somebody called...'

After a couple of seconds Chris looked up from his notepad, conscious that Neil had stopped talking and was sitting back in the chair, staring at the screen. 'What's the matter?'

Neil pointed at the screen. 'Take a look.'

Chris leant on Neil's shoulder again and looked at the screen for himself. Like Neil, he took a double take and stared in silence for a couple of seconds.

'Does that say what I think says?' asked Chris.

Neil nodded slowly, still taking it all in.

'Wow, that's a bit of a co-incidence isn't it?'

'You can say that again.'

Chris pointed to the bottom hand corner of the page. 'Look, there's a hyperlink there to a biography. Click on that and see what it says.'

Neil clicked on the link and read out the headline facts. 'Winchester College, then a double first from Balliol College, Oxford. Career civil servant. Joined as a Treasury Analyst and then moved to the Foreign & Commonwealth Office. Worked at the British Embassy in Vienna for a while. Ended up as Permanent Secretary to the Treasury followed by three years as Private Secretary to the Prime Minister and then finally appointed Cabinet Secretary four years ago.'

Chris blew out a low whistle. That was one serious CV. 'We ought to ring Matt and let him know. Or better still, we could ask him out for a beer tonight. That way he can tell us what he's found out about Jean Pettipher today. Maybe she works in the Cabinet Office as well.'

Neil pulled a face. He was more than happy to talk to Matt again, but he wasn't so sure that Matt would necessarily feel the same way about talking to them. He thought there was a good chance that Matt had woken up that morning with more than a few reservations about having said as much as he had. Still, like Chris, Neil was impatient to find out whether he had managed to identify the mysterious Jean Pettipher and there was no doubt about it, Matt would certainly want to be updated about their latest discovery. Not only had Aunt Hilary telephoned GCHQ and the Foreign Office but it also looked as though she may have known the most senior civil servant in the country.

Neil turned back and looked at the screen again. The whole thing just seemed too incredible for words, but it was too much of a co-incidence to be anything other than the truth. The photograph above the biography stared back at him, a proud, distinguished portrait of a successful and powerful bureaucrat; a hint of superiority in the old school tie and the upward tilting jaw-line.

Neil had never heard of him before but that wasn't surprising. What was important was that there was something very familiar and potentially important about the name. The current Cabinet Secretary was none other than somebody called Sir James Carlisle.

TWENTY-SIX

It was mid afternoon by the time Craven reached the outskirts of Beaulieu and found the correct lay-by and car park next to the New Forest. The whole area was a criss-cross of narrow country roads and sparse, open heathland and despite Buchanan's very precise instructions, every half-mile or so there seemed to be yet another designated area for the general public to leave their cars, each one virtually identical to the other and each one containing just one or two vehicles. He let out a sigh of relief as he finally saw Buchanan's Jaguar parked at the far end of an enclosure, waiting patiently for his arrival and confirming that he was in the right place.

There was only one other car in the vicinity which had been left near the entrance, a lone walker probably, enjoying the solitude of the forest and the warm September sunshine. Craven pulled up in between the two vehicles, switched off the engine and then wound down the window and lit up a cigarette. He knew that Buchanan would wait a couple of minutes before making a move, wanting to check first of all that no-one had been following him. There hadn't of course, but he didn't blame Buchanan for being cautious. Craven's second rule of fieldwork; *assume the best, plan for the worst.* He'd virtually finished his cigarette by the time Buchanan walked across the car park and opened the door, sliding into the passenger seat in his usual detached and formal manner.

'Craven, how are you?' Buchanan shut the door and wound down his window to let in some fresh air. It also gave him somewhere to lean his elbow.

Craven gave him a short nod. 'Charles. Sorry I'm late.'

The two of them sat in silence for a minute or so, both of them staring out of the windscreen at the heath and gorse in front of them, absorbing the stillness and tranquillity of the forest and enjoying the last throws of summer. A rare Montagu's Harrier fluttered silently on the wind high above their heads, a skilled predator hunting for smaller prey.

'I wonder what they eat?' asked Craven, staring up at the skyline.

'Anything that moves. Rabbits, lizards, small birds, voles...'

'Small birds?' Craven smiled ruefully to himself. 'They kill their own kind then?'

'Very efficiently.'

'Survival of the fittest I suppose.' Craven's head was now twisted at an angle, trying to follow the flight of the harrier as it hovered high above the car.

'Partly. It's more to do with the food-chain. Everything feeding off the layer below.'

'Whilst trying not to get eaten by the layer above.'

'Exactly. Basic law of nature. Eat or be eaten. Have you got the laptop?'

Craven nodded. 'It's in the boot.'

'Good. Everything okay?'

Craven nodded again, slower this time. 'Fine. Everything was straightforward.'

'Good. Has anybody had access to it since you got it?'

'No, nobody. No-one's looked at it. It's password protected anyway.'

Buchanan raised his eyebrows in surprise. 'How do you know that?'

Craven hesitated. It was always better to tell the truth. 'I switched it on, just to check.'

'Why would you want to do that?'

Craven shrugged. 'Don't know really. Curiosity?'

'Isn't that what killed the cat?'

Another moment of silence descended, both of them staring out of the front windscreen again, neither of them happy with the exchange but equally neither of them wanting to get into a confrontation. The noise of a car could be heard approaching from the distance, a faint, rumbling hum but slowly getting louder. Eventually, an old, beautifully restored saloon car droned past them on the other side of road. Craven looked in the rear-view mirror and smiled to himself. It was years since he'd seen a Triumph Herald in such good condition. It went past at no more than 20 miles an hour, carefully observing the speed limit. He could hear it fading into the distance, periodically slowing down for the speed humps and cattle grids that cut across its path.

Buchanan eventually broke the silence. 'So, what about the person that you got it from? You said he was with you yesterday when we spoke on the phone.'

Craven took out another cigarette and flipped open the Zippo lighter, thumbing the wheel to spark up a flame, the familiar smell of petrol catching his senses as it always did. He inhaled deeply and turned sideways to blow the smoke out of the window. 'What do you want to know?' I assume you don't want all the details?'

'Not really.'

'What then?' The two of them looked each other properly for the first time since Buchanan had got in the car.

'I just want to know that it's been resolved.'

Craven turned back and looked out of the windscreen again. 'It's been resolved. He won't be talking to anybody about anything. Ever again.'

Buchanan smiled to himself. *Good.* He didn't like loose ends. 'So who was he?'

Craven took another long drag on the cigarette. 'Graham Colley. He was a nobody. Just the wrong bloke unlucky enough to be in the wrong place at the wrong time.'

Buchanan nodded, acknowledging the vagaries of misfortune. 'And did he say anything before he died?'

'About what?'

'Anything. Teleios?'

Craven shook his head. 'No, nothing. He said he hadn't looked at the laptop. I didn't believe him.'

Buchanan nodded again. That was all he wanted to know.

'And Richmond?'

'What about him?'

'Did he say anything before he died?'

Craven flicked the ash out of the side window and smiled to himself. So that was it. Buchanan didn't know. 'About Teleios you mean?'

'Of course.'

Craven turned and looked at Buchanan again, wanting to catch his reaction. 'I don't know Charles, he was already dead when I got there.'

For once, Buchanan couldn't conceal his surprise. 'Oh, I assumed…' His words tailed off, too busy thinking through the implications of what he'd just learned. If it wasn't Craven, then who else could it have been?

'Someone got there before me. I think I probably disturbed them. They left a lot of money behind.'

'Money?'

'Cash. A lot of it. I'd say Richmond was trying to buy back the laptop.'

'From Colley?'

Craven nodded. 'I would think so.'

Buchanan fell silent for a moment, thinking through the implications of it being Colley rather than anybody else. Maybe Worsley's murder wasn't so worrying after all. 'And Worsley?'

'Definitely the same person. Whoever killed Richmond also killed Worsley.'

'Are you sure?'

'Positive. I've just been in there. The signature was identical.'

Buchanan smiled to himself. Earlier this morning it looked as if the whole thing was going to implode. Suddenly it looked completely the opposite. Worsley had been murdered in the early hours of Friday morning, so Colley must have killed him and then driven back home in time to go to work, just before Craven had caught up with him. The whole situation had gone from potential disaster to closure in a matter of seconds. The only loose end was the same one that had been there for the last couple of days. Neil Ashton. 'What about the nephew?'

Craven took another drag on the cigarette. 'I couldn't get near him. He's got someone staying with him for the weekend. Is it important?'

Buchanan pursed his lips, thinking about the risk of leaving the nephew to his own devices. It probably didn't make any difference. Richmond and Worsley would never have said anything of course, not unless they had been put under tremendous pressure – but Colley had been a real risk. As soon as he bought the laptop, the whole operation was in jeopardy. But now that they were all dead, it was probably safe again. The only people who knew about Teleios were going to keep their mouths shut – that was absolutely guaranteed. And if there was no-one else involved, then maybe he could close the file. Eventually he shook his head. 'No, it probably doesn't matter. He doesn't really know anything.'

Craven paused, thinking about Neil's conversation with Tom in *The Chequers* the day before, not convinced that he was as harmless and as "in the dark" as Buchanan thought. 'I'm not so sure Charles. He knows about Jean. I heard him talking about her yesterday afternoon.'

'I know. He telephoned her the other day.'

Craven frowned and turned to look at Buchanan again. He'd heard Neil talking about Jean Pettipher in the pub, but he didn't know that he'd actually rung her up. 'How did he manage that then? Where did he get the number from?'

Buchanan sighed. It wasn't a conversation that he wanted to get into. 'He must have got it from his Aunt.'

'So where did she get it?'

'She rang some old colleagues that she used to work with. One of them gave it to her.'

'Adam Saxby?'

Buchanan smiled, impressed at Craven's knowledge. He always was head and shoulders above the rest. 'Yes. There aren't many people outside the office who would know it but Adam is one of them.'

Craven tried hard not to look surprised and took a final drag on the cigarette. He flicked the butt out of the window, thinking about the original briefing document that Buchanan had showed him in *The Grapevine* at the beginning of the week. It didn't mention anything about Hilary Russell's background. It was typical of Buchanan. There was always something, some undisclosed piece of information which he always kept to himself. It was always the same. 'So who is he? A drone?'

Buchanan shook his head. 'Foreign Office. He worked on a Mossad operation a couple of years ago. We helped him out with some logistics.'

'And Daniels? I assume he works at the Doughnut?'

Buchanan nodded, impressed again at Craven's knowledge. 'He's a linguist. Spends his time listening to number stations. Spanish I think.'

Craven nodded and smiled ruefully to himself. For decades, staff at GCHQ did nothing other than tune into short wave radios, listening to dozens of stations on innumerable different frequencies, reading out seemingly meaningless blocks of numbers. Most of the stations were transmitted in Spanish, although occasionally they would be in German or Russian and for some reason, almost always broadcast by a woman's voice. Five-digit Spanish stations were the most common and were so called because they transmitted messages in blocks of five digits, normally beginning transmissions with something like "atención 273 68" repeated for several minutes. The three-digit group identified the recipient of the message and the second number indicated the number of five-digit groups in the message.

The other most common type was the 3/2-digit Spanish stations, so called because of the distinct pause between the third and fourth digit of each group. These normally opened with a three-digit group sent three times, again to identify the intended recipient, followed by "1234567890," this sequence repeated for several minutes. After ten tones, something like "grupo 137, grupo 137" would be sent to indicate the number of groups that were going to be transmitted.

Both formats followed two well known cryptological techniques. The five-digit sequences were transmitted to fit in with the one-time pad system in which both the sender and the recipient had copies of a code pad and the received numbers were added or subtracted from the numbers on the pad and the results then transcribed from a master code. The 3/2 stations used a variation of the dictionary code system, whereby both the sender and the recipient had an identical copy of the same book and the three digits represented the page number, while the last two digits were the position of a certain word on the page, usually counting from the upper left hand corner.

Both systems had been used for years and were somewhat slow and crude but were virtually unbreakable. Despite advances in computing and technology, they were still the preferred method for covert communication. The linguists at GCHQ spent hours on end, shift after shift, listening to monotonous broadcasts of indecipherable numbers and Craven couldn't imagine a more boring job in the world.

'And did Hilary Russell ring him as well?'

Buchanan nodded. 'Yes. She rang Daniels first actually. But he didn't have the number so she tried Adam Saxby.'

Craven shook his head. He was getting tired of always working in the dark. Normally he put up with it and kept his own counsel but this time it was starting to get to him. 'I didn't know Charles. Why didn't you tell me that she used to be in the service?'

Buchanan sighed again. 'It was a long time ago. She retired twenty years ago. Besides, it wasn't relevant to the assignment. Getting the laptop back was all that mattered. There wasn't anything that you or I could do to help Hilary Russell. It was too late for that.'

Craven looked out of the window again, unconvinced. 'So how did she know Jean?'

Buchanan shrugged. 'You know what secretaries are like. They all have a good network with each other. That's how they get things done. That's how they keep track of their respective bosses. They like to know where we are and what we're up to.'

'And does the nephew know?'

'I'm not sure but it doesn't really matter does it? At the end of the day she was just a low-grade civil servant who spent all of her career in the service and then left to enjoy a quiet and well-earned retirement in the country.'

'So there isn't anything you need me to do. No loose ends?'

'No, I don't think there is. I think everything has turned out better than expected.'

Craven paused for a moment, thinking about Winton Lodge and the police activity that he'd watched going on all morning. He hadn't recognised the girl; he'd never seen her before but the guy who was driving the car was definitely the useless detective who was leading the case back in Kent. It obviously hadn't taken him long to connect the two incidents. Still, no surprise really given that the same word had been sprayed in red paint in twelve-inch letters all over the murder scene. Even a semi-illiterate wooden-top was going to notice that. 'What about the police?'

Buchanan shook his head dismissively. 'They don't know anything. Lots of activity but it's not going to lead them anywhere.'

'They know that they're looking for something called Teleios. That local DCI must have worked a few things out.'

'I wouldn't worry about John Garrick. Even a stopped clock tells the right time twice a day.'

Craven pulled a face, still not convinced. 'The nephew's a journalist. He's inquisitive by nature. If they start talking to each other it could get difficult.'

Buchanan shook his head again. He wasn't worried. The only people that were going to say anything were dead. The circle had closed again and nobody was going to break the chain. 'It doesn't matter. They're not going to find out about Teleios and without that, there isn't any risk.'

'Sure?'

'Absolutely. One hundred percent.'

'Good. I can get back up to London then.'

'Yes, I think you can. Thanks for your help Craven, excellent support as always. By the way, I'm sorry to drag you down here and get you out of bed this morning. Worsley's situation needing checking out as soon as possible. I hope I wasn't interrupting anything.'

Craven smiled to himself. Buchanan's call couldn't have come at a more inconvenient moment. A picture of Sophie flashed across his mind, her naked body riding up and down with all the urgency and impulsiveness of an uninhibited teenager. He let the thought go almost as soon as it arrived. Now was not the time. 'It wasn't the greatest timing in the world to be honest Charles, but no matter – work comes first.'

'Oh, I'm sorry about that,' replied Buchanan, picking up the meaning in Craven's response. 'Maybe it's something you can get back to another time.'

'I don't think so Charles. Anyway, she wasn't really my type.'

Buchanan shook his head in despair. *The younger generation know nothing.* 'Take my advice Craven, there are only four types of women. *In Love, Hoping, Resigned, Bitter.* In terms of relationships, physical or otherwise, every woman falls into one of those four. There are no exceptions. Never have been, never will be. All you have to remember is not to waste any time on the first and last category.'

Craven's mouth was stuck in the open position but nothing was coming out, other than him slowly breaking into a wide grin and then into a disbelieving laugh. Buchanan's remark had been so out of character that it had completely stunned him into silence. Before he could say anything the passenger door had opened and Buchanan had got out, waiting for Craven to follow him and open the boot.

After a couple of seconds Buchanan stuck his head back into the car to see what the delay was all about. He smiled at Craven, enjoying the impact that his parting remark had made. It didn't hurt to keep the staff on their toes now and again. Especially the ones that thought they knew it all and knew him inside out. Anyway, it was good advice. *"Besides the noble art of getting things done, there is the noble art of leaving things undone. The wisdom of life consists in the elimination of non-essentials."*

'Come on then Craven. Let's get this laptop out of the boot and go and enjoy the rest of the weekend.'

TWENTY-SEVEN

Matt pulled up outside *The Chequers*, switched off the car engine and then turned off his headlights. As usual, the village was mostly in darkness. There were only one or two streetlights in Appleden which were located further up the lane, near the village hall, so the amber glow coming from the pub made it look particularly warm and inviting. He could hear the noise and laughter coming from the bar; a typical Saturday night full of people out socialising and enjoying themselves, halfway through the weekend and with the promise of a slow, leisurely Sunday to follow. A late breakfast followed by a lazy morning reading the Sunday papers perhaps, people taking their dogs for a walk, a pub lunch in front of a roaring log fire, maybe an old black and white film in the afternoon, curled up on the sofa. That's what Sundays were all about in this part of the world.

Matt had thought twice about whether meeting up again was a good idea but in the end curiosity had got the better of him. Besides, it had been a tough day at work. It wasn't often that he had to work at weekends and he felt as though he deserved a drink. Anyway, he liked Neil and Chris, they were all of a similar age and they were good company. Not like some of the philistines that he had to work with. He undid his seat-belt and opened the door to get out, just as his mobile started to ring. He pulled the door shut again and answered the phone, the courtesy light in the centre of the car slowly fading into darkness. 'Hello, Matt Isaacs.'

'Hi, Matt – it's Simon, how are you doing?'

Matt smiled. He could hear the sound of people laughing and glasses clinking in the background. It sounded like a London party in full swing. Obviously the social life for the boys in the Anti Terrorist Branch was a lot more cosmopolitan than it was down in the sticks. He could visualise the chrome and glass interior of some trendy bar or restaurant, probably in the West End, full of bright young things drinking cocktails or designer beer and talking about music or fashion or the arts. A million miles away from a sleepy, Kentish pub with its sloping floors and peg-tile roof. It was hard to believe that they were in the same country, let alone only an hour apart. 'Not bad Simon. Just finished actually. How did you get on?'

'Sorry mate, not very well. In fact not well at all to be honest.' Matt could hear the disappointment in Simon's voice. Part apology, part annoyance.

'Don't worry about it — it was a long shot anyway. It happens.' The party sounds seemed to be fading into the distance, as if Simon had wandered outside or into another room to continue the conversation.

'No, you don't understand Matt. I've drawn a complete blank. Absolutely nothing. It never happens. This number's got a security level on it that I've never seen before...'

Matt started to sit upright. Maybe there was more to this conversation than he thought. He watched the silhouette of a customer pushing open the door to the pub. It looked a bit like the guy that was sitting on the stool in the Bricklayer's Arms the other night.

'...I spent about four hours trying to trace it this afternoon and got precisely nowhere. I can normally track any number in about fifteen minutes. Thirty at the most.'

'Really?'

'Absolutely. I can get the mobile numbers of the grandchildren of the President of the United States in about ten minutes. The private line into Balmoral, the Iranian Embassy in Damascus, the husband of the Home Secretary's mistress. You name it, I can find it. But not this one.'

Matt looked out of the windscreen into the darkness, trying to work out the implication of what was being said. He was sure that the customer who had just gone into the pub was the same guy that had been in the *Bricklayer's Arms* the night they arrested Jamie Collins. He didn't know why it was bothering him — but it was. 'So what are you saying Simon?'

'Not sure Matt. I don't know what you're working on down there but whatever it is, it must involve someone very important or someone very senior.'

'Like the security services maybe?' Matt was already thinking through the connection with GCHQ and the Foreign Office.

'I doubt it. It's a mainline number and I've got every mainline number for every British Intelligence establishment in the whole country. I've got most of the foxholes and even some of the safe houses. If it's part of the security service then it's not one that's on the map and it's not one that I've ever heard of before.'

The two of them briefly exchanged some police gossip about old colleagues before promising to catch up with each other as they said goodbye; a commitment that both Matt and Simon knew was unlikely to happen. It was the nature of ex-colleagues parting. *We must catch up for a beer soon.* The need to offer continued friendship; an agreed pretence in the face of everybody being too busy and too focused with just getting on with their own lives.

Neil and Chris were sitting at one of the tables, just finishing off their first pint of the evening when Matt pushed through the door and came into the pub, a blast of colder air circulating into the bar. 'Don't forget,' said Neil, half whispering to Chris as he leant across the table, 'don't mention anything about me and Steph – she'd be in real trouble if anyone found out.'

Chris smiled to himself. It hadn't taken much to persuade Neil to tell him everything about Steph. In fact it had been hard to shut him up. 'Stop worrying, I won't say a word. Besides, Matt's not exactly in a position to throw stones is he? He told us virtually everything he knew about Teleios last night. I should think he's more worried about you and me not saying anything at the moment.'

Neil nodded. There was certainly some truth in that. Matt had made his way up to the bar and was gesturing over to them to see if they wanted another drink, which was greeted with lots of nodding and thumbs up of approval. Chris picked up both the empty glasses and went over to join him while he waited patiently to be served. Saturday night was always busy and there was a larger crowd than usual congregating around the bar. 'How's the head?' Chris asked, trying to squeeze into a space between a couple of locals.

Matt smiled as he gingerly touched the temple on the side of his head. Although the lump had gone down the bruising had come out and if anything, it looked worse than it did the night before. It was certainly still painful. 'I'll live. Anyway, it's doing wonders for my street-cred at the station.'

Chris smiled back at him, partly in sympathy and partly still in amusement at Neil's heroics. 'So, you had a busy day?'

Matt nodded. 'They're all busy at the moment.'

'Productive?'

'Yes, I think so. Lots of developments anyway. What about you?'

'Same. Let's get a drink and we'll tell you all about it.'

It took them about five minutes to get served and rejoin Neil who was still sitting at the table, staring into the middle distance and thinking about Aunt Hilary. He was trying to remember a time when she'd been working, but it was all too long ago, too distant a memory for him to be really certain about anything. He had a vague recollection of her coming in from work when he was small, but he couldn't be sure – he'd been much too young to really take any notice.

Matt sat down in the vacant chair and then swivelled round and looked nervously around the bar. He was still worried about being seen with Neil and Chris and wanted to double-check that none of his off-duty colleagues were in the pub. As he gazed across the room he spotted the familiar face again, the guy who had been drinking in the *Bricklayer's Arms*, propped up against the bar, slowly drinking a pint of Guinness and not seeming to take any notice of anybody else. Matt stared at him for a few seconds, trying to work out why he felt uncomfortable. There wasn't any logical reason for it – just a strange intuition, which for Matt was unnerving. He was much more comfortable dealing with facts. 'Do you know who that guy is over there?' he asked, nodding across the room towards Craven's direction.

'Don't ask me,' replied Chris, 'I've only just got here.'

Neil stared at Craven for a few seconds and then also shook his head. 'No, I don't think so. Why, who is he?'

'Don't know. I've just seen him before somewhere, that's all. Anyway, how did you two get on?'

Matt sipped his beer and listened patiently as Neil and Chris updated him on the day's events. They'd felt really pleased with the progress that they had made, but somehow it didn't seem to add up to very much when they went through it all and explained it to him out loud. Just an assumption about Aunt Hilary having worked for the Civil Service and then a possible identification of the name 'Carlisle' which had been written on the telephone pad. Not a place but a person. Neil had brought the piece of paper with him and pushed it across the table as he finished telling Matt about the Internet search. Matt picked it up and looked at the telephone numbers and words again, all written in a distinctive, backward sloping style with the artistic swirls and flourishes. He'd seen it briefly the night before, but now he was looking at it with a clearer head.

The GCHQ number was at the top of the list, followed by the Foreign Office number and then Jean Pettipher's. At the bottom of the page was the word Carlisle, followed by the word that none of them could read properly; it looked like Rawlings or Rowlands. Around the edge of the paper were a load of numbers, seemingly meaningless and mostly scribbled, some overwritten in bolder ink as though Aunt Hilary had been doodling whilst talking on the phone. 'What do you make of these?' asked Matt, pointing to a couple in the top right-hand corner. 'Have you any idea what these are?'

Neil shook his head. He'd already asked himself the same question but hadn't come up with anything. The telephone numbers in the middle of the pad were obvious but the others around the edge just seemed to be random scribbles. The two that Matt was pointing at, 131 and 313 meant nothing to him, other than the digits were obviously transposed. There was another pair of similar, matching numbers, 191 and 919 in the opposite top left-hand corner, but again, a complete mystery as far as Neil was concerned. At the bottom of the page Aunt Hilary had written a couple of dates, 1987 and 2003, which were probably significant and then finally there were four numbers scribbled up the left hand side of the paper, 2221, 3331, 4441 and 6661, all in a similar format but otherwise meaningless. Neil looked at them again, hoping for some inspiration.

'They must mean something,' said Matt, staring across at Neil and thinking out aloud. 'It's a bit like someone drawing a picture of a sun when they're on the phone talking about the fact that they've been to the beach. A sort of subconscious illustration of what they're thinking about. They must mean something – why else would she have written them down?'

Neil and Chris couldn't argue with that. Of course the numbers meant something – the problem was that none of them could work out what it might be. The three of them fell into a period of silence, slowly drinking their beer and thinking through the possible explanations for the cryptic message that had been left behind. They didn't notice Tom walk into the pub, his apparent late arrival greeted with much noise and laughter from the crowd of locals who were still congregated at the bar. Nor did they notice Craven quietly move away from where he was standing and sit down at the table behind them.

'Anyway,' said Chris, eventually breaking the silence, 'what about you Matt? You haven't told us how you got on today.'

Matt lowered his voice. 'A bit mixed to be honest. No luck on Jean Pettipher I'm afraid, but lots of progress elsewhere. Plus, everything seems to fit with your theory about your Aunt working for the Civil Service and Carlisle probably being Sir James Carlisle.'

Neil and Chris exchanged a knowing look and waited for Matt to take another sip of beer before updating them on everything that had happened. Like Matt had done earlier, they sat and listened without interruption as he told them about the day's events; the murder at Winton Lodge, the discovery of Aunt Hilary's journey to London two days before she died and the conversation with Matt's contact at the Anti Terrorist Branch. The pair of them slowly worked their way down their pints as they listened in growing disbelief to the story that was unfolding before them. A seemingly accidental death in a sleepy Kentish village had developed into something much bigger and more sinister than either of them could have imagined. The whole case seemed to have the fingerprint of the government or the security services all over it. Neil reflected on the absurdity of it all. Less than a week ago he was living and working in Cambridge, living a humdrum life and worrying about whether he ought to buy his first car or get on the property ladder. Now here he was, having a clandestine meeting with a local police officer and talking about intelligence establishments, stolen laptops, coded messages and security departments. It was positively surreal.

'So what happens next?' asked Chris, eager to understand where the enquiry was heading. 'Presumably you're looking for a link between Worsley and Richmond?'

Matt drained the last dregs of his pint and settled the glass carefully into the centre of his beer mat. 'Yes we are – but to be honest we already know what the link is…'

'Teleios.' interrupted Neil, also finishing off his pint.

'Exactly. It's the one link that connects all three of them. The problem is we don't what it means. Anyway, we're sending a team down to Hampshire tomorrow to find out as much as we can about Worsley. Other than that, it's still a question of trying to find Graham Colley and the laptop and then waiting until Monday until we can follow up the leads on your Aunt.'

'Nothing you can follow up tomorrow then?' asked Chris, unable to hide his disappointment, mindful that he was going back to Cambridge on Sunday evening and likely to miss all the excitement. It was like working on half a story and then moving onto something else.

Matt shook his head. 'You must be joking. This is the Civil Service we're talking about. A couple of us will be going up to London on Monday to interview Adam Saxby. He doesn't know that yet of course. We'll see if we can find out who Jean Pettipher is and more importantly, who Hilary Russell visited a week last Friday.'

Craven drank the last of his pint and decided to make a move. He'd seen and heard enough. The inquisitive nephew and his journalistic colleague were still in huddled conversation with the local CID plod, all of them too engrossed to take any notice of him making his exit. He lit a cigarette as he went out of the front door and wandered slowly up the lane, his footsteps sounding unusually loud as he walked past the rows of cottages towards his car, the only signs of life being the lighted windows behind drawn curtains. Craven stopped and listened for a moment, smoking his cigarette in the stillness and silence that seemed to pervade the whole village. He could hear the distant buzz of voices and laughter coming from the pub, but otherwise everything was deathly quiet, exactly as it must have been on the night that Hilary Russell had been murdered.

He finished the cigarette and walked slowly to his car, thinking about the conversation with Buchanan earlier in the day. He could have kicked himself. He'd been so preoccupied about talking about Graham Colley and Jean Pettipher that he hadn't concentrated properly on the details about Hilary Russell. They didn't make sense. He knew that as far as Buchanan was concerned the job was over – but something here didn't add up. Craven had been on the point of packing his bag and getting back up to London, but something had made him change his mind – and it wasn't the prospect of one more evening with the pneumatic Sophie that had made him book another night at *The Moon & Falcon*. He leant on the side of the car and pulled the mobile phone out of his pocket, pressing the green button to automatically dial the programmed number.

Charles Buchanan was sitting quietly at home, a glass of finest Burgundy in his right hand, reading the latest exposition on the life and death of Phillip Marlow and half listening to Gorecki's Symphony No. 3 building to its stirring climax in the background. He paused for a moment and looked around the room, a tastefully furnished study with an open fire, soft, comfortable leather chairs, a large, working desk and a wall-to-wall bookcase packed full of literary classics and expensive first and second editions. He smiled to himself as he reflected on his two worlds; the odd juxtaposition of work and home, of week and weekend, of cat and mouse. Rural Hampshire was the perfect antidote to SW1 of course, but it was the cut and thrust of political life that he had always enjoyed the most. The positioning of one's opponents, the laying of the traps, the deftly angled mirrors, and best of all, the cold, ruthless revenge, delivered long after everyone else had finished playing; the final, swift taking away of the chair.

Buchanan went back to his book and then seconds later looked up again. The mobile phone sitting innocently on the edge of his desk had started to ring. Reluctantly he put down the book and picked it up. 'Hello?'

'It's me.'

'Obviously.'

'I forgot to give you the phone back.'

Craven could hear the irritation in Buchanan's voice; the annoyance at having to discuss something that he thought was trivial, the impatience to get back to whatever it was he was doing. 'Don't worry about it. Destroy the SIM card – keep the phone if you like.'

'Thanks – but that's not why I'm ringing.'

'What then?' More impatience.

'There was something I wanted to ask you.'

'About what?'

'The case, obviously.'

'I've already told you, the case is closed.'

'I'm not so sure.'

There was a pause. Silence at both ends. Craven could hear Buchanan breathing. Controlled, measured, calculating. Unaccustomed to his authority being challenged. Subterfuge was easy. Direct challenge was much more uncomfortable. 'Like I said, the case is closed.'

'I don't think so. There's something I'm not happy about.'

'You're not paid to be happy.'

'I'm not being paid at all. The meter isn't running any more, remember?'

'Well then, whatever it is, forget about it. Move on.'

Craven paused again. Buchanan had already drawn a line under everything. He was going to have to force the conversation. Turn the wick up a bit. Ignore the usual protocols. 'Hilary Russell. Do you know who killed her?'

Buchanan winced. Craven had just broken a golden rule for the first time in his life. It was sacrosanct. 'I'd rather not have this conversation on the phone.'

'Well I'm happy to come round and have it face to face.' The tone of Craven's response left no room for any doubt. The threat was implied. A personal visit was not going to be a good idea. *Not on the payroll any more.*

Buchanan pushed back. 'I don't have anything else to say. The merchandise has been recovered. The case is closed. Anything else is a police matter.'

'Fine. I'll talk to them then.'

'Don't be so bloody stupid.'

'Then answer the question. Do you know who killed her?'

Buchanan hesitated. He'd worked with Craven long enough to know that he wasn't going to let this rest. He wasn't really going to talk to the police, of course, but the last thing he needed was Craven making a nuisance of himself. A maverick outside the tent, pissing in, was bad enough. A maverick inside the tent, pissing all over everybody else was unthinkable. Besides, there was nothing to hide. Buchanan didn't know who had murdered Hilary Russell. There were at least a dozen to choose from. He softened his voice deliberately. It was time to try and take back control. 'No, I don't know who killed her.'

'Is that the truth?'

'Absolutely, I have no idea.'

'Could it have been Colley?'

Buchanan winced again. It was only the thought of Craven knocking on his front door that stopped him from ending the call there and then. 'I doubt it. He probably didn't even know her.'

'Who then?'

'Like I said, I don't know.'

'Richmond?'

'Of course not.'

'Worsley?'

'He was a High Court Judge for god's sake. What's the matter with you? Stop reeling off names, anybody could be monitoring this call.'

'It doesn't make sense. Why has someone killed her?'

'I'm not having this conversation with you anymore...'

'She knew about Teleios didn't she?'

Buchanan hit the red button and slammed the phone down on the desk. Craven had gone too far. Talking about Richmond and Worsley was bad enough. Mentioning Teleios was another thing altogether. He sat back down in the leather armchair and took a large, hurried gulp of wine, cradling the glass in his hand while he thought through his options. He noticed that his hand was shaking. For once in his life he wasn't sure what he was going to do next. Eventually he picked up the mobile again and paged through the list of contact names until he found Carlisle. He hesitated. Craven had worked for him for a long time – they went back a long way. He knew where the bodies were buried. He was also one of Buchanan's most loyal supporters. Still, not anymore. *"No more important duty can be urged upon those who are entering the great theatre of life than simple loyalty to their best convictions."* The call was answered in a matter of seconds.

'James, it's Charles. Sorry to disturb you at the weekend. We have a problem.'

TWENTY-EIGHT

Garrick turned away from the window and stared across the CID room. It was nine o'clock on a Sunday morning and the place was as packed and as busy as any day in the middle of the week, a strange mixture of noise and silence; bursts of conversation and activity from some of the team and quiet, almost studious concentration from others. A few of them had disappeared for ten minutes to order a round of tea and bacon sandwiches but they were all now back at their desks, all working hard and none of them showing the slightest inclination to complain about having to work at the weekend. Most of them had been in all day on Saturday and Garrick knew that he would have to literally force some of them to leave tonight at a sensible time. He turned back towards the window again and gazed out across the park. It was going to be a glorious day. Warm, autumnal sunshine and not a breath of wind. It was bad enough having to work at weekends, but it was always worse when the weather was so good.

It was Steph who took the call from a couple of junior uniforms to say that they had found Colley's car, a silver Mercedes parked at the back of level five of the car park at Ashford International Station. Andy and a team of three others had just left to drive down to Stockbridge, so the CID room was quieter and less crowded than it had been for a while but the news of Colley's motor changed all of that, triggering an immediate response and a frenzied level of activity. Timetables for Brussels and Paris were suddenly being checked while a SOCO team and one of the police mechanics were immediately despatched to unlock the car and start searching for clues. Garrick didn't think that there was much chance of finding the laptop but he knew that they would have to go through the vehicle with a fine tooth comb before it could be moved. Either way, Colley was probably on the continent and long gone by now. Steph was already on the phone, talking to someone at Eurostar and trying to get a passenger list for the past 24 hours

Matt watched the flurry of activity with a frustrated, detached interest. Increasingly, the enquiry was heading in a direction which made him feel uncomfortable. Nobody seemed to be thinking logically anymore. They were all concentrating on chasing the wrong leads and they were all knee-jerking and getting over-excited at the slightest development or piece of news. He couldn't believe what he was seeing. Everyone in the office knew that Colley had left his passport at home, it was one of the first things that they had checked, so there was no way that he could have got a train to either France or Belgium. Besides, if he was on the run and didn't want to be followed, he was hardly going to leave his car in the International Car Park, advertising to the whole world that that he'd just disappeared on Eurostar. Not unless he was completely stupid. It didn't make sense.

Matt was just contemplating whether to say anything when suddenly, amongst all the noise and activity Steph was holding her hand over the phone receiver and calling across to Garrick, who was still standing by the window, still gazing out across the park and thinking about where Colley might have gone. It took her a couple of seconds to get Garrick's attention. 'Sir, it's Cheryl. Apparently Chief Superintendent Anderson is in. He wants you to go up.'

'What, now?' Garrick couldn't disguise the annoyance in his voice. Anderson never worked on a Sunday. What the hell was he doing coming into the office today?

Steph shrugged her shoulders in a sort of defeatist gesture, still holding her hand over the receiver. 'It sounds urgent Sir.'

Garrick rolled his eyes up to the top of his head and picked up his jacket. The last thing he needed was another cosy chat with the Chief Superintendent but it didn't look as though he had any choice in the matter. He left the team with a few instructions, including a very specific one to interrupt him if there were any developments and then made his way up to the executive suite on the top floor. The whole place was getting more and more like a corporate business every week. *We'll be calling the general public "customers" next.* The door to Anderson's office was shut when he arrived, which gave him a chance to have a quick word with Cheryl before he went in. She didn't normally work at weekends either so something had to be going on. She looked up and gave him a smile as he came into the office. She always looked genuinely pleased to see him. 'Hi John, how are you?'

Garrick smiled back. 'Fine thanks Cheryl. Busy obviously. Unusual for you to be working on a Sunday.' Half statement, half question.

Cheryl threw him a look which he couldn't quite read. 'It was all a bit sudden. The Chief Super's waiting for you.' She nodded towards Anderson's door, indicating to Garrick that he could go straight in. She hesitated for a second, as if she was unsure about whether to say something else or not. As he got to the door and was about to enter, she quickly made up her mind. A simple decision really. 'John?'

'What?'

'He's got the Chief Constable with him.'

Garrick looked at her for a second and frowned. What the hell was all this about? He'd seen the Chief Constable from a distance on a couple of occasions but he'd never actually met him or spoken to him before. The guy never normally left the inner sanctum of his office. Occasionally you'd see him at a conference or on television commenting on some social or political initiative, but most of the time he was holed up in his star chamber at County Headquarters, surrounded by sycophants and pen-pushers. Garrick already had a nasty feeling about what was going to happen next. He smiled at Cheryl in appreciation and then gave the door a couple of firm knocks and pushed it open and went in.

Anderson was sitting in his chair behind his desk, obviously waiting for Garrick to arrive, and Chief Constable David Hutton was standing behind him at the back of the office, gazing out of the rear window. Garrick could tell immediately that there wasn't any conversation going on, he could have cut the atmosphere with a knife. Anderson looked up and gave him a look which luckily Hutton couldn't see. Garrick interpreted the message, *this is nothing to do with me John*, and gave Anderson a short nod in return. 'You wanted to see me Sir?' Hutton turned round as the door opened and gave Garrick a thin smile.

Anderson opened his palm, gesturing to Garrick to take a seat. 'You know the Chief Constable of course?'

Hutton had walked across the room and was extending his hand in formal introduction. 'John, I don't think we've met have we?' He was still smiling but only with his mouth.

'No, I don't think we have.' *You know bloody well we haven't.* Garrick shook hands and settled himself into one of the seats in front of Anderson's desk, watching Hutton as he eased himself into the other one. He was a small, neat, tidy man and was wearing the smartest uniform that Garrick had ever seen. He couldn't stop staring at Hutton's shoes. He'd never seen shoes as shiny as that before and the creases in his trousers were positively razor-like. It was a wonder that he didn't cut himself putting them on every morning. Maybe he slept in a trouser press and never actually took them off.

'So, John, how's the enquiry going?' Hutton was staring across at Garrick, looking him up and down.

'Which enquiry is that Sir? We've got a few on at the moment.' Garrick knew as soon as he said the words that it sounded petulant, but by now he was beyond caring. He wasn't going to play those games. Whatever it was that Hutton had come to say, it had already been agreed and rehearsed and making polite, introductory small-talk wasn't going to change anything. They were just going through the motions.

Hutton continued staring at him and gave him another thin smile. Anderson groaned and put his head in his hands. This was going to get spiky.

'I understand you're following up leads with the Foreign and Commonwealth Office?' Hutton continued staring at Garrick; a cold, analytical stare, a hunter closing in on its prey.

Garrick smiled to himself. So that was what this was all about. Hutton reported directly to the Home Secretary. All the Chief Constables did. The Teleios enquiry was crossing a political line. Somebody, somewhere was getting upset. Either that or they were getting nervous. *Never mind about solving three murders. Just make sure that you don't upset anybody in the establishment.* 'Yes Sir, there's a line of enquiry relating to the first murder in Appleden which requires us to visit the Foreign Office.'

'Requires us?' Hutton raised his eyebrows at Garrick's choice of words. 'What does that mean exactly?'

Garrick stood his ground. 'It means that we need to eliminate a number of people from our enquiries and that one of them works at the Foreign Office.'

Hutton said nothing and continued staring, as if he were trying to read Garrick's mind; work out what he was thinking. The silence became uncomfortable in a matter of seconds. Anderson poured himself a glass of water, for no reason other than it gave him something to do. Something to fill the space.

'Why, is that a problem Sir?' asked Garrick, deciding to push back and get straight to the point. Whatever all this was about they might as well get on with it and stop fannying about.

'I've been speaking to the Chief Constable in Hampshire.' continued Hutton, ignoring the question and looking at Anderson as much as he was looking at Garrick, 'Obviously we have some inter-force coordination to think about.'

Garrick gave him the slightest of nods. 'Obviously.'

'And it's important that we have absolute clarity about where the investigation is being led from, otherwise there is the potential for things to fall between the gaps.'

Garrick nodded again but said nothing.

'So I have to tell you that I have agreed with Peter Brolin this morning that his force will take over responsibility for directing the enquiry with immediate effect.'

Anderson, who knew what Hutton had been about to say watched Garrick like a hawk, waiting for the explosion that didn't happen. Garrick said nothing. He wasn't going to give them the satisfaction of losing his temper. Besides, they were playing poker, not snap – and anyway, he wasn't surprised. He could see it coming a mile off. It was much better to sit there and say nothing for the moment, listen to the puerile justification, even though he was seething inside. A tightly screwed lid on top of an overheated pressure-cooker.

'It's nothing personal of course.' added Hutton, trotting out the platitudes with not even a half-hearted attempt to sound as though he actually meant what he was saying. 'I wouldn't want you to think that it's anything to do with the way the enquiry has been handled to date. It's simply that we need to coordinate across two forces and Worsley's murder is by far the more sensitive and the higher profile, so it makes sense to let our colleagues in Hampshire direct everything from there.'

'Even though the first two murders were committed in Kent and there's only been one in Hampshire?' Garrick stared across at Hutton with a cold, blank expression.

'It's not a question of numbers John, or about which incident happened first. The important thing is that we resource ourselves appropriately and then work in an open and collegiate way with our colleagues under clear, unambiguous direction.'

Garrick continued looking at him with the same cold, blank expression. The management speak was unbelievable. 'Can I ask who is actually heading up the enquiry Sir. I assume it's not the Chief Constable personally?'

Anderson groaned and put his head in his hand again.

Hutton ignored the sarcasm. There was no point in getting riled. He held all the cards and was going to get his own way. Besides, he hadn't played the Ace yet. That was still to come. 'Superintendent Fowler will be heading up the enquiry.'

Garrick's mouth dropped open in disbelief. Suddenly the calm and controlled response was in danger of going out of the window. 'What, Brian Fowler?'

Hutton nodded. There was almost a flicker of a smile on the corners of his mouth. Garrick looked at Anderson, hardly able to contain his anger. 'Brian Fowler? You're going to let Brian Fowler head up a triple murder enquiry? Are you serious?'

Anderson could hardly look Garrick in the eye. Again, the same, embarrassed look. *This is nothing to do with me John.*

Hutton crossed one leg over the other and then casually brushed the nap off the material on his trousers, feigning disinterest in having to answer Garrick's concerns; the art of conveying indifference mastered to perfection. 'Brian Fowler is an experienced and dedicated officer who I am confident will bring a great deal of focus and professionalism to the enquiry.'

Garrick stood up, unable to maintain his composure any longer. 'The only thing that Brian Fowler will bring to this enquiry is a maverick, cavalier approach to police-work and a large bottle of scotch. The guy couldn't run a bath. Asking him to head up a murder enquiry is like asking Herod to look after the children. Do you seriously expect me to work for Brian Fowler?'

Hutton allowed himself a smile. *Checkmate.* It was like taking candy from a baby. Time to play the Ace. 'No, actually John I don't, that would be unfair. Which is why I've agreed with Chief Superintendent Anderson that it's probably better if you take some leave for a couple of weeks...' again, the thin smile, '...on full pay of course.'

Garrick stood in the centre of the office, staring in turn at Anderson and then at Hutton, unable to believe what was happening and desperately trying to control his temper. 'I've just been on holiday Sir, I don't need another one thank you.'

Hutton stared back at him, cold and expressionless. 'That's a matter of opinion. Anyway, we need to give Brian Fowler the best possible start. The last thing we need is your team struggling with divided loyalties. Much better if you're not around for a couple of weeks.'

Garrick looked at Anderson who was still staring down at his desk. Too embarrassed and too ashamed to even look him in the eye. It told Garrick all he needed to know. This wasn't a decision that was up for debate. Anderson must have already tried to argue his case and had obviously lost. He looked back at Hutton and stiffened his back, almost standing to attention. 'Do you want my warrant card Sir?'

Hutton smiled, a smug, self-satisfied smile of victory. 'That won't be necessary Chief Inspector. We're asking you to take a couple of weeks' leave to give Superintendent Fowler a clear run at everything. You're not suspended. Try and book a late deal somewhere and find a beach and get some sunshine. Hopefully the enquiry will be finished by the time you come back – but if not, there are plenty of other things you can work on.'

Garrick looked back at Anderson again who was still saying nothing, still staring down at the desk. 'What about the team Sir? What would you like me to tell them?'

'Chief Superintendent Anderson and I will talk to them. You just make a discreet exit and we'll update them as soon as you've gone. We probably won't get much out of them today, but it'll be business as usual tomorrow.'

'What about the Foreign Office Sir? Matt Isaacs and I were going up to London tomorrow. He'll need someone more senior to go with him.'

Hutton stood up and started to walk back towards the window at the rear of the office, indicating that the conversation was over. 'Like I said Chief Inspector, try and find some sunshine and forget all about the enquiry. I'm sure Superintendent Fowler will pick up anything that's in progress.'

'And contact with the team?' Garrick already knew the answer but he wanted to hear it for himself.

Hutton turned and looked at him in silence for a couple of seconds. They were both playing games, both following a script that had been played out many times before. 'Best avoided I think. I always find that a couple of weeks holiday is a much more civilised arrangement than suspension, don't you think?' Again the thin smile. 'A more elegant way of finessing the situation. I trust we understand each other?'

Garrick smiled back, a cold, calculating smile. *I wouldn't bet on it*. 'Thank you Sir. Understood.'

TWENTY-NINE

There had been a principle inn and hotel in Beaulieu for hundreds of years, enjoying the same prime, central position in the heart of the village since the middle of the 16th century. Originally called *The Ship* and then *The George*, it had been known under its current name, *The Montagu Arms* since the 1740s and during its history had established itself as a meeting place for local farmers and parish officers, as well as a centre for timber auctions and lectures. The village fairs, originating from 1607 were held there every year, as were annual cattle markets until around 1809. At one time the inn even owned its own farmland.

The fact that it was on Buchanan's own doorstep was a coincidence, but a happy one nevertheless – it had always been one of his favourite hotels. From the outside it looked more like an old-fashioned country house rather than a commercial enterprise and in his opinion it was that mixture of tradition but informality that gave it such an individual and special character. Every time Buchanan visited the place he was always struck by the solidity and comfort of it all. An oak floored and panelled hall with an old brick fireplace led into a beautifully proportioned oak panelled dining room with French windows and then out into an "old world" cottage garden with paved paths, roses and cottage plants. From another door in the hall one could enter the Magnolia Lounge, the essence of quiet, traditional, comfort with a roaring log fire and huge, comfortable sofas and armchairs. Visitors would often while away a lazy couple of hours, taking morning coffee or afternoon tea while reading the daily newspapers, oblivious to the machinations of the world outside.

Buchanan had never actually stayed at *The Montagu Arms*, but he knew that the rooms were all generously proportioned and all properly furnished with traditional, high-quality English furniture. The perfect combination of style and functionality. There were also a number of suites and four-poster beds which were obviously popular with visitors and tourists. The Terrace restaurant on the other hand was one of his more regular haunts, as was the book-lined Library Bar complete with magazines, playing cards and a selection of board games. The restaurant was noted as one of the finest in the county and Buchanan frequented it often, normally on a Saturday evening with his wife or with a party of friends, or as on this occasion, for Sunday lunch.

The restaurant was nearly full, mid autumn being a popular time for tourists. Beaulieu was an ideal location from which to explore the delights of the New Forest, the famous *National Motor Museum* owned by Lord Montagu, or *Bucklers Hard*, the historic shipbuilding village where Lord Nelson's fleet was built. Visitors could walk through the back of the hotel to a public footpath which ran all the way to *Bucklers Hard*, an enjoyable and undemanding stroll which was perfect exercise before taking Sunday lunch. Buchanan looked around the room with a sense of satisfaction and then scanned the wine list with the same, confident familiarity. Much like the service, the food and wine were always of the highest quality.

'Could you manage some wine, James?' he asked, flipping the pages with a casual, nonchalant flourish, mindful that his guest had driven down that morning and that it was bad form to encourage anyone to drink and drive.

'I could manage a glass probably,' replied Carlisle, picking up his napkin and folding it across his lap. 'White perhaps, as it's lunchtime?'

Buchanan nodded and turned back to the list again. He knew it off by heart of course, but it didn't hurt to double-check. 'How about a Loire? Sancerre or Pouilly Fumé?'

Carlisle nodded as he looked around the restaurant at the other tables. 'Sancerre will be fine Charles, thank you. I have to say this is very pleasant. It's a long time since I've been to *The Montagu Arms*. It's hardly changed at all.'

Buchanan smiled. 'Exactly. And long may it continue.'

The pair of them paused as the waiter arrived to serve some bread and then take their order. Buchanan ordered warm pheasant mousse with morel cream followed by fillet of John Dorey with shrimps and saffron potatoes. Carlisle ordered fillet of sea bass with onion and orange confit followed by peppered New Forest venison with sultanas in Armagnac sauce. The wine arrived within minutes, appropriately chilled and left by the table in a large bucket of ice.

Buchanan picked up the jug of water and poured a large measure into each of their glasses. 'Thank you for coming down James, particularly at such short notice. I really appreciate it.'

'Not at all,' replied Carlisle, picking up the glass and taking a small sip. It's not like you to ask for help Charles, so I assume it must be serious?'

'Unfortunately, yes.'

Carlisle gave him a sympathetic smile. He'd known Buchanan for several years now and he had always been a lone operator – sociable enough in a fairly cool and detached sort of way, but definitely someone who worked to his own agenda. It was understandable of course. *Vector* wasn't even on the radar screen to most people in Whitehall, so secrecy and discretion were an absolute pre-requisite. Normal, business-like networking was impossible, in fact it was prohibited. It wasn't until his appointment as Private Secretary to the PM that Carlisle first became aware of Buchanan's existence, or of his department for that matter. Making the phone call yesterday evening must have been particularly difficult for him. 'How's Margaret?' he asked, trying to keep matters sociable and informal, at least until the first course arrived.

Buchanan smiled to himself, realising his indecent haste at almost jumping into the murky world of intelligence before the first glass of wine had even been poured. 'She's fine thank you James. Busying herself with furniture restoring at the moment.'

'Good, good. Important to let the ladies have their enthusiasms, I always think.'

'Indeed. And how's Caroline?' asked Buchanan, maintaining the charade. 'Still painting?'

Carlisle nodded, waiting a second or two to answer until he'd finished chewing a piece of bread that was staving off his hunger. 'Absolutely. She had a couple of watercolours at the Summer Exhibition this year. We were all very proud of her.'

Again the pair of them paused as the waiter arrived to serve the first course, also enquiring to see if they wanted him to open the wine. Buchanan nodded his agreement and then took a small sip to taste, allowing the waiter to pour a decent measure into both glasses.

'So, you'd better tell me what this is all about,' said Carlisle, picking up his wine and taking an appreciative mouthful.

Buchanan took a precautionary glance around the room to make sure that no-one could hear their conversation and then lowered his voice. 'It's Teleios I'm afraid.'

'Go on.' Carlisle was now eating the pheasant mousse with morel cream, concentrating on the food but at the same time listening to Buchanan. Two pleasures at the same time. Delicious food plus the schadenfreude of hearing about somebody else's problem. Exquisite.

Buchanan picked up his own glass and took an equally appreciative sip. The temperature was causing the glass to mist and form rivulets of cold moisture which were running over the surface and down the stem. The wine tasted clean and crisp. 'As I said on the phone James, I think we have an emerging problem which I need to alert you to.'

Carlisle stopped eating for a moment and stared at Buchanan across the table, looking him straight in the eye. 'Get straight to the point Charles. What's happened?'

Buchanan nodded, the pre-amble over. Time to get to the detail. 'On one level it's good news. We've recovered the stolen laptop and are reasonably certain that no-one has accessed it – or to be more precise, the only person who did access it is no longer with us.'

Carlisle nodded as he continued to eat, waving a hand contemptuously towards Buchanan indicating that he wanted him to get on with it.

Buchanan lowered his voice even further, almost to a whisper. 'We're also confident that the person who accessed the laptop was the same person who murdered both Stuart Richmond and Sir Julian Worsley. We believe he was blackmailing Richmond, possibly trying to sell the laptop back to him.'

'Remind me, which one was Richmond?' Carlisle was still clearing his plate. Obviously the cuisine in rural Hampshire was meeting with his approval.

'The Fashion Designer. Lots of High Street retail outlets. Always on the television. Rather pretty wife.'

Carlisle pulled a face, unimpressed, a vague recollection of who Buchanan was talking about. 'I'm surprised they let him in. He's not exactly in the same league is he?'

Buchanan shrugged his shoulders. It was certainly true that Richmond was probably the most junior member but they all had a lot to lose. Besides, he was one of the country's most successful businessmen. A real entrepreneur who promoted the spirit of free enterprise and the value of UK plc. Something of a pin-up at the Treasury, he would have thought. Not that any of that mattered anymore. The guy was dead.

'So basically, the threat to Teleios died with him?' added Carlisle, putting his knife and fork down for the first time in several minutes.

Buchanan nodded. 'Exactly. One of my team recovered the laptop and … let's just say he tidied up all the loose ends.'

Carlisle smiled to himself, interpreting immediately what Buchanan meant. 'Good. Well done.' Then he frowned, obviously confused. 'So what's the problem then Charles?'

'The problem,' replied Buchanan, leaning forward across the table and keeping his voice down, 'is that I think my officer has gone native.'

Carlisle allowed himself a faint smile and relaxed back into his chair. So that was it. He'd spent the whole morning worrying that the contents of the laptop had got into the wrong hands and in actual fact it was just Buchanan worrying about one of his team having thrown a hissy fit. He wiped the corners of his mouth with his napkin and then folded it neatly into a triangle and replaced it carefully across his lap. Poor old Charles. There he was, spending his whole life orchestrating subterfuge and betrayal onto other people and then suddenly, after all these years, somebody was threatening to do exactly the same to him. No wonder he was worried. 'Well, I can see why that's inconvenient Charles, embarrassing even, but I don't see why you need my help. Why don't you just haul him in and get him back onside?'

'It's not that simple. He's not on the payroll anymore. He's been freelance for a while.'

Carlisle shrugged, still not really understanding the problem. 'Well put one of your other team onto it. Get your best man on the case and get it sorted out.'

'He was my best man.'

Carlisle shook his head again, clearly frustrated that the conversation wasn't going anywhere. He also leant forward across the table and lowered his voice, the tone slightly impatient and spoken through gritted teeth. 'Charles, I understand your problem but I really don't see how I can help. The implications of Teleios becoming public are unthinkable. If one of your people has gone native, then you need to get them back into line as soon as possible – or if that isn't possible, arrange for a more permanent solution.' He stared at Buchanan to make sure that the implication of what was being said was fully understood. 'Either way, no-one is better positioned to sort that out than you.'

Buchanan gave him a cold smile. Time to shift the balance. 'I know. I don't actually need your help James. I just wanted to let you know what was going on...'

'Well, thank you, I appreciate that.' Carlisle moved his plate to one side and looked around the room to see where the waiter had gone. He was ready for his main course now.

'...and to warn you that he's likely to come and pay you a visit.'

'Me?' Carlisle looked genuinely surprised and for the first time a little uncomfortable. Spending his whole life in the Civil Service meant that he had led a safe, cocooned existence for more years than he cared to remember, slightly detached and protected from the real world. And having been a Private Secretary and then the Cabinet Secretary for the last seven years, he was used to getting his own way. Accustomed to controlling events, not waiting for things to happen. Buchanan's world was completely the opposite. Unpredictable, dark and slightly dangerous. Not something that he could control at all. 'What does he want to come and see me for? Teleios was in place long before I was around. If he's got some moral dilemma that he's struggling with, there's no point talking to me.'

Buchanan watched Carlisle's agitation with contempt. They were all the same. In fact the mandarins were worse than the politicians – at least some of the MPs actually had some balls. The Civil Servants were despicable. There wasn't a decent vertebra in any of them. As far as Buchanan was concerned they were all egotistic bureaucrats, obsessed by the hierarchy and the status and the privilege of office and only interested in maintaining their own power-bases and progressing their own careers – and Carlisle was one of the worst. Buchanan gave him another cold smile, just to let him know who was in control. 'He hasn't gone native because of Teleios, he doesn't know what Teleios is. I decided not to tell him.'

Carlisle raised an eyebrow, trying to maintain his composure and not appear over-concerned. He'd seen Buchanan dissect people before – it was like watching someone perform an operation without an anaesthetic. A mouse being played on the end of a cat's claw. He puffed out his chest slightly, unaware that it only made him look all the more absurd. 'So what's his problem if it's not Teleios. What's he's getting so bloody principled about?'

Buchanan picked up his glass and took a long, slow sip of wine, the crispness of the dry, flint after-taste merging with the hint of gooseberry and nettle on his palate. This was always the moment he savoured most. He would have preferred the Pouilly Fumé of course, more rounded and much more subtle but no matter, the important thing was that it was Carlisle's choice. Much better to have him relaxed and content before the kill. He spoke the words slowly. 'Hilary Russell. Hilary Russell is what he's getting so upset about.'

Carlisle sank slowly back into his chair and stared across the room, looking at nothing in particular. Suddenly he knew that this wasn't a game. Buchanan wasn't bluffing. He fiddled nervously with his cufflinks for a moment, trying to think of something to say. They were a birthday present from his son – expensive, gold, oval links. Un-monogrammed. They matched the signet ring that he wore on the little finger of his left hand. Stupid really, wearing cufflinks on a weekend. All part of playing the role. The Cabinet Secretary. The quintessential English gentleman. He picked up the wine and took a large gulp. Bugger the licence. Suddenly it tasted thin and sharp, much too acidic. He looked up at Buchanan who was staring intently at him across the table. Poised to make his move. 'Did he know her?'

Buchanan shook his head but said nothing.

'Just a loyalty thing then. Colleagues sticking together and all that?' The words came out in almost a sneer.

'Something like that.'

The two of them stared across the table at each other, the silence amplified by the noise and laughter of the other guests around them. Carlisle reached over and pulled the bottle of wine out of the ice bucket, not bothering to try and stop the excess water dripping all over the tablecloth. He poured a large slug of wine into his own glass and then leant forward and offered the same to Buchanan. Buchanan raised his hand, politely declining any more. Carlisle shrugged and stuffed the bottle back into the ice.

'So what happened?' asked Buchanan, leaning back into his chair and taking a relaxed, authoritative pose.

'What do you mean "what happened?" How should I know?'

Buchanan circled his wine glass on the tabletop and then took a small sip, holding his temper and choosing his words carefully. 'Hilary Russell came to see me on a Friday morning two weeks ago and two days later she was dead. The only person I told was you…'

Carlisle shifted uncomfortably in his chair.

'… I hadn't seen her for nearly twenty years and the only reason she came to see me was to tell me about Richmond's burglary and to warn me about Teleios. We wouldn't have known otherwise…'

Carlisle fiddled with his cufflinks again. Where the hell was that waiter?

'…She didn't need to do that. She took the time and trouble to come and tell me because she knew it was important. We owed her a debt of gratitude and instead, two days later she was dead. I want to know what happened.'

Carlisle shook his head. 'I don't know Charles. It was as much a surprise to me as it was to you.' He picked up the napkin and dabbed the top of his brow. Suddenly the restaurant seemed to have got very warm.

Buchanan leant forward across the table again. 'Who did you tell James?' There's a leak somewhere and if Hilary's death is nothing to do with you, then you must have told somebody else. Who was it?'

Suddenly the waiter appeared out of nowhere and started to clear away the dirty plates. Buchanan leant back and refilled his glass of water, waiting for the main course to be served, all the time watching Carlisle across the table, watching his every movement like a hawk. He didn't trust him. He didn't trust him one inch. No doubt going to Winchester and Oxford must have helped, but the simple truth was that the only reason Carlisle had risen to the dizzy heights of Cabinet Secretary was because he played the political game better than anybody else. There were other people who worked harder, or who were more intelligent, but admirable as those qualities were, they were not the defining qualities for ultimate success. It was the guile and the cunning and the ruthlessness that had got him where he was. That and the fact that he was a cock-sucker.

Carlisle waited for the waiter to depart and then picked up his knife and fork with anticipation. The New Forest venison with sultanas in Armagnac sauce looked positively mouth-watering and despite the sparring with Buchanan, it had done nothing to diminish his appetite. In fact the interruption from the waiter had given him a few seconds to collect his thoughts. He was feeling a bit better than he had a moment ago. Time to push back. 'Maybe Hilary Russell told somebody else,' he ventured, waving his fork in an animated gesture and looking across at Buchanan for the first time in several minutes. 'Perhaps she mentioned it to somebody else after she spoke to you.'

Buchanan almost snorted in derision. 'You obviously never knew her. The reason she came on the train was because she didn't trust the telephone and she wouldn't risk speaking to anybody other than me. She was a professional. Thirty-five years service. She told me what we needed to know and then she got back on the train and went home. Full stop. The end. It's inconceivable that she would have said anything to anybody else.'

Carlisle raised his eyebrows again, trying to delay the point at which he had to admit to his indiscretion.

'You may as well tell me James.' continued Buchanan, adding a thin smile just to emphasise the threat. 'Treat it as a sort of rehearsal for when my man turns up.'

Carlisle gave him a hollow smile in return. He needed Buchanan onside, if only to get his Rottweiller off his back. He knew it and Buchanan knew it. He took a deep breath. 'Okay Charles, I told Robert Bellamy. I thought he ought to know in case something blew up.'

Buchanan looked at him with disdain. 'When?'

'The Friday afternoon. A couple of hours after you told me.'

Buchanan shook his head in despair. 'Anybody else?'

Carlisle dropped his head and looked down at the table. Personally he wasn't that bothered but he knew he ought to have the good grace to appear embarrassed. Pretend that he was struggling to look Buchanan in the eye. Sackcloth and ashes. 'No, nobody. I promise, I only mentioned it to Bellamy.'

Buchanan turned away and looked across the room, thinking about what he was going to do next. Carlisle had obviously been covering his own back and hadn't given a second thought to the consequence of his actions. He probably didn't even know Hilary Russell and he certainly didn't care. Buchanan turned back and looked at him across the table again, his head still down, enjoying his lunch, oblivious to the chaos and mayhem that he had caused. A vile, obsequious parasite who spent his whole life fawning to his paymasters and stabbing everyone else in the back. Buchanan could have killed him. Still, there was no point wasting time thinking about that. Craven was probably going to do that for him. 'I told you it was classified James. For your eyes only. What on earth made you go and tell Bellamy?'

Carlisle gave him an apologetic shrug. 'I thought he ought to know. He's the Home Secretary for god's sake. I'm sorry Charles – about Hilary I mean. Please believe me, I had no idea, honestly.'

Buchanan put his knife and fork down for a second and gave Carlisle a grave and serious look. 'It's a bit late for that. Anyway, let's just hope that my man believes you if he decides to pay you visit.'

Carlisle picked up his glass of wine and looked back across the table. He'd had enough of being bullied by Charles Buchanan. Obviously what had happened was regrettable, but it was too late to change any of that now. Time to recover the situation and restore a bit of normality. *"We have to distrust each other, it is our only defence against betrayal."* 'Your man, he has a name does he?'

'Yes. His name's Craven.'

Carlisle took out a fountain pen and an old envelope from his inside jacket pocket and quickly scribbled the name on the back of the envelope. 'And he knows that you told me about Hilary's visit does he?'

'No, not yet – but it won't take him long to find out. If he asks it's going to be hard not to tell him. He can be very persuasive. Besides, he'll probably ask Jean – she wouldn't know not to say anything.'

'Jean Pettipher, your PA?'

Buchanan nodded, suddenly wishing that he hadn't told Carlisle that particular point.

Carlisle put the top back onto the fountain pen and clipped it back into the inside pocket of his jacket with a flourish. 'Well, thanks for the tip-off Charles. I'll let you know if he turns up.'

Buchanan picked up his own glass and smiled. 'James, trust me. If he turns up, you won't even see him coming.'

THIRTY

Despite their best intentions to make the most of the weekend, Neil and Chris ended up spending a very lazy Sunday doing not very much other than getting up late, going to *The Chequers* for a swift couple of pints and then enjoying a leisurely afternoon at Tom and Doreen's. Doreen had kindly invited them both to lunch and after tucking into a meal of roast beef and Yorkshire pudding, the pair of them spent the rest of the afternoon lounging about reading the Sunday papers and generally putting the world to rights. Tom had slumped himself into one of the armchairs in front of the fire and was working his way through a couple of bottles of Light Ale, whilst Neil and Chris were still sitting at the table, polishing off a bottle of red wine that Doreen had bought especially for the occasion.

As ever, Doreen was busying herself in the kitchen, washing up and giving the worktops and the flagstone floor a good clean, more than happy to have cooked Sunday lunch for a couple of very appreciative guests. Usually it was just her and Tom, which meant that they didn't normally bother with a roast dinner, so it was genuine pleasure for her to cook a proper meal for once, with roast potatoes and buttered parsnips and real, home made gravy. She hadn't met Chris before but as far as Doreen was concerned, any friend of Neil's was a friend of hers. In fact she had taken to him straightaway. He had a sort of mischievous, boyish streak which made him instantly likeable and which made her smile.

Tom flipped the top off a second bottle of Light Ale and carefully poured the beer into his glass, holding it at a 45 degree angle to make sure that he got the perfect head. 'So, any progress on this Teleios thing?' he asked before taking a sip and putting the beer carefully down on the hearth in front of the fire.

'No, not really,' replied Neil, staring at the flames which were spitting and crackling under a new bit of wood that Tom had just tossed onto it. 'We think it's something to do with where Aunt Hilary used to work, but beyond that we're not really sure.'

Tom chuckled as he stretched over and picked up his tobacco tin and lighter which were sitting on top of the mantelpiece. 'Sounds to me like you're asking the wrong question,' he said, opening the tin and pulling out a cigarette paper, 'a bit like asking, "so where has the other pound gone?"

Maybe you need to look at everything from a different perspective?'

Neil and Chris exchanged a puzzled look, neither of them too sure exactly what Tom was talking about. 'What do you mean, "where has the other pound gone?"' asked Chris, obviously not familiar with Tom's famous liking for anecdotes and silly stories. Neil groaned. He knew Tom well enough by now to know that there was another London Underground teaser or something similar coming. He could see the twinkle in his eye.

Tom stuffed some tobacco into the cigarette paper and rolled-up a smoke, slowly licking the gummed paper and using the silence to full effect. Eventually, he flicked his lighter and inhaled deeply, blowing a thin cloud of smoke towards the fireplace. 'Well, you must have heard the story about the three men who booked a hotel room for the night?'

Neil groaned again. Tom was definitely in storytelling mode.

Chris grinned, quickly cottoning on that this must be one of Tom's yarns or shaggy dog stories. It didn't matter. He couldn't remember the last time that he had felt so contented. Doreen's Sunday lunch had been just perfect and it was a lovely way to spend a lazy afternoon; sitting in front of a real log fire, drinking red wine and talking about nothing in particular with Neil and Tom.

Tom took another sip of beer and then started his story, as always enjoying the build-up before dropping the punch-line or posing the impossible question. Neil and Chris both listened attentively.

'Well, there were three blokes who suddenly had to book a hotel room overnight. They didn't have much money so they found a cheap hotel and asked the receptionist if she had a room that all three of them could share...'

'Okay,' said Chris, sipping his wine and still grinning in anticipation of the punch-line that was about to come.

'...and as luck would have it, the receptionist said that she had a cheap room and that they could have it for one night, for thirty-pounds. So the three men each gave her a ten pound note and then went upstairs to check in and unpack...'

Chris and Neil both nodded, indicating that they were keeping up with the story. Neither of them had heard it before.

'...Well, after about five minutes there was a knock at the door and the receptionist was standing there with five, one pound coins in her hand. "I'm sorry," she said, "I made a mistake, the room wasn't thirty pounds, it should have been twenty-five pounds so I've brought you five pounds in change." So the men each took a one pound coin and then one of them said to the receptionist, "thank you – and as you've been so honest, you can keep the other

257

two pounds as a tip." So, the receptionist kept the two pound tip, said "thank you" and then left. Got all of that?'

Both Neil and Chris nodded. It wasn't exactly complicated.

'So, how much have the men spent?' asked Tom, picking up his glass again.

'Twenty-seven pounds,' said Neil without even thinking. 'Nine pounds each. They each spent ten pounds and they each got a pound back.'

'Exactly,' said Tom starting to enjoy himself. 'So the question is; there was thirty pounds to begin with. If the blokes spent twenty-seven pounds and the receptionist has got a two pound tip, where has the other pound gone?'

Neil and Chris looked at each other in confusion for a couple of seconds while Tom broke into a broad grin and took a long, satisfied couple of puffs on his cigarette.

'Hang on, that can't be right,' said Neil, trying to work out the problem in his head, you must have said something wrong.'

'Not at all.' replied Tom, chuckling to himself as he drank his beer and watched Neil struggling to try and work out the conundrum. Maybe it was the effects of the red wine but as hard as he tried, he really couldn't get his head around it. *So much for a university education* thought Tom, still grinning and still enjoying himself. Even Chris, who was a lot more streetwise and quicker on the uptake was still looking confused.

'So what's the answer then Tom?' asked Neil, starting to get frustrated that he couldn't work it out.

Just like a couple of days before, Tom tapped the side of his nose with his forefinger in a silent, knowing gesture. 'You'll have to work it out lads. It shouldn't take you long, a couple of bright sparks like you!'

'Well, it's obviously the wrong question,' said Chris, remembering Tom's earlier comment, 'we're obviously looking at the problem from the wrong perspective.'

'Exactly,' replied Tom, pointing a finger towards Chris and nodding in approval. 'Now you're thinking. And once you've worked it out maybe you should try and use the same logic to look at ...' He stopped in mid-sentence as all three of them heard the front doorbell. 'I wonder who that can be?' he said, pulling a face and as he flicked his cigarette butt onto the fire.

'Whatever you do Tom Webster,' said Doreen, bustling past them with more than a hint of sarcasm in her voice, 'don't stir yourself out of that chair. I wouldn't want you putting your back out.'

Tom looked at Neil and Chris and pulled a sheepish face as Doreen disappeared into the hall on her way to answer the door. After fifty years of marriage he knew well enough when to keep his mouth shut and just keep his head down. Doreen on the warpath was not a woman to be reckoned with. The three of them listened for a moment or two, trying to identify the voice and work out who she was talking to. Within a couple of seconds Doreen was back, poking her head around the door and looking at Neil who was finishing off the last dregs of wine in his glass. 'It's DC Page Neil, she says she wants a quick word with you. I asked her to come in but I think she wants to speak to you next door.'

Neil and Chris exchanged a knowing look. Obviously something had happened which Steph didn't want to talk about in front of Tom or Doreen. Either that or it was personal. 'Time we were going anyway.' said Neil, putting his empty glass on top of the mantelpiece and indicating to Chris to follow suit. 'Thanks for a wonderful lunch Doreen. It was excellent.'

The two of them said their goodbyes and let themselves out, finding Steph still waiting patiently on the front door step, looking surprised and slightly uneasy to see that Neil wasn't on his own. He quickly did the introductions as they all walked down the path to the front gate and then back up the front path to *Yew Tree Cottage*. 'Actually,' said Chris, suddenly sensing that he ought to make himself scarce, 'I need to go and get some petrol. 'I ought to be getting back and I'd rather fill up now than stop on the motorway.'

Neil gave Chris an appreciative nod as he opened the front door and then gave him the front door keys. Chris was obviously disappearing just to give him and Steph a bit of time on their own. 'Here, take these. Save you ringing the bell.'

Chris smiled. 'Thanks. I'll be about ten minutes. I'm not sure if you'll still be here when I get back' he added, looking at Steph who still seemed to be uncomfortable in his presence, 'but if not, it was really good to meet you. Neil's told me all about you!' He didn't dare look round as he walked back down the path, a huge grin on his face as he imagined the two awkward, embarrassed people that he'd left behind.

'Ignore him,' said Neil, eventually breaking the silence and closing the front door. 'Come on, I'll make us a cup of tea and you can tell me whatever it was you came to talk about.'

Steph smiled at him, albeit it a little nervously as she followed him down the hall and into the kitchen. Chris's parting comment was still playing on her mind. 'Have you really told him everything about you and me, Neil?'

Suddenly it was Neil's turn to look slightly uncomfortable. 'Well, not *everything*,' he replied, unable to stop his face from blushing. 'Anyway, I'm beginning to think that maybe I shouldn't have said anything at all. What with work and everything.'

Steph pulled a face – half smile, half grimace. "Well, actually that's what I came to tell you. I don't think we're gong to be able to see each other for a while, at least not until the enquiry is over.'

Neil couldn't disguise the disappointment in his face. Meeting Steph was one of the best things that had happened to him in a long time. Almost instantly his expression changed as another thought occurred to him. 'Why, has someone found out?'

Steph shook her head and smiled. 'No, it's not that. We're under new management. And I think we're all going to be under the spotlight for a few weeks. We're all going to have to play everything by the book.'

'Under new management? What does that mean?' Neil frowned as he filled the kettle under the tap and started to make a pot of tea, listening attentively as Steph began to tell him about the day's events. Unlike Matt, she took care not to give Neil any details about the actual investigation, but as the two of them sat at the kitchen table and drank their tea, she updated him on Garrick's sudden departure and on the new regime which was now in place.

'So what's the new boss like?' asked Neil, leaning back in his chair and looking at Steph across the table. She was a looking tired. Too much overtime and working at weekends probably. That and the constant struggle of trying to balance a career with being a single mother.

Steph shrugged. 'We don't know yet. He starts tomorrow morning. But the signs aren't good.'

'What does that mean?'

'Let's just say his reputation precedes him. He's not exactly known for his up-to-date, modern policing methods. Or for his clearance rate for that matter.'

'And what was Garrick like?' asked Neil, trying to work out why he would have been removed. Obviously he must have done something wrong, or maybe he just wasn't up to the job.

Steph smiled to herself. 'He was brilliant. Best boss I've ever worked for. And he got results.'

Neil frowned again, obviously still confused by what Steph was telling him. 'But why would they replace a perfectly good copper with somebody less effective? It doesn't make sense.'

Steph let out a long sigh. 'This is the police force Neil. It doesn't have to make sense.'

The two of them sat in silence for a couple of seconds, thinking through the absurdity of Steph's last remark when suddenly they heard the sound of Chris turning the key in the front door lock and letting himself in, his arrival accompanied by a loud and excitable announcement as he walked down the hall. 'Hey Neil, guess who I found waiting on the front doorstep again! Matt's popped round to update us on what's been happening and you'll never guess what's…'

Chris stopped in mid sentence as he and Matt reached the kitchen doorway and saw Neil and Steph still sitting at the kitchen table, Neil's face the picture of acute embarrassment and Steph's not far behind him.

'Oh, hello Steph,' said Matt, thinking on his feet and trying to bluff his way through it. 'What are you doing here?'

As hard as she tried, Steph couldn't stop her face from blushing, her neck and cheeks instantly turning a bright shade of crimson. Matt looked at her for a second and then suddenly the penny dropped. The body language between her and Neil was unmistakeable. 'Why didn't you tell me?' he said gently, giving Steph a warm, sympathetic smile. 'You know I wouldn't have said anything.'

Steph gave him an embarrassed smile back. There wasn't much she could say. She'd decided not to tell Matt partly because it was private but also because she knew it was wrong and she didn't want to get him involved. Either way, it was nothing to do with him not being able to keep a secret. But somehow, any explanation now seemed rather lame. Too little, too late. 'Anyway,' she said, deciding to push back a bit, 'never mind me. What are you doing here? And what's all this about updating Neil and Chris on what's been happening? What's been going on?'

Matt and Neil and Chris all looked at each other for a moment, each of them waiting to see if somebody else was going to speak first. 'Mmm. I think we'd better have another cup of tea,' said, Neil, eventually breaking the silence and sensing that there was a lengthy and rather guilty explanation about to take place. 'I think it's about time that we all had a more open and honest conversation about everything.'

'Amen to that,' said Chris with some feeling. 'I've had enough of all this subterfuge. Particularly since we're all meant to be on the same side. I'll put the kettle on. You two can update Steph on what's been going on.'

Chris duly made the tea while Neil and Matt brought Steph up to date with everything that had happened since Matt had broken into the cottage on Friday evening. To her credit, she tried not to laugh too much at Neil's description of how he attacked Matt with the frying pan – but most of all she was just relieved that all the secrecy that had been there between them was now out in the open. It felt as though a weight had been lifted off their shoulders and that suddenly, the process of personal disclosure had created a special relationship between the four of them, a sort of shared understanding and a common purpose.

'So, what happened today then?' asked Neil, conscious that Matt had come round to tell them something specific.

'It's not particularly good news.' replied Matt, pulling out a chair and sitting down next to Steph. 'It looks like the only line of enquiry that's still open is the one in London; following up the phone calls that your Aunt made to Adam Saxby and Jean Pettipher a couple of days before she died. All the other leads have dried up today.'

'What about Colley?' asked Chris, 'I thought he was your primary lead.'

'He was,' replied Matt grimly, 'until we found his car this morning with his body in the boot.'

Neil and Chris exchanged a worried glance. That was the fourth dead body in the space of just over a week. 'And no laptop I presume?' asked Neil.

Matt shook his head. 'No, no sign of the laptop. We found a couple of CDs in the glove compartment which belonged to Stuart Richmond but otherwise, nothing. Unless we can find the laptop, the trail on Graham Colley has gone cold. A bit like him really.'

'And what about Worsley?' asked Chris. 'Wasn't there anything there?'

Again Matt shook his head. 'Not a thing. We've spent most of the day trawling through his bank details, credit card transactions, telephone records but we've found absolutely nothing. The guy didn't have so much as a parking ticket. Plus we sent a team down to search his house today and they've been through his desk and all of his papers with a fine tooth comb but have also drawn a complete blank. They've checked his emails, his on-line address book, his Internet history, in fact they practically took his computer apart and put it back together again, but it's as clean as a whistle. We can't find a single thing to connect him to Stuart Richmond, let alone to something called Teleios.'

'So what are you going to do next?' asked Neil.

Matt took a deep breath in anticipation of what he was about to say. 'Well, that's why I came round. The reason I wanted to see you was to try and persuade both of you to go to London tomorrow to see Adam Saxby.'

'Us?' Neil and Chris looked at each other with a mix of bewilderment and amusement. 'I don't think there's much point in us going to see him,' said

Chris, not realising for a moment what Matt had in mind, 'he's hardly likely to talk to a couple of journalists.'

'That's not what I meant actually.' replied Matt, hardly able to believe himself what he was about to suggest. 'What I had in mind was you going to see him pretending to be a couple of police officers.'

Neil and Chris looked at each other in stunned silence again and then burst out laughing. 'Police Officers ? Us?'

'I'm serious,' said Matt, more than a little offended at their slightly frivolous response to his proposal. 'That's what I've been trying to tell you. The visit that I was going to make tomorrow with Garrick has been cancelled – courtesy of Superintendent Fowler. This is the only lead that we've got left. Everything now depends on you two following up the telephone numbers on that piece of paper.'

'Us?' replied Neil, rather indignantly. 'You're meant to be the police officer Matt. Isn't that what we pay taxes for?'

'Can I have a look at the piece of paper?' asked Steph, suddenly interrupting to try and diffuse the situation. For a moment it looked as though the boys were about to get into an argument. 'I haven't seen it before.'

Neil went off into the dining room to get it out of the bureau where he'd put it for safe keeping, handing it over to Steph as he sat back down. 'The telephone numbers are the ones down the middle.'

'I'm really sorry Matt, I can't go to London,' said Chris, getting up from the table to put his empty cup on the draining board. 'I have to be back at work tomorrow.'

'Can't you take another day off?' asked Matt, trying to stress how important it was. 'It's really crucial that we follow this up.'

Chris shook his head. 'There's no way that I can take another day off. I'm not just doing my own job, I'm covering for Neil as well. If I don't go in we won't make the copy deadline.'

'What does that mean?'

'It means I'll probably get the sack.'

'Well, you'll just have to go on your own then,' said Matt, looking at Neil across the table. 'I can tell you how to behave and what to say.'

'You must be joking!' replied Neil, pulling a face to indicate that it wasn't going to happen. 'I'm not sure that I would have agreed to it, even if Chris was able to go, but there's absolutely no way that I'm going to London to see Adam Saxby on my own.'

'Which one of these is Saxby's number and which one is Jean Pettipher's' interrupted Steph, still staring at the piece of paper and not taking much notice of the conversation.

'Saxby's is the middle number' replied Neil, 'and Jean Pettipher's is at the bottom. The 01242 number at the top is GCHQ. We assume that she rang them in that order.'

'And what are all these prime numbers for?' she asked, pointing to the numbers that had been scribbled around the edge of the notepaper. 'Are they significant at all?'

Chris stopped what he was doing at the sink and Neil and Matt suddenly stared at Steph across the table. 'What do you mean, prime numbers?' asked Matt, leaning across and looking at the piece of paper again. 'Which ones are prime numbers?'

Steph raised her eyebrows in surprise, suddenly aware that everybody was staring at her as though she'd just said something important. 'Well, these four definitely are, 2221, 3331, 4441 and 6661. I recognised them straight away. Why, do they mean something?'

'We don't know,' replied Neil, 'we didn't know what they were. Are any of the others prime numbers?'

Steph looked at the note again and frowned for a moment as though she was trying to work out something in her head. 'Well this one certainly is,' she said, pointing to the number 131. 'It's well known because it's a three-digit prime number which is also the sum of three, two-digit prime numbers; 41, 43 and 47.'

'How on earth do you know that?' asked Matt, suddenly seeing a side to Steph that he'd never witnessed before.

'I did double Maths at A level. Pure and Applied. I was also interested in number theory quite a bit. I think they could all be prime numbers actually.'

'I'll go and get the laptop,' suggested Chris. We can get on the Internet and check them out fairly easily.'

'There's no need to do that,' replied Steph, suddenly enjoying her new found role as group expert. 'Just get me a calculator and I can do it quicker.'

Neil went back into the dining room again and got a calculator out of the bureau. 'So how do you check whether a number is prime or not?' he asked as he handed it over to Steph.

'Easy,' replied Steph, tapping in 313 to check the first of them. 'You multiply the number by itself, subtract one, and if the answer is divisible by 24, then it's a prime number.' She quickly did the calculation and then proudly held up the calculator so that they could all see. 'There you are, 313 squared is

97969, which minus one is 97968, which then divided by 24 is 4082.'

'Are you sure?' asked Matt, pulling a somewhat disbelieving face. 'I've never heard of that before. I thought you had to use really complicated algorithms to work out prime numbers. Why does squaring a number and then deducting one and dividing by 24 work?'

Steph didn't even bother to look up as she continued tapping figures into the calculator. 'I could explain it to you Matt, but I'm not sure that you'd understand.'

Matt pulled an indignant face. It was almost as if Steph was implying that he was stupid. 'Try me,' he said with just a hint of arrogance.

Steph suddenly stopped and looked up at him and smiled. 'Okay. All prime numbers can be expressed as either $(6n+1)$ or $(6n-1)$. This factorises to either $12n(3n+1)$ or $12n(3n-1)$ and ...'

'Stop, stop stop.' Matt had his hands held up high in front of him in absolute surrender. Both Neil and Chris were grinning from ear to ear. 'Okay, I believe you. Just crunch the numbers.'

It took Steph no more than a minute or so to check them all, including 1987 and 2003 which the boys had previously thought were dates. Like all the others, they both turned out to be prime.

'So the question is,' asked Neil, 'why was Aunt Hilary writing down prime numbers on the phone pad? Is it some sort of code? Does it have anything to do with Teleios?'

'You know what I think,' said Chris, suddenly getting excited. 'I think it's exactly like Matt said the other day. It's a bit like someone drawing a picture of a sun when they're on the phone talking about the fact that they've been to the beach. A sort of subconscious illustration of what's in the back of their mind. I don't believe she was thinking about prime numbers at all. I reckon she was on the phone thinking about Teleios and for some reason, also thinking about the word Prime. And we know where we've seen that before, don't we Neil?'

Matt and Steph didn't really understand what Chris was talking about, but Neil had suddenly caught up with Chris's line of thinking and was becoming equally excited. 'You're right. It was on the Internet, when we were looking at GCHQ. Geoffrey Prime. He was a spy or something.'

Matt and Steph exchanged another confused look. 'What on earth are you talking about?' asked Matt. 'Who is Geoffrey Prime?'

'Geoffrey Prime used to work at GCHQ,' replied Chris. 'There was a high-profile court case back in the 1980s. I can't remember any more than that but it was a huge scandal at the time. Maybe, just maybe, Teleios has got something to do with GCHQ and with Geoffrey Prime.'

Matt frowned, not convinced by Chris's logic at all. 'I'm not sure. It's a hell of a coincidence. A few scribbled numbers on a phone pad having the same name as something that you happened to see on the Internet? The link is tenuous to say the least. It's hardly likely, is it?'

Neil looked slightly disheartened at Matt's response but nothing could dampen Chris's belief in what they'd discovered. 'It's got to be worth checking out though Matt. And it's a lot more to go on than we had ten minutes ago. Maybe it's something you can follow up tomorrow?'

Matt smiled. 'Yes, of course I can. Especially now that I'm not going up to London and I've got a free day. Anyway, maybe the combination of me checking up on Geoffrey Prime and Neil seeing Adam Saxby will finally give us a breakthrough.'

'I told you before,' said Neil, starting to get more than a little irritated, 'there is no way, absolutely no way, that I am going to go up to London to visit Adam Saxby, pretending to be a copper. It's not going to happen, so let's just forget about it and let's talk about something else...'

THIRTY-ONE

Things weren't looking that good for Neil as he drove Steph's car into the car park at Headcorn Station and hurriedly tried to find somewhere to park. Not for the first time since he'd arrived in Appleden, he had overslept and it had also taken him longer than expected to sort out the suit and shirt that he'd brought with him for the funeral. Luckily Matt had lent him a brighter tie so at least he looked the part, even though he'd never actually been a commuter before. The real problem was that he was running late and he hadn't bargained on the amount of traffic that was on the roads at seven o'clock in the morning. Headcorn was a small rural village in the middle of Kent, but the number of cars and buses converging on the railway station was unbelievable. While the rest of the country was still asleep or still eating breakfast in its pyjamas, Headcorn was experiencing its own mini rush-hour; hundreds of people all arriving at the same time, all trying to get a head-start on the working week.

Neil eventually found a parking space, fed endless amounts of loose change into one of the pay machines and then walked quickly over to the ticket office. Luckily there wasn't much of a queue. Everybody else seemed to be a regular commuter, which meant that most of them already had season tickets. Neil bought a return ticket to Charing Cross and then got himself a newspaper before crossing over the bridge to the platform on the other side.

It didn't take him long to work out that most of the people around him seemed to be on autopilot. Most of them looked tired and grey and worn out and certainly none of them were making conversation with their fellow passengers, despite the fact that they probably saw each other every day and had presumably travelled together day in, day out for years on end. They all stood motionless on the platform, all locked in their private, silent worlds and all gazing into the distance with a sort of sad, glazed expression. Neil watched a seemingly endless line of them coming over the bridge, the last few passengers timing their arrival down to the last minute, all of them walking purposefully up to a particular point on the platform as if they stood in exactly the same place every day.

The trains from Headcorn ran alternately to Cannon Street and Charing Cross and inexperienced as he was, Neil quickly worked out that you could tell which commuters were travelling to which station, just from their appearance. The Cannon Street passengers, who obviously worked in the City were predominantly wearing pinstripes and cufflinks and looked slightly different to the West End passengers, who were a touch more bohemian. Nevertheless, irrespective of where they were going, they were all dressed in black and were all about to sit in a fluorescent-lit, air-conditioned metal tube which conveyed them up and down a metal track, presumably to work in a fluorescent-lit, air-conditioned cubicle somewhere in the middle of London. It was positively Orwellian. Neil shuddered at the thought of ever having to do this on a regular basis. They had to be mad.

The 07.15 to Charing Cross duly arrived on time and Neil found himself a window seat and settled himself down for the hour or so journey to London. He had always walked to work in Cambridge so the prospect of some uninterrupted time to sit down and read the morning paper was something of a novelty for him and in truth, was rather appealing. He noticed that most of the other commuters who had started off the journey either reading or listening to music soon dozed off and that by the time they got to Sevenoaks, which was the last stop before London, there were not many people in the carriage who were actually awake. Inevitably, the guard came round to check everybody's ticket, just at the point when most of them had fallen asleep.

One thing Neil did notice was how narrow the seats were these days and paradoxically, how fat or obese some of the passengers were. He watched with a sort of morbid curiosity as some of the large, fat-arsed women tried to squeeze their massive, wobbling frames onto a seat that was made for somebody half their size. Inevitably, some poor, normal-sized commuter was squashed into the window and had to suffer the discomfort of an unpleasant, cramped journey, just because the person sitting next to them was too ignorant or lazy to eat less or do any proper exercise. And of course it was the huge, fat commuters that were stuffing their faces with croissants or some other sort of breakfast which was also stinking out the carriage. It was appalling. It occurred to Neil that nobody took personal responsibility for their own actions anymore and made him wonder whether they ought to vary the ticket prices depending on how big or heavy the passengers were. He remembered reading a story about a guy in America who had spent the last twenty-five years eating virtually nothing but junk food, who was now trying to sue the hamburger outlets because in his opinion, they were responsible for the fact that he was overweight and unhealthy. It was positively breathtaking.

Neil finished reading his newspaper and spent the final part of the journey gazing out of the window, fascinated by the rows and rows of Victorian terraced houses which backed onto the railway line, following the route which snaked all the way into London. Thousands of grimy, decaying properties with small, untidy back gardens, dark and mostly overgrown, some of them still with the remnants of cold back-yards and dilapidated outhouses and most of them with no more than a loose and rusting chain-fence to protect them from the rush and noise of the hurtling trains.

Neil checked his watch as they pulled slowly through London Bridge and headed towards Charing Cross. It wasn't even a quarter-past eight. In a couple of minutes they would be there and it wouldn't take more than ten minutes to walk down to King Charles Street. He could either go down Whitehall and pass Downing Street on his right or cut through Horse Guards and come round the back. Either way he was going to be early.

As the train finally drew into Charing Cross he let most of the other passengers get off first. They were all clearly in a hurry to get to work, all dashing off like ants, probably to some important meeting or another and he was in no rush at all. Eventually he stood up and put on his coat, glancing around the carriage at the one or two passengers who were also taking their time. Probably best to find somewhere to grab a cup of coffee, give himself half an hour or so to collect his thoughts and decide exactly how he was going to play it. Neil had never impersonated a police officer before and the closer he got to actually having to do it, the more nervous he was starting to feel.

*

Jean Pettipher was by her own admission, something of a creature of habit. Too many years living alone meant that she had become too accustomed to her own company and to her own conventions, and one of the defining hallmarks of her life as a confirmed spinster was that everything had a place and every activity had an established order and routine which had to be followed. Every morning she would wake up to the alarm clock, religiously set for 06:53 and then lie in bed, listening to the last few minutes of music before pushing off the blankets on the stroke of the last pip that heralded the seven o'clock news. Without fail, come rain or shine, she followed the same, familiar ritual; putting on her slippers and dressing gown and then going downstairs to switch on the kettle and feed Fleurie, her beloved Russian Blue, who slept curled up in the armchair rather than in the cat basket, which lay empty beside her, still as clean and new as the day it had been bought.

Jean turned on the radio in the kitchen and then went off to shower while Fluerie finished eating and disappeared through the cat-flap into the small courtyard garden. Jean often wondered whether cats could tell the difference between weekdays and weekends, the earlier, faster schedule of Mondays to Fridays as opposed to the relaxed, slower pace of Saturdays and Sundays. If they could, then Fluerie would certainly have guessed that this was a Monday morning, the first, crisp sequence of activities after a couple of long, leisurely days of doing nothing. Everything suddenly timed down to the last second.

Jean left the house as usual at 07.40 and walked down to the bus stop at Crouch End Broadway. The No. 41 left at 07.51 and went down Hornsey Rise towards Archway Station, past *The Nags Head* on the Holloway Road and then followed a route through Highbury and Islington before going through Holborn and then onto the West End. By the time it got to Tottenham Court Road and Leicester Square it was standing room only, but traffic permitting, it normally managed to arrive at Trafalgar Square just before half-past eight. For Jean, it was then just a short, five minute walk to the office in Carlton Gardens. Sometimes she walked along Pall Mall and cut through Waterloo Place and other times, just to be different, she took the route under Admiralty Arch.

For a number of reasons, Jean always sat on the top deck, not least because it meant she could avoid the hustle and bustle of people pushing and shoving as the bus got into central London. Providing it was free, she also liked to sit in the same seat, about halfway down on the left-hand side. She knew the journey from that perspective and always felt uncomfortable if for some reason she had to travel sitting on the other side. Like all the other women on the bus that morning, Jean sat motionless in her seat, clutching her belongings on her lap and staring out of the window at nothing in particular.

The bus was fairly empty when it got to Crouch End Broadway, which meant that she normally started the journey with an empty seat, in fact it wasn't until the Angel at Islington or maybe even Mount Pleasant that she would have someone sitting next to her. Sometimes it was the same person although of course they didn't speak – that would have been far too familiar. Jean heard the faint ding of the bell but was still staring out of the window, not really taking any notice when she became aware that someone had got on and was now sitting down beside her.

'Hello Petty. How are you?'

Jean twisted round in an instant and couldn't hide her shock at seeing Craven, particularly the fact that he was sitting on a No. 41 bus. The last time she'd seen him was in the enclosure at Goodwood, suited and booted and holding a glass of wine. Her mouth dropped open in surprise. 'Craven, what are you doing here?'

'I thought I'd come and see you. I guessed you'd be on this one. Same old Petty.'

Jean blushed. Then she smiled. She liked everybody who worked at *Vector*, they were her family, *"her boys"* as she liked to call them. But Craven had always been her favourite. No one else called her *Petty*. No one else came close. Then she frowned. She knew him of old. 'So, what are you after? It must be pretty serious for you to get on a bus.'

Craven pulled a face, pretending to be offended at the suggestion that there could be an ulterior motive. 'I just wanted to see you Petty, see how you are.'

Jean gave him an old fashioned look, not taken in for one moment by his pretend innocence. She was open to flattery, possibly – but stupid? Definitely not. 'Come on Craven, I'm busy. What do you want?'

Craven grinned. 'Do you fancy a coffee?'

Jean shook her head in mock despair and then looked at her watch. She had no idea what this was all about, but she guessed that it must be important. 'You can have ten minutes. Then I have to get to work.'

Craven smiled and leant across and kissed her on the cheek. 'Thanks Petty. You always were the best.'

Jean blushed again and pushed him away, giving him the naughty schoolboy look. He was incorrigible. The problem was, she already knew that she was going to tell him everything. Everything she knew and anything he wanted to know.

THIRTY-TWO

Matt eased himself back into his chair and looked around the CID room, trying to imagine how on earth anybody from another force was going to re-energise and motivate the team now that Garrick had gone. The shock of yesterday's announcement had started to fade, but if Anderson and the Chief Constable were expecting things to simply return back to normal, then they couldn't have been more wrong. He gazed across at his colleagues, all of them in the office since the crack of dawn and all diligently working on their separate lines of enquiry. At first glance the CID room looked like it always did – busy, crowded, industrious – but the whole place had an odd, subdued feel about it, as if they were just going through the motions, everybody waiting for something to happen or for someone else to give them some direction. Suddenly all the commitment, all the appetite, all the energy seemed to have disappeared. It was going to take one hell of a personality to lift the team out of its current mood and what was worrying Matt was that by all accounts, Brian Fowler was not the man for the job.

Matt checked his watch again. They were expecting Fowler at any time but more importantly, he was still waiting for the file that he'd arranged to be couriered down from London first thing that morning. He leant forward and clicked the mouse, re-reading the email that confirmed that it had been despatched at 7.10 am. It had to be there soon – in fact, as far as he knew the courier could be coming through the front doors of the station at that very moment. Matt drained the last dregs of coffee out of a plastic cup and decided to wander downstairs and see what was happening. The waiting was becoming unbearable. He was beginning to regret asking Simon for a copy of the Anti-Terrorist Branch file. Maybe he should have just checked out whatever was on the central database. He dismissed the thought almost as soon as it went through his mind. The security file was gong to be much more detailed and besides, the national database had a tracking system which monitored and recorded what everybody was looking at. For some reason, particularly since Garrick's departure, he wanted to keep what he was doing to himself – at least for the moment.

As usual, Phil Edwards was sitting behind the front desk, not doing very much other than drinking a cup of tea and tidying up some paperwork. He glanced up, looking slightly guilty as he saw Matt come through the double swing-doors into the main waiting room. 'Oh, hello Matt, I was just about to give you a ring.'

Matt gave him an unconvincing smile. 'Why? Has a parcel come for me Phil?'

Edwards nodded towards one of the desks behind him, a large yellow-jacket courier bag sitting next to a pile of unopened post. 'A guy on a bike brought it in about five minutes ago. I was just about to walk it up to you.'

Course you were. Matt resisted the temptation to get into an argument and simply picked up the delivery and went back upstairs. The courier bag felt heavy and thick, which meant that the file inside was probably substantial. It was going to take him quite a while to read through everything properly, which meant that he really needed to find some privacy away from the rest of the team, not to mention some peace and quiet. He decided to check out the interview rooms on the way back to the CID room and predictably, all of them were empty. It was too early in the morning for any sort of activity and besides, virtually everybody was working on the Teleios case. Everything else seemed to have ground to a halt.

Matt got himself another cup of coffee and then made himself comfortable in Room three and settled down to do some serious reading. He clipped off the security tag on the side of the yellow-jacket, unzipped the bag and then pulled out a large, manila file which was crammed full of papers, all carefully photocopied and all neatly sorted into different categories, each section separated by a plastic, coloured divider. Matt quickly flicked through the file, firstly an executive summary typed on Home Office paper and then six or seven different sections, mostly consisting of copies of original documents. There was a biography with several photos of Prime at various ages, copies of his RAF service record, a transcript of police interviews together with photographs of evidence, a section of newspaper cuttings, a transcript of the trial, some prison records and probation reports and finally two A5 sealed envelopes, one marked RHYOLITE and the other one marked ECHELON, both of them stamped CLASSIFIED in bold, red ink. In the front of the file, stuck to the first page of the executive summary was a yellow "post-it" note and a hand-scribbled message from Simon. Matt smiled to himself as he read it. *"Hope this helps. Good luck mate. You owe me a beer!"*

Matt took a sip of coffee, shuffled his backside into the chair a couple of times to make himself really comfortable and then took out the executive summary and started to read.

"Geoffrey Prime left St Joseph's Catholic College in Stoke-on-Trent at the age of 16 with a handful of O Levels and no immediate prospects other than a job offer to start work at a local factory as a junior wages clerk. Two years later, in 1956, he was conscripted as a National Serviceman into the RAF and like most new recruits, wanted to make the most of that opportunity, expressing an ambition to become a member of Flight Crew. Unfortunately, colour blindness ruled him out and eventually he was consigned to ground duties and became Aircraftman II (Stores) GA Prime.

Two of Prime's O Levels were in Spanish and Latin and the RAF Selection Officer soon noticed that his new recruit had a flair for languages. With the Cold War at its zenith and the pressing need for Russian linguists, the Selection Officer forwarded Prime's name onto the relevant office and he was soon despatched from Alton to the special services college, RAF Crail, in Scotland to begin a Russian language course. One of the conditions of enrolment was that Prime was required to sign up for regular service, but this was not an issue for him – he was being offered the opportunity to gain professional qualifications and he willingly signed up for nine years.

Prime's initial progress was good, advancing to Aircraftman 1 and then to Acting Sergeant in the space of a few months. At the age of 19 he moved to London University on an advanced Russian Language course, but for some reason, possibly because of the distractions of London life, his work started to suffer and he left university after only three months. Inevitably, his rank and privileges were withdrawn and he was soon returned to the mundane life of ground duties and working in the stores. After a period of time he was lucky to secure a posting to Kenya and at the age of 21 was promoted to the rank of Corporal, filling his spare time by learning Swahili, which he spoke fluently with the native labour used on site.

Prime returned to Britain in April 1962, initially working for the Air Ministry in an office in Surrey. By this time, several years in the RAF had made him more mature and on returning to the UK he decided to try and resurrect his career in languages, applying for a training course at the Joint Technical Services Language School at Tangmere in Surrey. After a year of study, he left with an O Level in Russian and in May 1964 was posted to RAF Gatow, in Berlin. Prime was employed as a voice wireless operator in signal intelligence, monitoring Russian voice transmissions, and was in due course promoted to Sergeant.

At that time, Berlin was surrounded by East Germany and accessible by sealed train. It was during one of those trips that Prime made his first contact with the Russians by throwing out a message at a checkpoint, at the boots of a sentry, as the train moved slowly past him. Having volunteered his services, the KGB contacted him and arranged to meet him, initially at the Friedrichstrasse subway station and then subsequently at a flat in Potsdam, where he was trained in spycraft and indoctrinated by the Soviet Intelligence services. The two Soviet Intelligence officers that he met used the names "Igor" and "Valya" and instructed Prime in the techniques of using invisible inks, one-time pads and microdots. He was also given a Minox camera, which he later used to photograph sensitive documents, as well as £400 in cash, which he carried along with the rest of the espionage paraphernalia in a briefcase with a cleverly concealed false bottom.

In 1968, Prime left the RAF after 12 years' service and attended a two-month resettlement course at RAF Innesworth, Gloucestershire, where he was interviewed for a post as a Linguistic Specialist, Grade IV with GCHQ. On demobilisation he was offered the job and started work at the London Processing Group in St Dunstan's Hill, a London outstation of GCHQ, on 9th September 1968. Prime's job was to provide a transcription service from Russian broadcast intercepts, where he learned much about the secret methods and operations of the signal intelligence organisation.

Inevitably, Prime was able to inform his KGB handlers exactly what GCHQ were monitoring and what electronic eavesdropping methods were being employed. This led to false messages being transmitted to confuse NATO and to real secrets being smuggled through alternative routes. The Russians were so impressed with the information that in October 1969 they sent Prime an 'allo message which he received on a short wave receiver, in a form used for the one-time pad, instructing him to seek out a dead letter box in Esher, Surrey, where he found £400 in cash and a letter of congratulations.

Throughout his time at GCHQ, Prime continued with his double life, visiting Vienna, Dublin and Rome to meet his controllers and to pick up supplies of one-time pads, secret writing articles and payment for his work. In 1972 he visited Cyprus, again to meet his controllers. Unfortunately on his return to the UK he lost his one-time pads and wrote to his controllers in East Germany informing them of the unfortunate mishap. An 'allo message confirmed receipt but also, because of the risk, the transfer to his new status as a sleeper. After a couple of years of inactivity, Prime received a briefcase from the KGB in December 1974. It again had a false bottom, which when removed revealed spying equipment as well as a further £400 in cash. There was also a letter that invited him to Vienna in 1975.

In March 1976 Prime transferred to the GCHQ site at Cheltenham, accepting the appointment as a Higher Linguist in 'J' Division and then, within a matter of months, promotion to the position of section head. As a GCHQ translator and section head he was party to discussions about some of its most sensitive operations and was given Byeman clearance to work on Rhyolite material, a top secret spy satellite with unparalleled capabilities. The entire system was compromised by Prime for just £800. In fact, a similar betrayal was proceeding in the USA. A known drug addict by the name of Andrew Lee was passing virtually every technical detail of Rhyolite onto the Soviets.

When Prime first moved to Cheltenham he took up residence in a house owned by a 33 year old divorcee, Rhona Ratcliffe, and on 18th June 1977 they married. Apart from a wife he also inherited three young children who benefited greatly from the male, fatherly presence around the house. Perhaps Prime was also affected by his new found responsibility; he was certainly respected by the children and provided adequately for them. Aware of the danger of being discovered and without the courage to defect, on 28th September 1977 he resigned from GCHQ and after a short but disastrous attempt at selling quality wines, he became a taxi driver.

Despite his departure from the security services, Prime maintained periodic contact with the Soviets. Prior to his leaving GCHQ he had taken a number of photographs and on 16th May 1980 he handed over fifteen reels of film to the KGB in Vienna in return for £600. He also visited Berlin in November 1981, where his stock of espionage equipment was replenished and he received a payment of £4,000.

In 1981, Prime was questioned by the local police about an unrelated offence and realising that his house was about to be searched, took his wife out to a local beauty spot and confessed to everything. She decided to stand by him and the next day, just as Prime had feared, he was arrested and his car and house were searched. Amongst other items, a black leather briefcase was seized, which was later opened by Prime in the presence of police officers to reveal the secret compartment.

On 23rd May 1982, Rhona Prime contacted the local police to tell them that she had found a carrier bag containing a quantity of envelopes addressed to places in East Germany, two cellophane-like pads bearing columns of five figure numbers and some typewritten notes about microdot production. A team of specialist searchers entered Prime's home and after a detailed search found a harvest of evidence relating to his espionage activities. These included a list of frequencies and schedules that Prime had noted down, a shortwave radio, a Grundig reel-to-reel tape recorder and a number of top secret documents from GCHQ.

On 25th June DCS Cole interviewed Prime and laid out the East German envelopes, the one-time pads and the radio schedules. He also switched on the tape player and the monotonous drone of a coded number message, broadcast in German, filled the room. Prime initially offered the weak excuse that his hobby was listening to shortwave radio transmissions, but he soon realised that ultimately he would have to disclose the truth. On 26th June 1982 at approximately 4.30pm, Geoffrey Prime made a full confession that he was a Russian spy.

Throughout his time working for the KGB, Prime's codename was "Rowlands".

It is interesting to note that Prime had been given a Minox camera by his *controllers, which he had concealed in his loft beneath the fibreglass insulation next to the joists adjacent to the chimney, and he reasonably asked DCS Cole where it was, given that everything else had been produced as evidence. DCS Cole was unable to offer any explanation as to why it had not been found and a second subsequent search revealed nothing. As Prime knew it was secreted in the loft and the police did not discover it during their searches, its whereabouts and the reasons for its disappearance remain unknown.*

At the Old Bailey, on Wednesday 10th November 1982, Geoffrey Arthur Prime, then aged 44, pleaded guilty to seven counts against the Official Secrets Act and was sentenced to 35 years imprisonment. The information Prime disclosed was publicly represented as being damaging to the UK and beneficial to the Soviets but the details were not released and remain unknown, the Attorney General, Sir Michael Havers QC, simply declaring that his activities had caused "exceptionally grave damage and had threatened NATO plans for defending Western Europe."

Prime's sentence was the second-longest jail sentence in British legal history, but the trial itself lasted little more than two hours. The judges at both his trial and his later appeal said that if Britain had been at war with the Soviet Union, his crimes would have made him eligible for the death penalty and that they would have had no compunction in using it. The death penalty, although abolished for all other offences in 1965, remained in force for acts of High Treason until the Criminal Justice Bill was passed in July 1998. On sentencing, the Lord Chief Justice, Lord Lane, said: "By your treachery, you have done incalculable harm to the interests and security of this country and of our friends and Allies."

Prime would have been 82 on his release in 2020, had he served the full term. In July 2000 he was moved from the high-security Whitemoor prison in Cambridgeshire to a low-security prison in Rochester in Kent and eight months later, on Tuesday 13 March 2001, he was released from prison after serving only half his sentence. His release was controversial and caused public outcry, GCHQ making representations to both the parole board and to the Home Secretary before his release.

Prime now lives quietly at an undisclosed address, although the Daily Mail *has disclosed his whereabouts on at least one occasion."*

Matt sat back in his chair and blew out a low whistle. Whatever Prime had been selling to the Russians, it was clearly of the highest sensitivity. A 35 year sentence following a trial lasting barely two hours was absolutely without precedent. It was small wonder that they hadn't thrown away the key. He put his hand in his pocket and pulled out the piece of paper that Neil had given him the night before; the notepaper that Hilary Russell had written on the day that she had made the telephone calls to GCHQ and to London. He looked at the two names again, which were scribbled at the bottom of the sheet – one was Carlisle and the other was definitely Rowlands. Matt turned back to the executive summary and found the sentence that he was looking for towards the end of the paper.

Throughout his time working for the KGB, Prime's codename was "Rowlands".

There was no doubt about it. Connecting Hilary Russell's doodles with Geoffrey Prime had been a huge assumption, a real shot in the dark based on not much more than Steph's knowledge of pure mathematics and his own hypothesis that people subconsciously drew or wrote down what they were thinking about while they were talking on the phone. It was pure guesswork, an absolute leap of faith, but the word *Rowlands* had suddenly confirmed everything. It wasn't a coincidence. Hilary Russell had made three telephone calls a couple of days before she died and during one or maybe all of those, whatever she had been talking about, she'd been thinking about Geoffrey Prime.

'Oh, there you are Shylock – I've been looking everywhere for you...'

Matt looked up startled, Steph's sudden interruption jolting him out of the past and back into the present. He'd been so absorbed in reading Prime's file that he hadn't noticed her stick her head around the door.

'...Fowler's here. He wants us all in the incident room – five minutes.'

Matt nodded and closed the file in front of him, frustrated that he had to stop. It was just starting to get interesting and having immersed himself in Prime's background, all he wanted was to be left alone so that he could get on and read the rest of it. In particular he was dying to open the envelopes and read the stuff on Rhyolite and ECHELON – but he knew that it would have to wait. The new boss had turned up, which meant that they all had to be on their best behaviour. Matt wasn't looking forward to that one iota.

He folded the piece of notepaper and put it carefully back into his pocket. All evidence was supposed to be bagged, catalogued and held centrally to the enquiry, but there was no way that he was going to do that at the moment. Other than Steph, and Garrick of course, he wasn't sure who he could trust. The word *Rowlands* meant only one thing. The answer to Teleios, and therefore the answer to Hilary Russell's murder, was in some way connected to Geoffrey Prime.

Which meant that the answer to everything they were looking for, was probably somewhere in the file.

THIRTY-THREE

The Aruba Coffee House in Orange Street was a small, privately owned café tucked away in a quiet, secluded corner, just behind The National Gallery; a bright, modern coffee shop with contemporary, minimalist décor and easy-to-clean furniture. It was slightly off the beaten track for most tourists, so much of its trade came from local businesses, most of its customers working in the offices and shops in the immediate neighbourhood between St Martin's Lane and The Haymarket. Jean had used it occasionally, but it wasn't one of her regular or more favoured haunts. It was just a bit too far from the office in Carlton Gardens. Today though, it was perfect. Just far enough away to be discreet.

The place was fairly empty and Jean secured a table for four in the window while Craven went up to the counter and ordered a couple of coffees, a cappuccino for her and a black regular for himself. Jean took off her coat and put it over the back of the spare chair next to hers and then sat down, putting her handbag and gloves on the end of the table. She gazed over at Craven who was standing at the counter, getting into a lively conversation with the owner. Something about the Italian football team as far as she could make out. It didn't seem five minutes since he had been at *Vector*, both of them working in the same building, but then again, in another sense it seemed like an age since the two of them had last spoken. She smiled at him as he walked towards her, carefully balancing a large cup and saucer in each hand.

'There you go Petty,' he said, putting the coffee on the table in front of her, 'one cappuccino, no sugar, just as you like it.'

Jean smiled again. 'Thanks Craven, I'm impressed. I'm surprised you remembered.'

Craven smiled back as he put his own cup and saucer on the table and then sat down in the chair opposite her. 'Hey, how could I forget? Anyway, how are you Petty? Have you missed me?'

'Missed you?' Jean pulled a face, pretending that she'd hardly noticed that he'd gone. 'It's been wonderful. Peace and quiet for months on end. A real joy.' She picked up her spoon and scooped up some froth across the top of the cappuccino, popping it into her mouth with obvious pleasure. It was always the best bit about having a cappuccino. 'Anyway, how's the sordid world of free enterprise?'

Craven cupped his own coffee with both hands and blew gently across the surface. 'Not as lucrative as the sordid world of politics I'm afraid. I assume you heard that I've been doing some freelance for Buchanan?'

Jean put her cup carefully back into the saucer and frowned at him across the table, clearly surprised at what he had just said. Normally she knew everything that was going on. 'Freelance? No, I didn't know that. What have you been working on?'

Craven leant forward across the table a little, just to make sure that he couldn't be overheard. Not that there was anyone sitting near enough to actually listen but the whispered response added to the subterfuge. Petty would appreciate that. A one word explanation was all that was needed. 'Teleios.' He dropped the name like a pebble thrown casually into the middle of a pond and then leant back into the chair, watching the ripples with interest.

'Ah.' Jean gave him a knowing look and also leant back into her chair, conscious that they were about to have a conversation on a subject that was never spoken about. She should have guessed. The visit from Hilary Russell, the mysterious phone call from the nephew, the private calls to Carlisle. Suddenly it all made sense. 'And are you still working for Buchanan?'

'Not exactly.'

Jean nodded her head up and down very slowly, trying to figure out exactly what Craven meant by the last response. She checked her watch. Buchanan would be starting to wonder where she was. She could blame the bus for a ten or fifteen minute delay but no more than that. 'I've got about five minutes – literally.'

Craven leant forward again, his demeanour suddenly turning serious. Time to get straight to the point. 'Thanks Petty. I need your help. I need to know what Teleios is.'

Jean shook her head. An immediate, instinctive response. Not something done for effect. 'I'm sorry Craven, I can't help you. I don't know anything about it – never have done. If I did, I probably wouldn't be able to tell you, but as it happens, I don't know anything. Nothing at all.'

Craven looked at her across the table. He'd known Jean for most of his working life and he knew instinctively that she was telling the truth. He smiled at her and deliberately softened his approach; part flattery, part pleading for help. 'Come on Petty, you must know something. You know everything that's going on.'

Jean smiled back at him. On most things that was true. In fact on virtually everything that was true. But not Teleios. Teleios was different. She gave

Craven a quizzical look, wondering what he was working on. What was it that Buchanan had hired him to do? She let the thought pass – maybe it was better not to know. 'Buchanan keeps it to himself. It doesn't happen often, but this is one of them. Don't ask me why. He keeps the file locked in his drawer. Always has done.'

'And you've never seen it?'

Jean shook her head again. 'Never. And I'm sure nobody else has either – nobody at *Vector* anyway. It's like the Lucan file – and the one on Diana. I think Carlisle knows about it. Beyond that I don't know. Maybe the PM.'

Craven raised his eyebrows. As far as small, select groups went, they didn't come much smaller or more select than that. He decided to try again. Anything, any intuition, any sliver of information could possibly make a difference. 'Please Petty, there must be something. Isn't there anything you can tell me that will help?'

Jean gave him a gentle smile, the small creases around the edges of her eyes somehow lighting up her face. It was a genuine, warm smile to an old and valued friend. She wanted to help him if she could, but as hard as she tried, there was nothing, absolutely nothing that she could say. Teleios was a complete mystery. 'I'm sorry Craven, honestly, I can't think of anything. Teleios was around long before I started. It was years before I even knew it existed.'

Craven smiled back, recognising that she was trying her hardest but that the conversation was going nowhere.

'Hilary knew of course,' she added rather wistfully, giving the cappuccino an absent-minded stir, 'not that that's going to be of any help to anyone anymore.'

Craven pulled a face, part grimace, part sympathy. He was dreading raising the subject, so to some extent was relieved that Jean had done it for him. 'I was going to ask you about that. Did you know that she rang Buchanan the other week?'

Jean took a sip of coffee and nodded. 'Yes, it was me that took the call. I don't know why she wanted to speak to him though. I asked her, of course, but she just said it was confidential and that it was urgent. I made her an appointment to see him the following day.'

Craven put his cup down and frowned at her across the table, not sure whether he had heard her correctly. 'An appointment? Do you mean she came up to see him?'

Again, Jean nodded in silence, a mouthful of coffee stopping her from speaking for a couple of seconds. 'Yes, she came up on the Friday morning. Didn't you know? Didn't Buchanan tell you?'

Craven smiled ruefully to himself. *No he bloody didn't.* 'All he told me was that she had phoned you. He didn't tell me that he'd actually seen her.'

'She didn't phone me Craven, she phoned Buchanan. I just answered the call, that's all.'

Craven nodded, acknowledging the distinction. 'How long was she with him?'

Jean shrugged and pursed her lips, trying to remember the events of a couple of weeks ago. 'About forty minutes I think. Forty-five perhaps. Then she left. I got the impression that she was going straight back.'

Craven said nothing and drank his coffee for a minute or two, trying to sort out the timeline and the sequence of events in his own mind. Eventually he looked up at Jean who had finished her cappuccino and looked as though she was ready to leave.

'Did you know her very well Petty?'

Jean smiled, a faint memory of briefly working with Hilary many years ago suddenly coming back to her. 'Not particularly. We had a handover for a couple of months, but that was it really. I had to ring her a couple of times to ask her a few things, but that was years ago. I hadn't spoken to her for…'

'Handover? What do you mean a handover?' Craven had pushed his cup and saucer to one side and was suddenly leaning right into the middle of the table.

Jean looked slightly taken aback by the force of Craven's interruption. 'What do you think I mean? A handover. You know – how to do the job, where everything's kept, how everything works. What do you think I mean?'

Craven's mouth appeared to be stuck in the open, gobsmacked position. 'Are you trying to tell me that Hilary Russell worked at *Vector?*'

Jean raised her eyebrows in surprise at Craven's lack of knowledge. 'Yes of course she did. She worked there for over twenty years.' Jean suddenly stopped, recognising the look in Craven's face. A mixture if incredulity and disappointment, both at the same time. 'He didn't tell you did he?'

Craven let out a snort. 'No, he didn't. He said she was a secretary…'

Jean smiled to herself. *Well, she was really. Same old Buchanan.*

'..so was she Buchanan's PA before you?'

Jean nodded emphatically. 'Absolutely. In fact she was his first PA. By all accounts he was the green, inexperienced drone who thought he knew it all and she was the quiet, unassuming secretary with all the knowledge and experience about how things were actually done. On paper, she was meant to be working for him but by all accounts, for the first couple of years it was the other way round. Apparently she spent most of her time making sure that he didn't make a complete idiot of himself...'

Craven couldn't help smiling at the thought of that. Buchanan making a complete idiot of himself was not a concept that had ever occurred to him before.

'...The generally held view is that if it hadn't been for Hilary, he probably wouldn't still be there. Certainly not in the position he is now. There was a Baker Street heritage in there somewhere – and Bletchley I think. I never asked. Her father probably.'

Craven blew out a low whistle. It was an impressive pedigree to say the least. 'What does it say on her personnel record?'

'Department of Employment. Human Resources.'

Craven nodded. That's what it said for any of the female staff employed at *Vector*. Human Resources for the women, Facilities Management for the men. 'What happened after she left?'

'I don't know, other than...' Jean hesitated, suddenly having second thoughts about what she was going to say next.

'Other than what?'

'I'm not sure Craven...it might not mean anything.'

'Come on Petty, help me out here. What happened after she left?'

Jean's head dropped down to the table. It felt like a betrayal. Buchanan was her boss. 'He rang Carlisle.'

Craven fell silent for a moment and stared out of the window, already thinking through his options. 'I'll kill him.'

'Carlisle?'

'Buchanan.'

Jean checked her watch again. It really was time to go. She leant forward and took hold of Craven's hand. 'Listen to me. I don't know what happened, but there's no way that Hilary's death has got anything to do with Buchanan. He thought the world of her.'

'He looked okay to me.'

'You know what he's like. Trust me Craven, this isn't Buchanan's doing. If you want to follow this up, go and talk to Carlisle. Besides, Buchanan won't tell you anything, you know he won't. Apply a little pressure and Carlisle will tell you anything you want to know.'

Craven nodded. As ever, Jean was right. He had to forget the emotional, knee-jerk response. Tactically there was only one sensible option. He needed to pay Carlisle a visit. Not only would he find out what happened to Hilary Russell but he'd also find out what the hell Teleios was all about. At last he was making progress. 'Have you got an address for him?'

'Probably. Home or office?

'Either. Both.'

Jean nodded. 'I'll text you. Give me your number.'

Craven scribbled down his mobile number on an old business card and slid it across the table. Jean had pushed her chair back, indicating that she needed to leave and had picked up her handbag and was putting on her gloves. They were *Dents* of course, the finest kid leather with 100 percent silk linings. She took the card and put it in her handbag. 'Thanks. Give me a couple of hours, I'll send you something by lunchtime.'

Craven stood up, conscious that she needed to rush off and get to work. 'Thanks for your help Petty. It was lovely to see you. You shoot off, I'll go and pay the bill.'

Jean gave him another warm, genuine smile as she stood up and put on her coat, doing the buttons up to keep out the cold. 'It was good to see you too. Look after yourself, Craven. Make sure that you keep in touch.'

Craven smiled back and gave her a gentle wave as she walked out the door. For some reason, something inside him made him wonder if he would ever see her again.

THIRTY-FOUR

The Foreign Office was first established in 1782 and initially, its small numbers of staff were easily accommodated in two houses located at Cleveland Row in St James's. During the rest of the 18th century, with increases in both headcount and business, the Office moved briefly to the Cockpit, Whitehall and then eventually to Downing Street, where Lord Sheffield's house had recently been acquired. By the late 1820s, the Foreign Office had taken over more houses in Downing Street, and also in Fludyer Street, which at the time ran parallel with it, while the office of the Secretary of State for War and the Colonies was housed in an adjacent property, Nos. 13-14 Downing Street, which looked back onto St James's Park.

Downing Street and its environs was, at that time, far from being the select and salubrious home of central government that it would one day become. The narrow streets and alleys were full of public houses, such as the Cat and Bagpipes and the Rose and Crown, some of which could trace their origins back to medieval hostels set up for pilgrims seeking the shrine of Edward the Confessor at Westminster Abbey. These rubbed shoulders with livery stables, dressmaking establishments, cheap lodging houses for Irish and Scottish MPs, a number of private houses and several major and minor departments of state. Both ministers and parliamentary clerks worked to an accompaniment of carriage wheels, horses' hooves and hawkers plying their wares. Stories flourished about the Foreign Office clerks' unofficial activities – buying strawberries via baskets suspended on strings of red tape, throwing hot pennies to street singers and signalling with mirrors to pretty dressmakers across the way, all of which gave rise to the comment that they, like the fountains in Trafalgar Square, "played from ten to four". Critics seemed to forget the long hours and weekend working imposed on the clerks, especially during the period when Lord Palmerston was Foreign Secretary.

Worse than that, however, was the instability of the houses themselves. An underground stream made the area very boggy and the foundations of some of the houses in Downing Street were so poor that one had fallen down and the rest of the Foreign Office was shored up with wooden posts. Added to this, the vibration from printing presses placed in the attic storeys meant that some of the houses were not expected to survive beyond the length of their leases, at best some twenty years. Dangerous cracks appeared in walls and ceilings and the Office librarian was especially afflicted by noxious odours wafting into his room from a faulty sewer nearby.

There were several plans to build a new Foreign Office on the Downing Street site but nothing came of these until the 1850s, when it was decided to centralise the major departments of state in Whitehall and to replace the warren of fine houses and tumbledown courts with purpose-built ministries. The first building, designed by George Gilbert Scott in classical, Italianate style was opened for business in July 1868, and by 1875 there were four buildings providing premises for four separate departments; the Foreign Office and the India Office occupying the western or park end of the complex and the Colonial Office and the Home Office occupying the Whitehall end.

For many years this arrangement proved satisfactory, but eventually the growing complexity of public administration led to severe overcrowding and in 1963, Geoffrey Rippon announced that the whole of Scott's building had come to the end of its useful life and that demolition was proposed as part of a major redevelopment plan for the area drawn up by the architect, Sir Leslie Martin. A public outcry ensued which led to the redevelopment being prevented and ultimately, the buildings becoming Grade 1 listed. The merger of the Foreign and Commonwealth Offices in 1968 and the removal of the Home Office to Queen Anne's Gate in 1978, led in time to the occupation of the whole of Scott's building by the Foreign and Commonwealth Office. This allowed the formulation of plans to transform what had been four separate ministries into one interconnected and modernised block, while at the same time restoring historically significant areas to their original glory. With a new sense of the building's historic value, it underwent a 17-year, £100 million restoration which was completed in 1997.

Neil stood in the middle of the entrance hall and gazed up at the ceiling, his mouth open in awe at the sheer grandeur and magnificence of the architecture. He had never seen anything like it. To all intents and purposes it was a stately home – in fact the most luxurious and well-preserved one that he had ever seen. All courtesy of the taxpayer of course but nonetheless, the most un-businesslike office accommodation that he had ever set eyes on. He wandered over and stared up at a portrait of George Gilbert Scott, which was hanging proudly above the chimneypiece, and then went to look at a statue of a Gurkha soldier by Richard Goulden, circa 1929, standing in the entrance hall to the former India Office, commemorating the Gurkha regiments of the British Army.

'Detective Sergeant Ashton?'

Neil suddenly realised that the question was being directed at him and turned round to find himself facing an enquiring security officer, a guy in his middle to late fifties who despite the rather official uniform, looked to be out of breath and not particularly fit and healthy. More concierge than security. 'Detective Sergeant Ashton?' he asked again patiently.

Neil nodded. It was too late to go back now. 'Yes, your front desk asked me to wait here. Apparently someone is going to escort me to the second floor reception.'

'This way Sir.' The security officer waved his arm to one side, indicating to Neil to follow him towards the Grand Staircase which swept majestically up towards the first floor. Neil duly followed, walking a couple of paces behind and deliberately going slowly enough to look at the paintings and furniture and artefacts which adorned the building. The two of them climbed the huge, broad staircase, the security guard periodically looking behind him to make sure that his visitor was still there and Neil, gazing in wonderment at the works of art which surrounded their ascent; a collection of murals painted by Sigismund Goetze at his own expense to commemorate the triumphs of the British Empire leading up to the Covenant of the League of Nations.

'This is amazing, imagine working somewhere like this!' Neil's head was twisting and turning like an awe-struck child on bonfire night, captivated by the sheer elegance and refinement of it all. He'd spent half the night lying awake worrying about the visit, not least because he was nervous about having to impersonate a police officer, but any apprehension that had been there when he arrived had suddenly disappeared. He was totally mesmerised by the surroundings. The security officer ignored him, other than making a derisory grunt to convey his own succinct and personal comment on the merits of the building as a workplace. *You wouldn't be so impressed if you had to climb these bloody stairs a hundred times a day.*

Neil followed him down various corridors and past countless rooms until eventually they reached a staircase leading to the second floor, the walls lined with portraits of Emperor Napoleon III and the Empress Eugénie, painted by Mélincourt and presented to the East India Company in acknowledgement of its contribution to the Paris Exhibition of 1855. By now he had completely lost his bearings and had no idea which part of the complex they were in or whether they were facing north, south, east or west. Finally they reached a door marked Reception Room C, which the security guard pushed open and ushered Neil through.

'Good morning,' said Neil, striding up to the reception desk with as much confidence and authority as he could muster. Walking through the building had been a wonderful distraction but suddenly, the harsh reality of what he was doing had kicked back in. Pretending to be a police officer was fairly daunting, not to mention illegal – and he was working without a safety net. He hadn't a clue what he was going to do if he was found out.

The receptionist looked up from the paperwork on her desk and gave him an efficient smile. 'Good morning. Can I help?'

Neil gave her a half-smile in return, polite but firm. The sort of greeting that he imagined a police officer might give. 'Detective Sergeant Ashton – Kent CID. I'm sorry, I don't have an appointment but I'd like to have a word with one of your employees if that's possible – Adam Saxby.'

The receptionist gave him an odd look, which he couldn't quite read and then twisted the visitors' book around so that it was facing the right way for him to complete. 'Of course. Could you fill in the register please.' She pointed towards a pen which was lying to one side.

Neil picked up the pen and filled in his name and contact details, checking his watch to put in the correct time of arrival. When he'd finished he put the pen back in the holder and twisted the register back the other way so that the receptionist could read it. He was expecting her to ask to see some identification, a possibility that he and Matt had sat up for most of the previous evening discussing and trying to find a solution for. In the end they had decided that confidence and bluff were the best approach. According to Matt no-one ever looked at police ID warrants. Most of the time they could just have easily flashed a British Rail season ticket or a membership card to the local gym. Apparently anything in a small, black leather wallet with a colour photo and a printed card was all that was needed.

To Neil's surprise, the receptionist didn't ask him for any identification at all, nor did she check to see what he'd written in the visitor's book. It was almost as though she'd been expecting him. She simply stood up, handed him a plastic visitor's badge and then walked over to the door that he'd just come through. 'If you'd like to follow me please.'

Neil didn't have a clue where they were going, but dutifully followed her out of the reception and down the corridor, past a number of offices and meeting rooms on either side until they finally reached a door on the right marked *Sir Anthony Eden*. Neil knew enough about 20th century politics to know that Sir Anthony Eden had been Foreign Secretary on three occasions between 1935 and 1955, as well as being Prime Minister from 1955 until 1957.

Eden was generally ranked as one of the least successful Prime Ministers of the 20th century, so the Foreign Office unsurprisingly held his memory in much higher esteem than they did over at Downing Street. The *Sir Anthony Eden* room was obviously a meeting room named in his memory. Either that, or it was his original office, frozen in time and covered in dust and cobwebs.

Neil smiled to himself at the absurdity of that final thought. However, the one serious thing that was going through his mind was that he couldn't understand why the receptionist hadn't rung Adam Saxby to tell him that there was someone in reception wanting to see him. Still, maybe she was going to do that in a minute.

The receptionist stopped outside the room and put her hand on the doorknob, on the point of twisting it and opening the door. 'I've put you in here Sergeant Ashton. Mr. Saxby will be down in about five minutes…'

Neil smiled at her and then frowned, unable to hide his confusion. He was sure that she hadn't telephoned Saxby to ask him to come down.

'…your colleague arrived about five minutes ago, so he's already here.'

Neil froze on the spot. In the space of a split second his heart started pounding and his legs began to feel weak and started to shake. Suddenly his shirt collar felt tight and very warm. He could feel the top button pushing against his Adam's apple and the perspiration dripping down the side of his neck. 'Colleague?'

'Yes. Chief Inspector Adams from Hampshire CID. I assume you two know each other?' At that point she opened the door and gently guided Neil into the room ahead of her, addressing the guy who was standing by the window at the far end, pouring himself a glass a water and looking every inch of exactly what he was – a dyed-in-the-wool copper. 'Chief Inspector, your colleague from Kent CID is here. Mr. Saxby will be five minutes.'

The *Sir Anthony Eden* room was a conventional meeting room with a rectangular table and chairs in the centre and a sideboard with glasses and bottles of water at the far end. Neil thought about simply turning round and getting the hell out of there but he knew it was useless. Firstly, he couldn't actually remember the way out and secondly, even if he could, there was no way that his legs were going to carry him. What he desperately wanted to do was sit down and have a glass of cold water.

The receptionist hovered, wondering whether to ask Neil if he wanted a cup of coffee while the copper at the end of the room finished pouring the water and then turned round and gave him a long, hard stare across the table. He'd never seen Neil before but one thing was certain. If the guy who had just walked in the room was a police officer, then he was Vincent Van Gogh. 'I'm sorry, I didn't catch the name?'

Neil practically fainted on the spot. He just wanted the ground to open up and swallow him.

The receptionist frowned. Suddenly something didn't feel right. The chemistry in the room was all wrong. Female intuition. She thought they were both together but now it seemed as if they didn't know each other. Neil sensed her discomfort; the hesitation to leave the room, quickly looking backwards and forwards between the two of them, trying to work out what was going on. He exchanged a quick glance with the guy across the room, a flicker of something in the copper's eyes, a transaction invisibly transmitted. The slightest of nods but it was there. *Say something*, it said, *for god's sake say something.*

Neil decided to keep going. There was nothing to lose now. He looked at Chief Inspector Adams and held his gaze, trying to read any signals that were coming back the other way. 'DS Neil Ashton – Kent CID.'

The copper gave him a short nod and the faintest of smiles. 'Of course, Neil, we met at the conference the other week. Good to see you again. How are you?'

'Fine thank you Sir. Sorry I'm late.' Neil didn't dare look at the receptionist, it was as much as he could do to stop his voice from trembling and just concentrate on looking at the copper at the other end of the room and keep the conversation going. He'd never met or even seen Garrick before. He'd met Steph of course and Matt obviously, but the closest he'd come to seeing Garrick was when he was sitting in the waiting room at Ashford police station, waiting for Doreen – and in fact it had been Steph who had come out with Doreen that day, not Garrick. He'd never actually met the Chief Inspector who was heading up the enquiry into Aunt Hilary's murder.

Likewise, Garrick had never set eyes on Neil before. Neil Ashton wasn't a suspect and he'd always been happy to leave the primary contact to Steph. Besides, there were more important people to concentrate on – like Graham Colley for example. But he knew the name of course, he'd heard it every day for the past week and he'd recognised it instantly as soon as Neil had introduced himself. He didn't have a clue what was going on but the last thing he needed was someone blowing his own cover. Garrick had never impersonated a member of Hampshire CID before and now was not the time to get found out.

'I'll leave you to it then,' said the receptionist, backing out of the door, apparently now satisfied that everything was okay.

Garrick waited a couple of seconds to make sure that she had gone and then walked across to Neil, who had slumped himself into one of the chairs halfway down the table, his legs having finally given way to the stress of it all.

'Neil Ashton? As in Hilary's Russell's nephew?'

Neil looked up at him and nodded sheepishly, waiting for the admonishment that he felt sure was coming next. As far as he was concerned, Chief Inspector Adams from Hampshire CID was the real deal and he was about to get the biggest bollocking of his life.

Garrick smiled and held out his hand. 'John Garrick – Kent CID. I don't know what you're doing here but we've got about three minutes for you to tell me what the hell is going on and for us to get our act together. So you'd better start talking…'

THIRTY-FIVE

Matt and Steph exchanged a silent, knowing look as they filed out of the incident room and made their way back to the office, conscious that everybody else was saying nothing and that they were probably all thinking exactly the same thing. If this was what the future under Brian Fowler was going to be like, then life was suddenly going to become a lot tougher. Garrick's sudden departure had been hard enough to take, but being led by someone like Superintendent Fowler was going to make matters a whole lot worse. The guy was a complete nightmare; a sort of prehistoric dinosaur who had somehow survived from an age when policing was all about chasing villains, tearing around in unmarked police cars and doing whatever it took to get a conviction. It had about as much relevance today as the 1980s double-breasted suit that he was wearing. According to Andy, Fowler thought that DNA stood for the National Association of Dyslexics.

Matt still had the Prime file tucked under his arm and gave Steph a slight nod as they turned into the corridor, indicating that he was going back to the interview room to finish off his reading. Steph took the signal and followed a couple of paces behind him, impatient to find out what sort of progress he had made. As Matt walked over to the window he undid the top button of his shirt and loosened his tie, still recovering from the previous fifteen minute "team-talk" that had gone down about as well as a pork sandwich at his brother's wedding.

'So, what do you think?' asked Steph, quickly checking that no-one had been following them before closing the door behind her.

Matt turned away from the window and held up the file that was still in his hand, his whole body language tense and angry. 'I'll tell you what I think. I think we need to finish reading this so that we can solve this case and get rid of Superintendent Fowl-up as soon as possible.'

Steph smiled to herself. *Superintendent Fowl-up* was hardly original but she knew that it was going to stick. A lot of the team had been upset by Garrick's suspension, but Matt had taken it worse than most. She nodded towards the file that he was still holding firmly in his hand. 'Anything so far?'

Matt pulled a face in a sort of "yes and no" response and then passed her the summary that he had been reading earlier. 'See what you think. It's definitely something to do with Prime. I haven't found any reference to Teleios yet, but whatever it was that Hilary Russell was discussing on the phone, she was definitely thinking about Geoffrey Prime.'

Steph pulled up a chair and sat down on one side of the interview table, eager to find out what Matt had discovered. She started to read the summary while Matt sat opposite her and turned to the back of the file, opening up the envelope marked RHYOLITE. He pulled out two pages of closely typed text on what looked like Cabinet Office notepaper.

"RHYOLITE / AQUACADE – SIGINT Spacecraft Series
(NRO/CIA/ NSA Programme AFP-720, 472)

Information regarding Rhyolite, later named "Aquacade" is restricted, security classification A03. Ministerial clearance or GCHQ "Blackstone" authority is required for any access to information over and above that set out below:

Rhyolite, later renamed "Aquacade," was a breakthrough in the world of signal intelligence (SIGINT) developed by the CIA and the National Security Agency (NSA) during the period from 1967 to 1985. In its time Rhyolite was the most sophisticated satellite surveillance programme ever deployed, having the capability to intercept lower frequency signals in the VHF and UHF band, as well as monitoring microwave transmissions used extensively by the Soviet Union for its most secure transmissions.

Specific launch details remain classified, but the first prototype launched in the early 1970s, carried an experimental test package into space for the most advanced surveillance system ever developed. The first operational launch placed a satellite into geosynchronous orbit positioned above the Horn of Africa, approximately 24,000 miles from earth with a speed exactly matching the turning of the globe. From that location, Rhyolite monitored transmissions from western Russia, as well as intercepting telemetry signals transmitted from liquid-fuel Intercontinental Ballistic Missiles (ICBMs) launched from the Tyuratam missile-testing range and solid-propellant missiles, including the SS-16 and intermediate-range SS-20, launched from Plesetsk.

When packaged and ready for launch, Rhyolite resembled a large, shiny box, approximately half the size of a railway goods carriage. Once released into orbit, the box unfolded to reveal a gold-meshed, seventy-foot parabolic antenna designed to pick up fragments of distant microwave transmissions, which were then refocused onto its receiver. Each microwave circuit was capable of carrying hundreds of conversations. Years of development and billions of dollars were required to develop systems capable of handling the unprecedented amounts of data that Rhyolite received.

The British security services were full partners in the deployment of Rhyolite, NSA passing much of the information to GCHQ for transcription and analysis.

Subsequently, NSA constructed numerous listening stations on friendly foreign soil, including the Menwith Hill facility in North Yorkshire, which has since become the cornerstone in the satellite surveillance program known as ECHELON.

No further details are available. Information in the public domain is classified as sensitive. Dissemination of any information to external parties requires Ministerial clearance. Ends."

Matt put the papers down and looked across at Steph who was still reading, still engrossed in learning about the history of Geoffrey Prime. He looked back at the file again, suddenly realising how out of their depth they all were. Country police officers playing at being security agents or intelligence officers. It was nonsense. He didn't understand half of it, in fact he hardly understood any of it. He'd never heard of Rhyolite and reading the summary that Simon had sent had made virtually no difference whatsoever. He was still none the wiser. Besides, what on earth did a satellite surveillance system from thirty years ago have to do with Stuart Richmond or Sir Julian Worsley, let alone Hilary Russell? It didn't make sense. He gazed over towards the window for a moment and wondered how Neil was getting on. Hopefully he was seeing Adam Saxby by now. Maybe he was having better luck.

Are you alright Shylock?' Steph had looked up from her papers, suddenly aware that Matt had stopped reading and was staring out of the window.

'I was just wondering how Neil was getting on.'

Steph smiled. 'So was I. Why don't we give him a ring?'

Matt looked at his watch, not sure whether they should call Neil or not. 'Perhaps we should give him another half an hour. Besides, it probably makes sense to ring him once we've finished going through the file. We might be able to tell him something by then.'

'Okay.' Steph gave him a nonchalant shrug and went back to reading the summary. Matt turned back to the file and opened the second envelope marked ECHELON. Again, he pulled out what looked like copies of documents written on Cabinet Office paper.

"ECHELON – SATCOM intercept component of the US SIGINT System (NRO/CIA/ NSA Programme MBSC-388, 191)

Information regarding ECHELON is restricted, security classification A05. Ministerial clearance or GCHQ "Redwood" authority is required for any access to information over and above that set out below:

Designed and coordinated by NSA, ECHELON is the surveillance system which intercepts and analyzes virtually every phone call, fax, email and telex message carried over the world's telecommunications networks. ECHELON is controlled by NSA and is operated under the terms of the 1948 UKUSA agreement in conjunction with GCHQ in Great Britain, the Communications Security Establishment (CSE) in Canada, the Australian Defence Security Directorate (DSD), and the Government Communications Security Bureau (GCSB) of New Zealand. Unlike many of the electronic spy systems developed during the Cold War, ECHELON is designed primarily for non-military targets. It affects every person communicating within and between all countries, anywhere in the world.

The ECHELON system is fairly simple in design, consisting of position intercept stations located all over the world to capture all satellite, microwave, cellular and fibre-optic communications traffic, plus a network of computing capability to process and analyse the information.

The primary components of the ECHELON network are those stations specifically targeted on the international telecommunications satellites (Intelsats), used by the telephone companies of most countries. A ring of Intelsats is positioned around the world, stationary above the equator, each one serving as a relay station for tens of thousands of simultaneous phone calls.

The secondary components of the ECHELON system are those stations which have the capability to monitor the range of satellite communications not carried by Intelsat, such as fax, telex and voice messages, plus all Internet and email traffic. Menwith Hill in northern England is the largest spy station in the world with 22 satellite terminals and five acres of buildings, and has the capability to listen to vast chunks of the communications spectrum throughout Europe and the old Soviet Union. Further stations are at Shoal Bay, outside Darwin in northern Australia, Leitrim, which is located south of Ottawa in Canada, Bad Aibling in Germany and Misawa in northern Japan.

The ability of ECHELON to intercept most of the communications traffic in the world is unparalleled in its scope. However the real power of ECHELON resides in its ability to decrypt, filter, examine and codify all communications traffic into selective categories for further analysis by intelligence agents from the various UKUSA parties. As electronic signals are transmitted into stations, they are fed through supercomputers such as SILKWORTH at Menwith Hill where voice recognition, optical character recognition and data information engines look for keywords known as the ECHELON "dictionaries." Each of the five stations' Dictionary computers has a codename to distinguish it from others in the network. For example, the Yakima station located in the desert country between the Saddle Mountains and Rattlesnake Hills has the COWBOY Dictionary, while the Waihopai station in New Zealand has the FLINTLOCK Dictionary. Codenames are recorded at the beginning of every *intercepted message before it is transmitted around the ECHELON network, allowing analysts to recognize at which station the interception occurred.*

No further details are available. Information in the public domain is classified as confidential and dissemination of any information to external parties requires Ministerial clearance. Ends."

Matt slumped back into the chair and blew out his cheeks again. This was worse than ever. If anything, the information on ECHELEON was even harder to get his head around than the stuff on Rhyolite. He looked over at Steph, who seemed to have finished reading the summary on Geoffrey Prime but was still engrossed in the papers, trying to work out something on a calculator. 'What do you think, Steph?' he asked, impatient to find out if she had reached the same conclusion.

Steph looked up and pulled a face, still looking as though she was confused by something in the report. 'I agree with you Matt. Teleios must have something to do with Prime, although I still can't see what the actual connection is. But there's something here that doesn't add up.'

Matt frowned. Everything had seemed pretty clear-cut to him. It was the stuff on the satellite systems that was complicated. The summary on Prime was straightforward wasn't it? 'What do you mean there's something that doesn't add up? What doesn't add up?'

Steph was still turning the pages back and forth and tapping numbers into the calculator. It looked as though she was checking and re-checking the same calculation over and over again, but was obviously getting the same answer. 'The dates. The dates don't add up. They don't make any sense.'

'What dates? What are you talking about Steph?' Matt was starting to get irritated and it was starting to show.

Steph twisted the papers round so that he could read what she was talking about from across the other side of the table. She pointed to a sentence, about four paragraphs from the end of the report and read it upside down. 'Look, here, it says, *"At the Old Bailey, on Wednesday 10th November 1982, Geoffrey Arthur Prime, then aged 44, pleaded guilty to seven counts against the Official Secrets Act and was sentenced to 35 years imprisonment."* If he was aged 44 and sentenced to 35 years, that means he would have been 79 when he came out.

Matt nodded, quickly doing the same calculation in his head. 'So?'

'And if he was sentenced in 1982, then he would have been released in 2017.'

Matt was still frowning, not sure where the conversation was going, or whether it meant anything or not

'So, right at the end of the report, here…' Steph turned the sheet over and pointed to the penultimate paragraph, '…it says that "*Prime would have been 82 on his release in 2020, had he served the full term.*"

Matt studied the paragraph and quickly did the maths again in his head. Steph was right, the dates didn't add up. He was irritated that he hadn't spotted it himself, but he still wasn't sure whether it really affected anything. The important thing was the information about Prime's spying activities, not the number of years that he'd been sent to prison, or his actual age when he was convicted. 'Maybe it's just a mistake,' he said without much real conviction, 'maybe they just got their dates mixed up. Or maybe it's just a simple typo. Perhaps it should read 38 years instead of 35. Then it would make sense.'

Steph frowned, obviously not convinced. 'This is an extract from an official government document Matt. It would have been checked and re-checked by a whole army of different people. There's no way it can be a mistake. We're definitely missing something. There must be something else in the file that explains it.'

It was Matt's turn to pull a face and look unconvinced. He picked up the file and passed it across the table. 'I'm not so sure Steph, but if you want to keep ploughing through it then be my guest. Personally I need a break from reading all this stuff. I'm going to ring Neil.' He picked up his mobile and dialled Neil's number, the phone ringing half a dozen times before suddenly going into voicemail.

*

'Sorry about that,' said Neil, fumbling inside his jacket pocket, 'I should have switched it off before we started.' He could feel his neck going slightly red with embarrassment.

Garrick gave him a withering look across the table as Adam Saxby held up his hand to wave away the apology.

'So you were saying, Mr. Saxby,' continued Garrick, trying not to lose the momentum on the conversation, 'you didn't actually know Miss Russell?'

Saxby took another sip of coffee, putting the cup down carefully back into the saucer before he spoke. 'No, not at all. She retired about twenty years ago. Twenty years ago I was still at university. The only time I ever spoke to her was when she rang me the other week.'

Garrick nodded, recognising that Saxby must be telling the truth. The guy looked about 35 or 40 at the most. Twenty years ago he hadn't even started work. 'And she didn't come and see you a couple of weeks ago? Friday 22 September?'

Saxby shook his head again. 'Sorry. I never met her. Like I said, the only time I ever spoke to her was when she rang me for the phone number. The only reason she called me was because Guy Daniels gave her my name.'

'Do you know if she knew Daniels very well?' asked Garrick, trying to get a fix on the relationships.

Saxby shrugged. 'I assume so. Daniels has been there donkey's years. He must be close to retirement. Besides, he wouldn't have given her my name if he didn't know her.'

Garrick nodded again. That certainly made sense. 'And you say she worked in the Department of Employment?'

Saxby nodded in return. 'I rang Personnel and checked up on her after she called me. She was in Human Resources apparently. Red Lion Square I think.'

Garrick shook his head, none the wiser. This was going nowhere. Saxby obviously didn't know anything. 'And you're not able to tell me who she was trying to contact, or why?'

'I don't know why Chief Inspector, she didn't say and I didn't ask. And you already have the phone number and a contact name.' Saxby held his hands up in apology. 'I'm afraid I can't help you anymore than that.'

'An address would be helpful,' grunted Garrick, knowing instinctively what the answer was going to be. Saxby shrugged again and gave him an apologetic smile.

'Why is it so confidential?' asked Neil, saying something for the first time in several minutes. 'Surely if it's part of the Civil Service it should be in the public domain?'

Saxby shrugged for a third time. 'I don't know what else I can say. The number she was after isn't even known to GCHQ. That must give you some idea of the problem I have…'

'Although it didn't stop you giving the number to Hilary Russell – a complete stranger.' Garrick had spotted a chink of light and was trying to apply as much pressure as he could. 'If everything is so confidential, how come you were happy to give it to someone that you'd never spoken to before, someone who worked in the Department of Employment over twenty years ago?'

Saxby shifted uncomfortably in his chair and said nothing.

'This is a murder enquiry Mr. Saxby,' said Neil, suddenly getting into the role of Detective Sergeant Ashton and starting to enjoy himself, 'we can always do this down at the station.'

Garrick smiled to himself. Neil was actually starting to sound like a real copper.

Saxby shifted again, looking more and more uncomfortable by the second. 'She asked for somebody by name. It was enough to satisfy me that it was okay to give her the number. That's all I can tell you.'

'Whose name?' asked Garrick, ignoring the last comment.

Saxby said nothing and stared down at the table-top, trying to avoid any eye contact.

'Obviously not Jean Pettipher then?' Garrick was determined to keep pushing for an answer.

Saxby shook his head and mumbled into his chest. 'No, obviously.'

The three of them sat in silence for a minute or so, Saxby determined not to say anything that he wasn't allowed to and Garrick and Neil trying to figure out how to move the line of questioning forward. All they needed was a name and an address.

'So where does Jean Pettipher work Mr. Saxby?' asked Garrick, trying a different tack. 'Presumably if I contacted your Personnel Department and asked them to look her up, they'd be able to tell me?'

Saxby shrugged. 'Yes, I suppose so.'

'Well then, save me the trouble. What will it say on her personnel record?'

Saxby shifted in his seat again. Without knowing it Garrick was inching closer and closer to the truth.

'Come on Mr. Saxby, like I said, I could ring them now and get the information myself.' Garrick held up his mobile phone as if he was considering calling them there and then.

Saxby let out a sigh. 'It will say that she worked for the Department of Employment. Human Resources.'

Garrick frowned at him across the table, trying to work out whether he was trying to be clever or not. If he wasn't, then it was a huge coincidence – and Garrick didn't believe in coincidences. He leant forward to show his irritation, running out of patience at playing cat and mouse. 'I need the contact name and address Mr. Saxby and I'd like it now please.'

Saxby looked up from the table and held his palms open, trying to convey that there wasn't anything he could do. 'I'm sorry Chief Inspector. I can't, I just can't. You'll have to go to a much higher authority than me.'

Garrick let out a long sigh and turned sideways to look at Neil. He knew when he was beaten. Saxby wasn't holding out on them because he was concealing something. He just didn't have the authority to tell them what he knew. It was obviously classified – covered by the Official Secrets Act probably. He snapped his notebook shut and nodded to Neil, indicating that he'd had enough and that it was time to go. No point in going any further. Neil nodded back, taking the signal but also spotting that Saxby was watching their silent exchange, trying to interpret what it meant. Neil didn't know where the idea came from; some hackneyed cops and robbers television programme probably – but as the words came out of his mouth, they sounded like the real thing. He turned towards Saxby and looked him straight in the eye.

'Okay, have it your own way. Adam Saxby, I am arresting you in connection with the murder of Hilary Russell. You do not have to say anything, but it may harm your defence if you do not mention when questioned something which you later rely on in court. Anything you do say may be given in evidence and…'

'Whoa, whoa, whoa…' Saxby was suddenly on his feet, more animated than he had ever been in his whole career. 'Wait a minute, wait a minute, you can't do this!'

'We can do anything we like!' shouted Garrick, sensing that Neil's impromptu speech had suddenly got the desired reaction. 'Finish the caution DS Ashton.'

'Hang on a minute, hang on a minute…' Saxby was holding his hands up, slowly sitting back down in his chair. 'I'm not trying to be difficult. This information is highly confidential…'

'Frankly I'm not interested in your protocols Mr. Saxby,' said Neil, still adopting the formal, dogmatic manner of CID officer about to make an arrest. 'This is a triple murder enquiry and either you give us the information we need or I will charge you with obstruction.'

It was as much as Garrick could do to not look at Neil and burst out laughing. The lad was much too young to remember Charlie Barlow but his style of interrogation was frightenly similar. Saxby meanwhile was staring back down at the table-top, trying to work out the repercussions of either option. He was damned if he said anything and damned if he didn't. Rock and a hard place. He looked at Garrick and then at Neil, trying to work out whether they were really going to arrest him. After what seemed like an eternity he eventually made his decision. 'Okay, the address is Number 1, Carlton Gardens.'

Garrick gave him a short nod in appreciation. 'Thank you. Where is that exactly?'

'Just behind the Mall.'

'Thanks. And the contact name?'

Saxby hesitated and took a deep breath. Divulging the name somehow seemed a lot harder. 'Buchanan, Charles Buchanan.'

Garrick quickly scribbled the name down in his notebook. 'And who is he?'

'Good question.'

Garrick frowned at Saxby for a second before realising that he was being serious. 'Well, which department then?'

'Likewise, good question.'

Garrick frowned again. 'Home Office? Foreign Office? Treasury?'

Saxby smiled ruefully to himself. 'Unaffiliated, is probably the correct answer.'

Garrick pulled a face, not sure what to make of that. 'So what does he do?'

Saxby thought carefully for a moment before answering. 'He runs a department known as *Vector*. Beyond that I can't say. Arrest or no arrest Chief Inspector, that's as much as I can tell you.'

'Okay.' Garrick snapped his notebook shut again and stood up to make his leave. He sensed that there was no point in pushing it any further and besides, they'd got exactly what they had come for. 'Thank you very much Mr. Saxby, we'll pay Mr. Buchanan a visit. And if it helps, I'm happy to be discreet. I won't let him know that I got his details from you.'

'Thank you,' said Saxby, holding open the door, 'that's very kind of you. That would be much appreciated.' He smiled at Garrick as the three of them filed into the corridor. *But there's no need really. I'll be ringing him as soon as you've gone.*

THIRTY-SIX

Craven's knowledge of London was usually pretty good but the area just north of Paddington, known as Little Venice, was not one that he was particularly familiar with. Technically, it ran from the point where the Paddington arm of the Grand Union Canal met the Regents Canal, but the name, coined by Robert Browning who lived there from 1862 to 1887 was now generally applied to much of the neighbourhood that occupied about a square mile to the south of Maida Vale.

When the Grand Union Canal was opened in 1820, the area was home to artists, writers and prostitutes, but today it was much more genteel and was now regarded as one of the most exclusive, residential districts in central London. As the name suggested, the area was interspersed with picturesque waterways and comprised of about ten tree-lined streets with beautiful 17th century white stucco homes, plus a collection of chic and trendy shops on Formosa Street and Clifton Gardens. An assortment of restaurants, bars and waterside cafés gave the whole quarter a cosmopolitan, laid-back vibe and its proximity to Regents Park and its easy access to Oxford Street and to the West End meant that it had become a much coveted and fashionable address.

Tourists could take a scenic boat trip or follow the towpath on foot and discover how the winding waterway snaked its way through the heart of the city, heading downstream past the charming regency streets of Maida Vale onto Regents Park and Camden beyond, or alternately following the peaceful corridor upstream to the west, enjoying the tranquillity of the waterways that felt a million miles from the hubbub of the city roads and streets nearby.

It took Craven a little while to find the right address, Number 3, Leith Gardens; a small but elegant property tucked discreetly behind one of the main tourist areas in an exclusive, private mews. He quickly checked his mobile to make sure that he had the right place. Jean's text had arrived quicker than he thought and with better news than he had dared hope for. Waiting around all day for Carlisle to leave the office would have been a real pain, but as luck would have it, an evening engagement at *the Mansion House* and therefore a late night, probably with too much alcohol, meant that he had decided to work at home today. Home on Saturdays and Sundays was apparently somewhere in rural Suffolk, but during the week it was a smart and fashionable townhouse in Little Venice.

Craven decided to walk around the property and the adjacent streets a couple of times to get his bearings and to check out the lay of the land. He wanted to make sure that he had a map of the immediate vicinity in his head and in particular, that he had memorised the optimum escape routes. Craven's third rule of fieldwork. *Luck is what happens when preparation meets opportunity.* It took him about ten minutes to walk around the block a few times and get a plan of the surrounding streets and buildings committed to memory. He would have liked longer, but he knew that time was of the essence. Besides, a good plan, violently executed now, was going to work much better than a perfect plan put into action next week.

The major problem was that Carlisle's house was in the middle of a row of identical terraced properties, all butted up to one another and all with tiny, courtyard gardens at the back that were only accessible through the properties themselves. All of which meant that the only way into Carlisle's house was through the front door. Standing on the front doorstep and ringing the bell wasn't exactly going to create the element of surprise that Craven had in mind.

He lit a cigarette and wandered fifty yards down the road towards a small, private car park which was tucked behind the end property, the large "Residents Only" sign confirming that this was a facility reserved for the exclusive use of Carlisle and his neighbours. There were ten or so spaces neatly marked out in clean, white paint and Craven took a long, thoughtful drag on his cigarette as he looked at the four very different vehicles that were parked there. One of them had to be Carlisle's. If the guy travelled to and from home every week then he had to come by car. The Cabinet Secretary probably had more power and influence than almost anyone else in the country, but it wasn't as though he was a Government Minister with his own driver. Civil servants had to make their own travel arrangements and Carlisle had to ferry clean clothes down from Suffolk every week, probably on a Sunday night or Monday morning, and then take the dirty laundry back the other way, probably on a Friday evening. Not something that he would do on the train. Not someone as busy and important as him. Craven finished his cigarette and flicked it across the car park towards the perimeter fence at the back. No, one of them definitely had to be Carlisle's – the question was which one?

He discounted two of the cars immediately. The small, rusting Peugeot was too old and too dilapidated to belong to Carlisle. Sure, people with money often ran cheap, old runabouts whilst the expensive Jag was kept safe and sound at home in the garage – but that was just for running around locally; to and from the supermarket or down to the village pub. There was no way that he was going to do a regular commute up and down the M11 in a clapped out old Peugeot; not without his fingers crossed for most of the way. The thing looked as though it was running on a wing and a prayer. The other car that didn't fit was the ubiquitous silver Ford saloon. Maybe, just maybe, someone as high profile as Carlisle would opt for the guaranteed anonymity that a mid-range Ford provided but it was the interior of the car, particularly the child seats in the back that made Craven reject it. He peered through the windows at the untidy mess strewn all over the seats and the floor. This didn't belong to Carlisle. It was owned by a typical, middle-income family; some poor mortgaged-up-to-the-hilt husband with a screaming wife and two screaming kids.

The obvious choice of course was the large, gleaming BMW that was parked in the centre of the car park, a three-litre engine and pristine bodywork polished to perfection – but there was something about it that just didn't feel right. Craven wandered over and walked around it a couple of times. It was intuition really, but it was almost too perfect, a poser's car; the slightly tinted windows, the immaculate interior, the colour coordinated tax disc. This was owned by someone whose status was defined by the sort of car that they drove. It couldn't be Carlisle. Carlisle got his status from his job. Every time he walked into a meeting it must have stroked his ego. He was the most senior civil servant in the country. He rubbed shoulders with the Prime Minister and the Royal household for god's sake. The guy must have had a permanent erection whenever he was at work.

No, the car that really interested Craven was an Audi estate, slightly mud-splattered over a gun-metal grey finish and parked discreetly in the corner. Understated, practical, über reliable. Built with ruthless German efficiency. *Vorsprung durch Technik*. He held his hands over his eyes and peered through the windows. This was more like it. A 4x4 estate car, perfect for the country retreat but equally at home on the more fashionable streets of central London. There were also what looked like bits of wood in the back and an old dog blanket thrown over the rear seat. Craven could picture it in his mind. Carlisle poodling around the country lanes on a Saturday afternoon, going to buy some logs for the fire, the black Labrador sitting in the back. This had to be his car. It just had to be.

He lit another cigarette and felt the nicotine kick-in instantly, as he worked out a crude but effective plan in his mind. He watched with interest as a couple in a blue Mazda drove in and parked in one of the spaces. He could see the girl in the front passenger seat pointing towards the "Residents Only" sign and the guy shrugging his shoulders and then looking at his watch. They obviously weren't residents. The pair of them got out of the car and looked around nervously, trying to decide whether to risk parking there or not. Craven pulled out his mobile and paced up and down a few times, pretending to be deep in conversation. Eventually, the guy hit the remote control and the pair of them walked off towards the shops on the main road. Craven couldn't tell how long they were going to be, but all he needed was five minutes – ten at the most.

It took him only a matter of seconds to find a large stone on the edge of the car park and smash the glass on the front nearside indicator of the Audi. The alarm, a distinctive, high-pitched warble went off immediately, perfectly synchronised with the amber hazard lights, which were now flashing on and off. He checked his watch and then leant casually on the wing of the blue Mazda and began to wait. The alarm was certainly loud enough. If that was Carlisle's car, then he was going to be out of the house almost immediately.

Carlisle was sitting in his small but elegantly furnished living room, drinking a cup of coffee and still nursing a hangover from the night before. The official function at *the Mansion House* had been tame enough, but he'd decided to leave early and go onto *White's*, his club in St. James's. That was normally a safe and uneventful refuge on a Sunday evening but he had bumped into an old friend from university and had drunk far too much, the end result of which was now a blinding headache and a rather fragile stomach. He smiled ruefully to himself. He was getting too old for this. He was actually meant to be working at home today, but he felt too unwell to do anything but just sit in the chair and take things easy for a bit.

Still, it was always hugely entertaining to meet up with his old pals. He smiled again as he thought about Charlie Roxbrough, the 7th Earl of Stranmoor, blundering into *White's* dining room and knocking over the furniture, already three sheets to the wind having enjoyed far too much wine and brandy. Typical. Charlie always was a "Buller man" to the core, ever ready to uphold the ancient reputation of *the Bullingdon Club* for a bit of calculated hedonism and debauchery, despite his advancing years. Carlisle finished his coffee and mused about his time at Oxford with fond affection. Halcyon days He had made a good many friends at Balliol of course but it was the invitation to join the notorious *Bullingdon*, a socially exclusive dining club, that would always have the greatest and most lasting impact on his life.

Without any permanent rooms and infamous for its members' wealth and destructive binges, membership was limited to around 20 students at any one time and inevitably, was by invitation only. Naturally, it was prohibitively expensive for most and whilst non-Etonians were not necessarily barred from joining, it certainly helped to have attended the school. As a Wykehamist and not blue-bloodied at all, Carlisle had always felt enormously flattered and privileged to have been invited.

The Club was founded over 150 years ago and a vestige of its hunting heritage still existed in its support for the Bullingdon point to point, for which the Club President presented the winner's cup each year. Membership elections were held twice a year and the club still maintained an extraordinary secrecy; most undergraduates having no idea who was actually a member. New members were visited in their rooms, which were then ritually 'trashed' as a symbol of their acceptance, the newly elected "Buller man" then required to organise one of the club's infamous jaunts.

Members traditionally dressed for their annual dinner in specially made tailcoats in Oxford blue with offset ivory silk lapel facings, brass monogrammed buttons, and a mustard coloured waistcoat. With a reputation for drinking prodigious quantities of alcohol and for causing considerable drunken damage, a night in the cells was regarded as something of a par for a "Buller man", as was debagging anyone who attracted their irritation.

Carlisle smiled to himself as he remembered the antics of the annual Bullingdon Golfing Match, inevitably played with complete disregard for conventional rules and bourgeois conditions, such as daylight or proper links or greens. Members much preferred the purity which could be achieved at night, ideally between 1am and 2am, whilst attempting to drive from quad to quad – a challenge made all the more invigorating as the ball smacked into honeyed, eighteenth century stone and rebounded at potentially fatal speeds.

Charlie Roxbrough's commitment to *the Bullingdon* had always been joyously self-evident, often storming into the room of some pimply theology undergraduate in the small hours of the morning to haul its occupant downstairs and plunge him into the ice-cold fountain in the middle of the lawn. Carlisle, on the other hand had always managed to retain a degree of autonomy from the pack, enjoying the cachet which membership conferred whilst proving adroit enough to ensure that he was not too closely associated with the more abrasive of its celebrations.

He touched his temple as his head started thumping again, the sound of splintering woodwork and breaking glass still a faint memory from all those years ago. Or was it something else? Not a memory but the faint, distant sound of something equally familiar. A car alarm. Yes, a car alarm – he could hear a car alarm going off in the distance.

He picked up his front door keys and then put on a jacket and walked the short distance down to the residents' car park, the sound of the alarm getting louder and louder as he got nearer to his car. The first thing he saw as he turned the corner was the Audi, the alarm blaring in perfect harmony to the hazard lights which were flashing on and off, and then Craven, leaning on a blue car with his arms folded, a relaxed, unworried pose as if he was waiting patiently for someone to turn up.

Carlisle hit the remote button to turn off the noise and then turned towards Craven, who had already started walking towards him. 'What the hell's going on?'

Craven had his hands open, the briefly rehearsed apology spoken in his poshest, friendliest voice. 'I'm awfully sorry, it's entirely my fault, I must have bumped into your car.'

Carlisle frowned at him and then nodded towards the sign at the front of the car park. 'This is meant to be residents only.'

'I know, I know. I only stopped to make a phone call.' Craven held up his mobile phone as if it were proof of what he was saying. 'I really am terribly sorry. Obviously I'll pay for any damage.'

Carlisle grunted but said nothing else, squatting down to inspect the car more closely. There didn't seem to be any damage to the paintwork – just the indicator, but it was still a bloody nuisance. It wasn't the cost that was really bothering him, it was the inconvenience of having to get it fixed. Plus of course the car was probably illegal now. This was the last thing he needed. 'Any damage to yours?' he asked, standing up and nodding towards what he thought was Craven's car.

'No, I must have caught it at the right angle. I think mine's okay.'

'Mmm...' Carlisle grunted again. 'So, have you got some insurance details?'

'No, not on me,' replied Craven, telling the truth for the first time, 'but it's probably not worth making an insurance claim – I'd rather just pay for the repair to be honest. I'll give you my name and address and my telephone number.'

Carlisle nodded. That made a lot of sense. It was only the price of a bulb and a new reflector. Not worth losing your no-claims bonus over. 'Okay, give me your details and I'll call you later this evening.'

'I don't suppose you've got a pen and paper have you?' asked Craven sheepishly, patting his pockets to indicate that he hadn't got anything with him.

'No, of course I haven't,' snapped Carlisle, unable to hide the irritation in his voice. 'Haven't you got anything in the car?'

Craven gave him an apologetic shrug. 'Sorry.'

Carlisle muttered something under his breath and looked at Craven as if he was a complete idiot. 'I've got some in the house. Wait here, I'll be back in a minute.'

'I'll come with you.' offered Craven following a couple of paces behind and with as much obsequiousness as he could manage, 'save you walking back.' Carlisle said nothing and showed no signs of objecting to being accompanied, not bothering to turn round or respond in any way.

It took them less than thirty seconds to walk back to the house, an uncomfortable silence developing between them. Two strangers with nothing in common, momentarily united by a simple act of fate – or so Carlisle thought. 'I'll wait here,' said Craven, as they got to the front door, not wanting to make him too suspicious or wary.

Carlisle nodded as he put the key in the lock and pushed open the door. 'Okay, I won't be a minute.'

Craven watched him through the front door that had been left ajar. Carlisle walked a couple of paces down the hall and then turned left into the living room. He knew that he had left his fountain pen on top of the desk, but he wasn't going to give that to a stranger to write with, the nib would be ruined in a matter of seconds. He pulled open one of the drawers, looking for a biro or a pencil. For some reason he'd also run out of paper. He had some in his briefcase of course, but it was quicker just to take a blank envelope and use that. He picked up a pencil and a white envelope and walked back to the front door, only to find that Craven had gone.

For a moment he didn't know what to think. He hadn't been more than thirty seconds and the guy had completely disappeared. He stepped forward a couple of paces and looked up and down the road, just in case Craven had wandered off somewhere. Nothing. Then it hit him. The guy had vanished. Scarpered. How could he have been so stupid? It was a con. A simple con, but flawlessly executed. The guy had obviously run back to his car and driven off – and now there was no way of tracing him. No name, no phone number. Carlisle could have kicked himself. He was so convinced that he was going to get his name and address that he hadn't even thought to look at his registration number. How stupid was that? He'd been totally hoodwinked. What a bloody day it was turning out to be.

He shut the front door and walked down the hall and into the kitchen. He needed something to drink after that. Hair of the dog. As he walked towards the refrigerator, Craven stepped out from behind the door and thrust the black bin-liner over his head, wrapping his arms around his chest in one swift movement and then picking him up in a crushing, vice-like bear hug, his feet dangling several inches above the floor. The shock and violence of the instant blackout almost gave Carlisle a heart attack, the effect of which would not have been unlike the excruciating pain he felt as Craven squeezed his ribcage harder and harder, pushing every last breath of air out of his body. Carlisle tried to scream but it was no use, it was impossible to breathe and he was starting to faint and suffocate inside the plastic bag. He would never forget that moment. The sudden, absolute violence, the sheer terror of not knowing what was going on, the uncontrollable panic of not being able to breath. And the darkness, the silent, enveloping darkness…

Craven kept squeezing him, maintaining the pressure and waiting for the exact point at which to stop. Eventually he dropped him to the floor and pulled the bin-liner off his head. Carlisle was barely conscious and lay curled-up and motionless as Craven tied some plastic handcuffs on his wrists and then around his ankles. It took a good sixty seconds before he started to regain consciousness and work out what was happening. It was the unmistakeable sound of someone opening a kitchen drawer and rifling through the cutlery that finally brought him round.

Craven put the tip of the knife under his chin and pressed it gently. 'Know who I am?'

Carlisle looked up at him and thought for a moment. *Buchanan's boy. Craven, it has to be Craven.* Then he shook his head gently. No point in admitting anything.

'Know why I'm here?'

Again, Carlisle shook his head and said nothing.

Craven knelt down so that their faces were almost touching, the tip of the knife still firmly wedged underneath Carlisle's chin. 'Well, let's get straight to the point. You're going to tell me everything you know about Teleios – and then I'm going to disappear.'

Carlisle said nothing but pulled a face, half frown – half confusion, as if trying to indicate that he didn't know what Craven was talking about. Craven smiled and gently pushed the knife a bit further, so that Carlisle was now staring up at the ceiling. Then he jabbed it hard, without warning, puncturing the skin just above the Adam's apple. Carlisle yelped as the sudden horror and realisation of what was happening became all too real, his blood spurting out and running down his neck.

Craven walked over to one of the worktops and tore off several sheets of kitchen towel which he scrunched into a ball. Then he squatted down and pressed it firmly against the cut on Carlisle's neck to try and stop the bleeding. Carlisle held his gaze for a couple of seconds, as if trying to say thank you, his hands still firmly handcuffed behind his back. Maybe the guy had some compassion after all.

Craven gave him a cynical smile, dabbed the kitchen towel on his neck a couple of times and then stuffed it into his mouth, forcing him to breathe through his nose. 'Nothing to say? Well, we'll see about that.'

Carlisle started to tremble, his eyes wide open with fear as he watched Craven go over to the cutlery drawer again and rifle about for something else. He tried to shout but all that came out was a muffled, stifled sound.

Suddenly the noise stopped. Craven held up a pair of nutcrackers, the old-fashioned sort that people used to have at Christmas. They never really worked in his opinion. His memory as a child was of his Mum, always buying a box a dates and a bag of nuts on Christmas Eve; usually a string bag full of walnuts, almonds and brazil nuts that were impossible to crack. All he ever ended up with were tiny bits of nuts and shell, all mixed up and totally inedible. But the dates…now they were fabulous. There was always a picture of a camel on the front of the box…

He leant down again and put the little finger on Carlisle's right hand into the nutcrackers. Fingers were always effective. For some reason people seemed to have a much higher pain threshold when it came to other parts of their body, but in Craven's experience, fingers were normally the quickest route to getting someone to talk. Sometimes it took two attempts, but with most people, just like Ray Holland, one was usually enough.

Carlisle started to panic, the sweat literally running down his face. He started to hyperventilate. He knew what was going to happen next. The pain was going to be unbearable. Craven squeezed the nutcrackers gently for several seconds and then suddenly, without warning, clenched them together as hard and as violently as he could. The bone in Carlisle's finger snapped in an instant and he let out a blood-curdling howl, which as before, was totally muffled by the kitchen towel that was still stuffed in his mouth. *Merry Christmas Mr. Cabinet Secretary… Merry Christmas.*

Craven picked up the knife again and found a fresh piece of skin on Carlisle's neck, slightly closer to the jugular this time. 'Now, let's try that again. You're going to tell me everything you know about Teleios. Yes or no?'

Carlisle had nearly fainted from the shock, but he looked up at Craven and nodded without hesitation. The repercussions of Teleios becoming public were unthinkable but right now, he couldn't have cared less. It might have all sorts of ramifications for the government and for his own career, but none of that meant anything if he wasn't alive. The most important thing in Sir James Carlisle's life was Sir James Carlisle. The pain in his hand was almost unbearable and the knife was still digging into his skin and the blood was still trickling down his neck. Everybody else could go to the dogs. It was time to look after Number One. He was about to tell Craven absolutely everything there was to know.

THIRTY-SEVEN

It was mid morning by the time Steph had finished reading through the file and had found what she was looking for. Matt had given up some time ago and had gone back to the CID room, leaving her with some peace and quiet to trawl through the transcripts from the police interviews and the trial proceedings, plus all the local press cuttings. She smiled to herself as she put the documents back in order and gazed out of the window, thinking about what life must have been like in Britain in the 1960s and the 1970s. Reading the papers had transported her back to another time – to an era when life was a lot simpler and seemed to be more innocent. A time when people were certainly less affluent, but appeared to be much happier and somehow, when society seemed to be more tolerant. Strange really, given what she had just read.

She picked up the phone and dialled Matt's number, which was answered in a matter of seconds. 'Shylock, get yourself down here. I think I've found something.'

'Okay, thanks very much, thanks for calling,' said Matt, feigning disinterest as he put the phone down and leant casually back into his chair. Superintendent Fowler and DCI Stenning from Hampshire CID were floating about somewhere and the last thing he wanted to do was alert them to what he and Steph were up to. After a couple of minutes he picked up his mug and wandered over towards Andy who was leaning hunched-up over his desk, hanging on the end of the phone and looking decidedly bored, obviously listening to something not very exciting at the other end.

'Have you got change for a fiver for the vending machine?' Matt half-whispered.

Andy said nothing, still listening to the person on the phone, but pulled open his drawer to check and then shook his head, waving Matt away with his hand. He was trying to concentrate on a telephone conversation and Matt hovering over him was putting him off.

Matt wandered out of the CID room, still carrying his mug as if he was heading for the canteen, and quickly made his way down to the interview room. Steph was leaning against the windowsill, waiting patiently but beginning to wonder where he was. 'At last, what kept you?'

Matt pulled a face in frustration. 'Don't ask. Anyway, what have you found? Something on Teleios?'

Steph shook her head. There was nothing on Teleios, but there was something else. She could barely disguise the excitement her voice. 'I've found something which explains why those dates don't add up.'

Matt looked at her for a second and tried hard not to show his disappointment. Anger almost. Did the dates really matter? The important thing was that they had made a connection between Hilary Russell and Geoffrey Prime. What they needed to do now was find a connection between both of them and Teleios, not waste time trying to work out why a set of dates didn't add up. He took a deep breath, sensing Steph's impatience to show him what she had found. 'Go on, what is it?'

Steph opened the file again, looking for the document that she was about to quote. 'Do you remember that in one of the summaries it said something about another offence?' She thumbed through a few papers and then suddenly pulled one out, running her finger down the page, trying to locate the right paragraph. 'Here it is. *In 1981, Prime was questioned by the local police about an unrelated offence and realising that his house was about to be searched, took his wife out to a local beauty spot and confessed to everything.*' Do you remember that?'

Matt nodded. It was only a couple of hours ago that he read it himself. 'So, what's the significance of that?'

'What do you think it means when it says he confessed to everything?'

'Well, the spying, obviously.'

Steph shook her head. 'I don't think it does. We know from the police interviews that he didn't actually confess to being a spy until he was in police custody, several months after he was arrested. What he was confessing to his wife was the other offence. That's the whole point Matt. Prime was so notorious, in fact so infamous for being a spy that no-one took any notice of the other offence. It's almost as though it's been completely forgotten...'

Matt frowned at her, still trying to work out where Steph's line of reasoning was heading.

'.. .and more importantly, I think there's a real possibility that it's the unrelated offence which is the link to Teleios, not the spying. I don't think it's got anything to do with espionage or Rhyolite or ECHELON or whatever else it was that they were working on at the time. It's just all too far fetched.'

'So what was the other offence?' asked Matt, suddenly realising that he had missed something really important.

'He was a paedophile.'

'A paedophile! You're joking?' Matt looked at her with disbelief.

'Apparently he had a liking for young girls. And if you dig hard enough in the file it tells you that in addition to the 35 year sentence that he received for spying, Prime also received three years for the unrelated offence, which wasn't to run concurrently. That's why the dates didn't add up. He was actually sentenced to 38 years...'

'Jesus!'

'... but the GCHQ case was so sensational that it absolutely dominated the front pages. All he's ever remembered for is being a spy.'

Matt looked at Steph in stunned silence, trying to work out the implications of what she was saying. 'So why do you think it's the other offence that is the link to Teleios?'

'Well, it's only a theory,' replied Steph, 'but at the moment, we don't have anything that links Stuart Richmond and Sir Julian Worsley. As far we know they'd never met, they were different ages, they didn't move in the same circles and they were at opposite ends of the social spectrum. Worsley was old school; a privately educated lawyer and successful barrister, whilst Richmond was a self-made fashion designer and high-street retailer. They had absolutely nothing in common with each other, unless ...'

'Unless they were both paedophiles.' interrupted Matt, suddenly catching up with Steph's line of thinking.

'Exactly. Hilary Russell was obviously connecting Teleios to Geoffrey Prime in some way, but maybe it didn't have anything to do with what he was famous for. Maybe it's something as simple as him being a paedophile.'

'Which might explain the laptop. added Matt, starting to construct a logical sequence of events in his mind. 'It might also explain why Richmond was so keen to buy it back – and at such a high price.' He pulled out a chair and sat down at the table, eager to look at the documents himself. 'So what does it say exactly, Steph?'

Steph also sat down and thumbed through a few more papers, eventually pulling out another document, which she started to read out loud.

"Geoffrey Prime was also a convicted paedophile whose treachery was only discovered because of a string of sexual assaults on young girls. During 1981 Prime had indulged his liking for adolescents and had tried his luck with a 14-year-old Herefordshire girl in her own home. Prime had phoned her, claiming to be a 'Mr. Williams' and visited her house the next day pretending to be a painter and decorator. He made indecent suggestions and threatened her with a tin opener, but the girl was

different to the others and made a fight of it.

She screamed and made as much noise as she could, struggling against Prime's perverted wishes. Prime left the house when she screamed and ran off to his brown two-tone, Mark IV Ford Cortina, which was parked nearby in a small farm access. He drove away, unaware that one of the local farmhands was something of a car buff, who on interview with the police was able to give a detailed description of the vehicle. Whilst he was unable to recall the entire index mark he was able to state with certainty that the car was an 'S' reg.

Subsequent investigations through the PNC revealed that there were 426 owners of 'S' reg Ford Cortinas in the immediate surrounding area, all of whom would need to be interviewed. However, further inquiry revealed that the colour of the suspect's car was "Roman Bronze" which narrowed the quantity of registered keepers considerably.

During the offence Prime had exposed his face to the young girl, who gave a good description of him as well as describing his checked shirt. He also left a part fingerprint of high quality on the toilet cistern. The resultant "identikit" bore an uncanny resemblance to Prime. Eventually two detectives from Hereford CID, a DS Wilkes and WDC Miriam Rhodes arrived to question Prime about his ownership of the two-tone 'S' reg. Cortina which was parked in his drive outside. DS Wilkes also noticed that he was wearing the same style of checked shirt described by the victim of the assault.

Prime was aware that he had been identified as a prominent suspect and became extremely agitated when DC Wilkes asked him for his fingerprints, "purely for elimination." DC Wilkes and WDC Rhodes then made their leave but told him that they would return at around 6.00pm that evening to speak with Mrs. Prime. It was at that point that Prime decided to confess everything to his wife, who in turn persuaded him to give himself up to the Police.

The next day Prime was arrested for the offence and his car and house were searched. The police found 2,287 record cards containing the names and addresses of young girls, which were bagged and taken away as evidence, together with the black leather briefcase with the secret compartment.

On Wednesday 10th November 1982, Geoffrey Arthur Prime pleaded guilty to all charges; seven counts against the Official Secrets Act and three further counts against the Sexual Offences Act. Prime was sentenced to 35 years for High Treason plus a further three years for the sexual offences, and his name was placed on the sex offenders' register.

There is some evidence that Prime was a member of the Paedophile Information Exchange, a pro-paedophile activism group which used secret codes to communicate and which was being watched by the British government. There is also some conjecture that Prime was being blackmailed by the Russians, which is how they persuaded him to work as a translator at GCHQ – although that theory has never been proved.

On his release in 2001, a Home Office spokeswoman said that the Parole Board was satisfied that Prime no longer posed a threat to children, but that his name would remain on the sex offenders' register."

Steph put the document carefully back in the file and closed it gently, looking at Matt for some sort of reaction. 'So, what do you think?'

Matt gave her an appreciative nod. As far as he was concerned, Steph's perseverance in wading through Prime's file had absolutely paid off. Not only had she made the connection with the prime numbers, but she'd now identified a whole new line of enquiry. Steph was making a bigger contribution to the case than anybody else. 'I think it could be really significant. Like you said, all that stuff about GCHQ and surveillance systems was just too far fetched. This is much more credible. At last we've got some sort of explanation which might provide a connection between Richmond and Worsley.'

'Well, it's only a theory,' said Steph, looking pleased but still slightly confused, 'but if that is the connection, why was Hilary Russell ringing people at GCHQ and at the Foreign Office? If it's got nothing to do with spying or satellites, what does the murder of a couple of paedophiles have to do with the British government?'

Matt looked equally confused. 'I don't know. But given that's where Neil is right now I think we ought to ring him and let him know what we've found.'

Steph nodded. She couldn't have agreed more. She checked her watch as Matt pulled out his mobile phone and dialled Neil's number for the second time that morning. He half expected it to go straight into voicemail again but this time it was answered in a couple of seconds.

'Neil Ashton.'

Matt could hear the sounds of birds singing and what sounded like traffic in the distance. Neil was obviously outside somewhere. He sounded cheerful enough. 'Hi Neil, it's Matt. How are you doing? Where are you?'

'Hiya Matt. I'm sitting on a bench in St. James's Park. How's the research going?'

'It's going well actually. I think we may have found something. Have you seen Saxby yet?'

'Just finished, although not much help I'm afraid. He was a nice enough bloke, but he doesn't know anything. Just a contact name that Aunt Hilary was given. Someone who knew the next number that she was after.'

'Jean Pettipher's?'

'Exactly, although according to Saxby she's just a secretary. The person we need to speak to is someone by the name of Charles Buchanan.'

Matt scribbled the name down as Neil was speaking. Any information was worth following up. Steph looked over Matt's shoulder to see if she recognised what he was writing down, but it meant nothing to her. 'So what are you going to do next? Are you going to go and see him?'

'Absolutely. 'We've got his address and phone number so we're just about to ring him up and will try and see him this morning.'

Matt frowned at the other end of the phone, clearly confused by Neil's choice of words. 'We? I thought you were on your own. Is Chris with you?'

Neil couldn't help smiling to himself. 'Er… no. Actually it's somebody else. I'll put him on.' He passed the phone across to Garrick, who had been listening to one end of the conversation and who was grinning as he took the handset, imagining the reaction that he was going to get at the other end.

'Hello Matt. What the hell have you been playing at?'

Matt practically dropped the phone when he heard Garrick's voice. He was the last person he expected to be sitting on a park bench with Neil Ashton in the middle of London. How on earth did that happen? 'Sir? I thought you were on holiday?'

'I am. I'm being a London tourist today. Have you been discussing the details of a confidential police enquiry with a potential suspect?' Garrick was still grinning and could only imagine the goldfish impression that Matt was doing on the other end, trying to get his explanation out. 'Anyway, never mind all that now. I guess we've all got a bit of explaining to do, but it'll have to wait. What have you managed to find out?'

Matt breathed a sigh of relief. The last thing he wanted to do was try and explain how he had burgled his way into *Yew Tree Cottage* and how that had led to him telling Neil and Chris absolutely everything about the enquiry. By comparison, explaining the link to Geoffrey Prime was going to be a complete doddle. He kept it brief and straight to the point. 'We're certain that Hilary Russell was trying to speak to someone about Teleios and that there's a link between Teleios and Geoffrey Prime.'

'Anything else?' Matt could visualise Garrick on the other end of the phone, sitting on a park bench, writing everything down.

'It's possible that the link with Prime could be to do with the fact that he was a paedophile, rather than the fact that he was a spy.'

317

Garrick raised his eyebrows in surprise. 'Really? I didn't know Prime was a paedophile.'

'Neither did we. Steph made the connection about half an hour ago.'

'Good. Anything else?'

'There was a paedophile group which mentioned a government connection.' Matt nodded at Steph and clicked his fingers several times towards the file, indicating that he wanted her to get out the document so that he could refer to it. She passed it over to him in a matter of seconds. 'Yes, something called the *Paedophile Information Exchange*, which was an activist group, apparently watched by the British government.'

Garrick pulled a face. He'd never heard of it. 'Okay. Anything else?'

'No, I think that's it Sir.'

'Excellent. Thanks Matt. That sounds like good progress.'

'Will it be enough do you think?' asked Matt, conscious that much of what he'd given Garrick was largely supposition without any shred of evidence. The whole thing was built on nothing more than coincidences, hunches and intuition. All of which had put him way outside of his comfort zone.

Garrick looked at Neil who was sitting next to him and smiled. 'Don't worry Matt, it'll be enough. I've got an expert interrogator with me. A real professional. I'll keep you posted.'

THIRTY-EIGHT

It was a long time since Craven had received a round of applause, in fact he couldn't actually remember the last time people had stood up and clapped in celebration at something that he had done. Perhaps there was a presentation somewhere on some dim and distant training course, but failing that, it was probably a school play; a faint recollection of a brief and indifferent performance in a 6th form revue, too many years ago than he cared to remember. But as his foot connected with the cycle frame and he watched the lycra clad beanpole skid across the zebra crossing, the crowd of watching pedestrians erupted into a spontaneous and appreciative round of applause.

There was something about London cyclists which annoyed Craven intensely. The journey back from Little Venice had been straight-forward really, the Bakerloo line ran directly from Warwick Park to Westminster which meant that he didn't have to change tubes, and then it was just a quick walk up Great George Street to St. James's Park. London was always crammed full of tourists of course but it wasn't the traffic or the pedestrians that were the problem. As usual the roads were congested with cars and taxis and buses, and the pavements were crowded with too many people, especially at junctions where everybody was trying to cross – but overall people gave each other enough time and space and with a little bit of give and take, everybody got by. Everybody except for the cyclists that is.

Craven had never worked out whether it was something that had built up gradually over time or whether it was some new, overnight phenomena but either way, all of sudden, he had become aware that London cyclists no longer observed the highway code. In particular, they often rode the wrong way down one-way streets and seemed to totally ignore traffic lights, even if pedestrians were crossing under the direction of a green man. It wasn't the first time that a cyclist had nearly hit him on a zebra crossing, weaving through a crowd of startled and confused tourists, but today the beanpole in the lycra shorts and stupid helmet had actually gone through at speed, yelling obscenities at people to get out of the way. Craven timed his kick to perfection and caught the frame midway between the rear wheel and the saddle – the ideal point to spin the cycle over and send the rider smacking into the central kerb at high speed and with some force.

He didn't even bother to look round to see what damage he had caused as he crossed the road and went into the park, the sound of people clapping and cheering fading behind him. The bike was definitely crumpled and he reckoned that there was a decent chance that the guy had broken something. Either that or he was going to have a serious headache for the next couple of days. Craven wandered down the path towards the bridge and spotted Buchanan sitting on a bench near the central lake, reading a newspaper and waiting patiently for his arrival.

'Hello Charles, sorry I'm late.'

Buchanan looked up from his paper and gave him a hollow smile. If his manner was a little terse, it was because he was still smarting from their telephone exchange a couple of days earlier. He gestured towards the empty space beside him, indicating to Craven to take a seat.

'Why the park?' asked Craven, sitting down at the end of the bench and twisting round so that he could look at Buchanan properly. St. James's was busy with people and he quickly scanned around to make sure that none of them were too close to hear anything.

'I have a couple of unwanted visitors coming over.' replied Buchanan, folding up the newspaper and putting it to one side. 'Better if I'm not around.'

'Unwanted visitors?'

'DCI Garrick and Hilary Russell's nephew. They saw Adam Saxby earlier, pretending to be a couple of police officers.'

'They're working together?' Craven's voice was almost incredulous.

Buchanan pulled a face and shrugged. 'Looks like it. God knows how that happened.'

Craven shook his head in disbelief. It was always a possibility of course, after all they were all chasing the same clues. But he didn't really think that the useless wooden-top and the inquisitive nephew would actually end up working together. It was worrying to say the least. Coppers and journalists sharing information was not a good combination. 'Won't they just wait or come back later?'

Buchanan shook his head. 'No, I've arranged a welcome party for them. They won't be coming back in a hurry.'

Craven raised his eyebrows and smiled at Buchanan's turn of phrase. A welcome party didn't exactly do what it said on the tin. After a couple of hours with Buchanan's goons they wouldn't be going anywhere in a hurry. Not for a few days at least. 'Do they know anything?'

'Not really. They know Hilary made some phone calls before she died, but beyond that, not a lot. They're trying to work it out of course, but there's not much chance of that happening. Anyway, what did you want?'

'I've been to see Carlisle.'

'Good. How is he?''

'Talkative.'

Buchanan smiled ruefully to himself. He could just imagine the sort of exchange that had gone on between Craven and the Cabinet Secretary. They weren't exactly from the same side of the street. 'And what did he have to say?'

'Lots. But he said that he didn't know as much as you.'

'He knows most of it. You don't need to know anything else.'

'I could always go to the papers.'

Buchanan snorted in derision. 'I doubt it. Besides, they wouldn't touch it with a bargepole. Anyway, I'd have a D-Notice on it before they could even write it up.'

'I don't think a D-Notice is going to cut much ice in Paris or Berlin Charles. I'm sure the continentals would love to run the story...'

'I don't think so. They wouldn't take the risk.'

'...maybe the nephew could ghost-write it. I'm sure he'd be keen to see it published. I could always have a word with him...'

'You're bluffing.'

'...and then of course there's always the Internet. Nothing like the world-wide-web to get something into the pubic domain.'

'Like I said, you're bluffing.'

'Try me.'

The two of them stared at each other for a moment, an uneasy, hostile silence as they both waited for the other to break the Mexican stand-off.

'Don't try and play poker with me Craven. And don't try and hold a gun to my head.'

Craven took out a packet of cigarettes and lit one up, thumbing the Zippo lighter and snapping the lid shut in one, swift movement. 'You started this game Charles, not me. It's your call. And by the way, if I was holding a gun to your head, I wouldn't be able to shut you up.'

Buchanan looked across the park and let out a sigh. Craven was like a dog with a bone. He always was. He wasn't going to give up until he'd found out everything there was to know about Teleios – which meant that holding out on him was just delaying the inevitable. He thought through his options for a couple of seconds and then took a deep breath. There wasn't any point in trying to stonewall him any longer. He already knew most of it anyway. 'Okay, what do you want to know?'

'You know what I want. I want to know who killed Hilary Russell.'

'We've already had that conversation.'

'So?'

'So the answer is still the same. I don't know.'

Craven looked at him for a moment and held his gaze, trying to work out whether he was telling the truth. That was the trouble with Buchanan, the expression was always the same. You could never tell what hand he was playing. Buchanan stared back and said nothing, waiting for Craven to say something else or move on to the next question.

'Okay. Let's leave that for the moment. Tell me about Teleios. Tell me who they are.'

Buchanan raised his eyebrows in surprise. The Cabinet Secretary obviously had more backbone than he gave him credit for. 'Carlisle didn't give you the names then?'

'No. He was surprisingly resolute about that.'

Buchanan nodded in appreciation. 'Well for once I agree with him. I can't tell you the names either. Not under any circumstances.'

Craven took another drag on the cigarette, trying to decide whether it was worth pushing the point any further. 'You must be able to tell me something Charles. How many of them are there?'

Buchanan paused and thought about the question for a second. Maybe there wasn't any harm in divulging the numbers. It was hardly critical. It wasn't as if he was disclosing the names. Knowing how many there were wasn't going to affect anything. 'There are always twelve, although obviously two of them are now dead. They keep the number at a dozen. If one drops out they simply find a replacement.'

'And you know who they are?'

'Of course.'

'So why don't you arrest them?'

Buchanan took a deep breath. This was the bit that wasn't going to be easy. 'Because the country would never recover from the shock.'

Craven looked at him with disdain. 'They should be locked up. It doesn't matter what the reaction is going to be.'

'You don't understand. Teleios has been allowed to exist for over twenty years. It's too late to do anything now. There'd be an absolute riot.'

'Twenty years! Why the hell has it been allowed to go on for twenty years?' Craven took a final drag on the cigarette and stubbed it out viciously with his right foot.

Buchanan shook his head in frustration and then looked at his watch. It was nearly lunchtime and he knew this wasn't going to be a quick conversation. 'Okay. Let's start at the beginning. Did Carlisle mention something called the Paedophile Information Exchange?'

Craven nodded. 'Briefly, although he didn't say much about it.'

Buchanan took a deep breath. 'The Paedophile Information Exchange, or PIE as it was known, was a special interest group established in the 1970s to promote the views and rights of paedophiles. At the time their strategy was to develop a media campaign in order to attract attention to themselves. They believed that the only way that they could further their cause was to make paedophilia a real public issue.'

Craven raised his eyebrows in surprise. 'What, they actually put themselves in front of the cameras?'

Buchanan nodded. 'Absolutely. It's unthinkable today of course but I can remember their Chairman making an impassioned speech at an annual conference in Sheffield. It got a lot of publicity at the time and was all over the national press.'

'And people put up with it?'

'Yes they did. Society was more tolerant then. PIE set themselves up as a sort of academic, intellectual, lobbying group who wanted to challenge conventional thinking on sexual equality. At one point they submitted proposals to a Home Office Criminal Law Revision Committee on the age of consent. They produced a lengthy research document with clinical evidence to support their view that it should be abolished.'

Craven blinked at Buchanan in disbelief. 'Abolished? What, no mandatory age at all? You're kidding?'

Buchanan shook his head. 'Their view was that there should be a distinction between consensual sex and child abuse, and that the criminal law should concern itself only with sexual activities to which consent wasn't given. Needless to say, it was revolutionary at the time.'

'Revolutionary? It's obscene! Why weren't they arrested?' Craven was starting to get agitated at Buchanan's cool and dispassionate summary of events.

'They weren't arrested because they hadn't done anything wrong. They were expressing a point of view. It was an intellectual argument. We live in a democracy Craven, in case you hadn't noticed. You can't lock people up just because you disagree with their views.'

'How can you defend not having an age of consent? It's ridiculous!'

Buchanan shrugged his shoulders. 'Their view was that the acts themselves harmed no one and that the emotional and psychological harm came from the "after the fact" intervention from police and social workers, who tried to artificially create a "victim" and a "perpetrator" where none actually existed. Their belief was that as a society, we had created a child abuse industry which took children who had enjoyed pleasurable and consensual sexual experiences, and then traumatised them in an attempt to convince them that what they had done was wrong.'

Craven screwed his face up in disgust. 'That's just psychobabble Charles. You can't defend not having an age of consent. It's abhorrent.'

'I'm not trying to defend it, I'm just telling you that was their view. What you've got to remember is that paedophiles believe that it is perfectly acceptable to have sex with children and that it's the rest of us who are completely out of step. They view their preferences as a sexual orientation, not a psychological disorder. And they certainly view the criminalisation of paedophilia in the same way that we now view the criminalisation of homosexuality.'

'That's bollocks.'

Buchanan cringed at Craven's lack of vocabulary. 'They also believe that there is no possibility of society ever having an intelligent and reasoned debate on the issue because of the irrational and hysterical reaction to the subject. *Paedhysteria* is the fashionable term I think.'

'*Paedhysteria?*'

'Ask any *Daily Mail* reader. Paedophiles, gypsies, illegal immigrants. Probably in that order.'

'You sound as if you're defending them.' Craven was starting to feel uncomfortable with the tone of Buchanan's response.

Buchanan gave him a withering look across the length of the park bench. 'I'm not defending them at all. I'm simply telling you what happened. PIE was set up to campaign for the acceptance and understanding of paedophilia by producing thought provoking and controversial documents. If you're not able to have this conversation objectively I'll go back to the office. I didn't particularly want to have this conversation at all.'

Craven held his hands up in apology. 'I'm sorry Charles. Go on, what happened next?'

Buchanan maintained the withering look for another couple of seconds and then took another deep breath. 'PIE eventually disbanded in the 1980s, 1984 I think. Their original objective to legalise child pornography and to relax the age of consent became unachievable. Society was changing and there was increasing public disapproval of paedophilia, which meant that there was more stringent legislation and stronger criminal penalties. Over time the focus of the group changed. Its activities extended to giving advice and support to members who wanted it, and to providing a network for paedophiles to contact one another. Inevitably, some of its members found themselves on the wrong side of the law.'

'And presumably you were monitoring them all of the time?'

'Of course. Some of them were using secret codes to communicate but there was a small team at GCHQ who worked on it almost full-time.'

'Including Guy Daniels I presume?'

'Exactly, although it has to be said a lot of their activities were in the public domain anyway. The whole point of PIE was to bring the issue of paedophilia out into the open in an attempt to influence public opinion and stimulate an informed debate. What they wanted to achieve was pro-paedophile status as a valid political or civil rights movement. They had a whole range of articles and publications as well as a regular magazine.'

Craven shook his head again in disbelief. 'It's unbelievable. You just couldn't imagine that happening today.'

'Quite. Anyway, there was a full scale investigation towards the end of the 1970s and there were regular prosecutions after that, mostly for possession of child pornography or for magazine advertisements which were deemed to incite indecent contact between adults and children. The group eventually closed down in 1984.'

'And Teleios?'

'Teleios was borne out of PIE. The group formally disbanded but of course all that really happened was that it went underground. The movement had lost the political battle, but some of the members wanted to continue the network arrangements, mainly to exchange material.'

Craven screwed his face up in disgust. 'Child pornography you mean.'

'Exactly. Teleios was a small, exclusive and very private club. No more than a dozen members, all of whom had something in common; something in addition to the fact that they were paedophiles.'

Craven gave him another look, part disgust, part disbelief. 'It doesn't matter how important they are Charles, you can't have one rule for society and another rule for the privileged few.'

Buchanan shook his head. 'It was nothing to do with having separate rules, it went way beyond that. These people were different. They were so famous, so powerful, so influential in their own right, that none of them could afford to get caught. But more importantly, neither could we. We just couldn't take the risk that any of them would be identified. Teleios goes to the very heart of the establishment – and I don't just mean the government. The reaction would be catastrophic. The public would lose faith in the whole system.'

Craven let out a sigh and dropped his head towards the ground. He was getting fed up with this. Again, he looked up and stared at Buchanan. 'I still don't understand. Who the hell is going to get worked up because Stuart Richmond is a paedophile? It doesn't make sense.'

Buchanan waved a hand dismissively. 'Richmond was a mistake, they should never have let him in. The others are different. I keep telling you, the implications are unimaginable.'

'Like who for instance?'

Buchanan shook his head again. 'I can't tell you. Trust me, it's better for you not to know.'

Craven frowned and looked at him, still confused at Buchanan's explanation. 'Give me an example Charles. It just doesn't make sense. Not based on Stuart Richmond.'

'Well, you already know about Worsley. He was one of the most senior judges in the country.'

Craven pulled a face, unimpressed. 'Most people have never heard of him.'

Buchanan shook his head in frustration. He was revealing more than he intended, but he knew that there was no alternative. 'Okay. One of them is a member of the cabinet.'

Again, Craven pulled a face, the sarcasm in his voice confirming what he thought of Buchanan's disclosure. 'Forgive me if I don't look too surprised at the fact that there's a senior politician in the cabinet who's sexually deviant.'

Buchanan took another deep breath. He'd already passed the point of no return. 'Okay, one of them is a Chief Constable…'

'You're joking…'

'…and one of them is a member of the Royal family.'

'Jesus!'

'Exactly. The public's faith in the monarchy, not to mention the police force, is fragile enough as it is. This could destroy it forever.'

'A minor royal or someone in the immediate family?'

Buchanan ignored the follow-up question. 'You see the point. Cabinet minister, senior judge, chief constable, royal family. It's a conspiracy that's been condoned at the highest level for over twenty years. Trust me, people would be on the streets. The repercussions are unthinkable.'

Craven suddenly jumped to his feet and raised his voice, oblivious to the two or three tourists who were wandering along the path and were within earshot. 'But they're paedophiles Charles. They're bloody nonces. They're a risk to children. You can't let it continue. It doesn't matter who they are, it's appalling!'

'Sit down and keep your voice down for god's sake!' Buchanan gave him a murderous look that Craven had only seen two or three times before. 'Do you really think that I would allow it to continue if there was a risk to children? There's no evidence of any child abuse, in fact there's no evidence of any contact with children at all. All they do is look at photographs. They don't present a risk to anyone.'

Craven paced up and down several times before reluctantly sitting back down. He stared venomously at a couple of Americans who had wandered past in front of him, their accents, a loud, southern drawl jarring on his nerves. The park was usually busy of course, it was too much of a tourist attraction to be anything else, but the late, autumnal sunshine was always guaranteed to bring them out in their droves. Craven didn't have much time for tourists. Life was generally a lot easier when they weren't around. They tended to get in the way. Some of them were harmless perhaps, but he certainly didn't have any time for Americans. They didn't travel well. Loud, brash, camera-snapping philistines, more intent on taking a photograph or buying a T-shirt than actually enjoying the experience. He pulled out the packet of cigarettes again and lit another one, tilting his head back to blow the smoke up into the air. 'There's no excuse Charles, child pornography is still illegal.'

'Yes it is – but like I say, all they're doing is looking at photographs. They're not actually hurting anybody.'

Craven practically exploded again. 'How can you say that! If it wasn't for people like them, there wouldn't be any photographs in the first place!'

'What I mean is, the group is totally passive. They get sexual gratification from looking at pictures of adolescent girls. That doesn't make them child abusers and it doesn't mean they are a danger to the public.'

'It's outrageous! They're sick. They should be locked up.'

Buchanan took a deep breath. 'Have you ever been to the National Gallery?'

Craven took another long drag on the cigarette. 'Yes, of course I have. Why?'

Do you know how many pictures there are of naked children there?'

'Don't be ridiculous, that's different.'

'Why, because it's art?'

'No, because they're not real children.'

'Actually, I suspect many of them were real children.'

Craven flicked the ash off the cigarette several times in irritation. 'You know what I mean. They're pictures, paintings – not photographs.'

'Oh, so if someone made a cartoon of a middle aged man having sex with a thirteen year old girl that would be okay would it? – on the basis that they're not real people.'

'No of course it wouldn't. It's obscene.'

'Why? Nobody's getting hurt, it's just a cartoon.'

'It doesn't matter, it's vile. Besides, it makes it look as though it's acceptable.'

'So where would you draw the line?'

'I wouldn't draw it anywhere.'

'What about literature then? Is it okay to write about it? How about Nabokov? Is that literature or is it pornography?'

Craven looked at Buchanan and said nothing. *Lolita* was one of the finest books that he'd ever read.

'Come on Craven, tell me what you think. We could go on the internet now and in half an hour find photos of every kind of sexual depravity imaginable; rape, beastiality, necrophilia, S&M. Whatever you think about the subject matter, looking at pictures of them isn't illegal. Why is paedophilia so different?'

Craven continued looking at Buchanan, still uncertain as to what to say. It wasn't a logical argument that he wanted, it was an emotional one. How could anyone possibly defend it?

Buchanan snorted in frustration at Craven's refusal to get into a debate. 'Well, I don't think we need to explore the meaning of p*aedhysteria* any further do we?'

'What do you mean?'

'Do you know how many men enter the teaching profession each year to teach in infant schools?'

'No idea.'

The female to male ratio is about twenty to one. Infant and primary schools are desperate for more men to join the profession. Do you know why they don't?'

'The pay?'

Buchanan gave him a scathing look. 'Don't piss me about Craven, I'm not in the mood to play games.'

Craven held his hands up. 'Okay, I think I get the point.'

'Good. It's exactly the same reason why a grandfather can't give his granddaughter a bath anymore, no matter how young she is. Or why an uncle will no longer put his niece on his lap and read her a story, or give her a cuddle. Parents can't even take photographs of their own kids at a swimming pool these days for fear of accusations from other parents. *Paedhysteria*. It's as if even the most innocent relationship between a grown-up and a child is no longer allowed.'

'That's different. There's nothing innocent about Teleios.'

'They look at photographs Craven. That's all they do.'

'It's not a victimless crime. Don't try and make out that it is.'

'Do you know that in Reading last weekend, a young man was waiting at a bus stop with his girlfriend at about midnight and two thugs, fuelled on premium lager and high strength skunk launched an unprovoked attack on him and repeatedly kicked his head as if it was a football until he was unconscious. The victim has lost the sight in one eye and is likely to have a speech impediment for the rest of his life. The two thugs have been charged with actual bodily harm.'

Craven took another drag on the cigarette, using the pause to try and take some of the heat out of the discussion. 'So?'

'So, at about the same time about a mile down the road, a senior lecturer at the university was arrested for downloading indecent images of children. In the privacy of his own home he sat at his computer and looked at pictures on the Internet and then saved them onto the hard drive of his computer. He wasn't sending them onto anybody else or encouraging anyone else to look at them, he was just saving them for his own personal use.'

'So?'

'So which of them do you think has committed the more heinous crime?'

'It's not a competition is it? They're both serious offences.'

'Okay, so which of them do you think will get the more extreme reaction from the local community when their names are reported in the local paper…?'

Craven said nothing for a moment.

'… or which of them will get the longer prison sentence, or the worst treatment from other prisoners?'

'What's the point you're making Charles?'

'The point I'm making is that a large percentage of paedophiles never act on their sexual feelings and don't present any risk to society. And likewise, many sex offenders against minors are not actually paedophiles. The people who belong to Teleios are harmless. We've been monitoring them for years.'

'You can't condone it Charles, not under any circumstances.'

'I'm not condoning it, I'm simply saying that there isn't any risk, which is why it's been allowed to continue. There are a lot worse crimes in the world than looking at a photograph that someone else has taken. Looking at a photograph of the holocaust doesn't mean that you believe in genocide. The crime is committed by the people that were there – not by the people who look at it afterwards.'

Craven took a final drag on the cigarette and then stubbed it out on the path in front of him. There was no point in arguing with Buchanan – the two of them obviously had completely different views on the subject. And there was certainly no point in waiting for him to disclose the names. 'So, what happens next?'

Buchanan picked up his newspaper as if he was about to go, indicating that the conversation was coming to an end. 'Nothing happens next, the case is closed. The laptop's been recovered and the risk of any leak died with Colley. Draw a line under it Craven. This time next week you'll be working on something else.'

'But Colley didn't murder Hilary Russell did he? He might have killed Richmond and Worsley but he didn't murder Hilary. He probably never even knew her.'

Buchanan hesitated, not sure whether to agree with Craven's assertion or not. 'Maybe he did, maybe he didn't. I suspect we'll never know. The important thing is that Teleios is safe. Trust me Craven, things will quieten down now. There won't be any more incidents and in a couple of weeks, everyone will have forgotten about Teleios and everyone will have moved on. You need to do the same.'

Craven looked absent-mindedly across the park at the crowds of people; groups of tourists wandering along the paths and parents and children playing innocently in the sunshine. 'Are you sure about that Charles? No more incidents?'

Buchanan gave him a reassuring smile. 'Of course I'm sure. Trust me, the case is closed. Nothing else is going to happen.'

THIRTY-NINE

The diocese of Oxford was first established by an act of parliament in 1542 when Henry VIII, acting as the head of the church in England created six new dioceses throughout the kingdom, mostly out of the spoils of the suppressed monasteries. This intervention by Henry saw a new see located at Osney in Oxfordshire before it was moved to its present location in the city of Oxford in 1546, the seat being sited at the Cathedral Church of Christ, which uniquely among English dioceses was also the chapel of Christ Church College, Oxford.

Dr. William Reid, the current Bishop of Oxford was a busy man. The modern day diocese covered the counties of Oxfordshire, Berkshire and Buckinghamshire with parishes also in Bedfordshire, Gloucestershire, Hampshire, Hertfordshire and Warwickshire. In fact, the Oxford diocese was the fourth most populous bishopric in the Church of England and had by far the largest number of parishes and also the most church buildings of any district, the majority of which were Grade I or II listed. All of which meant that Dr. Reid was by habit an early riser, invariably wanting to get a head start on trying to fit all of his wide-ranging responsibilities for ministry, worship, church estates and pastoral re-organisation into what was always a busy schedule.

The Bishop's formal residence was the Diocesan Church House in Oxford but Dr. Reid had always been an independent man, both in thinking and in action, and some years ago had taken the decision to buy his own property, a small but quintessential stone cottage in the historic market town of Woodstock, some eight miles north-west of Oxford. The purchase had originally been made as an investment, a prudent piece of long-term planning designed to ensure his long and comfortable retirement, self-sufficient from the governance and constraints of the church. But much to his surprise and satisfaction, it also offered a number of shorter-term advantages, not least the opportunity for seclusion and anonymity; a quiet and peaceful refuge away from the pressures and demands of his official role.

There was something about the history of the town that had always appealed to Dr. Reid. Before the Norman Conquest, when the Wychwood Forest stretched from the Cotswolds all the way to London, English Kings had kept royal hunting lodges in Woodstock, its name meaning "a clearing in the woods." King Alfred was reputed to have stayed there in 890 and King Ethelred the Unready was said to have held a council in the town, suggesting that by the eleventh century its size and importance had grown fit to accommodate a King.

The Domesday Book described "Wodestock" as a royal forest and by 1179, when Henry II gave the town a Royal charter the market was firmly established. It was at Woodstock that Henry courted Rosamund Clifford and where, according to common folklore, Eleanor of Aquitaine discovered the affair and ultimately poisoned the Fair Rosamund. Edward, the elder, son of Edward III and apparent heir to the throne was born in Woodstock Manor in 1330 and Queen Elizabeth I, then Princess Elizabeth, was kept a prisoner in the gatehouse of Woodstock Manor in 1554 whilst she was under suspicion of colluding with traitors, the Manor itself by then being too dilapidated to house her.

Glove-making was once Woodstock's chief industry, but the town now prospered more from the thousands of tourists who flocked each year to visit Blenheim Palace, the impressive stately home designed by Sir John Vanbrugh in heavy Italio-Corinthian style and given in gratitude to John Churchill, 1st Duke of Marlborough, in recognition of his victory over the French and Bavarians at Blenheim in 1704. The deer park surrounding the house was landscaped by "Capability" Brown and Sir Winston Churchill, who was born at Blenheim Palace in 1874 was buried in nearby Blaydon churchyard.

Florence Cottage was situated in Park Street, a hundred yards or so from the Parish Church of St Mary Magdalene and only two or three doors down from Chaucer's House, once the home of Geoffrey Chaucer, the English poet. Fred Solly had lived in Woodstock all his life, man and boy, inheriting the cottage from his parents when his mother finally passed away, shortly before her eighty-seventh birthday. And whilst Dr. Reid had only been a neighbour for just over three years, Fred knew instinctively by mid morning that something was wrong. The curtains of Mill House were never closed during the day and there'd been no sight or sound of the good Bishop since the previous evening. Usually, he was up with the lark, buying a paper from the newsagent at the bottom of the High Street, often stopping to get some bread or milk on the way back. But not today. Dr. Reid's car was still parked on the road outside, but there was no sign of him at all.

Fred bent down and peered through the letter box, trying to see if there were any signs of life, but everything was still and quiet, all he could see was the narrow hall, spartan and carpeted in an oatmeal twist, and then the first few steps of the stairs at the end of the hall, heading straight up in front of him. He'd already been round the back and had let himself into the small courtyard garden, hoping to peer through the rear windows to try and catch a glimpse of anything that might explain the situation – but the dining room curtains were also closed and even the roller-blind on the kitchen window had been pulled down. Fred shouted through the letter box a couple of times but by now he knew it was pointless. Something was definitely wrong and it was time to call the police.

Woodstock police station was on the Hensington Road and luckily, it was open on a Monday for three hours, from ten until one o'clock. Small rural stations were only manned part-time, which meant that if anything happened outside of opening hours, the public had to ring the station in Oxford or even the one at Cowley, both of which were miles away. *Not much use in an emergency,* thought Fred as he checked the times in the local telephone directory and started to dial the number. It also made him wonder what on earth he was paying council tax for these days. Even the bin men only came once a fortnight now. In the event it took about forty minutes for PC Lamb to finish whatever he was dealing with at the station and to cycle the short distance across the main road and then up Market Street, which led straight into Park Street. Fred was waiting patiently on the front door step as the full might of the local police force pulled up on his bike and stood it carefully against the wall. 'Morning Fred, how are you today?'

'Fine thanks Toby,' replied Fred. You alright?'

'Not bad, thanks,' replied PC Lamb, taking off his cycle clips and slipping them in his pocket. 'Now then, what's all this about Dr. Reid?'

The pair of them had a brief conversation on the front doorstep and then Toby went through exactly the same process that Fred had gone through before, only in reverse order; peering through the letter box, banging on the large, heavy, black door knocker, ringing the front door bell and then finally going round the back of the house to try the back door and look through the kitchen window.

'Like I said, I've tried all this already,' said Fred, starting to get impatient. 'Maybe he's collapsed or something.'

PC Lamb rubbed the stubble on his chin and tried to peer through a gap in the curtains again, but it was too small to really see anything. 'Mmm, I don't like the look of this Fred, I think I'm going to have to break in. You sure you haven't seen him this morning?'

'Of course I'm sure,' replied Fred indignantly, 'I wouldn't have called you out if I'd seen him would I?'

'Spose not. I just don't want to start smashing his back window if he was up and out extra early this morning. Maybe you didn't see him go. Maybe he just forgot to draw the curtains.'

Fred pulled a face, unimpressed at Toby's dithering. He was like that even when he was a kid. The pair of them had known each other for nigh on fifty years. 'Of course he didn't forget to draw the curtains. Anyway, his car's still parked outside. There's something wrong here, I know there is. I'll smash the window if you're that worried about it.'

PC Lamb gave Fred a disapproving look, just to remind him who was in charge and then took out his baton. 'Okay, stand back then. Cover your eyes.'

Fred stepped back a couple of paces and watched Toby turn his back on the kitchen window and then tap it several times in reverse with his baton. The glass was old, it might even have been original, and it shattered fairly easily, splintering into half a dozen large, jagged pieces. It took him a while to carefully knock out all the fragments and then reach through the window to undo the catch, which was half-way up, where the two sash frames met. PC Lamb was no longer a young man, so it took him a good couple of minutes to lift up the bottom frame and then climb gingerly through the window, taking care to lift up the roller-blind which was in the way. As soon as he was inside he found a bunch of keys in one of the kitchen drawers and unlocked the back door. 'You'd better come in Fred. I might need a witness.'

Fred nodded and walked into the kitchen, quickly looking around to see if anything looked unusual. Everything looked spick and span, exactly as it always did. There was a cup and saucer on the draining-board and a half empty packet of biscuits on one of the worktops, but otherwise, everything was neat and tidy. Almost as if no-one was living there.

'We'd better check all the rooms,' said Toby, pushing the door on the left which led into the dining room. 'Like you say, he might have collapsed. He might still be upstairs…' He stopped in mid sentence and also in mid stride as he walked into the dining room and saw the Bishop of Oxford, fully robed and crucified to the wall, two large nine-inch nails drilled through the palms of each hand. A third nail had been driven through his throat, pinning his head firmly to the wall. 'Bloody hell…'

Fred was walking immediately behind him and bumped into Toby's back as he stopped abruptly and without warning. He looked straight over Toby's shoulder, noticing the blood first of all, the sheer volume of which made it

334

look as though someone had filled buckets with the stuff and literally thrown it around the room.

'Don't touch anything Fred,' ordered Toby, suddenly regaining his composure and remembering to follow procedure. 'I'll have to ring Oxford.'

Fred stepped to one side for a moment, partly to let Toby move back into the kitchen to make the call and partly to get a better look at Dr. Reid. The Bishop's eyes were open and his face seemed to have frozen in an expression of absolute pain and terror. This was not a man at peace. Fred quickly scanned around the room and noticed the word "Teleios" sprayed on the far wall in bright red letters. He wondered for a moment whether it was written in blood, but then he realised that it must have been sprayed in paint, the colour was slightly different from the blood that was splattered everywhere else. In the corner of the room was a small desk and chair. There was a telephone and a large computer monitor on top of the desk, which was still on, a selection of brightly coloured fish swimming backwards and forwards in an aquarium.

'Come on Fred, we'd better wait outside.' Toby was standing right behind him and getting nervous about them contaminating the murder scene.

'What do you make of that then?' asked Fred, pointing to the word "Teleios" and ignoring Toby's request to leave the room.

PC Lamb looked at the painted wall and frowned, obviously none the wiser. 'No idea. Never heard of it.'

'There's a computer over there,' added Fred, pointing into the other corner. 'It's still on. That's a screensaver.'

'How do you know that?' asked Toby, looking at the fish swimming backwards and forwards. The thing was almost lifelike.

'My niece has got one just the same. We ought to see what's on the computer.'

'We ought not to touch anything and get out of here,' replied Toby. 'SOCO will be here in a few minutes. Come on, let's wait outside.'

'Don't you want to know what's on the screen? It might be significant.'

'Not really. Come on. We shouldn't be in here.'

Fred threw him a frustrated look. 'What's the matter with you Toby? Come on, give me a pencil or something and I'll just tap one of the keys. It won't affect anything.'

Toby gave him a sideways look in return. Fred always was a mischievous bugger. He could still remember the pair of them when they were kids, getting caught scrumping in old Mrs. Wilson's garden which backed onto the school playing field, him stuck half-way up a pear tree with nowhere to hide and Fred, standing at the bottom with his pockets stuffed full of Sweet Williams. Mrs. Wilson had gone absolutely mad and marched the pair of them back to the school and straight into the Headmaster's office. Toby smiled to himself as he remembered him and Fred waiting in the outer office whilst old Mrs. Wilson was in with Mr. Coulston, giving him what for about how the children at St. Phillips weren't supervised properly anymore.

All Toby could think about was the fact that they were going to get caned but Fred, mischievous as ever, had decided to get his retaliation in first. He'd found a couple of hole punches on the Secretary's desk, a two-hole punch which she used most of the time and a big, four-hole punch that was obviously for special folders. Fred took the back off both of them and then emptied the contents into a large, empty ash-tray which was also on the desk. Toby then watched in disbelief as Fred went over to the hat stand, opened up Mr. Coulston's black umbrella and emptied the contents of the ashtray into the middle of it. 'That'll sort him out,' Fred had said, closing up the umbrella and putting it carefully back in place.

The pair of them each received four strokes of the cane, the pain and ignominy of which Toby could still remember – but even he had to admit that it was almost worth it to witness Mr. Coulston about three weeks later, walking out of school one October lunchtime with Miss Frances, the snooty, stuck-up English teacher, and opening his umbrella on the front porch, the pair of them absolutely covered in thousands of snow-like paper dots. It still made him chuckle after all these years.

Go on then,' said Toby, taking a biro out of his top pocket and passing it over to Fred, 'but be quick about it. And mind you don't touch anything with your fingers.'

Fred gave Toby a playful grin and then stepped forward a couple of paces and stabbed the top of the biro onto the enter key on the right-hand side of the keyboard. The aquarium full of brightly coloured fish disappeared in an instant to reveal a coloured photograph which filled the full size of the screen. Fred's cheeky smile disappeared in the same instant, immediately replaced by a mixture of shock and confusion. 'Bloody hell Toby, that doesn't look good.'

Toby was also looking at the screen with a mixture of shock and disgust. 'No it doesn't. Come on, let's get out of here. Let's go and wait outside.'

FORTY

David Hutton put the phone down and leant slowly back into his chair, holding his hands together in a prayer like pose as he reflected on what he had just heard. Things were starting to unravel faster than he'd ever imagined. Years of guarded anonymity were coming to an end and the whole network looked as though it was going to implode within a matter of days. The prospect was nerve-racking to say the least. He glanced at his diary again which stared back at him from the computer screen, and then quickly checked his watch. It was nearly 3.30 which meant that the car was probably already outside, the engine running and the driver waiting patiently, expecting the Chief Constable to be ready and punctual as he always was.

Hutton leant forward and clicked the mouse to close down the computer. The conference was a bloody nuisance and the timing couldn't have been worse. The whole situation was fast running out of control. Just when he needed to be around and alive to everything that was going on, he was going to be cut-off from the outside world for the next 48 hours, stuck behind some medieval moat and an impregnable drawbridge. The whole thing was a bloody nightmare. He wondered momentarily whether he could get out if it, but he let the thought pass almost as soon as it entered his head. It was nonsense of course. They were all in the same boat. Everybody was busy; everyone had a gold-plated excuse not to attend if they really wanted to. Besides, he was hosting the bloody thing. He was the one person who absolutely had to be there.

Hutton tidied up the last few papers on his desk and then locked the drawers, trying to work out whether he had any other options as he put the keys in his briefcase. He couldn't think of any. God only knew what was going to happen over the next couple of days but all he could do was carry on as normal and let events run their course. He didn't have any choice. As he picked up the briefcase to go, he took out the slim, coloured folder which was hidden discretely in the middle of a pile of papers, wedged neatly at the back of the case. He pulled out the top sheet and looked at the carefully typed list of names, Richmond's and Worsley's already struck-out with a thin red line. It was stupid really, writing them down and then crossing them off, but it was the habit of an introvert. Neat and tidy. Everything labelled, everything in its place. He picked up a red pen. It had to be exactly the same colour red of course, and then he drew a line through Dr. Reid's name. Victim number three. Not a casual, wavy line drawn by freehand but a clean, straight line drawn with a ruler which, as always, sat at a perfect right-angle on the edge of his desk.

'David – the car's waiting downstairs…'

Hutton looked up startled as his secretary poked her head around the door, giving him an efficient and impatient smile. He put the file back into the briefcase and nodded back to her, indicating that he was about to leave. Leaving the driver waiting was neither here nor there. Getting on the wrong side of his secretary was another thing altogether. Barbara Marshall was intimidation personified. Come to think of it, he was already working behind an impregnable drawbridge…

'…and I've got Chief Superintendent Anderson on the line. Do you want to take it or shall I get rid of him?'

Hutton glanced at his watch again. He had plenty of time. Most of them wouldn't be arriving until after five o'clock. 'No, I'll take it, put him through.'

Barbara nodded as she reversed out of the door and then Hutton waited a couple of seconds for the phone to buzz before picking up the receiver. 'Alistair, what can I do for you?'

'I was just ringing to check that you'd heard the latest.'

'The Bishop of Oxford? Yes, I've just had a phone call.'

Anderson's voice sounded surprised and almost disappointed, as if he'd wanted to be the first to let the Chief Constable know. 'Oh, I didn't realise you already knew. It's not good news.'

'Obviously. It's the fifth murder in under two weeks.'

Anderson hesitated. This wasn't a conversation that he was looking forward to. 'That's not what I meant. He was killed in the last 24 hours…'

'Yes, I know.'

'…and by the same person. It's the same signature as Richmond and Worsley. It means that Colley wasn't our man. You know what that means?'

'Yes, I think so.'

'It means we've got to re-examine every assumption that we've made so far and go right back to the beginning again. The team are absolutely on the floor.'

'Do the press know yet?' Hutton as ever had slipped effortlessly into politician mode, ignoring the details of the case and thinking about the messaging and the media repercussion that was bound to follow.

'No, but we'll have to let them know soon. It won't be long before it starts to leak.'

Hutton checked his watch again for the umpteenth time. 'Listen Alistair, I'm sorry but I've got to go. I'm going to be at Leeds Castle for a couple of days, which means I'm going to be out of circulation. I'll have my mobile with me, but switched off most of the time. I'll pick up messages when I can.'

'Actually, I wanted a quick word about something else,' replied Anderson, his voice suddenly more urgent. He needed to catch Hutton before he disappeared.

'Go on.'

'DCI Garrick.'

'What about him?'

'I think we ought to get him back.'

Hutton pulled a face. Getting Garrick back on the case was the last thing he wanted. 'Why would you want to do that?'

Anderson shook his head in frustration at the other end of the phone. Wasn't it bloody obvious? 'Like I said, the team are struggling. They respect Garrick. Plus he's an extra pair of hands. We need all the help we can get.'

'I thought we agreed, we need to give Fowler a clear run at things. Give him a chance to get the team onside.'

'I'm not sure we've got time for that. He's not made much of an impression so far.'

'Well he won't make any impression at all if Garrick comes back. Nobody will take any notice of him.'

'That's fine by me.'

Hutton stood up straight, adopting the position of someone about to make a final decision. 'It's out of the question. We agreed that Fowler would head this up and we need to give him the space to get on with it.'

'But it doesn't make sense. Garrick is a much better officer. It feels like we've downgraded the enquiry – not stepped it up a gear.' Anderson was starting to sound more and more frustrated. He'd seen some bad decisions in his time but this was ridiculous.

'I don't think you're being fair Alistair, or objective. Fowler's a good man. Give him a couple of days and he'll be fine. Besides, wasn't it Garrick who led us up the wrong path chasing Colley?'

'Well, anybody would have reached that conclusion. I don't think you can …'

'And how much time have we wasted chasing the wrong suspect?' interrupted Hutton, sensing that he'd found a chink in Anderson's argument and that there was an opportunity to close off the discussion.

'I'm not sure anything's been wasted…'

'And how many people have been murdered by the real suspect whilst you've been chasing the wrong man?'

Anderson fell silent on the other end of the phone. He always knew it was going to be difficult to get the Chief Constable to change his mind but suddenly he realised it was hopeless. It just wasn't going to happen.

Hutton nodded again at Barbara as she poked her head around the door for a second time, mouthing 'You need to go now!' and tapping her forefinger urgently at her wristwatch. 'Like I said Alistair, it's out of the question. Garrick's on paid leave and in my view that's the best place for him. Besides, he's probably lying on a beach somewhere enjoying himself. You'd probably struggle to get him back.'

Anderson literally bristled with indignation. 'I think I know John Garrick better than that. He'll be itching to get back to work.'

'Well, it's not an option. Leave Garrick where he is. And that's not a suggestion by the way. It's an order.'

Hutton put the phone down and took one last glance around the office before he left. Everything was neat and tidy and securely locked, exactly the way he liked it. And Barbara would make sure that it wasn't disturbed and remained exactly that way for when he got back. As he stood in the doorway and gazed across the room, for the first time he felt strangely composed. The conference couldn't have come at a worse time, but maybe in some bizarre way it was the best place to be. The next 48 hours were going to be critical. He smiled ruefully at the irony of the situation. Despite all the advances in technology and all the developments in sophisticated defence and surveillance systems, the absolute, highest level of security that they could arrange was a 12th century Norman castle. Maybe it was for the best. Teleios was about to implode. There were nine more names and any one of them was potentially the next victim. Except of course he knew better than that. Hutton wasn't in any doubt at all. He knew exactly who was going to be next.

FORTY-ONE

The 17.12 from Charing Cross to Ashford International was a regular commuter train, a long, snaking procession of twelve, filthy-dirty coaches which crawled noisily out of London and then made their slow and overcrowded journey back to Kent. Craven had walked down to the front of the platform and had managed to get himself a table seat next to the window, settling himself down for what he hoped was going to be an hour or so of uninterrupted thinking time. Time to decide what he was going to do next. Certainly the free paper that he'd picked up on the station concourse wasn't going to take very long to read; the thing was a complete rag.

A seemingly endless succession of people got into the carriage until eventually, the last few passengers squeezed themselves into the central standing area and then the doors closed, signalling that they were about to leave. Craven folded up the paper and leant back into his seat, closing his eyes and starting to process everything that Buchanan had said. Maybe he was right. Perhaps it was time to draw a line under everything and move on. Time to let go. After all, nothing he could do now was going to bring back Hilary Russell.

The train heaved its way through London Bridge and then headed on towards Sevenoaks, a thirty minute or so journey before the first tranche of passengers would spill out onto the platform, checking their Blackberrys for latest emails or ringing their loved ones to let them know that they were nearly home. Craven folded his arms and leant his head against the window, the movement of the carriage making him feel drowsy. It had been a long and eventful day and he suddenly realised how tired he was. He was only going back to Kent to pick up the car, but on reflection, maybe driving all the way up to London afterwards wasn't such a good idea. Perhaps one more night at *The Moon & Falcon* was a more sensible option. In fact, maybe it was just what he needed. He smiled to himself as a picture of Sophie drifted into his mind, her naked body, arched and free and reaching higher...

He opened his eyes for one last glimpse around the carriage before submitting to the hypnotic rhythm of the train, happy to switch off and doze for part of the journey. Craven never passed up the opportunity to eat or sleep – years of experience had taught him that you never knew when the next chance would come along. As he drifted off he was oblivious to the fact that three or four carriages back, Garrick and Neil were sitting opposite each other in silence, also making their way home and also struggling to keep awake after a long and tiring day.

*

Neil stared out of the window, much as he had done over a week before, the grey, urban sprawl slowly changing to green, Kentish fields. It had been one hell of a day. A real rollercoaster. What had started optimistically with Adam Saxby had ended abruptly and violently in the basement of Carlton Gardens, the two of them suddenly separated and both of them totally out of their depth. Garrick in one room and Neil in another. He squeezed his arm a couple of times, the legacy of the exchange with Buchanan's minders starting to ache and gnaw into the bone. He looked across at Garrick, who was gazing out of the window, looking at nothing in particular and obviously processing everything that had happened. Garrick caught his gaze and gave him a sympathetic smile. 'How's the arm?'

Neil gave him a weak smile back. 'Okay. I'll live. How about you?'

'Likewise. Nothing that a good night's sleep won't cure.'

In truth, Garrick was in absolute agony. Both his arms had been twisted close to the point of breaking and his back felt as though it had been dislocated in several places. God knows what sort of bruises he was going to end up with. It was as if somehow they knew that he was the only real police officer and had focused all their attention onto him. Anyway, if Buchanan's reception committee was intended to warn them off, then it had worked. There was no way that he was going back there again.

'So, what happens now?' asked Neil, as if he was reading Garrick's mind.

'We need to talk,' replied Garrick, leaning forward and trying to keep his voice down, 'but not here. Where are you parked?'

'Headcorn.'

'Me too.'

*

The train hurtled on towards Sevenoaks and then through Tonbridge, before pulling into Paddock Wood, a small Kentish village which sounded prettier than it actually was; a disappointing mish-mash of poor, working-class homes

342

and modern, box-like housing developments for the newer commuters who had moved into the area. The noise and disturbance of two passengers getting into the carriage woke Craven up as a couple of local lads plonked themselves down opposite each other, one next to Craven and the other one next to the elderly woman who was sitting opposite him.

Craven pulled himself up from his slumped position and took a look at the kid who was sitting diagonally across from him, an archetypal feral yob wearing a white, shiny tracksuit with dark-blue piping and a scruffy, white baseball cap pulled low over his forehead. The obligatory gold chain and large gold rings completed the urban, council-estate look, as did the dirty fingernails and the ubiquitous white earphones, connected to an extremely loud MP3 player. Craven couldn't work out what the music was, some American rap or hip-hop rubbish as far as he tell, but one thing he was sure of was that the volume must have been damaging the kid's ears. The noise that was bleeding out of the earphones was loud enough for everyone to hear; god knows what it sounded like inside his head.

'Blinding fucking music!' yelled the kid at his mate, a similarly dressed Neanderthal in sportswear and trainers. The mate grinned back, a stupid lop-sided grin as he chewed noisily with his mouth open, the grey, discoloured chewing-gum visible for everyone to see. Craven looked at the elderly woman opposite and gave her a resigned, sympathetic look. Thank god he was getting off at the next stop. The woman gave him a relaxed, almost reassuring smile back, seemingly unaffected by the language and behaviour of the two yobs. Craven had expected her to look offended or even apprehensive but she seemed totally un-phased. Maybe she had a hearing aid and had it turned off. She certainly looked old enough. She must have been about seventy, maybe even seventy-five years of age, a typical grey-haired pensioner with round, metal-rimmed glasses and small, wrinkled hands which he noticed were covered in prominent blue veins and large, brown vinegar spots.

'Told yer, fucking brilliant init!' yelled the mate, more as a statement than a question.

The kid nodded his head up and down slowly, his feet tapping in time to the music, which was still thumping in his ears. 'Absolutely top mate. Absolutely fucking top!'

Craven raised his eyebrows in despair. The whole carriage was now squirming and twisting around to see what all the noise was about. Commuter trains were normally silent, the majority of passengers either reading or dozing their way through the journey but these two were shouting obscenities at the top of their voices. Craven thought about asking them to shut up but instantly dismissed it as a bad idea. The last thing he needed was a public altercation on a crowded commuter train.

'You got any fags moosh?' shouted the mate as if he was contemplating lighting up there and then, his legs jigging up and down in a bundle of nervous energy.

'Excuse me,' interrupted the old lady, suddenly leaning over and looking at the kid with the earphones who was sitting next to her, 'do you think you could stop swearing. And would you mind keeping the noise down please?'

The kid grinned and looked at his mate. 'What did she say?' he yelled, 'I can't hear a fucking thing with this music on!'

The mate grinned back, enjoying the game that they were now playing. 'She said, can you keep the noise down!'

'Sorry mate, I can't fucking hear you! What did you say?'

Craven was just on the point of intervening when he saw the old lady pull out a large pair of scissors from the handbag that was sitting on her lap and then watched in disbelief as in one swift movement she lent over and cut the earphone lead, halfway down the kid's chest and then stabbed the point of the scissors under his neck. 'Can you hear me now?' she asked, pressing the scissors into his skin and pushing his head upwards and backwards until he was looking up at the ceiling.

'Oi!' The response from his mate was as though he was on a two second delay, probably because he was so gobsmacked at what he had just seen. His eyes were literally popping out of his head. He lent forward to jump up and grab the scissors but in that same instant collapsed back in agony as Craven dug his thumb into the front of his neck and pushed him hard, back into his seat.

'I said, can you hear me now?' repeated the old lady, as cool and collected as if she was talking to somebody on the telephone, the scissors still digging firmly into the kid's neck.

'What the fuck are you doing?' yelled the mate, still pushed back into his seat, the words spat out between clenched teeth.

'Shut up.' Craven jabbed his thumb even further into his neck and then smacked him hard with his other fist, a fast, stinging punch that immediately had the desired effect. He looked across at the old lady and gave her an impressed smile. 'Where are you getting off?'

'Staplehurst,' replied the woman. 'I'm going to visit my son and grandchildren.'

Craven nodded and then looked at the kid who was sitting next to her, still staring up at the ceiling and not daring to move a muscle. 'Okay, I'm getting off at the next stop, you two are getting off with me.'

'Piss off!' snarled the mate, finding some fresh bravado from somewhere.

Craven gave him a withering look and pushed him even further into the back of the seat. 'Pardon?'

The mate said nothing else. The force of Craven's punch had told him all he needed to know about the capability of the stranger sitting next to him. Maybe it was time to keep his mouth shut.

'We're going to Ashford,' mumbled the kid with the earphones, speaking for the first time since the incident had started. Suddenly he didn't sound as cocky or arrogant anymore

Craven gave him a thin smile. 'Not anymore you're not. You're getting off with me. You can catch the next train.'

*

Garrick gazed out of the window as they pulled out of Marden and frowned in disbelief as he watched a couple of teenage yobs being pinned up against the wall by an older man, a full-scale disagreement obviously in progress. He could only see the back of the guy's head, but he felt sure that there was something familiar about him, as though he'd seen him before somewhere. He let the thought go as the train gathered speed and rumbled on towards Staplehurst and then onto Headcorn. There were more important things for him to worry about, not least what the hell he was going to do next.

Almost an hour after they had left Charing Cross, the train pulled into Headcorn station and Neil and Garrick got off, cutting their way through the car park and then walking about a hundred yards down the main road towards the first pub that they could see.

'This'll do fine,' said Garrick, pushing open the half-glazed door and walking into the bar. 'You grab a seat Neil and I'll get them in. What do you want, a pint?'

Neil nodded as he wandered into the lounge and bagged a table near the door. The pub was pretty much deserted, so there wasn't much danger of them being overhead, but nevertheless, he knew that Garrick would want to sit as far away from the bar as possible. To be honest, going to the pub and drinking alcohol was the last thing that Neil wanted to do, not least because he still had Steph's car, which he needed to drop off. Besides, all he really wanted to do was go home, get something to eat and then get an early night and forget about the whole miserable day.

Garrick ordered two pints of bitter and then leant on the bar and waited patiently for the beer to be poured. After a minute or so he gazed casually around the room and suddenly, out of the corner of his eye, noticed a woman sitting with two other people in the corner, staring at him and then giving him a friendly smile. It took him a couple of seconds to realise that it was Cheryl. She was out of her seat and joining him at the bar in a matter of seconds, her eyes and warm smile conveying how pleased she was to see him.

'John, what are you doing here? Are you on your own?'

Garrick smiled back, albeit a little cautiously. Cheryl's uninhibited enthusiasm always caught him off guard. 'No, I've just popped in for a quick drink with a friend.' He nodded towards Neil, who was sitting quietly at the other end of the bar. 'What about you?'

'I'm with my sister and brother-in-law,' replied Cheryl, unable to hide the disappointment in her voice and nodding towards the couple who were sitting at the table in the corner. 'We've come out for a meal. The food here is really good.'

Garrick nodded and smiled nervously, uncertain about what to say next.

Cheryl looked at him for a moment and then squeezed his arm gently. 'Are you okay John? I'm really sorry about what happened. They've treated you appallingly.'

He gave her a nonchalant shrug. 'Oh, I'm alright. Most people would give their right arm for an extra couple of weeks' paid leave. I can hardly complain.' Sensing that he'd left Neil on his own for long enough he turned round and picked up the two pints of bitter, taking the top off one and making sure that he didn't spill the other. 'Anyway, it was good to see you Cheryl, enjoy the meal.'

Cheryl gave him another warm, genuine smile as they turned to go back to their separate tables. 'It was good to see you too John. Pop over and say goodbye before you go.'

Garrick walked back towards the table by the door and put Neil's pint down carefully on the beer mat in front of him. 'Sorry about that,' he said, feeling as though he needed to apologise for taking his time. 'She's a colleague from work.'

Neil raised his eyebrows and gave him a wry smile. *A close colleague by the look of it*, he thought to himself. 'So, what happens next?' he asked, picking up the pint and taking a less than enthusiastic slurp.

Garrick frowned, indicating that he wasn't too sure. 'I don't know to be honest. Unless anything else has happened today, Charles Buchanan was our only lead. Without Colley or the laptop I don't know what else we can do.'

'What do you mean?' asked Neil, 'You're not thinking about giving up are you?'

Garrick gave him an apologetic shrug. 'It's difficult Neil. I'm not meant to be anywhere near this case at the moment. In fact, I'm not meant to be working at all. I can hardly go into work and admit that I've been to see Adam Saxby today, or complain that I've been roughed up by a couple of people working for Charles Buchanan.'

'No, I suppose not.'

'And I don't fancy going back there on my own, do you?'

Neil shook his head emphatically. He didn't fancy going back there at all – full stop. He took another sip of beer and thought about what Garrick had said for a moment. It was true. Charles Buchanan was the only lead they had but it was absolutely worthless unless they could follow it up.

The pair of them sat in silence for a while, drinking their beer and generally reflecting on the day's events and on what they were going to do next. The whole enquiry seemed to be stuck again, but as hard as they tried, neither of them could think of a way to move it forward. Neil checked his watch a couple of times and when he'd eventually finished his drink, decided that it was time to go. He didn't fancy another beer and besides, he was driving.

'I'd better just say goodbye to my colleague,' said Garrick, also standing up and emptying his glass. 'I'll ring Matt later and see if there have been any developments today. I'll give you a call tomorrow and let you know.'

Neil nodded and left Garrick to take the empty glasses back to the bar. He put them on the counter and then wandered over to the corner table where Cheryl was still sitting with her sister and her brother-in-law.

'Hello, John, have you come to join us?' asked Cheryl, looking up expectantly as he walked over.

Garrick smiled back but held his hand up to decline the invitation. 'No, I just came over to say goodbye.'

'Oh, that's a shame,' replied Cheryl, looking genuinely disappointed. 'Have you already eaten?'

'Well…no…it's not that, but …'

'Oh, well stay and have something to eat,' she insisted. 'We haven't ordered yet. It would be wonderful if you could. I always feel such a gooseberry when I'm out with my sister and her husband.'

'No really, I couldn't. I wouldn't want to intrude…'

'Don't be silly, you're not intruding. We'd love you to join us, wouldn't we Sarah?'

Garrick looked at Cheryl for a second and then at her sister and brother-in-law, trying to work out whether they were just taking pity on him and being kind, or whether they really wanted his company.

'This is my sister, Sarah,' continued Cheryl enthusiastically, making the introductions, 'and this is her husband Martin. Come on, sit down John and stop being so reticent. Besides, I expect Martin would appreciate some male conversation. He gets fed up listening to our girly chats, don't you Martin?'

Martin nodded at Garrick and winked. 'Come on John, save my evening and take a seat. I'll get you another drink. Pint of bitter?'

Garrick broke into a broad grin and held his hands up in defeat, settling himself down in the empty chair next to Cheryl. It wasn't a difficult decision really. For one thing he was starving; both he and Neil had hardly eaten a thing all day. But more importantly, enjoying a quiet, relaxing meal with good company in a relaxed, informal setting was just what the doctor ordered. Just what he needed to unwind.

An hour and a half later, he was easing himself into the back of his chair, a glass of red wine in his hand and with only a hazy recollection of the day's events in London. Suddenly, the combination of good food, fine wine and sitting beside Cheryl all evening made it feel as though it hadn't been such a bad day after all. Ups and downs certainly, but a memorable day nonetheless. Even the pain in his back had started to fade under the vintner's anaesthetic.

'So, what do you do for a job Martin?' asked Garrick, leaning forward and topping up their glasses while the girls had disappeared to the cloakroom.

'I'm a teacher, I'm afraid,' replied Martin. 'Highlands Community School.'

Garrick raised his glass and gave him a respectful nod. 'Well, here's to you Martin. I don't know how you do it. Not a job that I could contemplate doing under any circumstances.'

Oh, it's not so bad,' replied Martin, 'you get used to it like all jobs.'

Garrick pulled a face, unconvinced. 'I'm not sure I could ever get used to teaching a bunch of adolescent school kids. They must be a nightmare to control. All those hormones, all that Lynx deodorant…'

Martin smiled. 'Actually, the kids are what make it worthwhile. It's the politicians and the red tape and endless bureaucracy that drives you mad. The teaching is the fun part.'

Garrick nodded. That was a familiar story alright. If it wasn't for all the government targets and the endless paperwork they'd have a lot more time to carry out some real policing. Catch a few criminals.

'Actually, I might be getting a taste of your world soon,' continued Martin, swirling his glass on the tabletop to aerate the wine. 'Did Cheryl mention it?'

Garrick shook his head.

'I've been asked to attend court as a character witness for a couple of ex-pupils. Jamie Collins and Gary Parkes. I taught them both right through secondary school.'

Garrick smiled to himself in recognition at the names. 'Is that something you volunteer for Martin, or something that goes with the territory; something you're expected to do?'

Martin looked almost offended at the suggestion that he might be doing it under duress. 'No, I'm more than happy to volunteer. They weren't bad lads at all. A bit mischievous perhaps but not fundamentally bad. Both from single parent families of course, but aren't they all these days. They certainly deserve another chance.'

'So what were they like at school?' asked Garrick, picking up his glass and smelling the bouquet of the *Mascerello Barolo*. It was going down a treat. 'Were they good mates at school?'

'Absolutely,' replied Martin, nodding enthusiastically, 'they were inseparable. They were quite different individually but they were always together. They were as thick as thieves. '

'Actually, that's not a phrase I'd recommend you using as a character witness when you get to court,' teased Garrick, taking another sip of wine.

Martin blushed at his faux pas and then grinned. 'Mmm…I can see I'm going to have to get a bit of practice in before the real event.'

Garrick grinned back. He liked Martin, the guy didn't take himself too seriously. 'So what did you mean when you said they were different?' he asked. 'Different in what way?'

Martin thought for a moment before answering, as if he was now using the opportunity to rehearse his answers. 'Well, Jamie was the livelier of the two. I teach English and Drama for my sins and he was good at both. Drama particularly.'

'Good on his feet then,' commented Garrick, still teasing slightly but immediately spotting a possible connection with Jamie's ability to unload stolen property.

Martin smiled. 'Yes, I know what you're thinking John, but I can't comment on that. All I can say is what he was like when I taught him. He was a very confident, articulate student, even if academically he wasn't that bright. But underneath he was a decent kid. "Good on his feet" is probably a good way to describe him.'

'And Gary Parkes?'

'He was the opposite really. He gave the impression of being a bit more studious, but he wasn't really any brighter than Jamie. Just a lot quieter and not as confident.'

'Not a budding thespian then?'

Martin smiled to himself. 'No, Gary was never comfortable on stage – or under any spotlight for that matter. Computing was his main interest. He had a real flair for it. He had a sister, Becca, who was a couple of years older. They both went to Highlands, although she was…'

'Sorry Martin,' interrupted Garrick, suddenly leaning forward. 'What did you just say?'

Martin sat back, slightly taken aback at Garrick's interruption and by the sense or urgency in his voice. 'I said he had a sister, Rebecca, who was…'

'No, before that,' interrupted Garrick again, 'you said something about computing.'

'Yes, I said it was his main interest. He had a real flair for it.'

'Are you sure about that?'

Martin gave Garrick a quizzical look, suddenly worried that he may have said something that he shouldn't have done. 'Of course I'm sure. We've got a computer room at school with over forty PCs, all of which are networked. We didn't have to pay for any hardware or software support for over five years when Gary was there, he could take a PC apart and put it back together again with his eyes closed. In fact he did it regularly when we upgraded all the processors and memory boards. I can remember we once had a problem with one of the servers which meant that none of the…'

Martin was still talking, recounting some technical issue from the past which Gary had obviously resolved, but Garrick had stopped listening, his mind racing back to the conversation that had taken place at Gary's house on the previous Friday. 'He wouldn't have had any trouble getting into a laptop then?' he asked, interrupting Martin for the third time in about a minute, 'Even if it was password protected?'

Martin shook his head. He didn't even have to think about the answer. 'Not at all. He did it all the time. The kids were always forgetting their passwords. Gary could programme in about three different languages. The kid was a real expert.'

FORTY-TWO

Garrick stood outside in the pub car park and looked up at the night sky, trying his hardest to remember exactly what Gary Parkes had said when he and Andy had paid him a visit. In some ways it was a pity that it had been Andy that had gone with him that day; if it had been Matt he could have rung him up and asked him to check his notebook. But Andy was more difficult. He'd have to explain why he was asking. Explain that he was still working on the case. Not so easy.

He paced up and down the car park a few times, struggling to remember the conversation, but then again, maybe the precise wording didn't actually matter. The kid had definitely lied. There was no doubt about it. What he had actually said wasn't important. The question was, why? Why say that he didn't know how to open up the laptop if he was such an expert?

Garrick looked up at the sky again, his neck craned upwards as he rotated a complete 360 degrees to take in the full panoramic effect. It was a fabulously clear night and the blue-black canvas was a breathtaking myriad of thousands and thousands of stars, a romantic, humbling moment, which he suddenly wished Cheryl could have experienced with him. In truth, the process of swivelling on the spot with his head twisted towards the heavens was not made any easier by the pint of bitter and the best part of a bottle of red wine that he had just drunk – and the combination of the two events was making him feel decidedly light-headed, particularly now that he was trying to re-focus on the ground in front of him, which still seemed to be turning.

Still, that made the next decision easy. There was no way that he was going to drive. He felt the car keys, which were still in his right-hand trouser pocket. It was tempting, of course, but he knew that it was stupid. How could he have even thought about driving home, let alone going round to Gary Parkes's house? Either he ought to get a taxi and go home and get some sleep, or else he needed to ring somebody up and go and visit Gary Parkes now. Strike while the iron was hot.

He paced up and down again and made his mind up in a matter of seconds. It was an easy decision. If Gary Parkes was suddenly a suspect, then he needed to act now. He pulled out his phone and looked at Matt's mobile number. Matt was the obvious choice, but then something stopped him. Whatever the Chief

Constable had said about taking a holiday, the reality was that he was effectively suspended and getting someone else involved was going to end up being messy. He was already in serious trouble. The last thing he wanted to do was put Matt's career in jeopardy. He paged through the list of names again, searching for another number and then hit the send button. The phone was answered at the other end almost immediately.

'Hello, Neil Ashton.'

'Neil, it's Garrick. Where are you?'

'I'm at home.' replied Neil, surprised to hear Garrick's voice so soon. 'Why, what's up?'

'Have you still got the car?'

'Yes. Steph's still at work. I'm dropping it off later. Why?'

Garrick looked at his watch. It was nearly half-past eight. Something must be going on for Steph to be working so late. 'I need a lift. Have you had anything else to drink?'

'Only a mug of Horlicks.'

'You need to get out more.'

'Tell me about it.'

Garrick smiled. Neil Ashton was okay. For a journalist, surprisingly, they got on really well. 'I think I've stumbled upon something – a new lead. Can you come and pick me up?'

'Sure, where are you?'

'Headcorn. I'm still at the pub.'

'The pub!' Neil smiled to himself. *She must have been a very close colleague.* 'Okay. Give me ten minutes. I'll be there as quick as I can.'

Neil quickly rinsed out the empty mug that was in the kitchen sink, turned off a few lights and then picked up his jacket and left. As he turned to lock the front door behind him he didn't see the figure step silently out of the shadows, a hand suddenly clasped firmly over his mouth and then his body pushed violently from behind up against the door. Neil had never actually seen a real gun before, let alone felt one in the back of his neck, but somehow he knew instinctively that the sensation of cold, hard metal on his collar line and the soft click of a safety catch being switched into position was the real thing. He stood in absolute, terrified silence, not daring to move a muscle, his heart pumping loudly in his chest as the adrenalin kicked in and started coursing through his body.

As always, Craven spoke with calm and measured control. 'Stand absolutely still and don't make a sound. Do you understand?'

Neil nodded in silence. He didn't want to speak. In fact, he didn't even know if he could speak. It was as much as he could do to just stand still and stop shaking.

'Whatever you do, don't turn around.' Craven pushed the Glock gently into the back of his neck a couple of times, just to reinforce the message. 'I'll say that again. Whatever you do, don't turn around. Understood?'

Neil nodded again, trying desperately to control his breathing. His heart was pumping so quickly that he was struggling to catch his breath, the effect of him being forced to stand motionless like a statue whilst suffering a full-scale panic attack. The sweat was literally running down his body.

Craven removed his hand slowly away from Neil's mouth, satisfied that he wasn't going to make a noise or do anything stupid. 'Okay, open the door, go back inside.'

Neil fumbled with the keys and opened the front door, walking slowly into the hall with Craven immediately behind him, the Glock still pressed menacingly into the back of his neck.

Craven pushed the door closed behind him and then nudged the Glock again, indicating to Neil to keep going. The pair of them walked down the hall and into the kitchen, stopping in front of the kitchen table.

'Okay, sit there and put your hands on the table.'

Neil did exactly as he was told, pulling out a chair and then spreading his hands out, his palms facing downwards on the table-top.

Craven said nothing for a moment, wanting to give him the chance to get his breath back. He waited a full minute before eventually speaking, although not the words that Neil was expecting to hear. 'Are you okay?'

Neil frowned, showing his surprise at the change of tone. He didn't have a clue who was standing behind him but he wasn't expecting the guy to ask him how he was. 'Not really. I'd be better if you took that thing out of the back of my neck.'

'It's for your own good. A gentle reminder not to do anything stupid.'

Neil remained absolutely still, as if to accentuate the point. 'Don't worry, I'm not gong to move. I can guess what will happen if I do.'

Craven paused and then took the gun away. Maybe the inquisitive nephew wasn't so inquisitive anymore. 'So, where were you going?'

'When?'

'Just now.'

'To pick up a friend.'

'Girlfriend?'

'No. Just a colleague.'

Craven smiled to himself. He knew that Neil didn't have any colleagues – not in this neck of the woods. *Must have been the useless detective then, or maybe his sidekick.* 'So, what's your name?'

'Neil. Neil Ashton.'

'Hilary Russell's nephew, right?'

Neil's heart skipped a beat at the sound of his aunt's name. 'Yes. Why, did you know her?'

Craven shook his head, even though Neil couldn't see him. 'No, I didn't know her,' and then after a pause, 'but I'm sorry about your loss.'

Again, Neil pulled a face, still surprised at the empathy that was being shown. It didn't make sense. What the hell was going on? 'Thank you. Do you know who killed her?'

'No.'

'It wasn't you then?'

'No.'

Neil breathed a sigh of relief. By his logic, if this wasn't Aunt Hilary's murderer, there had to be less chance of the guy actually pulling the trigger. 'So what do you want?'

'I don't want anything. I've come to do you a favour.'

Neil said nothing in response. Being held up on the front doorstep with a gun shoved in his back didn't feel like someone doing him a favour, but he kept the thought to himself. Whoever was standing behind him, he knew instinctively that it wasn't someone that you argued with.

'Did you see Buchanan today?' asked Craven, still maintaining the cool and measured tone of someone in absolute control.

Neil frowned, wondering how on earth somebody knew so much about his movements. Surely they hadn't been followed? 'No, he wouldn't see us.'

'Bit of a wasted journey then.'

'I wouldn't say that. It wasn't completely wasted.'

'How's that?'

'We found out about Buchanan. We didn't know anything about him before today.'

'And what did you find out, exactly?'

Neil hesitated. In truth they'd found out absolutely nothing about the elusive Charles Buchanan, other than his name and where he worked. All they really knew was that he didn't want to speak to them and that he employed a couple of very nasty minders. Beyond that they didn't really know anything.

'We know he's the key to all this,' bluffed Neil, trying to pretend he knew more than he did.'

Craven smiled at Neil's choice of words. 'You're wrong. Buchanan's the lock. I'm the key.'

'I don't understand.'

'You're a journalist, right?'

'Yes.'

'Which paper?'

'A local paper, in Cambridge.'

Craven couldn't hide the disappointment in his voice. 'Not a national then?'

'No, why?'

'I've got a story for you.'

'What sort of story?'

'A story that's going to make the front pages.'

Neil nodded his head very slowly, suddenly realising what Craven meant. He didn't understand why, but that didn't really matter. 'A story about Teleios?'

'Clever boy.'

'So why me? What do you want from me?'

'They'll try to suppress it. You'll know how to get round that. It's a story that needs to be told. Whatever the consequences.'

Neil nodded again. He didn't understand Craven's comment about consequences but he did understand what he wanted. Front page headlines. *News of The World* exclusive 'Okay. If you tell me, I'll make sure it gets printed. That's a promise.'

Craven looked at the back of Neil's head, trying to work out whether he had any idea about how difficult it would be to keep that promise. Either way, they were about to find out. *"I shall tell you a great secret my friend. Do not wait for the last judgement, it takes place every day."*

FORTY-THREE

Matt leafed through the file for the umpteenth time and then tossed it casually onto his desk, gazing across the CID room as if looking for some sort of inspiration. For the first time all day the place was empty, a momentary period of peace and quiet for him to reflect on the day's events and maybe catch his breath. The calm before the storm.

He sat forward in his chair and looked at his computer again and at the photos of Mill House, the grim, horrific picture of the Bishop of Oxford, crucified to his own wall and the large letters spelling out the word "Teleios" sprayed in bright red paint. There was no doubt about it. Whichever way he tried to rationalise it, they'd been following the wrong lead. Chasing the wrong suspect. Whoever had killed Dr. Reid was definitely the same person that had murdered Sir Julian Worsley and Stuart Richmond – and Graham Colley suddenly had the perfect alibi. By the time the murder was being committed in Oxfordshire, he was already dead.

'So, what do you think Shylock?' asked Steph, suddenly walking into the CID room carrying two cups of coffee. 'Any flashes of inspiration?'

Matt looked up and shook his head. 'No, not really. But at least it explains one thing.'

'Which is?'

'Which is,' replied Matt, pausing to take a slurp of coffee out of the top of the mug, 'we know that Colley was blackmailing Richmond, so there's no way that he would have left all that money behind at Richmond's house. Even if he'd been disturbed he would have had time to take some of it. Not one single note was missing. It doesn't add up. In fact, it never made any sense. Why would Colley want to kill him in the first place? He didn't have a motive.'

'Well actually,' replied Steph, pulling up a seat and sitting down by the side of Matt's desk, 'his motive, if he ever had one, was probably the opposite. There's no point in killing a golden goose is there?'

Matt nodded emphatically. 'Exactly. I don't know how we could have been so bloody stupid. Whoever killed Richmond wasn't interested in the money at all. It could never have been Colley.'

'Anything else from Oxford?' asked Steph, also drinking her coffee and trying to move the conversation onto something more positive.

Matt shook his head again. 'Nothing. There's a medical report due sometime this evening but I don't think it's going to tell us anything we don't already know.'

'What about Garrick or Neil? Anything from them?'

Matt pulled a face and frowned. 'No. Funnily enough I was just thinking about that. Nothing since lunchtime, which is really strange. Perhaps we should give them a call before the others get back. What do you think?'

Steph nodded in agreement as Matt leant forward to pick up the receiver, just at the same time as the phone started to ring. He grinned at Steph as he picked it up. 'There you are, I expect that's them now. Hello, Matt Isaacs.'

'Matt. DCI Ward, Oxford CID. Is Superintendent Fowler there?' DCI Ward sounded tired and not in the mood for small talk or polite introductions.

'No, sorry Sir,' replied Matt, momentarily thrown by the fact that it wasn't Garrick or Neil on the other end of the phone. 'he's not here at the moment. Can I help?'

'What about DCI Stenning?' continued Ward, ignoring Matt's question. 'Is he around?'

'Sorry he's out as well.' Matt could almost feel the irritation and impatience at the other end of the phone.

'No offence Matt, but is there anybody more senior than you around at the moment?'

'Sorry,' replied Matt for the third time. 'There's just me and another DC holding the fort. They've all popped out for half an hour.'

Ward broke into a wry smile at the other end of the phone. 'Ah, you mean they've all gone to the pub?'

'Something like that.'

'How long are they going to be?'

Matt quickly checked his watch. Ward had only just missed them; they hadn't been gone more than about ten minutes. 'Half an hour maybe?' he offered, almost apologetically. 'Do you want me to get someone to ring you back?'

Ward looked at his own watch. It was nearly nine o'clock. Time he was somewhere else. 'No, I'm about to disappear – I just wanted to update somebody on what we found on Reid's computer.'

'I can do that,' volunteered Matt, leaning forward and picking up a pen and paper.

Ward said nothing for a couple of seconds, as if he was deciding whether that was a good idea or not. 'Okay, but make sure it gets passed on as soon as they get back.'

'Of course.' Matt was still poised, the pen hovering over the paper, ready to capture everything that Ward said.

'Okay, at some stage we'll need to do a forensic search with some proper system tools but for the moment, we've carried out an initial trawl on Reid's computer. There are a couple of things that I think you'll be interested in.'

'Go on,' said Matt expectantly, scribbling as fast as he could.

'Well firstly, there are lots of emails back and forth to a variety of different addresses, but crucially to a couple that have the same prefix; Teleios 3 and Teleios 5…'

Matt threw Steph a significant look as he continued to note everything down.

'…and in particular there's an email dated Wednesday 13th September from Teleios 3, which from the content is obviously from Stuart Richmond. If you give me your email address I'll send it to you now.'

Matt finished writing and gave Ward his contact details over the phone. 'What are the emails about?' he asked, 'Do they tell us anything about Teleios?'

Ward shook his head. 'Not exactly, although in another sense they tell us everything we need to know. Most of them are blank, that's why the one that I've just sent you is so unusual. The rest are simply file attachments. No subject heading and no message.'

'And the file attachments? Photographs presumably?'

'Exactly. That's the real breakthrough. From our first trawl there appears to be something in the order of 3,000 photographs on Reid's computer. There are probably more saved onto CD or memory sticks somewhere. We're still searching the house, but it seems pretty clear that Teleios is some form of paedophile group which exchanges material on an almost weekly basis.'

Matt's computer suddenly gave a soft pinging noise, just at the same time that a dialogue box appeared on the screen, indicating that a new email had been delivered to his inbox. Steph leant over his shoulder and clicked the mouse to open it whilst Matt continued to hold the phone in one hand and write with the other. Both of them looked intently at the screen as the email popped up:

From: Teleios 3
Sent: 13 September 2006 11:02
To: Teleios 4
Subject: Urgent

Property burgled yesterday, Tuesday 12th September. Stolen items include personal laptop with address book and hard drive collection. Password protected but information is at risk. Police informed but not of laptop. Will advise of further developments.

Matt leant back into his chair and blew out a low whistle. After days of struggling with little more than intuitive assumptions and complete guesswork, suddenly everything they suspected was now being confirmed. Richmond must have been absolutely horrified when he discovered that his laptop had been stolen. No wonder he was prepared to pay £100,000 to get it back. Matt stared at the email again, trying to see if there was any information about the size of the group or how it operated but it was hopeless. The content of the email was self explanatory, but the distribution list told him nothing. In fact, it wasn't a list at all. 'So why did Richmond only send it to Reid rather than to the whole group? That doesn't make sense does it?'

'I don't know Matt. We wondered the same. Maybe he emailed them all individually.'

'And you're sure that there's no history of any email traffic other than to Richmond and one other?'

'Absolutely. Just Teleios 3 which is Richmond, and Teleios 5. Maybe it's a very, small, select group. Safety in numbers.'

Matt screwed his face up, clearly not convinced by Ward's response. He didn't know how many there were in Teleios but it had to be more than just a handful. 'And do you know who Teleios 5 is?'

'No idea Matt. Computing isn't exactly my forté. Besides, I expect we'll be handing most of this enquiry over to your lot tomorrow – but at least you now know why they're being murdered. Someone's taking this very personally. The crime scene here looks like a day of reckoning. Someone getting their revenge.'

I know, thought Matt, *Richmond's and Worsley's were exactly the same.* 'How bad are the photographs?' he asked, remembering the classification for paedophile pictures that went up to category 5 for the most serious offences. For the retribution to be so extreme, he assumed that they must be as hardcore as you could get.

'I've put a sample of about a hundred photos in a folder which I'll email over to you in a minute,' replied Ward. 'Obviously they're not very nice but I've seen a lot worse to be honest. Category 2 or 3 perhaps? We'll put the full collection onto CDs and get them biked over tomorrow.'

'Thanks.'

'Anyway, I've got to go. Tell Superintendent Fowler that I'll call him in the morning.'

Matt put the phone down and gave Steph an appreciative look. Her theory about Prime and paedophiles had been absolutely spot on. Without Steph they wouldn't be anywhere near up to speed. He was just on the point of updating her on exactly what Ward had said when they heard the sound of footsteps and voices approaching down the corridor. Matt glanced at his watch. Fowler and the team had only been gone 20 minutes but the sound of friendly banter and laughter echoing down the corridor meant that the trip to the pub had been brief but worthwhile. Certainly everybody sounded a lot more upbeat and positive than when they had left.

'Oh, there you are Shylock,' said Andy, leading the pack of CID officers back into the room, still grinning at some joke or remark that one of the team had just made. The unmistakeable smell of alcohol and recently smoked tobacco wafted in beside them. 'Everything alright? Do you and Steph want to take a quick break now?'

Matt nodded his approval to that suggestion. It had been a long day and it clearly wasn't over yet. 'Thanks. I just need to update you on a phone call that I took while you were out. A DCI from Oxford rang.'

Matt turned back to get his notes, just as his computer pinged for a second time, indicating that another email had been delivered to his inbox. He quickly opened it and saw that it was the folder of promised photographs from DCI Ward. He opened the attachment and waited a couple of seconds for the hundred or so photographs to load onto his screen By now the whole team had gathered around his desk and were looking over his shoulder.

'Were these found on Reid's computer?' asked Fowler, ever happy to ask the stupid question that everyone else was thinking.

'These are just a sample,' replied Matt, 'there should be about a hundred or so here. They reckon there are about 3,000 on his hard drive. Maybe more in the house.'

Fowler flinched as the first of the pictures popped up, a photo of a young girl aged eleven or twelve, perched on the edge of a single bed, her arms spread either side of her naked body as she leant back on her hands, her legs spread wide open and her breasts, showing the first, almost imperceptible signs of puberty; two small, raised mounds on her otherwise childlike torso.

A number of the officers shook their heads in disbelief. Steph put her hand over her mouth in shock.

'Put it on slideshow Matt,' suggested Fowler. 'We'd better see how bad they are.'

Matt put the programme onto slideshow and then the whole team fell into an awkward silence as photo after photo appeared, each one staying on the screen for five or six seconds before slowly fading into the picture that followed; a hundred anonymous victims, one after the other, all of them children but none of them in childhood anymore, all staring out of the monitor with the same haunting expression, the tragedy of stolen innocence somehow frozen in time by a silent, voyeuristic camera. The invisible thread of grace.

After about thirty or so pictures Fowler turned away, clearly affected by the images. 'Okay Matt, I think we've seen enough. Can you arrange to get them all printed. Sorry, but we're going to need hard copies for the evidence file.'

'Actually,' interrupted Andy, 'before you stop, can you just page back to the photo of the girl on the green sofa. It was about three or four pictures back.'

Matt halted the slideshow and paged back to the photo that Andy was talking about. It was a picture of a small, slim girl with long, dark hair, aged about nine or ten, sitting on a green sofa and wearing nothing other than a pair of white ankle socks and a necklace made out of seashells. The bright red lipstick on a child so young was particularly disquieting, as was the mixture of apprehension and bewilderment that was etched across her face. A nervous smile, forced and haunted by fear.

'What's the matter?' asked Matt. 'Something you recognise? The sofa? The room?'

Andy shook his head. 'No, the girl. I've seen a picture of that girl before. And quite recently. Not that picture obviously, but I've definitely seen her somewhere.'

The rest of the team looked at him, waiting for the punchline, waiting for the name. 'Recently as in the last few weeks?' asked Steph, trying to help Andy remember.

'Definitely. Recently as in the last few days.'

Again, the rest of the team stared at him and then back at the picture. It didn't mean anything to anyone else in the room.'

'Can you page back Matt,' suggested Andy 'and then page forward again so that it comes up as if I'm seeing it for the first time. Staring at it doesn't seem to be helping.'

Matt did exactly as Andy asked and paged backwards through a couple of photos and then forwards once more, until the picture of the girl popped up again. Andy stared at it for a couple of seconds, struggling to make the connection with something in the back of his mind. He was just at the point of giving up when suddenly he gasped in recognition. It was if someone had suddenly turned on all the lights, the implications of which were already racing through his mind.

'What is it?' asked Matt, sensing that Andy knew who it was. 'Do you recognise her?'

Andy continued staring at the screen and nodded. 'It's Becca Parkes. There was a photo on the mantelpiece when Garrick and I went out to see Gary the other day. No lipstick of course and fully clothed, obviously – but it's definitely the same girl. That's definitely Becca Parkes.'

FORTY-FOUR

Stella Parkes had got used to the sound of police officers banging on her front door over the years and the noise and commotion that was being made as she walked down the hall was unmistakeable. Nobody other than coppers made a racket like that.

Stella put the half smoked cigarette in between her lips as she reached up to pull back the security bolt and then opened the door. Her eyes were still squinting from the smoke as she peered out into the darkness, trying to see who was there.

'Hello Stella, can we come in?' said Garrick, pushing past her and not bothering to wait for a reply. 'DC Ashton,' he added, waving an introductory hand towards Neil who was still standing on the front step.

'Oi, what do you think you're doing?' yelled Stella, following Garrick down the hall in disbelief. 'You can't come barging in here just like that. Have you got a warrant?'

Garrick reached the living room and spun round to look at her, leaning forward into her face so that they were literally nose to nose. 'Nope. I'm not even on duty. Gary about?'

Stella looked at Garrick in confusion and then turned round and looked at Neil, who had walked in behind her. She'd dealt with Garrick plenty of times over the years but she'd never seen him like this before. And she'd never seen the DC that was with him. He didn't even look like a copper. 'I hope you shut the door behind you,' she said to Neil, taking a final drag on her cigarette and blowing the smoke towards him. 'because this is a bloody rough area you know. They'll pinch anything 'round here given half the chance.'

'No, I left it open for the riot squad and the dog handlers,' replied Neil with as much sarcasm as he could manage, 'they're right behind us.' Garrick gave him a wink behind Stella's back. It was exactly the right response. Exactly what a hardened, cynical cooper would have said.

'Who's he then?' asked Stella, looking back at Garrick but thumbing backwards over her shoulder towards Neil. 'You recruiting comedians all of a sudden?'

'Stella?'

'What?'

'Shut up. Just answer the question. Is Gary in?'

Stella looked at Garrick for a second and then walked over to the mantelpiece to stub out her cigarette. She could tell that something was up. She'd seen Garrick in a serious mood before but nothing like this. She turned round and looked at him, trying to read what was going on. 'No, he's out. Why, what do you want him for?'

'He's not upstairs then?' asked Garrick, not sure whether to believe her or not.

'I've just said, he's not here. What do you want him for?'

'Go and check upstairs would you DC Ashton,' said Garrick, looking at Neil and completely ignoring Stella's question. 'So, where is he? The Bricklayer's?'

Stella gave him a filthy look and then turned towards Neil, who was already in the hall and about to climb the stairs. 'And don't you dare bloody touch anything, do you hear? I'm going to make a complaint about this. You need a warrant to look 'round my house. I'm going to write to the Chief Constable and make a formal complaint. You wait and see. You two are going to be in real trouble.'

'Stella!'

'What?'

'Shut up and just answer the question. Is Gary at the Bricklayer's?'

Stella gave him another filthy look. 'No, he isn't, he's at work. He doesn't spend his whole life in the pub you know. Unlike some people I could mention.'

Garrick ignored the last remark, distracted more by the thought of Gary Parkes actually having a job. As far as he could remember Gary hadn't done a day's work in his life. 'Come on Stella, I haven't got time to muck about. Where is he?'

Stella shrugged her shoulders and walked over to the mantelpiece again, picking up the packet of cigarettes and taking out another one to light up. 'Suits me. It's no skin off my nose if you don't believe me.'

Garrick stared at her across the room, trying to work out whether she was telling the truth or not. She certainly didn't look as though she was lying. 'Okay,' he said, softening his tone slightly and giving her the benefit of the doubt, 'where's he's working?'

Stella shrugged her shoulders again and then lit the cigarette with a cheap, plastic lighter which she put back on the mantelpiece. 'Dunno. He went out about four. Said he'd be back after midnight. Probably around one o'clock.'

'That's an eight, nine hour shift. So why has he suddenly got a job?

Where's all this work ethic suddenly come from?'

'Dunno. He didn't say and I didn't ask.' Stella took another drag on the cigarette, her right elbow resting in the palm of her left hand, her left arm folded horizontally across her body. 'Anyway, what do you want him for?' she asked, tilting her head back and blowing the smoke up towards the ceiling.

Garrick ignored her and looked enquiringly over at Neil, who had just walked back into the room. 'Anything?'

Neil shook his head in silence. He didn't have a clue where Gary was, but he definitely wasn't upstairs.

Garrick looked back at Stella again who was still standing by the fireplace, still smoking and still feigning disinterest. 'Okay Stella, last chance. This is serious. We need to find Gary and we need to find him now. Do you have any idea where he is?'

Stella took another puff on the cigarette and shook her head. 'No idea. Anyway, what do you mean, serious? What's happened?'

'He means life or death.' said Neil, suddenly butting in for the first time and putting on a grave voice. 'He means someone's about to get killed.'

Stella looked at him and then back at Garrick again, wondering what the hell was going on. Suddenly she realised that they were serious. This wasn't any old run of the mill enquiry.

'Listen Stella,' said Garrick, softening his tone again and trying one last time, 'I can't tell you what this is about, but he's right, it is a matter of life and death. Trust me, your Gary's in a lot of trouble. And if it helps you understand how important this is, then one; no, we haven't got a warrant, two; I'm really not on duty and not meant to be here and three; actually, he's not even a copper.' Garrick nodded towards Neil as he finished the sentence and watched Stella's face start to change, part confusion, part worry. 'So if you know where he is you'd better tell us now. Before it's too late.'

Stella said nothing for a couple of seconds and then took a deep breath. Something inside her, some indefinable, maternal instinct suddenly told her that she needed to tell Garrick where her son was. And that she needed to do it now. 'Okay. He's got a catering job. Contract, through an agency. He started today.'

'Do you know where?' Garrick had already moved towards the door, ready to leave. In the distance he could hear the faint wail of police sirens, somewhere on the edge of the estate, slowly getting louder.

Stella nodded. 'He didn't tell me, but I saw it on some paperwork. 'Leeds Castle. He's got a job at Leeds Castle.'

FORTY-FIVE

The one thing that Craven hadn't expected to hear again was the sound of the mobile phone ringing. He actually thought that he had turned it off and he certainly hadn't bothered to recharge it for a couple of days, so it was a complete surprise when the screen started flashing and the familiar ring-tone burst into life.

He put down the glass of wine and picked up the remote control which was lying next to him, quickly switching the television onto silent. Watching TV was not something that he did very often and watching TV whilst lying on top of a hotel bed, slowly working his way through a bottle of red wine was almost unheard of. Still, as far as he was concerned it was probably time for a bit of indulgence. It had been a tough week and some good old-fashioned rest and relaxation was definitely in order. Having delivered everything that Buchanan had asked for, a quiet, celebratory drink before life went back to normal was just what he needed.

It was just a pity that Sophie didn't seem to be around. He'd checked with the hotel reception when he got back but it looked as though tonight was her evening off. Drinking on his own was all well and good, but sharing a bottle or two with Sophie would have been much more enjoyable. They would definitely have found a more interesting way to celebrate – in fact, after a couple of bottles of wine the possibilities were endless. *Still, maybe it was just as well*, he thought as he leant over and picked up the mobile from the bedside cabinet.

'Hello?'

'It's me.'

'Obviously.'

'I wasn't sure whether you still had the phone.'

'Only just.' Craven glanced at the handset, the yellow bar in the top right-hand corner of the screen indicating that the battery was almost flat.

'Where are you?'

'Kent. Still at the hotel.'

'I thought you were back in London.'

'I had to come back for the car. I decided to stay over.'

Buchanan smiled to himself at the other end of the phone. *In love, Hoping, Resigned, Bitter.* 'Not disturbing anything am I?'

Craven smiled ruefully to himself. *If only.* 'No, just having a quiet night in.'

'Good. Actually, you being down there is helpful.'

Craven frowned. He wasn't sure what Buchanan meant by that remark but it sounded as though he had another job lined up, which wasn't exactly what he had in mind. A few days rest was what he was really looking forward to; a bit of time to catch up on things and re-charge the batteries. 'Why, have you got something else for me?'

'Not exactly…'

Craven waited and said nothing. There was a pause at the other end of the phone. A hesitancy in Buchanan's voice, which was unusual. In fact it was unprecedented.

'…it looks as though I owe you an apology.'

'What for?'

Again the pause, the words still cautious and tentative. 'I was wrong about something I said earlier.'

'You were wrong about a lot of things you said earlier.'

Buchanan let out a frustrated sigh. Craven was the most obstinate person he had ever met. There had to be some Yorkshire blood in there somewhere. A grandparent perhaps. 'No, I didn't mean that. I was wrong when I said nothing else was going to happen.'

Craven was still lying on the bed, the pillows propped up against the headboard so that he could see the television, a black and white advert for some expensive perfume playing silently across the screen; a stick-thin girl with a fabulous bone structure looking all windswept and interesting on a beach. He picked up the remote control again and put the TV onto standby, suddenly realising that he needed to concentrate on what Buchanan was saying. 'Why, what's happened?'

'There's been another murder.'

'Where?'

'Oxford. Same signature as the others.'

'When was this?'

'Last night.'

'Jesus. You sure it's the same signature?'

'Positive. It's identical.'

'Not Colley then.'

'Exactly.'

'Jesus. Who was it?'

'Dr. William Reid.'

'Never heard of him.'

'Bishop of Oxford.'

'Jesus.'

'Not quite – although there was a passing resemblance at the end.'

Craven said nothing at the other end of the phone. Again, he didn't know what Buchanan meant by the last remark but he wasn't really thinking about that. He was too busy thinking about Graham Colley, a picture of those last few moments forever etched into his memory; Colley on his knees on his own kitchen floor, begging for mercy, his hands tied behind his back and his eyes bulging from the pressure of the plastic tie that was digging into his neck, slowly choking him to death. An innocent man. A blackmailer perhaps, but nothing worse than that.

'It gets worse.'

'Go on.'

'There was a computer at the murder scene. The local plod have been all over it.'

'So?'

'So, it's full of evidence, obviously.'

'And you're worried about it leaking?'

Buchanan shook his head in despair. Craven still didn't get it. 'Of course I'm not worried about it leaking. I can control that.'

Craven allowed himself a faint smile. *I wouldn't bank on it.* 'So what's the problem then?'

'The problem is that the police are now ahead of us. For all we know they might already know who the murderer is. They could be arresting him as we speak.'

Craven pulled a face, obviously confused by Buchanan's comment. 'Well that's good isn't it? The sooner they catch him the better, surely? The last thing you want is any more incidents.'

Again, Buchanan shook his head in frustration. 'Incidents I can manage. But the one thing I wouldn't be able to control is a high profile court case. Can you imagine the public reaction? The Crown trying to prosecute some poor vigilante who's been killing off rich, successful paedophiles. It'll be a circus. Not only are some of them employed by the Crown, one of them comes close to actually wearing the bloody thing!'

Craven smiled to himself. Buchanan was right. Whoever was working their way through the list of Teleios names was destined to become the most popular defendant in British criminal history. The prospect was unthinkable.

The government would fall, almost certainly but the real threat would be to the wider establishment, possibly to the point where the damage was irrecoverable. The implication for the police force, the judiciary, the royal family, in fact the whole political and legislative infrastructure, was just too serious to even contemplate. Still, it was all academic really, now that he'd told Neil everything. A court case, high profile or otherwise, was going to be neither here nor there. If the inquisitive nephew managed to publish what he'd promised, it would be like unleashing a tsunami. Craven was beginning to wonder whether he should have said anything at all. 'So what do you want me to do about it?'

'What do you think? I want you to find out who it is and deal with them. Permanently.'

Craven picked up a packet of cigarettes and took one out, waiting a couple of seconds before he lit it as he thought about Buchanan's request. 'That's not going to be so easy,' he said, snapping the lid on the Zippo lighter and blowing a thick cloud of smoke into the centre of the room, 'not with the police crawling over everything. Have you got any idea who it is?'

'No. But I can probably point you in the right direction.'

'Go on.'

'I think I know who's going to be next...'

Craven said nothing and took another long drag on the cigarette, waiting for Buchanan to offer up the information; the next piece of the jigsaw that he had probably known all along.

'...I think it's going to be the Chief Constable. And he's going to be at Leeds Castle for the next couple of days.'

'Leeds? What, as in Yorkshire?'

Buchanan shook his head in disbelief. Craven had travelled all over the globe and could name most of the capital cities of the world from memory, but his knowledge of British geography was just appalling. 'It's in Kent, near Maidstone. About half an hour from where you are now.'

'Oh, okay. You'd better give me his name then. I'll go and check it out.'

Buchanan took a deep breath and swallowed hard. 'Actually, I'd better give you all the names. The rules have changed in the last couple of hours. This whole thing could implode at any minute. Have you got a pen and paper?'

'How do you know he's going to be next?' asked Craven, leaning over to the bedside cabinet and picking up a pen and small notepad, the latter branded with the name of the hotel and a small, ink drawing of a four-poster bed.

'Reid wasn't tortured. No stun-gun marks.'

Craven frowned again, clearly confused. 'You've lost me.'

Buchanan looked at his watch. Time was of the essence and the explanation wasn't exactly straight-forward. 'Try and imagine Teleios as a circle, like the numbers on a clock. The group was originally set up by the person who still uses the pseudonym, Teleios 1. He knows the identity of all the other members but crucially, everybody else in the group only knows the names of two others; the person immediately before and after their own number. It's a security arrangement that's served them well. If something goes wrong, none of them can identify more than two others. They exchange material like "pass the parcel." Inefficient but very secure.'

'I still don't understand.'

'Richmond was the most recent member, recruited about four years ago. Not Teleios 12 as you might think. He replaced a previous member who died and therefore inherited his pseudonym, Teleios 3. That means he knew the identity of Teleios 2 and Teleios 4. Teleios 2 was Sir Julian Worsley and Teleios 4 was Dr. William Reid, both of whom are now dead. It's pretty clear that Richmond gave up both their names before he was murdered. That's why he was tortured so many times with a stun-gun.'

Craven raised his eyebrows in surprise. 'Worsley was number 2? Does that mean he'd been a member for a long time?'

Buchanan nodded, even though Craven couldn't see him on the other end of the phone. 'He was the second oldest member. He joined right at the beginning when he was a young, successful barrister making a name for himself in the Criminal Law Courts.'

'And the guy who started it all? Teleios 1?'

'A young, successful police inspector making a name for himself in the Met.'

Craven nodded slowly, the history of Teleios and the sequence of events suddenly making sense. 'Now a Chief Constable, presumably.'

'Exactly. Their paths crossed and the rest, as they say, is history.'

'And you're sure he's going to be next?'

Buchanan nodded again. 'Pretty much. There were eight pairs of stun marks on Worsley's body, virtually the same as on Stuart Richmond. My guess is that he talked before he died. He must have identified Teleios 1. The only other person he could identify was Teleios 3, which was Stuart Richmond, who was already dead.'

'And nothing on Reid's body?'

'Not a mark. It's as if the murderer didn't bother – as if he already knew where he was going to strike next.'

Craven blew out his cheeks. It looked like it was going to be a long night. 'You'd better give me the names then.'

Buchanan took another deep breath and nodded reluctantly. And then, against all his better judgement, he looked at the list again and started to read them out.

FORTY-SIX

Leeds Castle was built in 1119 by Robert de Crevecoeur, a descendent of one of William the Conqueror's warlords, replacing the earlier Saxon manor of *Esledes* which had been on the same site since 857AD. The castle was built as a Norman stronghold and held by the Crevecoeur family until 1278, when it became a royal palace for King Edward I, becoming part of the Queen of England's dower – the settlement widowed queens received upon the death of their husbands. In the three centuries that followed it became a royal residence for six medieval queens: Eleanor of Castile; Margaret of France; Isabella of France; Joan of Navarre; Anne of Bohemia and Catherine de Valois.

In Tudor times, Leeds was greatly enjoyed by Henry VIII who visited frequently and who transformed the castle for his first wife, Catherine of Aragon, adding many of the Tudor windows that still exist today. In 1520, an entire tented village was erected when Henry, accompanied by a retinue of 4,000 courtiers, stayed at Leeds on his way to his famous meeting with Francis I of France at the "Field of the Cloth of Gold," a painting commemorating the event still proudly displayed in the large Banqueting Hall. Henry's son, King Edward VI, granted the castle to one of Henry's courtiers for his services, and Queen Elizabeth I was also imprisoned there for a time before her coronation.

In the 17th century the castle was sold to the Culpeper family, who ensured that it escaped destruction during the English Civil War by managing to support both the Royalists and the Parliamentarians during the conflict and the subsequent Restoration. In later years, the castle was bought by the Wykeham Martin family and then, finally, in 1926 by the Hon. Olive, Lady Baillie, a wealthy American heiress and the last private owner. Lady Baillie spent considerable time and money refurbishing the interior and turning the living quarters into a sumptuous treasure trove stocked with ceramics, paintings, furniture and tapestries, first working with the French architect and designer Armand-Albert Rateau and then later, with the Paris decorator Stéphane Boudin. Following her death in 1975, the castle passed on to the Leeds Castle Foundation, a charitable foundation established by Lady Baillie to administer the estate and to promote and preserve the castle and grounds for future generations to enjoy.

The present day castle, described by Lord Conway as "the loveliest castle in the world", was now an important leisure destination in the county of Kent, attracting thousands of visitors each year who flocked to see the royal palace and to experience over one thousand years of English history. The 500 acres of beautiful parkland were landscaped in the early 18th century and many of the trees that were planted then, still remained. In the gardens, an aviary housed rare and exotic species from across the globe and after a break of over five hundred years, the fruits of the Leeds Castle vineyard were once again being used to produce fine wine. More popular still was the infamous maze, constructed in 1988, using over 2,400 yew trees and planted and trimmed to resemble a topiary castle.

The practice of using Leeds as a security venue, a tradition first established by Lady Baillie during the Second World War, had continued in more recent years. The castle's location, set on two islands and projecting into a large, natural moat made it an ideal setting for a high profile conference, guaranteeing its delegates peace, privacy and above all, absolute security. In July 1978, a meeting between the Egyptian President, Anwar Sadat and the Israeli Foreign Minister, Moshe Dayan took place in preparation for the Camp David Accords and in 2004, the Northern Ireland peace talks were hosted there by the then Prime Minister, Tony Blair.

Neil parked the car about a hundred yards or so from the entrance, switched off the engine and turned off the lights. The security presence at the main gate was discreet but formidable; three heavily armoured Land Rovers and five or six police officers, all dressed in heavy, protective clothing and carrying semi-automatic weapons. 'I assume they're not your lot?' he asked Garrick, peering through the windscreen and nodding towards the group of uniforms standing motionless by the main gate. Even from a distance Neil could see the outline of sophisticated, military style firearms and communications equipment, which somehow seemed at odds with the rural, Kentish landscape.

Garrick shook his head. 'No, they're not local. CO19 probably...'

'CO19?'

'...or CO6 perhaps. Either way it means they're from London.

'CO6?'

'SFOs. Specialist Firearms Officers,' added Garrick, suddenly realising that he'd slipped into jargon again and that Neil was having difficulty in keeping up.

'How can you tell?' asked Neil, struggling to see any distinguishing detail from the all-black uniforms, which blended perfectly into the deepening gloom.

'There are only a couple of units that wear that sort of gear, particularly the baseball caps and the combat helmets. And the vests are probably ballistic proof rather than just stab proof.'

'And are the guns real?'

Garrick smiled ruefully to himself. 'They're semi-automatic carbines. I can't see what type, not from this distance – but they're definitely real.'

'And they'd use them if they had to,' said Neil, more as a statement than a question, suddenly feeling uneasy about the level of security and firepower in front of them.

Garrick pulled a grim face and then nodded. 'Absolutely. We're not taking any chances here. Put the lights on and drive up very slowly towards the gate. No sudden movements.'

Neil took a deep breath and noticed that his hands were starting to tremble as he switched on the ignition and turned on the headlights. As he drew up slowly towards the main gate, two of the officers nearer the road began to visibly stiffen, staring intently at the approaching vehicle and cradling the submachine guns with slightly more purpose. Neil pulled up within ten yards of the entrance and then dipped the headlights and turned off the engine. The two police officers had already walked towards the car, making sure that it didn't get any closer, one walking round to Neil's window and the other one standing in front of the car.

The officer standing outside Neil's door made a circular motion with his hand, indicating to Neil to wind down the window. Neil pressed the button on the inside of the door, taking a second to realise that the electric windows wouldn't open with the ignition turned off. He leant forward to switch on the engine again, just as the police officer opened the door and put a firm and restraining hand on his upper arm. 'Don't start the car again please Sir.'

Neil leant back in the seat and put his hands up in front of him, palms facing outwards. There was no way that he was going to do anything that was likely to invoke a sudden response. Garrick meanwhile had put his right hand inside his left-inside jacket pocket to get out his warrant card. He suddenly froze in mid action as he heard the police officer at the front of the vehicle shout something and then saw the tiny, infra-red dot from the sight of a semi-automatic weapon spot precisely on the upper left hand side of his chest.

'I wouldn't make a move if I were you Sir,' said the officer, still leaning in through the driver's door and not sounding the slightest bit unnerved by the situation, 'not if you want to drive home in one piece.' He leant further into the car and then removed the keys from the ignition.

Garrick remained perfectly still, his hand still resting inside his jacket pocket. The night air was fairly cool, particularly with Neil's door open, but a bead of sweat was starting to form on his forehead. Everyone in the force knew the reputation of the boys from CO19. "Trigger happy cowboys." was the general consensus and "shoot first, ask questions later," was by all accounts, their normal modus operandi. 'DCI Garrick, Kent CID,' volunteered Garrick. 'I was just getting out my warrant card.'

'Thank you Sir,' replied the officer, still totally unfazed by the sudden flurry of activity. 'If you could take your hand out very slowly and pass the warrant card to me please.' And then he added in a calm, deadpan, matter-of-fact voice. 'My colleague will fire if you make any sudden movement.'

Garrick let out a deep breath and then withdrew his hand slowly, passing the black, leather card holder across the front of Neil's chest and over to the waiting officer. A small torch appeared from nowhere and then the warrant card was read in a matter of seconds. 'Wait here please,' said the officer, walking away from the car and back towards his colleagues at the main gate, the leather holder still in his hand.

Garrick peered through the windscreen and then turned to look at Neil, wiping away the bead of sweat that had formed across his forehead. 'Phew, what do you think of that then?'

'It's pretty impressive security,' replied Neil, also letting out a deep breath and staring at the huddled group of officers in the distance. One of them was speaking into a mobile phone, obviously making a call to take instructions or maybe check out Garrick's ID. 'I can't imagine anyone getting past that lot in a hurry.'

Garrick turned and looked out of the side window, staring into the darkness and at nothing in particular. The security was certainly impressive, but that was hardly surprising. That was the whole point. Tonight, Leeds Castle was a terrorist's dream. Fifty Chief Constables plus another fifty deputies, all under the same roof. Maximum risk, maximum security.

'And is it always held here, at Leeds Castle?' asked Neil, as if he was reading Garrick's mind.

Garrick shook his head and continued staring out of the side window; half listening to Neil but still reflecting on something that he had said earlier. 'No, each force takes it in turn to host it. It just happens to be in Kent this year. Anyway, tell me again what the guy said. The bit about the Chief Constable. What did he say exactly?'

Neil hesitated. He wasn't sure that Garrick wanted to hear the exact words. 'He just told me to tell you to watch your back and not to trust him.'

Garrick looked at Neil and gave him an encouraging smile. 'Just tell me what he said Neil, word for word. It might be important.'

Neil looked down at the floor, slightly embarrassed. 'Okay, he said, "Tell that useless detective to watch his back. Tell him to watch out for the Chief Constable. Tell him he can't be trusted." That was it. Word for word.'

Garrick turned to look out of the side window again. *Useless Detective. I'll show him who's bloody useless.*

'He's coming back,' said Neil, looking out of the front windscreen, suddenly spotting the police officer walking purposefully back towards them and trying to change the subject. The mood inside the car had started to darken and the last thing they needed was Garrick losing his temper in front a load of armed police officers.

Suddenly the passenger door opened and the officer leant forward into the car again, the warrant card being returned to Garrick now that his identity had been checked and verified. 'Thank you Sir, that's all in order. How can I help you?'

'We need to get up to the castle as soon as possible,' replied Garrick, putting the warrant card back into his jacket pocket and cutting straight to the chase. 'We've reason to believe a murder suspect is up there. I need to apprehend him as a matter of urgency.'

'Not possible I'm afraid,' replied the officer, squatting down on his haunches so that he was at the same level as Garrick. 'It's a security lockdown. Nobody gets in, nobody gets out.'

Garrick pulled a face, part frustration, part annoyance. 'This really is important. We wouldn't be here otherwise. It's a matter of life and death.'

The officer looked at him for a moment and held his gaze, trying to read what this was all about. Some country bumpkin murder enquiry probably. Hardly life and death. A couple of local woodentops getting all excited by a once in a lifetime investigation. Anyway, if there was a murder suspect up at the Castle, he wasn't going anywhere. 'I'm sorry Sir. We have a security cordon in place and we're under strict instructions not to break it, not under any circumstances.'

Garrick looked at him and shook his head in despair. This was impossible. If he didn't manage to persuade this uniform to let them through, there was going to be one less delegate drinking at the bar that evening. He was absolutely sure of it. 'What's your name officer? he asked, trying to make the question sound not too confrontational, but at the same time checking the epaulettes for his rank and number.'

'Blake Sir, Sergeant Blake.'

'I'm not trying to be difficult Sergeant Blake, but it really is critical that you let us through.'

The officer gave him a sympathetic smile, trying his best to diffuse the situation, but making it clear that Garrick's seniority didn't count for anything on this occasion. 'I'm sorry Sir, I can't make any exceptions.' He nodded towards the castle grounds behind him. 'We have a number of VIPs attending as well the Chief Constables. The Home Secretary opened the Conference this evening and is still on site.'

Garrick let out a frustrated sigh. There was only one way that he was going to turn this around. It was time to up the stakes. Apply a little leverage. 'Okay, Sergeant Blake. I have to advise you we have reason to believe that our murder suspect is likely to kill again this evening and that his target is one of the conference delegates. I understand your position and respect the decision that you have to make but just for the record, I will formally note that you have refused us entry three times this evening, despite me giving you very clear and detailed information regarding a specific incident that is about to take place.'

The officer looked at Garrick and held his gaze for a second, trying to work out what the hell this was all about. Suddenly his neck was on the line and he knew it. If he refused Garrick entry and anything happened there would be a formal enquiry. Then again, if he let him in and something got out of control... He was damned if he did and damned if he didn't. 'Do you know who the target is?' he asked, trying to get as much information as possible before having to make a decision.

Garrick nodded. 'Chief Constable David Hutton. Kent Constabulary.'

The officer looked at him again and nodded back. There was no point in delaying any further. On reflection it was an easy decision. Garrick's ID had been checked and if there really was a security threat in progress, then he had to act on it. He didn't have any option. 'Okay, I can't let you take the vehicle in, your colleague will have to wait here for you. But I can escort you up to the castle in one of the Land Rovers. It's the best I can do.'

Garrick gave him a short nod in return. 'Thank you.'

'I'll have to ring ahead and let them know that we're coming...'

'Of course.'

'...and you'll need to submit to a full body search.'

Garrick nodded again and then turned to Neil. 'No point in you waiting for me Neil. I'll need to ring for back-up anyway. You get out of here. Besides, you'd better drop this car back to Steph, she'll be wondering where you've got to.'

Neil had already taken the car keys back and wasn't going to argue. Hanging around in the dark waiting for Garrick to reappear, maybe after an hour or so wasn't exactly what he had in mind. He watched Garrick get out of the car and walk slowly with the uniform back to the main gate, the pair of them deep in conversation, presumably about what was going to happen next. Neil turned the keys in the ignition and switched on the headlights. Garrick was right. *Time to get out of here.*

Craven watched the events from a distance, parked a couple of hundred yards away across the other side of a small, stone bridge. Suddenly he had a decision to make. Follow Neil or stay with Garrick at the castle. He took one last drag on the cigarette and flicked the butt out of the window, just as Neil's headlights raised and dipped as he drove over the bridge towards him, on his way to Leeds village and then back to Appleden and Cranbrook.

Craven looked in the driver's mirror and watched Neil's red tail lights as the car drove past him and then faded into the distance. He had to make a decision now. Garrick was about to disappear into the castle grounds and Neil was already on his way home. Buchanan's instructions were unequivocal. Find the murderer and deal with him, permanently. That meant he had to follow Garrick and get to whoever the murderer was before the police did. That wouldn't be difficult. The security at the main gate was solid enough, but that didn't matter. The grounds were enormous and there were public footpaths and side entrances all over the place. There was no way that they could cover them all. There was even a public golf course for God's sake. All he had to do was get up to the castle and then pick his moment.

That made it simple. The obvious decision was to follow the useless detective. Except there was something nagging in the back of his mind. Something that Buchanan had said earlier. Something that didn't add up. Something that made him think that he ought to stick with Neil.

Craven looked in the mirror again and then checked his watch. An old military routine. And then something clicked. Suddenly it fell into place. Decision made. *"It is as true in everyday life as it is in battle. We are given one life and the decision is ours whether to wait for circumstances to make up our mind, or whether to act, and in acting, to live."*

FORTY-SEVEN

It took Matt less than ten minutes to drive out to the Connaught Estate, but it was time enough to clear his mind and reassure himself that it was the only sensible course of action. Certainly the last half-hour or so had been a complete waste of time; stuck in the office trying to find out something on Becca Parkes while most of the others had gone out looking for her brother. Still, that was situation normal these days. Him tied to a desk drowning in paperwork, whilst everyone else was tearing around the countryside, chasing up leads and getting all the glory.

Matt smiled ruefully to himself. Hopefully they were having better luck than he was. He'd searched the national database and then trawled through as many local records as he could find but there was nothing, absolutely nothing on Becca Parkes. In fact, other than one outdated vehicle offence involving Gary several years ago, there was nothing on any of them. For a family living on the fringes of the criminal underworld, they'd somehow managed to avoid any arrests or a formal police record.

Matt gazed out of the side window as he turned off the main road and into the estate, the rows of grey, anonymous flats looking more like some East European landscape than a housing development in the south-east of England. No wonder people like this turned to crime. What else was there for them to do? What chance did someone like Gary Parkes really have to get out of there and make something of himself? The prospects of a proper education and a decent job had to be pretty slim.

Matt found Stella's house without any trouble and then, just as Garrick had done a few days earlier, stood and waited patiently for a few moments before realising that the front door-bell wasn't working. Eventually he rapped the knocker and then watched the outline of Stella's head and shoulders appear through the frosted glass, the silhouette slowly getting larger as she walked down the hall towards him.

Stella opened the door and stared at Matt's warrant card which he was holding up in front of him, open and ready to confirm his identity. She looked at him with contempt, shaking her head in disbelief at the third visit in less than a couple of hours. 'What is this, some sort of competition?'

Matt frowned at her, totally thrown by what she had just said.

'You know, see how many times you can harass the same person in one evening? I've already told Garrick and that other lot – he's not here.'

Matt looked at her for a second and then smiled to himself, reflecting on the events of the last half-hour. Suddenly, the phone call from the CO19 Officer wanting to verify Garrick's identity began to make sense. Garrick must have got to Stella's house ahead of Fowler and the rest of the team.

'I said, he's not here,' repeated Stella, beginning to get impatient with Matt just standing on the doorstep and not saying anything in reply. Besides, the night air was turning chilly and a cold draught was blowing up the hall and into the house. She wanted to close the door and get back into the warm.

'I'm not looking for Gary,' replied Matt, suddenly coming to his senses, 'I wanted a quick word about something else.'

'What about?' asked Stella, her response suddenly shifting to guarded suspicion.

'Becca. Can I come in for a minute?'

Stella looked at Matt in surprise for a couple of seconds and then shrugged and walked back down the hall, leaving the front door open behind her as an invitation for him to follow. Whatever it was he wanted she wasn't really worried. Becca was a good girl. Always had been – always would be. She picked up a packet of cigarettes and quickly lit one before Matt closed the front door and caught up with her in the sitting-room. She looked at him with a mixture of distrust and irritation. 'Well, get on with it. What do you want a quick word about?'

Matt had thought long and hard about how best to handle the situation but in the end had decided that the direct approach was probably the best. He put his hand inside his jacket pocket and pulled out the folded piece of paper which he passed over to her. 'I wanted a quick word about this.'

Stella unfolded the paper and found herself staring at a photo of a small, slim child with long, dark hair, sitting on a green sofa and wearing nothing more than a pair of white ankle socks and a necklace made out of seashells. Suddenly, the aggressive, impatient mood dissolved as she gasped in horror and then put her hand over her mouth in shock, just as Steph had done an hour or so earlier. 'Where did you get it from?' she whispered, still staring at the picture and reversing slowly into the armchair behind her.

'We found it on a computer with a lot of …similar photographs,' replied Matt, trying to choose his words carefully. 'Can I ask, have you seen it before?'

Stella nodded, still staring at the photo but saying nothing, the tears starting to well up in her eyes as the pain of something long forgotten, some fragment of history which she thought had been locked away forever, suddenly flooded back. Eventually she gazed up at Matt and handed the sheet of paper back. 'I didn't think I'd ever see it again. Whose computer did you find it on?'

Matt hesitated. He wasn't sure whether he was allowed to say, but then again, it was probably going to be all over the newspapers soon. 'It belonged to somebody called Dr. William Reid. He was the Bishop of Oxford.'

Stella shook her head, indicating that she'd never heard of him. People like her didn't know people like that.

'Do you know who took the photograph?' asked Matt, folding up the paper and putting it back in his pocket.'

Stella looked up at him again, this time with a flash of anger, the words spat out through clenched teeth. 'Of course I know who took it. Her father took it. My ex-husband.'

Matt tried his best to hide his surprise and then decided to sit down, perching on the edge of the sofa and leaning forward to adopt an earnest, sympathetic pose. Somehow, standing up and staring down at her wasn't having the desired effect. 'Do you know where he is now?'

Stella almost snorted in derision and then shook her head. 'No idea. Don't you know?'

Matt frowned, momentarily thrown by Stella's remark. 'We might need to follow this up. When did you last see him or have any contact with him?'

She pulled a face. That was easy. 'The day we left. I haven't seen or heard from him since the day we walked out. I don't know where he is and I don't want to know. And I don't care.' She took a last puff on the cigarette and then stubbed it out viciously in the ashtray, as if she was stubbing out the memory of her husband's face.

Matt gazed around the room for several seconds, trying to give Stella's anger a moment or two to subside. The photographs of Becca and Gary were still proudly displayed on the mantle-piece, innocent smiles from an innocent age. 'Can I ask what happened?' he asked. 'Did you report it?'

Stella looked at him in disbelief. 'Of course I reported it! What do you think I was going to do, ignore it? I'm her mother for god's sake!'

'And what happened?' asked Matt, still leaning forward and trying to ignore the hostile response that he was getting back.

Stella let out a long sigh and leant back into her chair, her whole body seeming to visibly drain from the memory of it all. 'It was a waste of time. A complete waste of time. He got himself some posh lawyer – or his mates did, to be more accurate. They always stick together, as you well know.'

Matt frowned at her for a second time, again momentarily thrown by what she had just said. 'Do you remember the name of the lawyer?' he asked, suddenly following up a hunch.

Stella shook her head. 'It was years ago. I might recognise it if I heard it again, but I can't remember it now, not after all this time.'

'How about Worsley?'

Stella looked at him for a moment and then suddenly leant forward in the chair. 'Yes, that was it. Worsley. Julian Worsley. He was very…public school. You know, a bit of a toff.'

Matt took out his notebook and checked his watch before scribbling down exactly what Stella had said. 'And you're sure you don't know where your husband is?'

'Ex-husband. He was in London when we left but he could be anywhere.'

'I don't suppose you have a photo of him do you?' asked Matt, more out of hope than expectation.

Stella almost laughed at the absurdity of the question. 'You must be joking. I burned everything. Absolutely everything.'

Matt nodded. He understood exactly what Stella meant. He wanted to ask whether anything else had happened between Becca and her father, but he was too frightened to ask. Maybe there was more to it than just a few photographs. He stood up, ready to make his leave. 'Oh well, just a thought. Can you give me his full name and his date of birth. We'll follow it up from there.'

'Anthony,' replied Stella, also standing up. 'Anthony James. 14ᵗʰ March, 1963.'

Matt scribbled the names and date into his notebook. 'Thanks, I won't take up any more of your time. Obviously my colleagues will be in touch about Gary.'

'You've written the wrong name down,' said Stella, looking over Matt's shoulder and nodding towards his notebook, which he was about to shut.

'What do mean?' replied Matt, looking at what he'd just written down. It was exactly as Stella had just told him.

'Anthony James Parkes.' replied Stella, pointing to the words on the page. 'Parkes is my maiden name. You don't think I'd keep his bloody surname after what happened do you?'

Matt gave her an apologetic smile and crossed out the word Parkes on the page. No wonder he hadn't be able to find anything on the database, he'd been looking for the wrong person. 'Sorry, stupid of me. I should have realised. What's his surname?'

'Stenning,' replied Stella in a very matter-of-fact voice. 'Anthony James Stenning.'

*

Charles Buchanan looked at his watch for the third time in as many minutes and paced up and down the hall again, the mobile phone still clenched firmly in his right hand. This was always the worst part; the interminable waiting and the not knowing. It was almost an hour since he had spoken to Craven and he didn't have a clue what was going on. Everything was starting to unravel, that much was certain – but exactly how things would end up was much harder to call. That was the problem. The fall-out was always the bit that you could never predict. He glanced at the mobile again, willing the screen to suddenly burst into life but there was nothing, absolutely nothing.

He wandered back into the study and eased himself into one of the leather armchairs, the sound of *Mozart's Requiem* still playing quietly in the background. Instinctively he picked up the glass of finest Burgundy, a vintage *Chambertin Domaine Arrmand Rousseau* which he'd been saving for a special occasion and took a long, leisurely mouthful, savouring the complexity and elegance of the structure; the bright, assertive raspberry on the palate finely balanced with the warm, spicy, oak top-notes. It was exquisite. Not exactly the special occasion that he'd had in mind but no matter, whichever way it panned out it was going to be a night to remember. He looked around the room as he always did, admiring his own taste and the understated refinement of it all. It was something that money could never buy.

He took another gulp of wine, resigned to the thought of having to wait and then closed his eyes, letting the first soothing bars of the *Lacrimosa* wash over him. Suddenly, just as he began to drift off into the music the harsh tone of the mobile phone lying next to him started to ring, jarring into the *Sequentia* with unashamed modernity. Buchanan reacted in an instant, the urgency of the situation prompting him to stand up to take the call. 'Hello?'

'It's me.'

'Obviously. What's happened?'

'Nothing yet. Just surveillance.'

'Is everything okay?'

'Grey. Seventy-thirty white. But I need to ask you something.'

Buchanan sighed. That was the trouble with Craven. There was always something. 'Go on...'

'Something you said earlier – about Reid's computer.'

'What about it?'

'You said the police had been all over it.'

'So?'

'And that it was full of evidence.'

'So?'

'You said the word "obviously." You said "it was full of evidence, obviously." Do you remember that?'

Buchanan shrugged. 'Not particularly. But it would have been, wouldn't it? Full of evidence, I mean.'

Craven was nodding to himself in the darkness at the other end of the phone. 'Exactly. Richmond's laptop must have been the same. Full of evidence. That's why he was being blackmailed.'

'So?'

'So why didn't you say the same about Worsley?'

Buchanan thought for a moment and then shrugged again. 'I don't know. Nobody said anything about any evidence. Maybe he didn't have a computer.'

'Of course he had a computer. I went in there, remember? I saw it. Besides, he was part of the network. He had to have one.'

'Well maybe it was clean. Maybe he wiped it after Richmond got burgled. Maybe he was spooked.'

Craven shook his head, clearly unimpressed with Buchanan's line of reasoning. 'Worsley was a paedophile. He was just like the rest of them. They take years to build up their collections. That's how they always get caught. They never throw anything away.'

'So what are you saying?'

'Maybe somebody wiped it clean before anyone else got to it.'

Buchanan frowned. 'What, you mean the person who killed him?'

Craven looked out of the car window into the darkness and shook his head in frustration. For once, Buchanan was missing the point. 'No, I don't mean that. The person who killed him wanted the police to find as much evidence as possible – just like they did in Oxford.'

'You've lost me.'

'Where do they get the material from?' asked Craven, suddenly changing tack.

Buchanan smiled to himself. He'd wondered how long it would take Craven to get to that particular point. It was the one unanswered question, the final piece of the jigsaw. 'I don't know. We've never been able to find out.'

'Not the internet then?'

'Of course not, the internet is traceable. None of them can afford to go on the internet.'

'So somebody gets it for them and then loads it onto one of the computers?'

'I presume so. Why?'

'I think I know who it is. And I think it's the same person who killed Hilary Russell.'

Buchanan thought for a moment. 'And the same person who killed the others? Richmond, Worsley and Reid?'

Craven gazed out of the side window, suddenly distracted by a movement in the distance. It was time to go. 'I doubt it. Not unless they're killing their own kind.'

*

Matt stood outside Stella's front gate, his mind racing about what she had just said and trying to decide what to do next. The name was too unusual to be a co-incidence. If she had said Smith, or Brown he wouldn't have been concerned at all – but Stenning? It had to be the same person. It just had to be.

He shivered for a second and pulled his collar up, suddenly noticing the cold wind, which was whipping across the estate and cutting through his jacket. He quickly got back into the car and switched the engine on, turning the heater up to maximum and hoping that the hot air was still warm enough from the journey out. The problem was, he couldn't remember where Stenning was. He knew that Fowler had taken Andy and most of the others with him but he couldn't remember whether Stenning had gone with them or had stayed behind. He racked his brains trying to recall who was still in the station when he took the call from the CO19 officer. Steph was definitely in the building somewhere, still waiting for someone to give her a lift home. But Stenning... where the hell was he?

Matt looked in the mirror and then suddenly shook his head in disbelief. *Of course he didn't go with Fowler and the rest of them. He'd hardly go and see his ex-wife, would he?* He took out his mobile phone and paged through the address book, quickly thinking through his options and who he should call. Garrick was at Leeds Castle, probably out of bounds by now, and Fowler and Andy were almost certainly not far behind him. He looked in the mirror again as he made his decision. He didn't really have any choice. He had to ring the station and just hope that it wasn't Stenning who answered the phone. Matt dialled the number and waited for what seemed like ages before someone eventually picked up the call.

Sergeant Phil Edwards was sitting where he always sat at that time in the evening, at the small, side desk just out of sight from the front reception where he could put his feet up and read the paper and drink a mug of tea without being disturbed. The middle of the shift was always the best part of working lates. Everyone else was out and about and it was that nice, calm period before the storm; a couple of hours of peace and quiet before the pubs chucked out and the whole place turned into a bloody maelstrom again. Edwards took a long, slow slurp of tea and turned over the page of *The Daily Mirror*, wondering whether there was anything decent on the television for when he got home later.

As he immersed himself in the TV schedules it took him a couple of seconds to realise that one of the phones on the other side of the room was ringing. He pulled himself out of the chair with an air of tired resignation and then walked slowly across the office, still carrying the mug of tea and half hoping that the ringing would stop before he got there. He knew instinctively that it was probably someone for CID and that yet again, they had all buggered off somewhere and call-forwarded their phones to him. He picked up the receiver with an almost begrudging acceptance of his duty to answer it. 'Sergeant Edwards.'

Matt breathed a sigh of relief at the other end. 'Phil, it's Matt.'

'Hello Matt. What I can do for you?'

'Is DCI Stenning still there?'

Edwards took another slurp of tea. There was no point in letting it go cold. 'No, he's gone. He left just after you did. He's back in tomorrow morning. Do you want to leave a message?'

'No, not really. Is Steph still around?'

'No, she went with him. He gave her a lift home.'

Matt pulled a face. He didn't like the sound of that. Stenning was definitely in the office when they were looking at the photos on the computer – and he hadn't said a word when Andy identified the photo of Becca Parkes, his own daughter. There was no doubt about it, he had to be implicated. Matt glanced at his watch. He was stuck at Ashford and the journey to Steph's house in Cranbrook was going to take too long. Twenty minutes certainly, maybe half an hour. 'Phil, have we got any patrol cars in the Cranbrook area at the moment?'

Edwards shook his head. 'No, I don't think so. Why, what's the matter?'

'Oh, nothing,' replied Matt, suddenly thinking of another option. 'Just me panicking about something. Something and nothing probably.' He put the phone down and immediately paged through the list of numbers again until he found Neil's mobile. Unlike Edwards, Neil answered the call in a matter of seconds, the sounds of traffic and engine noise in the background confirming that he was out driving somewhere.

'Neil, it's Matt. Where are you?'

'I'm just dropping the car back to Steph's. What about you?'

'How far away are you?' replied Matt, ignoring Neil's question and conveying a sense of urgency in his voice.

'Five minutes, tops. Why, what's up?'

Matt hesitated. He wasn't sure himself. Something was definitely not right about DCI Tony Stenning, but for the moment he didn't have time to think it through and work it out. For once, he was just going to have to act on instinct and intuition, something that he was extremely uncomfortable about. 'I'm not sure. I just wanted someone to check that Steph was okay.'

'No problem,' replied Neil, turning off the main road towards Cranbrook. 'I'm literally five minutes away. Why wouldn't she be okay?'

'I don't know,' replied Matt. 'Just a hunch. It'll take too long to explain. Just give me a call when you get there and let me know that she's alright.'

'Okay. Stop worrying, I'm nearly there.'

'Oh, and look after yourself.'

Neil smiled ruefully to himself as he glanced over his shoulder and looked at the cricket bat that was lying on the back seat, the handle heavily bound in greying, black tape and the ageing wood dimpled and marked from years of use. He wasn't sure why he had brought it with him really. The experience with Buchanan's minders had certainly rattled him and then the incident with the guy on the front door-step had made him think that he ought to take something with him. A bit of insurance, just in case. Suddenly it was looking like a good decision. 'Don't worry Matt, I'll be fine.'

Matt hit the red button to end the call and almost instantly dialed Steph's home number. Maybe he should have thought about that before ringing Neil, but either way, he wanted to double check that she was alright. Anyway, she might know where Stenning had gone after dropping her off. He had to be staying in a local B&B somewhere. There was no way that he was going to drive up and down from Hampshire every day. The phone seemed to ring for ages before Steph eventually picked it up. Matt could tell immediately from the relaxed and cheerful way that she answered that everything was alright.

'Steph, it's Matt. How are you?'

'Oh hiya Matt,' replied Steph, as always sounding pleased to hear from him. 'I'm good thanks. Are you okay?'

'Yes, I'm fine. I was just checking that you got home alright, what with not having the car.'

Steph started to laugh, partly in appreciation at Matt's concern, but also because the knife that was pushed up hard against her throat was forcing her to pretend that nothing was wrong. 'Oh, I got a lift from work – I got in about ten minutes ago… Everything's fine.'

Matt breathed a huge sigh of relief at the other end of the phone. At least that was one less problem to worry about. 'Okay, I'll leave you to it. I'll catch up with you tomorrow.'

'Okay, see you tomorrow. Thanks for ringing Sherlock, I really appreciate it.'

FORTY-EIGHT

Garrick paced up and down the reception, waiting impatiently for Hutton to extricate himself from the after-dinner drinks reception which was obviously in full swing. He couldn't actually see what was going on but he could tell from the noise that was drifting out from behind the closed doors that it was a typical, boisterous gathering which appeared to be getting louder and louder by the second. He looked at his watch for the umpteenth time and gave Sergeant Blake, who was waiting discretely at the other end of the reception, a knowing look. These events were always the same in his experience. The serious business of conference wouldn't start until tomorrow, but for now the formality of evening dinner was being followed by the time-honoured tradition of an "all expenses paid" drinks reception; literally a free-for-all in every respect. He let out a disapproving sigh as one of the waiters came through the double doors and caught a brief glimpse of the room full of people; a hundred or so higher-ranking officers, their seniority and uniforms somehow at odds with the alcohol fuelled revelry that was well under way.

Sergeant Blake gave him a sympathetic smile in return, just as his two-way radio squawked into life, the call suddenly taking him by surprise. He wandered a few paces down the corridor, talking into his lapel and then looking back at Garrick a couple of times as he listened to his colleague and decided what to do next. Eventually he finished the call and walked back over to Garrick. 'We have some more visitors at the gate. Your colleagues from Ashford by the sounds of it.'

Garrick raised an eyebrow and then nodded in silence. It was probably better not to say anything, otherwise there was a risk that he might have to explain why they had arrived separately.

'I'm going to keep them there for the moment until you've spoken to Hutton. Otherwise this is going to turn into a bloody circus.'

Garrick nodded again. That suited him fine – not that he had any choice in the matter. Sergeant Blake was definitely in charge of security. He checked his watch again and noticed for the first time that day that he was starting to feel nervous. The adrenalin which had got him through the visit to London had long worn off and the relaxed, alcohol-induced haze that had developed nicely over dinner with Cheryl had completely disappeared. Suddenly, he felt tired and stone-cold sober and not at all looking forward to the prospect of seeing Chief Constable David Hutton again. This was the guy who had effectively suspended him and told him to go and lie on a beach for a couple of weeks. He wasn't exactly expecting a warm and friendly welcome.

Sergeant Blake wandered back over to the other side of the reception, just as the double doors behind Garrick opened and Hutton walked through, carrying what looked like the remnants of a gin and tonic in his right hand. He looked over at Garrick and gave him a short nod. 'John. I didn't expect to see you so soon. I assume it's urgent?'

'Yes Sir,' replied Garrick, standing slightly to attention and as always mesmerised by the crispness of Hutton's uniform and the mirror-like shine of his shoes.

Hutton stared at him for a second, holding his gaze as he tried to work out what this was all about. 'I assume it's to do with Teleios?' he asked, lowering his voice and looking behind him rather cautiously as another waiter came out through the double doors.

'Yes Sir,' replied Garrick again, not sure whether to launch straight into an explanation or wait until he was asked. He chose the latter.

'Okay, we'd better go down here, there's a syndicate room we can use.' Hutton gave him a grim smile and then headed off down the corridor, Garrick duly following a few paces behind. After thirty seconds or so they reached a small room on the left, a circular table with six chairs and the obligatory, ubiquitous flip-chart standing in the corner. On the opposite side of the room was a small table with half a dozen glasses and a couple of bottles of water. One still, one sparkling.

'This'll do,' said Hutton, unscrewing one of the bottles and pouring out two glasses of water. He passed one over to Garrick and then gestured to him to take a seat.

Garrick sat down and took the glass appreciatively. The bottle of red wine which he had drunk earlier was beginning to get its own back and that, combined with his nervousness at seeing Hutton again, meant that his mouth was really dry. He was also waiting for the admonishment that he felt sure was coming next. An Exocet probably, knowing Hutton's reputation.

'So, you didn't fancy the beach then?' said Hutton, more as a statement than a question, a faint smile playing across his lips. It was almost as though he found the situation amusing.

'No, not really Sir.' replied Garrick, slightly thrown by Hutton's demeanour.

'You'd better get straight to the point then. And make it snappy.'

Garrick took a deep breath. 'I think I've identified the murder suspect. But more importantly, I believe he's working here, at the castle, and I think he plans to strike again, tonight.'

Hutton took a sip of water and said nothing, his mind quickly processing what Garrick had just said. 'What's his name?'

'Parkes, Gary Parkes. He's the one who burgled Richmond's place and took the first laptop.'

Hutton shrugged, indicating that the name meant nothing to him. 'And you think he went back and murdered Richmond?'

'Almost certainly. And Worsley and Reid probably. They all have the same signature.'

Hutton took another sip of water, still working out the implications of Garrick's news and what they should do next. Not that they had many options.

'And do you know why? Why he would want to kill them?'

Garrick shook his head. 'No Sir, not yet.'

'But you know who his next target is?'

Garrick nodded slowly and then swallowed nervously, unable to hide the embarrassment in his response. 'Yes Sir, I think so.'

Hutton nodded back. Confirmation that they both knew what he was talking about, even though he didn't have to say the words. The time to stop talking was always when the other person was nodding their head in affirmation but saying nothing. He gulped down the last of the water and then stood up, the conversation obviously over. 'Right, well we'd better go and find him then. I assume you know what he looks like. Where's he working?'

Garrick also stood up and shrugged his shoulders, indicating that he wasn't exactly sure. 'On the catering side somewhere. That's all I know. In the kitchens probably, or maybe as a waiter?'

The pair of them left the room and made their way down the corridor towards the main restaurant, their logic being that the kitchens were the first place to look and that they were most probably located in that vicinity. The restaurant itself was relatively quiet, a handful of delegates opting to miss the after-dinner drinks reception in favour of a quieter conversation over a cup of coffee or a glass of wine. A couple of them had papers strewn across the table, obviously engrossed in a serious dialogue about something or other. Hutton and Garrick ignored them and followed their noses towards a pair of swing doors at the back of the room. Instinctively they knew that the kitchens had to be through there.

Garrick spotted Gary Parkes at the back of the kitchen almost as soon as they walked through the double doors. The black and white check trousers and the white apron made him look very different but Garrick had dealt with him too many times over the years not to recognise him instantly, even at a distance across a large, crowded kitchen. And likewise, Gary spotted Garrick as soon as he and Hutton walked into the room. He didn't know Hutton of course, but the uniform was unmistakeable and he realised immediately that he was in trouble. If Garrick had come all this way to look for him, then it meant only one thing.

Gary's first impulse was to defend himself and instinctively he picked up a large filleting knife that was lying on top of the worktop next to him, a nine-inch stainless-steel blade which was slightly curved and absolutely razor sharp. Garrick and Hutton immediately froze on the spot, as did the rest of the kitchen staff, conscious that two strangers had suddenly walked into the room and that something was about to kick off.

Gary reversed a couple of paces and then looked around him nervously, wondering if there was an exit anywhere near him through which he could escape. Garrick was just on the point of making a dash towards him when the fire door in the corner of the rear wall suddenly opened and a couple of contract staff sauntered through, returning from a quick, unauthorised cigarette break at the back of the building. Gary saw his opportunity and before anyone could say or do anything to stop him, darted through the door and out into the night air, the filleting knife still grasped firmly in his hand.

Garrick shouted something meaningless like "Stop him someone!" and then raced across the kitchen in hot pursuit, clattering a few saucepans out of the way and dodging the rest of the staff who were stood rooted to the spot, their mouths still open in amazement. By the time he reached the fire exit Gary had already jumped over a small terrace wall and was halfway across a lawn, heading towards the castle maze.

Garrick raced after him, running as fast as he could but losing ground with every step. The grass was damp and slippery and in truth, Gary was much younger and fitter than he was. The kid had already disappeared into the maze by the time Garrick reached the entrance. He stopped for a moment, partly to get his breath back but also to think about what the hell he was going to do next. The floodlights from the castle had lit up the lawns and gardens fairly well but the maze, which was further away was going to be much darker, particularly in the centre. Suddenly he began to question the merits of blindly following someone into the middle of a pitch-black labyrinth. Firstly, he had no idea how he was going to get out and secondly, the kid was a triple murderer carrying a nine-inch blade. Not exactly an ideal situation.

For a second, he wondered whether he should wait for back-up. The good news was that there was only one entrance in and out of the maze but in reality, Gary could easily climb any of the hedges and then disappear into the castle grounds. If he didn't act quickly the kid could escape within a matter of minutes – and then possibly for good. Garrick looked back up at the castle, the small crowd of kitchen staff still congregated around the back door watching what was going on but otherwise, no sign of any help or reinforcements. Ironically, there were a hundred or so police officers inside the conference but none of them had any idea about the drama that was unfolding outside. And surprise, surprise, there was no indication of Chief Constable David Hutton lending any support. And where the hell was Sergeant Blake when he needed him?

Garrick thought about the situation for a moment and then decided to act. There was no point waiting for someone else to turn up and help and besides, if he didn't move now, it might be too late. He stepped forward a few paces into the maze and then took a right turn at the end of the first hedge, listening as hard as he could for any signs of Gary being close by. He needn't have bothered. Gary had deliberately stayed close to the entrance and as he watched Garrick turn left at the next junction, he stepped out of the shadows and swung his arm silently around his neck.

Garrick stopped in his tracks, the unmistakeable feel of cold, polished steel on his throat. The pair of them stood in silence for a couple of seconds, Garrick not daring to move a muscle, his heart pounding loudly in his chest and Gary standing behind him, breathing heavily and trembling slightly as the adrenalin continued pumping through his body. He pressed the knife firmly into Garrick's neck a couple of times, just to make sure that they both knew who was in control.

Garrick swallowed hard and stood very, very, still. He had no doubt that Gary had the capability to kill him. A moment's impulse and it would be over in a matter of seconds. He stood motionless for what seemed like ages until he finally sensed a relaxation in Gary's breathing and then decided to speak. The only way he was going to get out of this was to try and talk his way out of it. 'If you put the knife down Gary, we can talk about this.'

Gary laughed to himself and then shook his head. 'You must think I'm stupid. There's nothing to talk about. It's too late for that.'

'It's never too late. Put the knife down and we can work this out.'

Gary snorted at the absurdity of Garrick's remark. Of course it was too late. He'd already killed three people. There was no way back from that. There was nothing to work out.

Garrick stood his ground, despite the disadvantage of circumstance. 'It'll be worse if you kill me. Whatever you've done, killing a police officer is different.'

Gary snorted again. 'Yeah, well maybe it will earn me some credibility when I get inside. Killing a copper will give me a reputation.'

'Don't be stupid Gary, there won't be any "inside" if you kill me. You won't get out of here alive.'

The two of them stood in silence again, Gary thinking about what Garrick had just said. Maybe he was right. The place was crawling with armed coppers.

'Besides, you won't get any credibility for killing me. Hutton maybe, but not me.'

Gary smiled to himself as another thought occurred to him. 'I could always take you hostage. Get myself a safe passage out of here.'

It was Garrick's turn to snort in derision. 'You've been watching too much television Gary. The only way you're going to walk out of here alive is if you walk out of here handcuffed to me. Otherwise it'll be in a body-bag.'

For the first time, Garrick felt Gary relax the pressure on his throat. 'I'm probably a dead man already. You don't know who these people are.'

Garrick twisted his head slightly so that he could look him in the eye. 'Yes I do, which is why you need to walk out of here with me, rather than with anybody else.'

'Do you know what they do?' replied Gary, looking back at him but already thinking that Garrick might be right. He was probably his safest route out of there. 'Do you know why they all protect each other?'

'Yes I think so.'

'And how difficult it will be to stop them?'

'I know.'

'You can't guarantee me anything.'

Garrick twisted around even more. By now, the knife was almost on his shoulder. "I promise you this Gary. If you give me the knife and walk out of here with me, I'll make sure that you don't come to any harm.'

'Promise?'

Garrick nodded. 'I'll take you in personally. No-one else will get near to you. I promise.'

Gary looked at him for another couple of seconds and then suddenly lowered the knife and turned it round, offering the handle to Garrick to take it from him. He knew it was over. Besides, holding Garrick to ransom wasn't going to get him anywhere. Garrick was as expendable as anybody else. They were all too far down the food-chain to be of any value.

Garrick let out a huge sigh of relief and then gave him a reassuring smile as he took the blade. 'Well done Gary. Good decision.'

'You got some cuffs then?' asked Gary, holding his hands out, his wrists held close together.

Garrick smiled at him again. 'I haven't got any on me. Hold your arms behind your back as if you're wearing some and I'll hold onto your arm. That'll be fine.'

The pair of them walked the short distance to the entrance and then emerged from the maze, the crowd of staff still congregated by the back door of the kitchen, waiting patiently to see how the drama was going to conclude. Garrick held Gary's left arm loosely with his right hand as they walked slowly up towards the terrace. 'Okay, we'll get back to the castle and then I'll ring for a car to pick us up.'

Gary nodded, resigned to whatever process was now going to take place. There was no point trying to resist anything anymore. At least he was with Garrick. Somebody he could trust. 'Who's Hutton then?' he asked, looking at Garrick as they started crossing the lawn.

Garrick frowned. 'What do you mean who's Hutton? That's the reason why you're here isn't it? David Hutton. He's next on the list.'

Gary frowned back. 'Never heard of him.'

Garrick suddenly stopped, the pair of them looking at each other in the cold, night air. A chill wind was whipping across the lake, causing them both to shiver. 'He's a Chief Constable. I thought that's who you were after?'

Gary nodded. 'Yeah, I am. Teleios 1. He is a Chief Constable. But his name's not Hutton. I don't know anyone called David Hutton.'

Garrick looked at him again in confusion. And then he saw the tiny, infra-red dot spotted precisely in the centre of Gary's forehead, the unmistakcable sight of a Heckler & Koch MP5 carbine. He turned towards the castle and shouted "NO!", a split second before he heard the rifle shot and then felt Gary slump to the ground, the pool of warm, crimson blood already seeping out into the cold, black turf beneath him.

Up in one of the bedrooms, located high above the courtyard and with a perfect view of the grounds, the Right Honourable Robert Bellamy, Secretary of State for the Home Department, gazed down at the scene below and took another sip of finest French Armagnac. He could see a man in civilian clothes, the second man who had run into the maze, now on his hands and knees, bending over the body. Either he was crying or he was trying to resuscitate him. Either way, it was too late. He picked up the telephone again, listening to the closing bars of the *Agnus Dei* playing quietly in the background and then he smiled; a smug, arrogant smile of someone accustomed to his position of superior, protected privilege. 'It's done,' he said, taking a long, satisfying puff on a large, hand-rolled Double Corona, 'target is down. Checkmate.'

FORTY-NINE

Stenning smiled to himself as he stood in the doorway and looked around the room. This was more like it. Exactly how a little girl's bedroom should look; lots of pinks and yellows and pastel blues and lots of soft, cuddly toys scattered everywhere. Chloe, as ever, was snuggled up in bed with the covers tucked up under her chin, clutching Mr. Rumpus and staring intently at the strange man who was now staring back at her, his heart and pulse already starting to quicken with anticipation.

'Is mummy coming up to say goodnight?' Chloe asked, her large, round eyes following Stenning's every move as he walked into the room.

He smiled back at her, trying to reassure her that everything was alright. 'No, mummy's busy. She asked me to come up and say goodnight.'

Chloe propped herself up on her elbows and looked down at Stenning who was now standing at the end of the bed, still gazing around the room in nervous excitement, savouring the moment so that he would always remember it. A hunter closing in on its prey. 'Will you read me a story?' she asked, already deciding that mummy was probably too tired to come up and tuck her in.

'Of course I will,' he replied, squatting down to look at the rows of books in the pine bookcase at the end of the bed. 'Which one would you like?'

Chloe smiled. '*The Three Billy Goats Gruff* please.'

'Is that your favourite?' he asked, quickly finding the title and then sitting on the end of the bed.

Chloe nodded her head very slowly, still unable to take her eyes off the strange man whilst all the time hugging Mr. Rumpus even tighter under the blankets. As usual she was dressed in pink pyjamas.

'But mummy said you've got to have a bath first,' continued Stenning, still holding the book but deliberately not opening it. 'Bath first, story later.'

Chloe suddenly put on her saddest, pouting face to show that she wasn't happy. 'I have a bath before I go to bed, not after.'

'I know. But mummy forgot. She's been at work all day.'

Chloe pulled another face to indicate that she still wasn't happy. The bottom lip got lower and the sadder face got even sadder.

'I'll tell you what,' said Stenning, getting up and walking to the door, 'I'll start the bath and we'll read the story while its running – and if you're good, I'll read you another one before you go to bed.'

Chloe maintained the sad, pouting expression but nodded reluctantly. She didn't really want a bath, but the prospect of two stories, plus of course the chance to stay up a bit later was too good to miss. Stenning walked out of the bedroom and found the small bathroom at the end of the landing, turning on the cold tap but making sure that the plug wasn't in. The sound of running water was all he needed. He walked back into the bedroom and found Chloe, still sitting up in bed and waiting patiently.

'Right, pop out of bed then and we'll take those pyjamas off.'

Chloe looked at him for a moment and then got out of bed, hooking her small legs out and over the covers without having to move the sheets. She stood by the side of the bed and then put her arms straight up in the air, waiting for Stenning to lift her pyjama top over her head. That's what mummy always did.

Stenning took hold of the hem of the pyjama top and lifted it gently over her head, the top ending up inside out and the electricity in the material causing her hair to rise slightly with the static. She quickly put her arms down to cover her body. Suddenly it was colder now that she had got out of bed.

'Right, now the bottoms,' said Stenning, trying to keep his voice as relaxed and as nonchalant as possible. Inside, his heart was starting to tingle with excitement.

Chloe pulled down her pyjama bottoms and then wiggled her legs and kicked them off, sending them flying across the room. That always made mummy laugh.

'Right, now come and sit on my lap and we'll read the story.'

Chloe leant back over the bed to pick up Mr. Rumpus and then climbed onto Stenning's lap. She shivered slightly as he put his left arm around her tiny shoulder, holding the book up in the same hand and resting his other hand on her right knee. The exhilaration of touching her smooth, silk-like skin was almost unbearable.

'*Once upon a time there were three billy goats who were called Gruff. In the winter they lived in a barn in the valley. When spring came they longed to travel up to the mountains to eat the sweet, lush grass.*'

Chloe started sucking her thumb and stared wide-eyed at the pictures in the book as he read the story. She knew the words off by heart.

The three Billy Goats Gruff had to cross a rushing river. But there was only one bridge across it, made of wooden planks. And underneath the bridge there lived a terrible, ugly, one-eyed troll. Nobody was allowed to cross the bridge without the troll's permission and nobody ever got permission. He always ate them up.

The smallest Billy Goat Gruff was first to reach the bridge. Trippity-trop, trippity-trop went his little hooves as he trotted over the wooden planks. Ting-tang, ting-tang went the little bell round his neck.'

Stenning started to gently trace his fingers up and down Chloe's right leg, moving in small, deft, circles from her knee up to the top of her thigh. Chloe cuddled up tighter as he gave her a reassuring squeeze with his left arm.

'"Who's that trotting over my bridge?" growled the troll from under the bridge.

"Billy Goat Gruff," squeaked the smallest goat in his little voice. "I'm only going up to the mountain to eat the sweet spring grass."

"Oh no, you're not!" said the troll. "I'm going to eat you for breakfast!"'

Chloe started kicking her legs backwards and forwards excitedly. That was always her favourite bit.

'"Oh no, please Mr. Troll," pleaded the goat. "I'm only the smallest Billy Goat Gruff. I'm much too tiny for you to eat, and I wouldn't taste very good. Why don't you wait for my brother, the second Billy Goat Gruff? He's much bigger than me and would be much more tasty."

The troll did not want to waste his time on a little goat if there was a bigger and better one to eat. "All right, you can cross my bridge," he grunted.'

Suddenly, Stenning stopped. Chloe's bedroom faced the front of the house and he was sure that he had heard a car pull up and then someone turn the engine off. He waited for a moment, listening intently to what was going on outside. Chloe looked up at him, wondering why he had stopped reading. He put his index finger over his lips, indicating that he wanted her to be quiet and then eased her off his lap and onto the bed. As he tip-toed over to the window he heard the car door slam and then the voice of a man talking, as though he was speaking on a mobile. Suddenly it sounded as though he was almost directly below the window. Whoever it was, was coming up the path.

Stenning stood to the side of the window and gently pulled back the curtain, just enough to see what was going on. The guy had stopped near the top of the path, too engrossed in his phone call to take any notice of anyone staring down at him.

'Okay, I'm here now,' said Neil, 'I'll call you back once I've checked everything is okay.'

"I really think you should wait," replied Matt, trying to emphasis how dangerous he thought the situation was. 'There's a car on its way. Just wait until it gets there.'

'Well how long is that going to be?' asked Neil, pacing up and down the path in frustration. This was ridiculous. If Steph was in trouble he needed to go in there now.

'I don't know. Ten, fifteen minutes maybe.'

'Jesus. We can't wait fifteen minutes. What did she say exactly?'

'She didn't say anything. She just called me Sherlock.'

'Sherlock?' Neil looked up at the sky in exasperation. 'What the hell does that mean?'

'It means she's in trouble.'

'Are you sure?'

'Positive. It wasn't a mistake and I didn't mishear her. She was trying to tell me something.'

'Right, then I'm going in. Make sure that car gets here as quick as possible.' Neil didn't wait to listen to Matt's protestations and switched the phone off before putting it back in his pocket. Then he walked back to the car, unlocked the passenger door and leant over to pick up the cricket bat which was lying on the back seat. Maybe it was going to come in handy after all.

Stenning watched him walk back up the garden path and then disappear from view. Chloe meanwhile had got back into bed, sensing that something was wrong. The storytelling had stopped halfway through and now she was getting cold.

'Where's mummy?' she asked, worried for the first time that she couldn't hear any noise coming from downstairs. Normally, she could hear mummy moving about or watching television, but tonight there was nothing, as if mummy wasn't there.

Stenning gave her another reassuring smile as he tip-toped across the room to the door. 'I'll just go and check she's alright. I'll be back in a minute.'

Neil skirted past the small side garden and then walked round to the back of the house. That way he would be able to look through the kitchen window and also try the back door. Maybe it was unlocked. As soon as he reached the small, rear patio by the back garden he could hear the cold water running, seemingly coming from the upstairs bathroom and flowing non-stop into the drain. That didn't look right at all. He looked through the kitchen window, just to make sure that it wasn't coming from the sink, and it was then that he saw Steph's body, lying prostrate and motionless on the kitchen floor.

Neil immediately tried the back door but it was locked. Then he heard the scream. A high-pitched, frightened scream that unmistakably had come from a child. Without hesitation he smashed the end of the cricket bat into the large, kitchen window, sending huge shards of glass onto the kitchen floor below. He jabbed at the corners in quick succession to get rid of the jagged edges and then without any thought for his own safety, threw the bat through the open window and climbed through after it.

*

Garrick slumped himself into one of the chairs in the bar and stared into the middle distance, oblivious to the noise and chaos that was going on around him. By any standards it had been one hell of a day. On its own, the visit to London had been as eventful and traumatic as anything he had experienced in years, but the events of the last hour had somehow exceeded even that – and had made it probably one of the worst days of his life. Strange really, that sandwiched in between those two events was also one of the most enjoyable couple of hours that he had spent in a long time.

Hutton eased himself into the chair opposite and looked at Garrick across the table, trying to choose his moment to get his attention. He didn't know him very well, but he could tell from Garrick's body language that he wasn't in good shape. Eventually he stood up again and headed towards the bar. 'Can I get you a drink John?'

Garrick looked up, for the first time realising that Hutton was there, and then shook his head and went back to staring into the middle of the room, still processing everything that had happened. Hutton ignored his response and walked up to the bar, returning a couple of minutes later with two large glasses of red wine, one of which he plonked down on the table in front of him. 'Cabernet Sauvignon. Largest glass I could find.'

Garrick looked up again and gave him the faintest of smiles.

'It's not your fault John,' continued Hutton, easing himself back into the chair and taking a sip of wine, 'so stop beating yourself up.'

'I gave him my word,' replied Garrick, still staring into space. 'I promised him that he'd be okay.'

Hutton raised an eyebrow, not convinced that that had been a very good idea. 'Well, maybe the promise was a little rash, however well intentioned. For what it's worth, I don't think there was anything you could have done to stop it.'

'We're meant to be protecting the public,' mumbled Garrick, putting his head in his hands and trying to pull himself together, 'not putting them at risk.'

Hutton took another sip of wine. 'He was a triple murderer John and he came here to murder again. You saved a life tonight, don't forget that. If it hadn't had been for you, Brolin would be dead by now.'

Garrick frowned and then looked at Hutton properly for the first time since they had sat down. 'Brolin?' He recognised the name but couldn't remember where he had heard it before.

'Peter Brolin,' replied Hutton, sensing Garrick's confusion. 'He's the Chief Constable for Hampshire. He's heading up the Teleios enquiry, remember?'

Garrick pulled an apologetic face, realising that he should have recognised the name.

'We were talking about him earlier,' continued Hutton, 'when I asked you if you knew who the next target was?'

Garrick started to look embarrassed and slightly flustered. Nothing made sense anymore. In fact, the deeper he got into this enquiry the less he understood. He picked up the glass of wine and took a large gulp. 'I don't think I can do this anymore.'

'Don't be stupid John. Of course you can. Anyway, this case is over, whether we like or not.'

'How can it be over? Someone's just been shot in cold blood. There's going to be an enquiry. A public enquiry. This is going to go on for months, years maybe.'

Hutton picked up his glass again and also took a large gulp. 'There isn't going to be any enquiry John. This isn't going to be in the papers tomorrow or make the ten o'clock news. It ends here, tonight. Behind closed doors.'

Garrick put his head in his hands again, still unable to work out what was going on and for once, not able to trust his own judgement or intuition. A couple of hours ago Gary Parkes wasn't even a suspect and now he was dead. And Hutton, who he was convinced was the Chief Constable implicated by Neil's mysterious visitor, now didn't seem to be involved at all. He tilted his head back and drained the last of the red wine in two or three large gulps. Getting drunk wasn't going to solve anything, but for the moment, he didn't really care. All he wanted to do was stop his mind from racing and try and blot out some of the detail.

Hutton gave him a sympathetic look across the table and then went back up to the bar, returning almost immediately with a bottle of Cabernet Sauvignon and a packet of cigarettes. He poured a large measure of wine into Garrick's glass and then sat down and refilled his own. 'Do you want a cigarette John?' he asked, peeling the cellophane wrapper off the freshly bought packet.

Garrick shook his head without looking at him. 'No thanks, I don't smoke.'

'Neither do I,' replied Hutton, pulling one out and putting it in his mouth. 'Not for about ten years anyway.'

Garrick gave him a knowing smile and then leant across the table and picked up the packet. 'Same here,' he said, also taking a cigarette and then picking up the complimentary book of matches which were lying in the ashtray. He shrugged casually as he lit his own and then offered the burning match to Hutton. 'Still, I suppose we can always give up again tomorrow.'

They each took a long, slow drag on the cigarettes and then relaxed back into their chairs, the effects of the nicotine kicking in instantly. Garrick picked up his glass again, this time taking a more measured sip, immediately feeling calmer and much less stressed. 'So what happens next?' he asked, suddenly seeing Hutton as a colleague for the first time in his life.

Hutton took another puff on the cigarette, the nicotine starting to make him feel slightly dizzy. 'I don't think anything happens next. You know, for a moment there, maybe a couple of weeks ago, I thought there was a chance, a real opportunity to expose this conspiracy and to close it down once and for good. But not now. That opportunity's gone, I'm afraid. Any prospect of dealing with Teleios died with Gary Parkes.'

Garrick shook his head in frustration. 'I don't think I understand anything anymore. In fact, I'm not sure I ever did. None of this makes any sense to me.'

Hutton gave him another sympathetic smile and picked up his glass. 'Peter Brolin and I go back a long way. We started our careers at about the same time and our paths crossed a great deal, particularly in London. We were both at West End Central for a while before I moved to the City and Brolin moved to Vice.'

'Vice?' Garrick couldn't help raising his eyebrows at the irony of that.

'Yes, I know. Prophetic really. Anyway, you get to know someone really well if you work with them for long enough, particularly in CID. Endless night shifts, hours of mindless surveillance. It's hard to keep anything private in this job. You run out of conversation far too easily...'

Garrick nodded in silent agreement. Hutton had obviously earned his rank by working his way up on the front line, which was more than you could say about most of the top brass.

'...and life was very different then of course. Much less regulation. Lots of officers had some very...' Hutton hesitated, trying to choose his words carefully, '...unorthodox relationships with some of the criminal fraternity...'

Garrick smiled to himself. He knew what that meant alright. Bundles of used notes in discreet, brown envelopes probably.

'...and Brolin certainly had some strange relationships. Stranger than most, in fact. He was very friendly with an up and coming barrister, a guy from one of the chambers in KBW. Coppers socialising with briefs was almost unheard of then.' He took another sip and thought for a second. 'Still is, I suppose.'

'Worsley, I presume?'

'Exactly. They used to drink in a club in Soho, a dingy little basement joint just off the back of Berwick Street. It was called *The Teleios Club*, run by a Greek-Cypriot who was part of the Soho mafia, long before the East Europeans moved in and ruined everything. They were all Maltese and Greek-Cypriots in those days.'

Garrick shook his head in disbelief. 'Is that all the name means? Just the name of a club where they used to go drinking?'

Hutton nodded as he took a final drag on the cigarette and then leant forward to stub it out in the ashtray. 'That's all it was. Just the name of the place where they used to meet. After a period of time there were four or five of them, a real strange mix of seemingly unconnected people. One of them was a MP. I could never work out what they had in common. I thought they were all Masons at first.'

'So how did you find out?'

'Brolin had a sergeant working for him who followed him everywhere. If Brolin got transferred anywhere, his DS always went with him.'

'Fowler, I presume?'

Hutton put his glass of wine down and burst out laughing. 'Bloody hell John, you really don't understand anything do you? Fowler hasn't got anything to do with this. He's just a useless copper who Brolin wanted to put in charge of the enquiry. Just to make sure that it didn't go anywhere.'

'So why did you let him?' asked Garrick, unable to stop the incredulity in his voice, 'and more to the point, why did you take me off it?'

'Simple. I needed someone to go off-piste. This conspiracy goes to the very heart of the establishment John, and conventional policing, carried out by the book was never going to get a result – not on this case. I could have put money on Brolin volunteering to head up this enquiry and to be honest, I was more than happy to let him. To push back would have put them all on their guard. What I needed was someone who was incorruptible – but someone who was also angry enough to disregard the rules and take some shortcuts. Somebody who could get in under the radar.'

'But if you knew who they were, why didn't you do something about it? Why didn't you just report it?'

Hutton shook his head and smiled at Garrick's naivety. 'To who? My boss, the Home Secretary? You don't understand the magnitude of this John. Too many people in high places rely on this conspiracy remaining exactly what it is. Besides, I don't know all the names. Once upon a time I made it my business to know as many as I could, but that was years ago. Some of them have changed since. I had no idea that Richmond was a member.'

'So what happened with Brolin's sergeant?' asked Garrick, dragging Hutton back to the previous conversation.

'He was accused of trading in child pornography. Apparently he was taking photos of his own daughter.'

'Jesus!'

'There were also some rumours about child abuse, although I'm not sure there was any evidence. Anyway, Brolin got Worsley to represent him. Worsley never handled cases like that. Suddenly the connection was obvious. Or at least it was to me.'

'And what happened?'

'He got off, which meant that he was probably in debt to Brolin for the rest of his life. As you can imagine, his prospects if convicted were unthinkable. God knows what would have happened to him if he'd got sent down.'

Garrick cringed. Unthinkable was right. Coppers and paedophiles needed the protection of Rule 43. This guy needed it twice over. 'So does he still work for Brolin?'

'Stenning? Absolutely. He wouldn't work for anyone else.'

'Stenning? As in Tony Stenning?'

Hutton nodded. 'Why, do you know him?'

Garrick ignored the question. Already he was sitting bolt upright, frantically searching his jacket pockets for his mobile phone. Suddenly, his energy for police work had returned with a vengeance. He needed to call Matt and he needed to call him now – before it was too late.

*

As soon as he climbed through the window, Neil knelt down to make sure that Steph was alright. He could tell immediately that she was unconscious but because of the way she was lying he couldn't tell whether she was breathing and he didn't want to risk turning her over, in fact he didn't want to risk moving her at all. He decided to try and check for a pulse, he'd seen people do that all the time on television, checking the cardoid pulse on the side of the neck but it was a lot harder than it looked. He put his index and middle finger into the small hollow between the windpipe and the large muscle, just below the jaw line but despite several attempts, he couldn't feel anything. That's when he started to panic.

He stood up and started to fumble in his jacket pocket, trying to find his mobile so that he could call for an ambulance. It was at that moment that he a caught a glimpse of something in the corner of his eye, something moving quickly across the room towards him. He glanced around, just in time to see Stenning stoop down and pick up the cricket bat, which was lying in the centre of the kitchen floor. Neil stepped back a couple of paces, retreating into the corner of the room, looking nervously all around him as he tried to find something he could use to defend himself. For only the second time in his life, he picked up a frying pan. Stenning stared at him and said nothing, his breathing rapid and erratic from the adrenalin that was now pumping through his body.

Neil edged slightly towards the back door. He could see that the key was still in the lock, which meant that if he could somehow disable Stenning for a couple of seconds, there was a chance that he could escape. Stenning gave him a thin smile and stepped forward a couple of paces, effectively cutting off his path. He had already made up his mind. Chloe was still waiting for him upstairs, frightened and in need of comforting, and nothing was going to get in the way of that. Neil Ashton wasn't going to leave the house alive.

Neil put his hand in his jacket pocket again, still trying to find his mobile. Maybe he could call for help. Stenning shook his head, indicating that he was wasting his time and then suddenly stepped forward again, unleashing a fast, powerful square cut, aimed at the side of Neil's head. Neil reacted in an instant, raising the frying pan in front of him just in time to parry the shot, the cricket bat clattering into metal, almost forcing the pan out of his hands which were gripping onto it for grim death.

Stenning took a couple of deep breaths and then raised the bat again, as if he was about to make another strike, and as Neil raised the frying pan once more to shield his upper body, Stenning suddenly kicked him hard and unexpectedly in between the legs. Neil let out a gasp and doubled-up instantly, dropping the frying pan onto the floor as he instinctively clasped both hands to his groin. It had been a long time since he had played cricket but the pain of being hit in the testicles by a thunderous hook shot would stay with him forever – and Stenning's kick had just brought the memory of that flooding back.

Stenning dropped the bat and pounced on him in an instant, knocking Neil backwards onto the floor and then wrapping his hands around his throat and squeezing for all he was worth. Neil tried in vain to struggle free but it was no use. Stenning was much heavier than he was and was sitting on top of him, his knees digging into his biceps, pinning him to the ground, and his thumbs digging harder and harder into the front of his neck, forcing the very life out of him.

Neil made one last attempt to get free, pushing and twisting as much as he could to get his arms out from underneath Stenning's legs, but the harder he tried, the weaker he became. The pressure on his neck was unbearable and after a minute or so of constant struggling he could feel his last reserves of energy finally draining away, his head starting to swim and his vision beginning to blur, as if he was floating in a dream, drifting effortlessly in some grey, swirling mist. He could hear Stenning on top of him, grunting and breathing but he couldn't see him anymore, his voice sounding muffled and faded in the distance. And then slowly the grey mist got darker and darker and then he started to fall, as if he was drowning, slipping deeper and deeper into an ever decreasing spiral until in the end he couldn't see or hear anything at all. And then finally, in the silence, in the still, empty, silence there was a white, shining light. And then there was nothing.

Stenning relaxed his grip as soon as he felt Neil's body go limp. Time was of the essence. He needed to get out of there and he needed to move quickly, but not before he had gone back upstairs to see Chloe again. The real prize, the once-in-a-lifetime opportunity was still waiting for him and there was no way that he was going to leave without finishing what he had started. He took a couple of deep breaths, the exertion of struggling with Neil beginning to take its toll. He didn't see or hear the movement behind him. In fact, it wasn't until he heard the single word, *"Howzat"* spoken in a cold, sarcastic voice that he realised that there was anyone there. He spun round in an instant, a millisecond before the cricket bat smashed into the side of his jaw, a shot delivered with such speed and ferocity that it practically lifted him off the floor.

Craven didn't like cricket very much, in fact he couldn't stand the sport. Football had always been his game. Ever since he had been a small child he had spent many a happy afternoon at White Hart Lane, watching his beloved Tottenham Hotspur playing the beautiful game. Not winning as much as he would like and never consistent of course, which was always the problem with Spurs but whether they won or lost, they always played the Tottenham way, which meant that they played with a style and panache like no other club in the country. And sometimes he enjoyed watching the occasional game of rugby now and again. Not club rugby obviously, but he liked to watch the *Six Nations* when it was on the television and it was always enjoyable to see the English giving the French a good hiding. And the Welsh of course.

But cricket was a different matter altogether. His father had always been an avid supporter but as far as Craven was concerned, everything about the sport was slow and boring. Other than the opportunity to spend a couple of hours in a reasonably good beer tent, he couldn't think of anything to recommend it. It was a wonder really that he even knew how to hold a bat properly, let alone make a decent stroke but as he stood in the middle of Steph's kitchen, it somehow all came very naturally to him. In fact, his father would have been proud of him. Stenning, who had been knocked sideways onto the floor was now trying to drag himself up and started to open his mouth, as if he was about to say something. Craven looked at him with contempt and then flexed his body again, unleashing another huge, bludgeoning drive, a vicious, brutal stroke which cracked into the side of Stenning's skull, knocking him unconscious before his head had even touched the floor.

Stenning wasn't too sure how long he had been knocked out, no more than a few seconds probably but as he came round, he realised that it had been long enough for his hands to be handcuffed behind his back and for his ankles to be tied together. He looked up at Craven in absolute terror, wondering who the hell he was and what was going to happen next. He opened his mouth again, about to say something for the second time in as many minutes and then almost choked as Craven suddenly stuffed a tea-towel into his mouth, ramming the cloth as far down his throat as he could manage. Already Stenning's eyes were starting to water as he struggled to breath and swallow properly. Then he watched in sheer, unadulterated horror as Craven took out another plastic tie and proceeded to loop it around his neck.

'This, is for Graham Colley,' said Craven, suddenly pulling the plastic collar tight, as hard and as firm as he could.

Stenning gasped in sudden, total panic, realising for the first time that he was going to die.

It was the least of his problems.

'And this,' added Craven, pulling out a long, ceramic, kitchen knife from the metal block on top of the worktop, 'is for Hilary Russell.'

FIFTY

It was mid afternoon by the time Neil woke up. It took him several seconds to open his eyes and then a few seconds more to focus on the surroundings, the whiteness of the room making him wonder for a moment whether he had died and gone to heaven. The events of the previous day slowly came back to him as he stared up at the ceiling and then gazed at the clean, crisp walls, suddenly realising where he was. His bed was in the middle of the room, equidistant from a closed door on the left and a large window to his right, the effect of the drawn blind giving the room an ethereal, ghostly hue. On either side of him were two small bedside cabinets, one with a plastic jug of water next to an empty, matching beaker and a half-empty box of tissues. Neil glanced around the room again and then looked down at his left wrist, the tell-tale identification bracelet with his name, hand-written in clear, blue ink resting just above the plastic tube which went into to the top of his hand via a small, pink cannula.

He squirmed around and followed the plastic tube backwards, up to a saline drip which was hanging from a tall, thin frame, standing beside the bed. Then he twisted the other way and looked at the wall behind him to his right, a collection of monitors and leads, all seemingly jumbled just above his head. Suddenly he saw what he was looking for, a large green button clipped to the outside rail of the grey, metal bed-frame, next to a pair of cheap, plastic earphones. He pulled himself up and then leant over and pressed the button hard, wondering whether it would make any sort of ring or buzzing sound as he pushed it twice in quick succession, holding the second push for several seconds. He rested back on the pillow and stared across the room again, noticing for the first time that there were two plastic, moulded chairs, one stacked on top of the other, beneath the window. He was just beginning to wonder whether anyone had heard the buzzer, when the door to his left opened and a slightly plump but very efficient looking nurse walked in.

Neil looked at her and gave her a weak smile.

'Mr. Ashton. You've decided to join us then?' she said, smiling back but not waiting for any reply, immediately getting into the routine of checking the saline drip and then plumping up his pillows. She took his temperature by putting a thermometer in his ear and then stood by the edge of the bed and took his blood pressure, pumping the monitor until his arm went stiff and then releasing the pressure in several short bursts until she was satisfied that she'd got the right reading.

'135 over 86.' she proclaimed, ripping off the Velcro armband with practiced efficiency and rolling it up into a scroll. She was obviously used to seeing patients in much worse condition than Neil. Then she lifted his wrist and took his pulse, gently holding his arm in position as she stared at the breast-watch which was pinned upside down on her uniform.

'Fit as a fiddle,' she said, not even bothering to tell Neil what the reading was. 'I think we can dispense with this now,' she added, stretching up to turn off the valve near the top of the bag of saline and then expertly removing the tube and the cannula from the top of his hand. Finally, she placed a small, flesh-coloured plaster over the puncture wound, just to stop it weeping. It reminded him of when he was a small boy, getting injections for measles or chicken pox, or whatever it was they used to inoculate children for when he was young. He half expected her to pop a *Smartie* into his mouth.

'Now then, do you fancy a cup of tea?' she asked, still bristling with well-organised efficiency.

Neil smiled and nodded approvingly. A cup of tea was exactly what he fancied.

'Oh, and there are a couple of policemen waiting to see you.' she added, tucking in the side of the bed as she tried to make it tidy again. 'They've been waiting for hours. Do you want to see them or do you want me to send them away? If you're not up to it I can always get rid of them.'

Neil shook his head. 'No, it's alright, send them in. I'll be fine.'

The nurse looked at him for a second and then for the first time gave him a sympathetic smile. 'Okay, just for fifteen minutes – but then they'll have to leave. You've had a close shave.'

Neil smiled at her in gratitude and then leant back onto the pillow and closed his eyes. Suddenly he felt drained and tired. He must have nodded off for a second because when he opened his eyes again, Garrick and Matt had moved the two plastic chairs and were sitting next to each other by the side of the bed, waiting patiently for him to wake up.

'Hello Neil,' said Garrick, giving him a friendly, reassuring smile, 'how are you feeling?'

'Oh, I'll live,' dismissed Neil, pulling himself upright and anxious to change the subject as soon as possible. There were much more important things to talk about. 'How's Steph? Is she alright?'

Garrick held his hands up, indicating that there was nothing to worry about. 'She's fine, absolutely fine. In fact she's ...'

'And what about Chloe?' interrupted Neil. 'Is she okay?'

Garrick held his hands up again. 'Stop worrying Neil, they're both okay. Chloe's with Steph's mum and she's safe and well. She was a little bit frightened when we found her, but otherwise totally unhurt.'

Neil let out huge sigh of relief and leant back into the pillow. 'I was afraid that she'd been...you know...'

Garrick shook his head. 'Unhurt and untouched. You got there just in time.'

Neil let out another huge sigh of relief. 'And Steph?' he asked. 'Are you sure she's okay?'

Garrick nodded and gave him another reassuring smile. 'In better shape than you think. She's in another ward just down the corridor. We promised to let her know as soon as you came round. She's been really worried about you – in fact we all have. I expect she'll want to pop up and see you as soon as we've gone.'

Neil smiled to himself. That sounded good. After all the trials and tribulations of the last few days, the only thing that really mattered was that Steph and Chloe were okay. Nothing was more important than that. He looked over at Garrick and then at Matt. They both looked tired and drawn, as though they had been up all night. Certainly they didn't look as though they'd had any sleep. 'And is it all over?' he asked. 'Can we all get back to normal now?'

Garrick exchanged a knowing look with Matt and then nodded. 'Absolutely. Normal would be good.'

'Do you remember anything about last night?' asked Matt, speaking for the first time.

Neil thought for a moment and then shrugged. He only had a hazy recollection of what had happened and was still trying to work everything out. 'I remember finding Steph laid out on the floor and then this guy appearing from out of nowhere but after that, nothing – other than I thought he was going to kill me. It's a good job you turned up.'

'Actually, it wasn't us,' replied Garrick, 'the ambulance was already there when we arrived.'

Neil frowned and looked at them both, obviously confused by the sequence of events.

'We think you must have been followed,' explained Garrick. 'Whoever it was not only stopped the attack but also called for an ambulance. They probably saved your life.'

411

'Really?'

'Absolutely. The paramedics got there just in time.'

'No, I didn't meant that. You really think I was being followed?'

Garrick smiled to himself at Neil's naivety. For a journalist, sometimes he seemed totally innocent about the real world. 'Of course. You were being followed earlier in the evening. It must have been the same guy.'

Neil fell silent for a moment, reflecting back on the confrontation on the doorstep of *Yew Tree Cottage* and then the discussion in Aunt Hilary's kitchen, the gun pushed menacingly into the back of his neck. He suddenly shivered, as if he could still feel the sensation of cold, hard metal on his collar line.

'Any idea who he might be?' asked Matt, trying to drag Neil back to the present.

Neil shook his head. He didn't have a clue. He thought for a couple of seconds, trying to recall the man's voice but it was no use. Too much had happened in the last 24 hours and his brain was already overloaded. He was still trying to remember everything and work out what it all meant. 'What about the guy who attacked me,' he asked, 'do you know who he is? Have you caught him yet?'

Garrick raised an eyebrow. He was wondering how long it would take before they got to that particular question. He looked at Matt again and then took a deep breath. 'His name's Tony Stenning. He was the person who killed your Aunt.'

'Oh.' Neil wasn't expecting that response and looked visibly shocked by the bluntness of Garrick's reply. He looked across the room for a second, uncertain about what to say.

'He was a police officer,' continued Garrick, 'not actually a member of Teleios but he was certainly involved. We think he was supplying the material. He had the connections from when he used to work in Vice.'

Neil let out a deep breath, still adjusting to the fact that Aunt Hilary's murderer had been identified. He'd spent much of the last seven days thinking about little else and now suddenly, it was all over. 'And you're sure it was him?'

Matt nodded. 'I've been up most of the night trawling through his police record. Less than a month ago he headed up a surveillance operation into illegal drug shipments being trafficked through Southampton docks. They seized over twenty kilos of a controlled substance called *Magic*; essentially a *Fentanyl* based narcotic mixed with heroin.'

'And is that what killed her?'

Matt nodded again. 'Unfortunately we'd been looking in the wrong places.

All the time it was in our own back yard. It seems that part of the consignment that was being held as prosecution evidence had gone missing.'

Neil shook his head in disbelief. 'I don't know what to say. Why did he kill her?'

'Because he was told to probably,' replied Garrick 'but beyond that, it's hard to say. My guess is that as soon as Richmond lost the laptop, everyone inside Teleios thought that their secret was about to be discovered and even worse, that their identities were going to be made public. They weren't prepared to let that happen – not under any circumstances. Anyone referring to the group by name was perceived to be a threat.'

Neil fell silent again and stared into the middle of the room, processing everything that was being said. Memories of Aunt Hilary suddenly came flooding back to him; the pair of them making biscuits in the kitchen at *Yew Tree Cottage*, Aunt Hilary stirring up a creamy looking mixture in a big, tan coloured bowl and him aged three or four, standing on a wooden chair waiting patiently to lick the large, wooden spoon. She had been like a mother to him. It was always her who cleaned his wounds and kissed them better and it was always her who made sure that he wrote his thank-you letters before the end of Boxing Day. She taught him how to play Bezique, how to make ginger beer from a funny looking plant and how to make coloured masks for Halloween. And it was Aunt Hilary who took him to the park and ran along behind him, holding onto his saddle until she was out of breath and could run no more, one day letting go and watching him pedal into the distance, shouting excitedly at the top of his voice that he could suddenly ride. But most of all he could remember her at home on a Sunday morning, listening to *The Archers* and then pottering about in the garden, picking the summer fruits that she would turn into jam before carefully labelling and storing them at the back of the larder. Some of the jars were still there. *"Behind the glass, under the cellophane, remains your final summer – sweet and meaningless, and not to come again."*

'The real tragedy,' continued Garrick, suddenly feeling the need to fill the silence, 'is that your Aunt was probably the last person they needed to worry about.'

'And have you caught him?' asked Neil, suddenly turning back and looking impatiently at both of them.

Matt and Garrick exchanged another look. 'We didn't need to catch him,' replied Garrick, 'he was lying on the floor at the other end of the kitchen when we arrived – although in his case waiting for the pathologist rather than a paramedic.'

Neil pulled a face, unable to hide any lack of sympathy in his response. 'Who killed him? The guy who was following me?'

Garrick shrugged. 'He must have done. It looked personal. The crime scene was a little...dramatic.'

Neil frowned, indicating that he wasn't too sure what Garrick meant by that remark.

'He had a plastic noose around his neck. It was exactly how Graham Colley was killed.'

Neil frowned again. That didn't sound very dramatic.

Garrick hesitated. He wasn't sure whether he should give Neil all the details or not. Matt nodded at him, indicating that he ought to continue. Neil was involved as much as anybody. He was entitled to know. Garrick took a deep breath. 'He also had a gaping hole in the front of his chest. His heart had been cut out and was skewered into the middle of the kitchen table...'

'Jesus!'

'...we'll have to wait for the post-mortem to confirm the exact cause of death but from the expression on his face, I'd say that it was cut out while he was still alive.'

Neil blinked a few times in stunned amazement. The crime scene must have been an absolute bloodbath. 'And are you going to arrest the others – the rest of the group?'

Garrick's head dropped slightly. 'No. The case is over, Neil. We won't be arresting anybody else.'

Neil stared at him in disbelief and then looked at Matt, as if he was looking for corroboration of what Garrick had just said. Matt's head had also dropped to the floor but he looked up momentarily, conscious that Neil was waiting for him to say something. 'It's difficult Neil. Any possibility of identifying the others died with Stenning and Gary Parkes last night. We don't know who they are and we don't have much hope of ever finding out. The group will have closed ranks already.'

'But that's ridiculous!' exclaimed Neil, 'there must be something you can do. How many people have been killed because of this?'

'Too many,' replied Garrick, with feeling, still embarrassed at the position that he was having to defend, 'but the difficulty is that Parkes and Stenning were responsible for four of those – and they're both now dead. And whilst the cases on Colley and Stenning will remain open, I don't think anyone inside Teleios had anything to do with them. Your mysterious visitor is the prime suspect and he's already disappeared into thin air – and I've a feeling we're not going to see him again.'

Neil let out a frustrated sigh, angry and disappointed at Garrick and Matt's acceptance of the situation. One minute everyone was chasing around the countryside trying to solve the case and then suddenly it had all stopped. 'But surely there must be something you can do?' he asked, 'otherwise they're going to get off scot-free.'

Garrick shook his head. 'We don't know their names, Neil – and even if we did, we probably wouldn't be able to do anything. None of them are going to talk.'

Neil scowled, clearly unimpressed with Garrick's response. 'Which means they've got away with it. Totally unpunished.'

Garrick shrugged. There wasn't much he could say. He'd put forward the same argument with Anderson only a few hours earlier.

'And, they'll be free to do it again,' added Neil, starting to get crosser and crosser. 'Teleios might struggle to survive but they're bound to surface somewhere else. A different name with a different supplier – but probably the same group of people.'

Garrick shrugged again, holding his palms out in front of him, indicating that there was nothing he could do.

'It's outrageous,' said Neil, crossing his arms in front of his chest and leaning back onto the pillow. Absolutely, bloody outrageous!'

Garrick and Matt exchanged a nervous glance. Neil was getting upset, which probably wasn't doing his blood pressure any good at all. 'We ought to be going,' said Garrick, standing up and indicating to Matt to follow suit, 'otherwise that staff nurse will be after us. I don't know about you but she absolutely terrifies me.'

Neil looked at them both and then smiled, his anger disappearing as quickly as it had come. He knew it wasn't Garrick's fault.

'We'll come and see you again tomorrow,' added Matt, also smiling. 'I'll bring you some grapes.'

Neil nodded in appreciation. 'Thanks. The liquid variety please – in a bottle.'

'Do you know what you're going to do next?' asked Garrick, hovering by the door as he waited for Matt to put the plastic chairs back under the window, stacking one on top of the other. 'Have you decided to stay in Appleden, or are you going back to Cambridge?'

Neil smiled to himself. That was easy. In fact, that was one of the easiest decisions he had ever made. He knew exactly what he was going to do next. Aunt Hilary had left him *Yew Tree Cottage* in her will and, for the first time in his life, he suddenly had the opportunity to put down some proper roots and create a brand new future for himself. Besides, there wasn't much in Cambridge for him now. He would miss Chris and Carol obviously, but it wasn't as if they were a million miles away – it was only a couple of hours by car. And whilst he had enjoyed working at *The Chronicle*, the job had more or less run its course and it was time to move on and do something else. An opportunity to do a bit of freelance perhaps? And then there was Steph of course. After all the secrecy and subterfuge of the last week or so, finally there was a chance for him to have a proper relationship that was going to be open and above board – which was exactly what he wanted. No more secrets and no more excitement. Just a period of simply enjoying life without any complications.

Garrick looked across at him and smiled, not bothering to wait for a reply. It was obvious from the wistful look on Neil's face what his decision was going to be.

Neil watched them both leave and then sank back into the pillow, suddenly thinking about Garrick's question. He knew that he was going to stay in Appleden but he didn't know exactly what he was going to do for the next couple of days, let alone the next couple of weeks. After a moment or two he leant over to one of the bedside cabinets and opened the drawer, hoping that someone had picked up his personal belongings and put them in a safe place. He guessed that his clothes had probably been ruined, particularly if the kitchen had been the bloodbath that Garrick had described – but he had a wallet and a mobile phone, plus some keys which he really wanted back.

He looked inside the drawer and then quickly closed it again, disappointed that it was completely empty. Everything had been in his jacket pocket and it was possible that it had all been thrown away. Then he leant over to the other cabinet and breathed a sigh of relief as he saw his mobile phone in the drawer. He quickly scrabbled around and found his wallet and then two sets of keys, one for *Yew Tree Cottage* and the other for Steph's car. He picked up the mobile to check whether he had any messages, but predictably the battery had gone flat. Then he opened his wallet, just to make sure that his credit cards were still there. He couldn't actually remember how much cash he'd had with him the previous day but as he looked inside to check, he noticed a piece of white notepaper, carefully folded twice into a small, neat square.

Neil frowned as he took it out and then put the wallet back into the drawer. He certainly didn't remember putting it there himself, but then again, a lot had happened in the last 48 hours. Maybe his memory wasn't what it used to be. He leant back into the pillow as he unfolded the paper and stared in confusion at the small, ink drawing of a four-poster bed at the top of the page, just below the name of a local hotel, written in old-fashioned, copper-plate lettering. Then he looked in amazement at the list of 12 names, written by hand, one underneath the other down the left-hand side of the page. His mouth dropped open in disbelief as he scanned down the list and immediately realised the implication of what he was reading.

'Are you all right Mr. Ashton?'

Neil looked up, startled, suddenly realising that the staff nurse was standing in the doorway, waiting patiently for him to notice that she was there.

'I'm...er... fine thank you,' he stammered, hurriedly folding the piece of paper and putting it discreetly under his pillow.

'Fine enough for another visitor?' enquired the nurse, smiling with a hint of something mischievous in her eye. 'I have a young lady out here who is very keen to come and see you.'

'Oh absolutely,' replied Neil, pulling himself upright and suddenly wondering whether his hair looked a mess. He quickly tried to flatten it down with the palms of his hands.

The nurse smiled at him again. 'Okay. Ten minutes though and then I think that will be enough visitors for one day. Understood?'

Neil nodded in agreement as he watched her turn and head out into the corridor. He quickly put his hand under the pillow and took a swift, second glance at the piece of paper, almost as though he couldn't believe his eyes and had to double-check what he had read the first time. His heart skipped a beat as he scanned the list of names again and thought about the article that he was going to write. Life was never going to be the same again. *So much for simply enjoying life without any complications.* After a couple of seconds he folded it up again and then opened the drawer to put it back in his wallet.

'Hello Neil, how are you feeling?'

Neil spun round in a flash, his heart skipping a beat for the second time in a minute. In fact, it was absolutely racing. The voice was unmistakeable, as was everything else about her; the petite, elfin like appearance, the slender, suntanned body and the earnest, impatient smile. He gasped as he looked across the room, a maelstrom of emotions pumping through his body and a hundred questions suddenly running through his mind. He half expected her to be wearing a tiny, grey sundress, holding a glass of wine in one hand and a pair of shoes in the other.

'Hello Jules,' he said, unable to think of anything else to say, 'What are you doing here? I didn't think that I'd ever see you again.'

Her smile softened as she walked towards him. 'Well, I'm here now. Welcome home Neil. Welcome home…'